COLD DEATH

ELLIE KLINE SERIES: BOOK NINE

MARY STONE

DONNA BERDEL

Mary Stone

To my husband.

Thank you for taking care of our home and its many inhabitants while I follow this dream of mine.

Donna Berdel

First, a big thank you to Mary Stone for taking a chance on me by collaborating on this story. I'm honored and indebted!And, of course, to my husband. Thank you for being you. You're my rock.

DESCRIPTION

Kill or be killed...

Despite her blossoming relationship with Clay Lockwood, Charleston police detective Ellie Kline will never find her happily ever after until Dr. Lawrence Kingsley is locked away for good...or dead. Not only did the sociopathic psychiatrist kidnap Ellie when she was fifteen, the serial killer has murdered or traumatized everyone Ellie has sworn to protect. She's no longer looking for justice...she's looking for vengeance.

Now, with Kingsley's protégé in a psych ward, it's up to Ellie to find Katarina's young daughter, Bethany, the latest victim of Kingsley's monstrous machinations, before he kills again.

But there's nothing Kingsley loves more than a game of cat and mouse, with Ellie as his unwilling opponent. Before long, Ellie is drawn into the doctor's twisted game as he leaves her clues that lead her on a dangerous hunt—one that could finally put an end to Kingsley...or to Ellie and everyone she loves.

Lock your doors, steel yourself, and hold on tight for Cold Death, the bone-chillingly nerve-racking and thrilling conclusion to the Ellie Kline Series.

1

Bethany flopped onto her side and wiggled deeper under the covers, pulling the blanket up to her chin. When rough fabric scratched her cheek, and a chemical odor tickled her nose, she frowned and tried to sink back into sleep, but the wrongness of the blanket poke-poke-poked at her brain.

What a weird dream.

The laundry detergent her mama used reminded Bethany of sunshine and flowers and made the covers soft. This dream blanket had been washed in something that smelled like chemicals and was itchy on her skin.

Eyes pressed shut, Bethany rolled onto her back and sniffed again. The blanket still smelled wrong. Plus, too much cold air was sneaking through and making her shiver. At home, the comforter was so nice and thick that she sometimes woke up sweaty, even when there was ice on her windows.

At home.

The thought squeezed Bethany's ribs like a giant's hands, the pain jolting her awake. She blinked her eyes open to darkness. No glow from the happy face nightlight her mama had plugged in by the door, no soft green numbers from her clock.

Bethany remembered now. This wasn't a dream. Or even a nightmare.

She wasn't with her real forever mama. The bad man had kidnapped her and trapped her in some icky old house.

Her tummy rumbled, reminding her that she'd gone to sleep hungry. Since the bad man always slept until after the sun came up, now might be the only chance she had to fix that.

The little room she slept in had two windows with wood nailed across them, so even in the middle of the day, it stayed gloomy and sad. Right now, there was no light at all peeking between the cracks in the boards. Bethany guessed it was still early morning.

Careful not to make the bed creak, she eased into a sitting position. She strained her ears, waiting for any noise from the hallway, and when none came, she relaxed a little and scratched her cheek.

Ouch!

The instant sting made her jerk her hand away and stuff her fingers into her mouth. Stupid windows. She'd forgotten that she'd cracked and torn her nails on those boards when she'd tried to claw them off yesterday. The wood hadn't moved at all, but now her fingers hurt any time she pushed too hard.

Bethany shivered, and her eyes burned. She wanted to go home.

When her fingers stopped hurting so much, she pulled the scratchy blankets up higher and hugged her knees to her chest. She hated the blankets and the cheap, uncomfortable bed with the mattress that somehow felt harder than the floor. She hated the ouchie boards on the windows and the bad man who'd put them there.

The entire room smelled funny and old, like this ugly brown rocking chair one of her adoptive parents had kept in the living room. It had supposedly belonged to the woman's grandfather, and her face had turned red when Bethany asked if he'd smelled bad too.

When Bethany complained to the bad man about those things, he just smiled his creepy smile and said the itchy blankets and hard bed were good for her. "Being too comfortable makes people complacent."

She scowled into the darkness. She didn't even know what complacent meant. Not that she was about to ask. Not him. Even when he smiled, he scared her because she didn't think he was happy for the same reasons that most people were.

The first man who'd taken her had been scary, but she could tell he'd liked her sometimes too. But this man...

She didn't think the bad man liked her at all, and when he talked about her mama, his face changed and his fingers stroked the knife in his pocket.

Bethany trembled and buried her face against her knees. "Where are you, Mama?" Her whisper was soft in the empty room, barely louder than a breath.

No answer from her mama, but her stomach growled, reminding her of why she'd woken up in the first place. The man never fed her enough, and she'd never been so hungry in her entire life.

A little bit at a time, Bethany scooted across the mattress. She eventually reached the edge and eased her bare feet to the wooden floor. When she went to stand, the blanket tangled around her legs, tripping her weight onto the wrong board. The wood creaked, and the sound was as loud as a scream to Bethany's ears in the silent house. Fear turned her legs to ice, and she sucked down a breath, waiting.

When the man didn't burst into her room by the time she counted to thirty, Bethany padded over to her discarded socks and slipped them on. Not so much because the wood floor was cold—even though it was—but because her mama had once told her that socks made footsteps quiet, and that was what Bethany needed to be right now. Quiet as a mouse. Or a burglar.

Socks on, she crept across the tiny room, choosing each step with care. She'd spent hours pushing her feet against each board to see which ones creaked, then she'd practiced walking while only touching the quiet spots enough times to memorize the path. It was kinda like the dance moves they'd had to practice over and over for a school musical last year.

Back then, though, she hadn't thought to practice in the dark. Or when her heartbeat filled her ears, and her hands shook with fear. Her mama had taught her that.

"Practice when you're happy and when you're sad. Practice when you're afraid and even when you're mad." Mama had taught her so many useful things in the short time they'd been together. "Be prepared for any situation at any given time, sweet girl. That's what will help you be a superhero."

Bethany touched her foot to the next board, relieved when nothing squeaked. The bad man had really good ears. Like superhero hearing.

She scrunched up her nose. No, not superhero hearing. Super*villain*. Because Bethany was one-thousand-percent sure that anyone who kept her away from her mama was a bad guy. She just wished this particular bad guy wasn't as sneaky as a cat. Sometimes, she'd turn around and scream because he'd be right there standing behind her, smiling his creepy smile while she almost peed her pants.

Bethany focused on her feet. *Forward, forward, to the left, forward, to the right, to the right, forward, forward.* When she reached the end, her hands shook so much that she almost turned around and crept back to the bed. This was too scary. What if the bad man caught her sneaking around?

The cramp in her stomach helped her swallow her fear. Once her hands stopped shaking, she reached for the doorknob and circled her fingers around the cold metal. *Careful.* She rotated to the left. A little more...a little more...there! The knob caught, but Bethany was ready, pushing the metal toward the door before it could make that loud screech.

After pressing her ear to the wood and waiting for a count of fifteen, Bethany eased the door open, just wide enough to squeeze her body through the crack. Any wider and the door would creak, and then the bad man with his supervillain hearing would appear like magic.

Bethany shivered as she slipped through the narrow sliver of space and chanted a reminder in her head. *Be sneaky, like Catwoman.*

Maybe the chant worked because Bethany didn't make any noise when she entered the hallway. Wonder Woman was still her favorite hero, but she had super strength and a magic lasso, and Bethany didn't have either of those things.

Neither did Catwoman, though. She mostly ran around wearing a tight black suit and broke into people's houses to steal stuff, and for now, Bethany needed to be more like her. Not with the black outfit, but with the sneaking and stealing stuff part, because all the bad man had given her to wear were three sets of the same pink pajamas.

That sounded bad, but her mama told her that sometimes people had good reasons to steal. Bethany figured that her empty belly counted.

Plus, secretly, she was pretty sure that Katarina—oops, she meant Katrina—was more like Catwoman than Wonder Woman, and her mama was tough.

If Bethany wanted to eat, she needed to be tough too. A Catgirl.

She pressed her body close to the wall as she crept down the hallway, testing each board with her toes before placing her full weight on it. In the darkness, she could barely make out the painted pictures that lined the walls. Most were of a little boy and a lady with big, poofy hair, like in one of those old TV shows. There were Polaroids too, but they were stuck in the middle of fancy gold frames with swirly designs, which Bethany thought was weird.

Then again, everything about this house was weird. And creepy. Like the layer of dust that covered the glass and metal picture frames and the furniture, and the cobwebs that hung from every corner. Almost as if the house had been empty for a long time before the bad man dragged her here.

Just thinking of the dust tickled her nose, and a sneeze built in Bethany's throat. Her eyes widened, and her lungs stopped working. Oh, no, not now! If she sneezed, the bad man would wake up.

Desperate, she shoved her fingers against her top lip and pressed hard. Another tip from her mama. The trick seemed too silly to work, so she was surprised when the need to sneeze disappeared after a few seconds.

Once her heart stopped drumming in her ears, Bethany began creeping down the hallway again. She passed an open doorway that led to the bathroom with its thin, ugly brown towels and even uglier brown-and-pink striped plastic shower curtain and didn't stop until she stood just outside the hateful man's bedroom.

In the dim light, her eyes took a couple seconds to find the lump in the bed and a few more to catch the rise and fall of the blanket with his breaths. She waited until she memorized the pattern before moving again, timing her footsteps the way Mama had taught her after that one time Bethany had tried to sneak up on her.

Her tummy turned warm when she remembered that day. She'd woken up early that morning and tiptoed into Katarina's bedroom, holding the *I like to poop* sign she'd drawn in purple marker. She was only a step away from taping the sign to Mama's t-shirt when Katarina had reached out and grabbed her before yanking her onto the bed.

At first, Bethany had shrieked, then giggled. Once she'd caught her breath, she'd asked her mama how she'd known.

Mama had tapped Bethany's nose. "Always time your footsteps to your target's exhalations. That helps hide any noises you might make."

Bethany was smart enough to know that exhalations meant breathing out, and target meant the person you were sneaking up on.

But her mama was even smarter because she knew how to sneak up on people in the first place.

Count to five, step. Count to five, step.

Walking that way was slow, but finally, Bethany made it out of the hallway and into the living room. She didn't even look at the front door as she snuck by. She'd tried all the doors lots of times, and they were always locked. Maybe sometime soon, she'd be brave enough to search the bad man's room for the keys, but for now, she just wanted food.

The living room was colder than the rest of the house but less stinky. Bethany tried to rub away the goose bumps on her arms, wishing she'd wrapped the scratchy blanket around her like a cape. But no, the fabric would have dragged on the floor or even knocked a lamp over, and that would be bad.

As soon as she got back to her room with her prizes, Bethany promised herself she'd jump under the covers and pull them over her head and have a mini feast until she was warm again.

For now, she had to keep going. She was so close. Almost there now.

At the entrance to the kitchen, Bethany stepped on the metal strip that divided the carpet from the stained floor that was peeling in spots. When she shifted her weight to that foot, something sharp stabbed the bottom, stinging like a piece of glass. A tiny whimper escaped before she could stop herself, and she cringed and covered her mouth. Tears prickled behind her eyes, but it was fear that stopped her breathing and cocked her head toward the hallway.

Several seconds passed. Nothing.

To be safe, Bethany waited another ten seconds before leaning one hand on the wall. When she was sure she hadn't made a peep, she balanced on one leg and lifted the other one to carefully pluck the small nail out of the meaty part of her foot. The sock felt wet now, and she wondered if she was bleeding. She shuddered. Hopefully, her sock was thick enough to keep the blood from messing up the floor.

Not that it mattered. Either way, she wasn't about to turn back now. Her stomach hurt too much to leave without food.

Bethany limped halfway into the kitchen before hesitating. Her head shifted from side to side. Refrigerator or pantry? The man kept all the dry food up on the highest shelves over her head, but refrigerated food went bad. If she wanted to bring snacks back to her room to hide for later, she needed stuff from the cabinets.

With a nod to herself, Bethany veered toward the pantry. She pushed her hands down on the counter slowly, checking for any loud noises first before pulling her knees up one at a time. With one hand on the wood for balance, she pushed up to her feet.

Twisting, she eased open the cabinet doors and gave a soft gasp.

The inside was crammed full of food. Everything from cooking stuff like dry spaghetti noodles and jars of sauce and tuna to all sorts of snacks. Potato chips! Cookies! Crackers! Cereal! Peanut butter! Bread!

Bethany's mouth watered, and her empty stomach growled. Suddenly ravenous, she stuck her hand in and latched on to the closest snack—peanut butter crackers.

Even though they sounded so delicious that she was almost drooling, Bethany forced herself to put them back. The plastic wrap they came in was too tight and noisy to risk opening. She grabbed an individual packet of cookies instead, using her teeth to carefully open the bag. The sweet chocolate scent hit her as she lifted a cookie to her mouth, making her dizzy with excitement.

The cookie was almost to her lips when hands grabbed her around the stomach and yanked her backward. Bethany jerked in surprise, and the cookie and bag slipped between her fingers.

No!

Bethany wanted to cry when the single cookie hit the old stained floor and cracked into little pieces. The bag landed near the man's foot, and she wanted to scream when he kicked it under the counter.

"Let me go!"

Bethany squirmed and wiggled and kicked, trying every move she could think of to escape, but the bad man was too strong. His hands tightened and dug into her tummy. As much as she wanted to fight, her energy disappeared quickly, like living in this house had turned her muscles into noodles.

No wonder she was so tired. The stupid, mean man didn't feed her enough. She knew because her teacher last year had taught them all about bodies and how their cells turned food into fuel. If kids didn't eat enough food, their cells got super tired.

Bethany was tired of being tired.

When she stopped struggling, the bad man sat her on the counter. "Sit."

Bethany was too weak and disappointed to disobey. Once her butt touched the cold surface, the man rested his hands on her shoulders.

"That was very naughty of you, trying to sneak food while I was asleep."

The man stood close enough that his nasty sleep-breath hit Bethany's nose. She tried to wiggle away, but his hands clamped down harder.

"You must learn self-control. A person should never allow themselves to be ruled by their stomach, so for your own good, your punishment will be smaller portions for the next two days until you learn how to put mind over matter."

Bethany's stomach clenched down hard. "That's stupid. How can I learn any lessons if I'm starving to death? My teacher said we don't learn well if we don't eat enough."

His soft laugh made Bethany bunch her fists in her shirt. "You're in no danger of starving to death, and I'm afraid your teacher is wrong. Sometimes, we only learn the lesson when we're forced to sit with our discomfort."

"I don't want to do whatever that is. I'm hungry!" Furious now, Bethany lashed out, shoving her palms against his chest before twisting her body to the side. She ducked free of his hands, long enough to leap to the floor and lunge for the cookies beneath the counter.

He grabbed her by the shirt and yanked her backward before her fingers could grab the bag. With rough hands, he whipped her around to face him. Bethany pulled back her leg to kick him in the shin when light creeping in from the gaps in the boarded-up windows struck silver.

Bethany's mouth went dry, and she forgot all about fighting.

Knife.

The man shook the weapon a few inches from her nose before tapping the blade against her cheek. Bethany shivered from both the icy metal and fear. She squeezed her legs together to stop her knees from shaking, and she didn't cry or yell, even though it was hard.

Never let them know you're scared. Unless acting scared gives you an advantage, in which case, use it.

Another of her mama's tips. Bethany got the feeling that the bad man *wanted* her to be afraid, though, so she swallowed hard and stuck out her chin. "You keep showing me your stupid knife, but I know you're not gonna kill me. You want to catch my mama and lock her up too, and you're using me to trap her."

This time, the man's soft laugh sent shivers down Bethany's arms. "Aren't you a clever girl? But who's to say I can't carve you up a little while we wait to snare your dear mama in our trap?"

Oh. She hadn't thought of that.

Bethany's lower lip trembled as the knifed dipped lower, down to her neck. The man pushed the flat side of the metal into Bethany's throat and used it to lift her chin.

He pressed harder, and the sharp edge bit into her skin. Just a teensy bit, but enough that Bethany was scared to breathe.

He laughed, and the sound was scarier than if he'd yelled. "Besides, I only need Katarina to *think* you're alive."

This time, Bethany couldn't stop her knees from trembling.

C lick, click, click, click.

Charleston Detective Ellie Kline hit the backspace key until the freshly typed words vanished off the page. After hunching over the report all morning, she'd hoped to have more to show for her efforts, but so far, every attempt to complete the write-up on Valerie Price resulted in the same pattern. Type, erase. Type, erase.

She blew a loose red curl out of her face and reached for the breakfast burrito by her mouse, grimacing at the shiny grease congealed on the yellow paper wrapper. She shoved the barely touched takeout to the far side of her desk without taking another bite, the sight turning her stomach.

Wrong. The breakfast burrito was wrong, her report was wrong, everything was wrong.

A snippet from the page caught Ellie's eye and punched her in the gut, stealing the air from her lungs.

Valerie Price: deceased

Valerie was gone, and Ellie wasn't sure anything would ever feel right again.

The cursor blinked at Ellie from the white screen, as if

taunting her to finish. But how? How could she be expected to condense Valerie's life down to a couple of pages? Especially when Val should still be alive right now?

Grief crashed over Ellie, ripping away the fragile veneer of control that Ellie clung to as easily as a schoolboy ripped the wings from a fly.

Val had been a survivor. A fighter. Careful, smart, and capable, she'd escaped a murderer's clutches once and deserved to live out the rest of her days safe from the human predators that prowled the earth. She was the one who'd got away. The woman who'd lived through the worst yet somehow persevered. After her traumatic experiences, she was supposed to go on to lead a long, happy life.

Except she couldn't now. Because, now, she was dead.

Fate was so cruel sometimes.

A bark of male laughter across the bullpen wrenched Ellie from the image reel flickering through her head. Two of the other on-duty detectives were shooting the shit in the corner, joking around like today was any other day.

Meanwhile, the cursor blinked at Ellie, reminding her that, sooner or later, the job required her to fill the blank page with facts leading up to Valerie's death a week ago.

With a soft snarl, Ellie shoved away from the desk and stormed out of the bullpen that housed the Violent Crimes Unit.

She paced the hallway a few times before flinging open the door and stomping down the stairs, the bang of her footsteps against concrete oddly satisfying. With her hands in her pockets and her chin tucked to avoid eye contact with curious coworkers, Ellie wandered the first floor.

This is a waste of time. You have a stack of cold cases to solve.

She wasn't sure why she bothered with the mental reprimand. None of them had helped so far.

She'd recently tracked down one of her cold cases, a man

named Luke Harrison. Luke had been snatched over a decade ago as part of an illegal child adoption and trafficking ring run in part by the now jailed Neil Burton, an attorney who had probably been stripped of his license to practice law by now.

After finding Luke, Ellie should have been eager to find the rest of the victims. Sold to the highest bidder by the corrupt lawyer, each and every one of them deserved to be found just as much as Luke did. But not even the folders full of missing children on her desk had worked as an effective motivator.

The most she could muster was a half-hearted scan of her voice messages and email to confirm that none of the detectives from other jurisdictions with possible matches to her missing kids had gotten back to her yet. But…nope. Nothing. And she wasn't expecting anything for days.

That left Ellie with a lot of spare time on her hands. Too much. Days she should spend chasing down other leads. Instead, she wasted hour after hour torturing herself with the last few minutes of Val's life.

Gunshots exploded, and the man who'd kidnapped Ellie crashed to the floor. Val screamed as she tumbled down the steps.

Ellie grabbed the dying man's gun and squeezed the trigger at the madman firing from the top of the stairs. She got off several shots before he fled, then raced to Val's crumpled body, falling to her knees by the woman's head. "You're going to be fine, you hear me? Just hold on."

But even as Ellie uttered the words, she knew she was lying.

Blood. So much blood. A bright red river pouring from her friend's chest, staining the perverse pink getup their nemesis had forced her to wear.

That brave, strong woman had died on that cold floor, wearing ruffled pink underwear and a matching cropped baby tee with little white socks. A toddler's outfit. A cruel reminder of the man who'd held Ellie prisoner years ago.

Val died with her blood still warm and slick on Ellie's hands.

Murdered at the hands of a vicious monster. The very same man who'd kidnapped Ellie when she was only fifteen years old and had never forgotten her since. One man responsible for so many deaths and so much pain. Some mornings, Ellie was surprised to wake up and find her heart hadn't exploded from the burden of containing it all.

Dr. Lawrence Kingsley, otherwise known as Abel del Rey. Psychiatrist, genius, and sociopath. Ellie wouldn't rest easy again until he was locked away for good or dead.

If there was any true justice left in the world, it would be the latter option, and by her hand.

"What did those Skittles ever do to you?"

Ellie jumped, and Val's face disappeared, leaving her glaring at the contents of the vending machine and the fuzzy reflection of a tall man in a cowboy hat. Funny, she didn't even remember stopping there. She definitely hadn't noticed Clay walk up behind her.

She grimaced. Some detective she was. So lost in her own thoughts that anyone could have snuck up on her. She needed to get her head on straight...and fast.

Shivering, Ellie rubbed her forearms as she turned to face Special Agent Clay Lockwood. With his usual casual aplomb, he leaned his shoulders against the wall, his favorite cowboy hat perched atop his dark hair. Most days, she allowed herself at least a few moments to appreciate the agent's lean, muscular grace.

Today, it was all she could do not to whirl back to the vending machine, beat on the glass with her fists, and scream.

"What are you doing here?"

She winced at the sharp edge of her voice, but Clay didn't miss a beat. "I'm picking up Luke Harrison's file so that I can use it to help find Caraleigh."

His tone was so matter-of-fact, he could have been discussing the weather, but Ellie wasn't fooled. When it came to the younger sister who'd disappeared on a family trip to the fair when she was only eleven and he was thirteen, the agent was a maelstrom of guilt and fear.

"You should probably leave her case to someone who's less emotionally invested."

Clay's eyebrows pinched together as he studied her face, and she thought he was going to say something about pots calling kettles black. Instead, he asked a simple question. "What's wrong?"

On the heels of her snappiness, his soft, gentle tone was almost more than Ellie could take. Her throat tightened, and that annoying burn kicked in behind her eyes. Another second of his concerned gaze would topple her over the edge, so Ellie stared at her shoes and blinked. "None of your business."

The hand that circled her upper arm and guided her into the closest empty room was gentle. Clay kicked the door shut behind them. "Go ahead, cry and get it all out."

The pressure in her throat intensified. "I don't need to cry. I'm...fine." The tremor in her voice contradicted her words, but Ellie didn't care.

She balled her fists, clenched her jaw, and fought off the pain. Crying was worthless. Not even an ocean of tears would bring Val back or rescue poor nine-year-old Harmony...*Bethany*...from Kingsley's clutches.

After the psychiatrist killed Val, he'd shot his former protégé, Katarina Volkov, and vanished with her daughter. The pair had been living under the aliases of Katrina and

Bethany Cook, courtesy of WITSEC and the federal marshals, but he'd found them anyway.

"I know you better than that."

Emotion exploded in Ellie's chest. Dark and furious and wild. She didn't want Clay to know her better than that. She didn't want anyone to. Letting people in always ended in pain. Relationships crashed and burned, and the people she was sworn to protect were murdered by sadistic serial killers. Each time, the outcome flayed another piece from Ellie's heart.

Why couldn't he understand that and leave her be?

"You might think you know me better, but you don't. Just because we slept together once and we work together doesn't mean you have a direct line to who I am or how I think."

She scoffed, the need to lash out coming stronger and stronger with each word.

Ellie waited for Clay to say something, and when he only looked at her with those tender brown eyes, she poked him in the chest. "I knew Nick my entire life, and I guarantee you he had no idea what made me tick, not really. So, stop pretending that we have this deep connection. Some people are just meant to be alone, and I'm one of them." She poked him again, harder this time. "This isn't a *Twilight* movie, and we aren't soul mates. Get over yourself. It's the twenty-first century now. Women don't need a man to feel complete."

When her fury and heartache were finally spent, the last of the fight drained from Ellie. Her legs wobbled like she'd just run a hundred miles. She grabbed a nearby chair to steady herself while shame seeped through her pores and filled her throat with a thick, oily residue.

A tear slipped down her cheek. Ellie bowed her head, searching for the words to apologize for lashing out.

Clay's finger was gentle as he lifted her chin. "Look at me."

Ellie didn't want to look at him. She'd rather crawl into a hole and hide away. From him. From Val's death. From Bethany's kidnapping. From her memories. From the world. But she was tougher than that. She had to be.

His face swam in front of her, thanks to the stupid tears filling her eyes, but she blinked and blinked and forced herself to meet his gaze anyway. Whatever rebuke he planned to deliver, she deserved it.

"I love you."

All Ellie could do was gape as Clay leaned in and pressed a featherlight kiss to her lips. The contact was there one moment, gone the next. When he straightened, she pressed shaky fingers to her mouth, which still tingled from the brief contact.

She tried to speak, but her vocal cords locked up. Probably for the best because she had no idea what to say. Her mind spun, and her emotions yanked her in every different direction all at once.

And curse him, Clay must have had an inkling of how she felt because he tipped his hat with a faint smile. "Shh, don't say anything now. I just needed you to know that whenever you're ready, I'll be here." His expression turned solemn. "And I mean it. When you're ready, and not a second sooner. Pressure and love don't mix, no matter how someone in your past might have acted."

Great. Now her eyes were burning again. Ellie nodded, afraid if she tried to utter even a single word, she'd collapse into a sniveling heap.

"Good, glad that's settled. In the meantime, I'll be filling every free hour by searching for Caraleigh." His voice turned to steel. "Luke is the first real lead I've had on her case in years, and I won't stop until I exhaust every damn resource and reach every dead end."

As if mentioning his sister was the reminder the agent

needed to get back to work, Clay headed for the door but paused when his hand touched the handle. "Any word on how long Katarina will be stuck in the psych ward?"

Still reeling from Clay's shocking declaration, Ellie's brain required a few seconds to process the abrupt subject change. When she did, she hugged herself and grimaced.

"That's entirely up to Katarina."

3

After Clay left, Ellie entered the corridor that led to a cluster of labs. She slipped inside the one that housed Carl's tiny office, breathing in the mix of chemical odors while she rapped on the open door. "You have a minute?"

The young man lounging behind a giant computer monitor didn't acknowledge her at first. His fingers raced across the keyboard while he hummed along to whatever song was playing on the oversized headphones covering his ears.

Rolling her eyes, Ellie stepped closer to the desk and clapped her hands. "Earth to Carl!"

With a screech of metal, the lab tech jolted upright in the chair and yanked the headphones off, his round-eyed expression almost comical. "Wha...oh hey, Ellie." He flashed her a sheepish grin and tapped one of the earpieces now dangling around his neck. "Sorry, I didn't hear you come in."

"I can see that." She returned his smile and waved a hand at the empty chair. "May I?"

Carl brushed his frizzy brown hair off his forehead and grinned. "Yes, of course. Come on in."

Ellie wrinkled her nose as she settled into the seat. "What's that smell?" Definitely not chemicals. Something sickeningly sweet.

Carl greeted her question with a blank stare before he slapped his palm to his forehead. "Oh, sorry. I forgot. I left a banana in here over the weekend, and it got a little funky. It's in the trash now. Is it bothering you? Because I can take the trash out now if it is."

He half rose before Ellie had a chance to wave him down. "No, it's fine. Please sit."

Carl flopped back into the chair like an exuberant puppy. "Actually, I'm glad you came by. I have a favor to ask."

"Ask away."

"I was hoping you could write me a letter of recommendation."

Another surprise coming on the heels of the last one. Whatever question she'd been expecting, it sure as heck wasn't that. Ellie's jaw slackened. "I…you want to leave CPD and go somewhere else?"

Carl nodded. "Yeah, I'm considering moving to Georgia. I…um…" The tech's pale cheeks turned pink as he fiddled with a notepad on his desk. "I've been seeing a woman who lives close to Savannah."

At first, Ellie was too stunned to do anything but blink. First Jillian, now Carl? Was everyone in her orbit managing a romantic life besides her? When she finally recovered, Ellie summoned a small smile. "That's great, Carl. I'm happy for you."

The tech's hazel eyes lit up. "Thank you, that means a lot. But it also means I need to find a new job."

"Well, we'll be sad to lose you, but I'd be happy to write you a rec. Without your help, I don't know where we'd be on some of our cases. Oh!" An idea struck Ellie. "I just remembered, Clay and I met a detective from Savannah recently. We could put in a good word for you if you like?"

His eyes widened. "Uh, yeah! That would be awesome."

Ellie regarded his unbridled excitement with a stab of envy. "Georgia, huh? You must like the heat a lot more than I do."

"I know, I know. Everyone keeps telling me that it's even hotter in Georgia than it is here." He groaned before placing a hand over his heart and heaving a theatrical sigh. "But I figured since Jillian is off the market now, then there's nothing keeping me in Charleston. It's time to move on and mend my broken heart, sweat or no sweat."

Ellie laughed at the lab tech's goofy reference to his old crush on her roommate and best friend, Jillian Reed. Carl had definitely been a little bummed when the evidence clerk had started dating Ellie's ex-partner, Jacob Garcia, but his feelings had been more of the puppy love variety than anything serious.

"I think your broken heart mended just fine if you're moving to be closer to a woman. I hope you'll like the change."

"Me too. Though I'll miss everyone here, you and Jillian especially."

"We'll miss you too. And speaking of missing you...any news on Katarina's phone?"

As the paramedics loaded her in the ambulance outside of Kingsley's parents' home the night he'd disappeared with Bethany, Katarina had grabbed Ellie's shirt, demanding she recover her cell phone. She'd ditched the bugged device behind a fire hydrant a few blocks away, hoping to mask her movements.

She'd failed on that front, but with a little luck, Carl would work his magic and persuade the tracking chip to reveal Kingsley's location.

The tech hunched his shoulders and twisted his lips to the side. "That phone is a giant pain in the butt. Whoever loaded that bug knew what they were doing. Tracing anything has been a real challenge."

When Carl heaved a loud sigh, Ellie's hopes wilted. That didn't sound very promising. "Were you able to get anything off it at all?"

Carl exhaled again before straightening with a wide grin, his eyes sparkling. "I said tracing was a real challenge, not impossible. Not when you've got skills like I do."

Part of Ellie wanted to scold him for pranking her like that, but the bigger, more excited part overruled the impulse. "So, you did get something?"

"Yup. That's what I'm saying. I found the store where the phone was bought and activated. Don't get too excited," he warned when Ellie leaned her elbows on the desk, "because I called already, and they don't have a surveillance system that works."

Ellie flopped back in the chair because video footage was exactly where her brain had gone. "Of course not. That would be too easy."

"But the cashier remembers the guy who bought the phone, says he paid in cash."

Ellie sat back up. Not the best news, but better than nothing. "Thanks for checking on that. I'll send a sketch artist over to see if we can't get a decent image. Anything else?"

"I managed to track a few IP addresses too."

Ellie frowned. "A few IP addresses? How many?"

"The number doesn't matter. Our guy is tricky. All the messages on Katarina's phone came from different addresses, so either he was hopping from one signal to the next, or more likely, running his internet through a randomizing proxy server." Carl spun his chair back and forth. "I'm still in the process of backtracing, but I should be able to get that information for you soon."

So, not a complete bust after all. "That's great news, Carl. You're the best."

"I know." Carl rubbed his knuckles on his shirt and grinned.

Ellie snorted. "So modest too. I'll be sure to add that to the letter of recommendation." She wagged a finger at him as she rose. "Which I'll gladly hand over to you the second you finish the backtrace and report to me with your findings."

"Yeah, yeah, I know."

He pretended to grumble, and after winking at him over her shoulder, Ellie headed out of the lab and wandered into the hall.

Lost in her own thoughts, Ellie didn't notice Chief Johnson until he called her name. "Good morning, Detective Kline. Mind if I take up a moment of your time?"

Ellie halted in the middle of the corridor. "Okay." Not like she could say no when he towered over her with that expectant gleam in his dark eyes. Sure, Marcus Johnson seemed to have a soft spot for her, ever since the day he'd struck her with his police car when she was fifteen and fleeing from Kingsley's clutches in the middle of the street, but he was still the chief of police. Ellie would remain eternally grateful that he'd found her, but she suspected the by-the-book, no-nonsense officer with a heart of gold had never fully let go of his guilt for almost running her over.

"This way." Chief Johnson waved his hand in a *hurry-up* gesture, so she fell into step beside him as he led them to his office. Her boss, Detective Harold Fortis, was already seated in one of the chairs facing the chief's massive desk.

"Go ahead, take a seat."

Ellie did as the chief asked, settling into the empty chair next to Fortis. The chief's chair groaned when he sat his muscular body down, and the wheels squeaked as he scooted in. Despite the trademark bright smile that gleamed white in his dark-skinned face, Ellie remained stiff as she glanced between her boss and the chief, wary of whatever topic might require a private meeting.

Chief Johnson steepled his long, lean fingers together on the desk. "We're still waiting on your report on Valerie Price. I hope you'd tell us if there were any problems?"

The gentleness in his deep voice made swallowing a challenge. "I'm almost finished."

Not a total lie, but not the full truth either. As much as Ellie hated to fib, there was no way she could face these two men and tell them how every time she went to type, she wanted to weep.

"Take all the time you need." Fortis turned in his chair to face her more fully, nodding somberly. "After everything you've been through, you deserve a damned medal."

Ellie blinked. That was…definitely not the reaction she'd been expecting. Especially from Harold Fortis. She turned to her boss, noting a few more gray hairs mixed into his brown curls than last time. "Thank you. I'll admit, the past few days have been rough, but it's part of the job."

"Constantly getting dragged into cases involving your own kidnapper isn't in any part of the handbook that I've read." Chief Johnson braced his palms on the desk. "Fortis is right. You deserve a medal, along with some time off to enjoy it."

In her lap, Ellie's hands balled into fists. Was that what this was all about? The two of them had teamed up on her? Conspired in some misguided attempt to convince her to agree to a vacation?

She chose her next words carefully. "I'd love to take some time off here soon, but it'd be a waste of vacation days if I took them before Kingsley is behind bars. There's no way I'd be able to relax, not until we catch him."

Ellie pretended not to see the look her boss and the chief exchanged. Chief Johnson sighed, his chair creaking as he leaned back and folded his hands behind his head.

"Detective Kline, I know it probably seems that way right now because of everything you've been through these past few months. Partly because your adrenaline kicks into over-drive when you're stressed, so you end up walking around amped up all the time, even when you're about to collapse on your feet. You won't do anyone any good if you end up sick or on psych leave for chronic sleep deprivation."

If the criminal in question were anyone but Kingsley, Chief Johnson's lowered brows and stern countenance might have cowed her into submission. But Kingsley was the person behind all of Ellie's stress, so she squared her shoulders instead. "For my sake, I hope we find that monster soon, because impending breakdown or not, I won't stop until he can't hurt anyone ever again."

Chief Johnson rubbed the crease between his eyes and groaned. "Fortis, can you talk some sense into her?"

Ellie fought the indignant burn beneath her ribs and shifted to face her boss, preparing to tell him not to waste his breath.

"I'm sorry, Chief, but I'm going to have to side with Kline on this one."

"I don't..." Ellie stopped when Fortis's statement registered, sitting there like a fool with her mouth dangling open for the second time since she'd entered the office. Either the sleep deprivation had already kicked in and triggered auditory hallucinations, or her boss had just backed her up. At the moment, she was leaning toward hallucinations. That seemed the likelier of the two scenarios. "I'm sorry, can you please repeat that?"

"Sheesh, no need to sound so surprised," Fortis grumbled before shrugging his beefy shoulders. "I might not have started out as your number one fan—"

"Or even my five hundredth fan."

Fortis ignored Ellie's muttered interjection while Chief Johnson stifled a suspicious-sounding cough. "—but despite that rocky start, you've turned out to be the best cop in this department. When you don't allow that reckless streak of yours to screw things up, that is."

Her boss glared at Ellie when he tacked on that last bit, stealing a little of the wind from her sails. Not enough to keep her chest from puffing up, though. Fortis didn't believe in coddling his detectives or handing out idle praise. A compliment from him was more valuable than ten from someone else. "Thank you, sir."

Fortis stared her down for a long, hard second before jerking his head in a curt nod. When he spoke next, his voice was gruffer than usual. "Don't make me regret this."

"I won't."

He met her bright smile with a scowl before grunting and focusing on the chief. "As much as it pains me to say this...if anyone's gonna bring Kingsley in, it's her."

Chief Johnson studied them both with his head cocked to one side like they were part of a particularly fascinating display at the zoo. "Okay, I guess that's settled then. Detective Kline can continue working for now." He tapped a finger to his chin, and his lips began to twitch. "Although, if she's as good as you say she is, Detective Fortis, then maybe she should throw her hat in for your job soon."

Oh boy, he's done it now. Ellie cringed while she waited for her boss to respond to Chief Johnson's jab.

To her relief, Fortis just laughed. "Hey, that works for me. Kline can have my job all wrapped up in a big, shiny bow... right after you hand me yours."

4

"Mama, help me! Please, Mama! Please!"

Katarina Volkov raced through the empty hallways, turning down corridor after corridor as she chased her daughter's high-pitched screams. "Bethany! Where are you, baby?"

Heart pounding, she threw open the first door, only to find an empty room. No furniture, nothing on the white walls. The wooden floors were bare too...and dark.

"Mama, help!"

Katarina raced to the next room, but Bethany wasn't there, either. Somewhere in the distance, a discordant rumble kicked off. The noise grew louder and louder with every footstep as she sprinted down the hall, each one intensifying an impending sense of doom. Katarina felt like a thousand scorpions were crawling across her skin with their tiny feet, curling their stingers in anticipation of a strike.

"Harmony? Bethany?" At the very end of the hall, the last door waited, glowing a bright, pristine white. Her baby was in there. She had to be. The rumble grew in volume, shaking the walls, the floor beneath her feet. Wordless, but somehow, Katarina understood anyway.

Hurry, or you'll be too late.

Frantic, Katarina sprinted toward the room. When she was only steps away, she spotted the blood. A rivulet of red snaked down the white wood like a river.

The rumble turned into a primal drumbeat. Too late.

Too. Late.

No. No! "Hang on, baby! I'm almost there!"

Katarina gasped as she pushed through those final steps and shoved the door open, her hands coming away wet with blood.

Inside, the ceiling disappeared. The walls weren't wooden. Instead, they were created from cages stacked upon cages, reaching up to the clouds from every side. In each cramped metal cell, faces plastered themselves against the bars.

"Mama, help me!"

"Please, Mommy, save me!"

"Don't let him take me, Mama!"

Katarina staggered back. So many children pleading with her to save them. But where was her own child? "Bethany?"

She ran toward the closest row of cages, searching each face for her daughter. Before her eyes, the images contorted.

"Save me." It was the woman known as Val. The same woman Kingsley had killed the night he'd escaped with Bethany.

"Save me." Katarina jumped back just in time to avoid Clayne's outstretched fingers grabbing for her through the bars. His eyes begged for mercy while his throat bled from the fatal wound she'd inflicted.

"Save me, save me, save me..."

Everywhere she turned were faces from her past. Her first kill. The adoptive parents Kingsley had murdered before taking her in. That man she'd killed in the hotel room with Eden. That long-haul trucker, Lucky, she'd sold at auction.

She clapped her hands over her ears. Not now. She couldn't do this now. "Bethany? Bethany!"

A mocking laugh from behind sent chills racing across her skin. Katarina whirled, and her heart froze in her chest.

Bethany was tied to a chair. Quiet and pale, with gaping, bloody holes where her eyes had once been.

Almost worse, though, was her outfit. Her sweet baby was dressed the same way as Valerie had been before she died. Pink ruffled underwear, a pink cropped t-shirt, and little white socks.

"Oh, god." Katarina tried to reach her, but her feet stuck to the floor. She opened her mouth to scream for help, but the cry locked in her chest.

The little girl's sightless eyes turned toward her. "You lied. You promised you'd keep me safe, but you're too late."

As her daughter spoke, blood began spurting from her neck, from the same spot where Katarina had stabbed Clayne. Faster and faster, while Katarina screamed and screamed...

A hand closed around her shoulder. Katarina's eyes jerked open, her gaze landing on the man's face that hovered a few inches from hers.

With one foot still trapped in the nightmare, Katarina noted the familiar hairline and suspicious build. That was the trigger her instinct needed to kick in.

"You," she breathed...one second before she lashed out and punched him in the throat.

While the doctor gasped for air and stumbled back, Katarina ripped off the sheets and bounded to her feet. "Where is she? What'd you do with my daughter?"

A sharp pain pinched and tugged the skin beneath her collarbone, and with a snarl, Katarina yanked on the rubber tube connected to her chest until the entire thing ripped free, spraying blood across the room.

The stranger in the white coat was still struggling to breathe when Katarina grabbed his collar and shoved him, hard enough that his spine slammed against the wall. A rolling desk careened away and crashed into the bed. She shoved her forearm across his throat, just beneath his Adam's apple, and the wheezing rattling from his lips filled her with savage satisfaction.

"Tell me where Bethany is, or I'll kill you right now."

Her gaze pinballed around the room, landing on a counter bearing a yellow plastic bin and a white towel. Next to them was a small pair of scissors. She released the pressure on his neck just long enough to lunge for the makeshift weapon. The next moment, he was pinned to the wall again.

Katarina's blood raced through her veins while visions of Bethany with her throat ripped and her eyes torn out flooded her. A strange buzzing filled her ears, banishing the weird beeps and voices and humming machines, infusing her with the calm she needed to force Kingsley to tell her the truth.

"Where. Is. My. Daughter?" She shoved the sharp tip of the scissors against his carotid, scraping the edge across his flesh with enough pressure to cause blood to well up along the scratch.

Through her red haze, she felt a firm tug on her shoulder. The pressure sent pain shooting through her chest. Surprised, she glanced down to find a red spot growing on the front of her blue shirt.

She frowned. Not a blue shirt. A hospital gown.

The pressure yanked on her shoulder again, and Katarina whirled and lashed out her hand, catching the wide-eyed woman in the upper arm. "Where's Bethany?"

More people flooded into the space around them, wearing scrubs and white coats.

Katarina's gaze bounced from face to face, but none of them was her daughter. "Where is she? Where?"

She punched and kicked with her bare feet, but there were too many of them. A big brute wrapped his arms around her from behind, trapping hers by her sides. "Calm down, you're going to be okay."

Katarina screamed and threw back her head, feeling the crunch when her skull connected with his nose. The second his grip loosened, she ducked down and wiggled free, her eyes locked on the doorway. That way. She had to escape this place and find Bethany.

Before it was too late.

Even though the pain in her chest spiraled and her gown stuck to her skin from all the blood, Katarina lowered her head and attempted to plow her way through. She made it a few steps before more hands grabbed hold, then made it one more before she felt a sharp pinch in her arm.

"I got her. She'll calm down in a few seconds."

Another hand reached across her face, so Katarina lunged and sank her teeth into the exposed skin.

"Jesus Christ!"

The person jumped away, leaving a narrow path to the hallway clear. On bare feet, Katarina darted for the opening, but her limbs grew more sluggish with every step. It was like someone had drained her blood and replaced it with cement.

The glaring white floors ahead began to spin and grow fuzzy. She stumbled, righted herself, and staggered another step toward freedom. "What did you do...where's...Beth..."

"Catch her!"

That was the last thing Katarina heard before the darkness claimed her.

She woke in the same damn bed she'd spent an entire week in, with her chest wound sore and re-bandaged, but at least the stupid chest tube hadn't been replaced. Hopefully, that meant she'd be released from this dungeon soon. Kingsley had Bethany, and the first thing Katarina was going to do was hunt that bastard down and rescue her daughter.

The bed clicked and hissed before the mattress shifted,

making Katarina jump, then yelp when the movement pulled on her fresh stitches. "I swear, I'm going to hunt down a baseball bat and beat the ever-loving shit out of you if you don't stop that," she hissed.

She stared at the white ceiling and groaned. Great. Apparently, she'd been stuck in the hospital for long enough now that she'd resorted to threatening beds. This one really did deserve a good beating, though, along with the genius who'd invented the damn thing. Stupid piece of junk moved on its own every fifteen minutes. She'd just be getting comfortable or dozing off, and then...*click...hiss*! The mattress she was pretty much chained to would self-adjust the air volume and wake her up.

Earlier in the week, she'd all but begged a gray-haired nurse to switch her to a different bed, but the frumpy woman had barely spared Katarina a glance as she'd bustled around the room, checking monitors and jotting notes into the keyboard. "We keep all of our ICU patients on these beds. They help prevent pressure ulcers and deep vein thromboses. And young lady, you've been through enough, as I'm sure you know. You keep ripping out those stitches and getting infections, you're never going to leave this place."

Upon further prodding, the nurse had simplified those terms down to "bedsores" and "blood clots."

Katarina gritted her teeth. Bring on the blood clots already. She'd happily trade one of those for a bed that minded its own fucking business and stayed put.

She sighed, opened her eyes, and found the ancient TV bolted to an adjustable stand on the wall. On the screen, a couple argued with dramatic hand gestures. Katarina curled her lip. Soap operas. Before last week, she would have bet money that they no longer existed.

She only wished that she'd been right.

Not only were the abominations to the TV world still

around, but here she was stuck watching this stupid, melo-dramatic crap. How many times could characters in one town suffer from amnesia, anyway?

Katarina cast a longing glance at the remote bolted to the table. A foot away, but with her hands in restraints, it might as well have been a mile.

The only way to watch a different show was if she called in the nurse to turn the channel for her. Katarina clenched her jaw and settled in. As bad as the acting was, she hadn't quite sunk that low yet.

Besides, she needed to spend all her waking moments coming up with a plan on how to get the hell out of this place. As annoying as they were, cringe-worthy dialogue and yet another plot twist where the main character came back from the dead was the least of her concerns.

Click. Hiss. The mattress moved again, inflating beneath Katarina's hips and deflating under her shoulders.

She growled deep in her throat. How could she possibly get anything accomplished with the monstrosity beneath her serving up constant interruptions?

After punching the mattress with both secured fists, she forced herself to concentrate. Bethany. How was she going to find her daughter?

Before she got very far in her planning, the door opened, and a man in blue scrubs walked in. Late twenties, with stubble on his chin, blue eyes, and brown hair just short of a buzz cut. Cute, in that Midwestern, corn-fed, broad-shoul-dered sort of way. He even had dimples when he smiled, as he was doing at Katarina right now, and the motion spot-lighted a small nick by the left side of his mouth, likely from a shaving mishap.

"How're you feeling this afternoon? Sore, I bet, after all the excitement. You'll be happy to know that you didn't do any lasting damage. In fact, the doctor said your pneumothorax was all drained, so we didn't even have to replace the chest tube."

Even his voice was warm and sweet, matching his twinkling eyes and reminding her nothing of Clayne. Neither did the way he fussed over her by adjusting her pillow and pushing the rolling tray with the water bottle closer. Still, now she couldn't stop thinking about Clayne and how he'd begged for his life in those last few moments before she'd slit his throat.

Beep, beep, beep.

The nurse frowned when the heart rate monitor picked up the pace. "Everything okay?"

A week ago, I killed my boyfriend to save my daughter's life, and now she's missing anyway. Kidnapped by the same vicious man who stole her from me at birth. What do you think, does any of that sound okay to you?

She asked a different question instead. "When am I going to be released?"

"Whenever the doctor agrees that you're ready." He laughed at the disgusted snarl Katarina made. "I know the hospital isn't much fun, but you have to remember that you were shot. In case you didn't know, that's kind of a big deal. We need to make sure you're okay before you leave. Otherwise, you'll wind up here again, only in worse shape next time."

The hell she would. "Can't I just sign some papers and leave against medical advice?"

"Someone's been watching too much *Grey's Anatomy*. Just kidding. That might have been an option...before you attacked the doctor."

Katarina punched the mattress again. "Oh, right. That."

The man shot her an amused look. "Yes. That."

So stupid. She hadn't meant to attack the doctor, not exactly. The nightmare had freaked her out, and when she'd woken, all she knew was that his hair and build reminded her of Kingsley, and it was like her brain had just snapped.

During the brief time she'd fought him, she'd been half out of her mind, convinced that the man wasn't an ICU doctor at all, but Kingsley. The entire time she'd been trapped in this hospital room, she'd been on edge, waiting for him to show up at her bedside in yet another new face.

"It's the stupid bed. I haven't been sleeping well." He shot her a sympathetic look, and she sighed. "So what, once I'm all healed up, they're going to throw me in jail or something?"

The man tapped the plastic bracelet strapped to her wrist with his pen. "Nah, you should be okay. Temporary insanity. You're headed to the Behavioral Health Unit after this."

Surprise was like a fist to her gut. "Yeah, no way. I need to get the hell out of here."

He chuckled. "I wouldn't get your hopes up."

With a sinking heart, Katarina noticed the bright yellow color of her new bracelet, which matched the new socks on her feet. A string of curse words flooded her mouth, but she choked them back with a valiant effort.

Dammit.

That damn doctor must like punishing people who got the better of him, the big wimp. The psych ward, seriously? The place the staff referred to as Crazytown when they didn't think the patients were listening.

Katarina was always listening, though.

She studied the man as he worked. "What's your name? This is the first time I've seen you around."

"Jasper." He flipped his name tag around so she could read for herself.

Jasper A. Matthews, Behavioral Health CNA

"I'm the one prepping you to move to the behavioral health unit. A bed just opened up."

"I swear, I'm not really crazy." Even to her own ears, her

voice sounded defensive, and Jasper's lifted brow reinforced her suspicions. She rolled her eyes and groaned. "Okay, fine, you've probably heard that one before."

"Three times today already, but who's counting?" He winked at her. "If it helps at all, your stay in the unit will be as short as it needs to be."

And who made those length-of-stay decisions? Some freaky old psychiatrist who worshipped Freud and wouldn't release Katarina until she agreed that penis envy was the root cause of all her problems? Fine, whatever. Give her a script, and she'd recite whatever BS was on the page verbatim.

Anything to get the hell out of there and find her daughter.

"Do the beds on the psych floor move?"

Jasper's laugh was deep enough to shake his entire body, and warm. A nice laugh. "No. Moving beds on the psych ward would cause more problems than they solved."

"Thank god for small favors."

He laughed again, and Katarina allowed the warmth to flow over her. The sensation faded all too quickly, though. Flirting with the cute CNA wouldn't do a damn thing to save her baby girl. "Please. I don't want to be transferred. I want to go look for my daughter."

"Is your daughter Bethany? The girl in all those Amber Alerts lately?"

Katarina's throat swelled up, and she nodded. "That's her."

Jasper stopped smiling, and compassion creased the skin around his eyes. He reached over the bed rail and patted her hand. "When you get up to the sixth floor, all you have to do is show the doctor that you're mentally competent and no danger to yourself or others. Then they'll let you go."

For some reason, his small bit of kindness made the lump in her throat grow larger. "Thank you."

"No worries, I'm here to help." He rose from the rolling

stool. "I'll be back in a few minutes, okay? I need to check on that bed."

Katarina's gaze stayed on him as he left. Kind, cute, young. Jasper could prove to be useful in her escape plan.

Or he might get in the way.

She closed her eyes. Yes, he was nice, but if he tried to stop her from going after Bethany, she'd kill him. Just like she had Clayne.

Her stomach roiled at the memory. As long as she lived, Katarina would never forget the stark horror and disbelief in Clayne's eyes the moment he'd realized she was going to kill him. Or the warmth of his blood when the liquid gushed over her hands. Or the blood that bubbled from his mouth right before he died.

Almost worse than that, though, was the smug little grin on Kingsley's face as he'd sat back and watched the whole thing. Like he was a proud dad, basking in the glow of his child's first win at a track meet.

Her stomach clenched down hard, and saliva flooded her mouth. She was still fighting off the last of the nausea when the door swung open again. "That was quick."

She'd expected Jasper, but the tall man who'd entered her room wore a white lab coat instead of scrubs.

Katarina frowned at the newcomer. The tanned skin and brown eyes beneath square-shaped glasses looked familiar. Even the voice reminded her of Kingsley, though the doctor didn't enunciate as clearly, almost like he spoke with marbles in his mouth or had a slight speech impediment.

But the jaw and mouth were all wrong. She relaxed, reminding herself of what happened earlier. Maybe she really was losing her mind if she kept finding Kingsley in every single male doctor's face that entered the room.

The doctor straddled the stool and rolled closer to the

bed. "On a scale of one to ten, what's your pain level this afternoon?"

"Two."

"Any problems urinating or defecating on your own?"

"No."

The next few questions were more of the same, routine checkups on her recovery that she answered multiple times a day. Katarina could have answered them in her sleep by now.

"How does it feel to be in the hospital when your daughter is out there missing?"

Katarina's inhalation hissed louder than the bed, but the doctor wasn't even looking at her. Her pulse eased when she remembered the transfer. The psych ward, right. This was probably just a tiny taste of the kinds of intrusive questions she could expect up there. "Awful. Scary. Any chance you could decide to let me go now and schedule an outpatient appointment instead?"

"I'm afraid not." The doctor skipped right ahead to the next questions. "How are you feeling mentally, besides that? Any nightmares from being shot?"

"One or two," Katarina lied. More like multiple nightmares every night, but she was afraid admitting as much would end in her being held prisoner here for an indefinite time period.

"How did you feel when you killed Clayne, and his blood spilled on your hands?"

Katarina went still for a heartbeat while a loud whoosh roared through her ears.

Had he really just...holy shit!

Her head whipped to the side. The doctor's smile was like a razor now, and a cunning gleam sharpened his eyes. Even though he looked different now than he did when he took her daughter, Katarina *knew*.

"You bastard! Where is she? Where's Bethany?" Katarina's

fingers curved into claws, and she launched herself at his face, but the restraints held tight, yanking her back to the bed. She screamed, ripping at the bindings again and again, thrashing and kicking her legs so hard that the metal head-board banged against the wall.

"There's my beloved girl, always so full of piss and vine-gar." Kingsley leaned over the rail and brushed his knuckles across her cheek. "Bethany's blood is so much sweeter than yours ever was."

With a howl of pure rage, Katarina bared her teeth and snapped. He yanked his hand away with a low chuckle before she could sink her canines into his flesh.

"You sick fuck! I swear I'll kill you if you hurt so much as a single hair on my daughter's head, do you hear me?"

As Katarina continued to thrash and spew hate at the smirking monster from her nightmares, two scrub-clad men rushed to either side of the bed and grabbed her arms.

"That's him! That's the man who—"

"Calm down, or we'll have to call the nurse to give you another sedative. Do you understand?"

When Katarina nodded yes, Jasper turned to Kingsley. "What happened?"

"I was just walking by when I heard a woman moaning in pain, so I popped in to check. When I got closer, she attacked me, ranting about some missing daughter?" Kingsley raked a hand through his hair and flashed the CNA a sheepish grin. "Sorry, I was trying to help, but it seems I only made things worse. I best get back to my own patients and leave you two to this one."

Katarina wanted to scream, but she couldn't afford to lose more time to a sedative. Not now. Not when he was so close.

She dug her fingernails into her palms until they bled, forcing herself to let him walk away without a fight. When he reached the threshold, he glanced over his shoulder and winked at her. "Good luck."

As he disappeared from view, Katarina fumed with helpless rage. The heart rate monitor beeped faster, in time to her galloping heart.

Laugh now, but I promise that if you've hurt Bethany, I'll be the last one laughing when I carve you up one centimeter at a time and feed you your own flesh.

But before she could make good on her threat, she had to figure out a way out of here.

5

D etective Harold Fortis checked the time on his computer and logged out with a weary sigh. Two and a half hours past shift change. He should be home already, cracking open his second beer with his feet kicked up, catching that new comedy on Netflix. Instead, his chump ass was still stuck behind the desk like a true sucker. Guess that's why they paid him the big bucks…half of which would start heading straight into his wife's pockets if he signed those divorce papers she kept pestering him about.

He cracked his neck to both sides and arched his back in a deep stretch, but his spine still complained when he first stood up. Christ. He was only in his forties but already creaking like a damned rocking chair. At this rate, he'd be walking as stiff as a robot by the time he hit fifty if he wasn't careful.

After gathering his bag and jacket, Fortis walked out of his office and into the bullpen. A curly headed detective with pale skin and a crooked nose waved him over to a desk near the door. "Yo, Fortis, long time, no see. Must be rough, working that nine-to-five grind. You sure you don't want to clock in late with us big dogs? I'd even be willing to sacrifice myself and trade shifts. That's how much you mean to me."

The detective plastered his hand across his heart like he was reciting the Pledge of Allegiance.

Fortis grinned as he detoured over to the desk. "Whatever. You're all talk, O'Reilly. You moan and groan about the night shift, but deep down, we all know you crave the excitement."

The brown-skinned detective sitting two desks over swiveled his chair toward them. "He might, but I'd pay good money to sleep normal hours again. My wife has been busting my balls lately, waking me up in the afternoon to do shit around the house or help the kids with their math homework. That woman, I swear."

He shook his fist while Fortis and O'Reilly cackled.

"Please, Willis, you're not fooling anyone. We all know you'd clean the floor with your tongue if Rita asked you to and say thank you afterward." O'Reilly grinned as he made the jab. Fortis laughed and shook his head.

Willis flipped them both off. "Yeah, and so what if I would? That's why I'm married with kids, and your ass is single."

O'Reilly rolled his eyes at Fortis. "Because I won't lick the floor on command? I think I'm okay with that trade-off."

Fortis chuckled at their banter. "I can't believe I'm saying this, but I miss seeing you two clowns."

"Same here." O'Reilly grinned. "We should try to get together for a round of golf soon if our schedules ever cooperate."

"Sounds good to me." Even with taking the kids a few times a week, Fortis had a lot more down time on his hands now that he'd moved into that crappy little apartment. It'd be nice to shoot the shit with the guys again. "I'll send a text this week. Let's see if we can make it happen."

"Perfect." O'Reilly shot him a quick salute. "You out of here?"

"Yeah. Gotta get my ass home before I turn into a pumpkin."

"Too late for that." Willis snickered after Fortis as he headed for the corridor. Fortis flashed them the middle finger, and their laughter followed him into the hall.

He considered the stairs before pressing the elevator button. Tomorrow. He'd start taking the stairs tomorrow. Right now, he just wanted to get home and ease his aching muscles under a hot shower. Too much sitting. That was his problem. That, and too many damned reports to type up, along with all the bullshit meetings. Time kept marching on, and unless Fortis did something about it, he'd start accruing more aches and pains and keep getting slower.

He hated the notion of giving up his family here, but one day, he'd have to think about retirement.

Fortis yawned as the elevator dinged and the doors slid open. One day, but not any time soon. Not at his age. He was still a few years away from the big five-oh. That joke with Chief Johnson earlier about stealing his job had been just that, a joke.

Fortis pushed the button for the lobby and debated calling his kids. Hearing their voices always lifted his spirits, even though he couldn't believe how fast they were growing. Eddie was nine, and his baby girl was almost a teenager.

He still remembered the day they'd brought her home from the hospital, bald and toothless, with an angry red face and the softest skin. Forever ago now, but some moments, it seemed like only a week had passed.

Fortis reached for the phone in his pocket but stopped short of pulling the device out. Yeah, the kids were great, but calling them meant talking to his wife. He wasn't in the mood for Marie to rake him over the coals about signing the stinkin' divorce papers. Not tonight, and if he had his way, not ever.

Sure, he and the old lady had their fair share of problems, but so what? Name him one marriage that didn't. Every last person he knew, detective or otherwise, had struggled at some point.

And okay, so a lot of police officers' marriages went bust, but he didn't care. His Marie was different. Special. The best damn thing that ever happened to him, even if he hadn't always been the best at conveying that feeling.

The hell if he was giving her up without a fight.

Flowers. Maybe he'd grab some flowers and run by to see her as a way of showing her his appreciation.

Although, deep down, Fortis knew what she'd really appreciate was him picking a different career. Retirement was out of the question, but there was always the private sector. Security, or a P.I. Some of the guys who'd retired a few years ago were raking it in now.

The elevator dinged its arrival to the first floor. As Fortis exited, he tried to picture himself as a private dick. Hiding in the bushes while he snapped photos of cheating spouses through grimy windows or hunting down scumbags to help put them behind bars. Making his own hours, picking and choosing the cases he accepted. He could wear one of those fedoras, kick his legs up on his desk, and wait for a leggy blonde with a mystery to sashay in.

"Is Detective Kline in?"

The hourglass blonde in the tight red dress fizzled away as Fortis neared the man who'd asked the question. The stranger stood in front of the front desk, wearing a baggy gray sweatshirt and a black knit beanie on his head.

"I'm sorry, she's gone home for the day, but I'm happy to take a message."

Fortis slowed his pace. His gaze shifted from Loretta, the

night clerk who sat behind the desk with a polite smile on her face, back to the stranger.

"No, I won't put you through the trouble. It's not an emergency. I merely stumbled across some information on an old case the detective was working." The man sidled closer to the desk and flashed Loretta a smile. "I don't suppose you could tell me when she'll be back in? Or perhaps share an email address?"

The man's face didn't look familiar, and yet, something about him didn't sit right with Fortis. His gut insisted that he was missing something.

Fortis never ignored his gut. When he'd been a rookie, back in the dark ages, his first boss had pulled Fortis aside and told him a story about how his dad's old partner had ignored his gut once and ended up with a bullet to the head. The grizzled old veteran had glowered down at Fortis when he'd growled, "Ignoring gut instincts is how good cops die."

In all his years on the force, Fortis had never forgotten that lesson. He wasn't about to start now.

He strode up to the desk, positioning his body between the stranger and Loretta. "I was on my way out and over-heard you asking our desk clerk about Detective Kline. I'm her direct superior, Lead Homicide Detective Fortis, and I'll be happy to take that information on the old case down and pass it along."

He studied the stranger's reaction for any hint of emotion, but apart from a brief tightening of the man's jaw over the interruption, his pleasant expression never changed.

Despite that, the hairs rose on the nape of Fortis's neck. Smooth. This guy was smooth.

In his world, the slickest people were usually the ones with the most to hide.

"Thank you, Detective Fortis. How very helpful of you.

I'm sure Detective Kline appreciates having such a conscientious boss."

Was this asshole fucking with him? Fortis narrowed his eyes, but the man's body language gave nothing away. The smile never left his face, and without anything concrete to go on, Fortis decided to drop it. The guy had a weird way of talking, but maybe he'd been educated at one of those fancy-schmancy schools abroad.

In that same smooth manner, the man relayed a story about the times he'd spotted a teenage boy begging for money in downtown Charleston many years ago but had only recently realized the boy had been declared missing. "So, of course, the first time I found myself back in Charleston, I wanted to do my civic duty and report this information to the proper authorities."

"Of course you did." Again, Fortis studied the stranger's face. Beyond sounding like a hoity-toity prick, the man hadn't said anything alarming enough to drag him into one of the interrogation rooms.

His gut pinged again, making its disagreement clear. "Well, you'll be happy to know that that particular case was already solved."

Since Fortis was watching him closely, he caught the stranger's initial reaction. Or more like, the lack of one. The man showed no response to the news, which Fortis found weird. "For someone who came in to do their civic duty, you don't seem all that excited about hearing the good news."

Another tightening of that chiseled jaw, almost imperceptible, before the smile widened. The man clutched his hands together in front of his chest. "No, that's wonderful news! My apologies. It sometimes takes me a few moments to process information, especially after a long day of travel. That's my cue to retire to my hotel, I think. Thank you for your time, Detective. Enjoy the rest of your evening."

Without waiting for a reply, the man pivoted and headed for the exit. When the door whisked shut, Fortis made a decision, his heart beating like a drum in his chest. He strode toward the door that the man had just disappeared through, calling over his shoulder to the desk clerk. "See you tomorrow, Loretta."

"Night, Detective Fortis."

Fortis emerged into the brisk night air with damp palms. The glow spilling through the lobby doors and from the streetlights that lined the parking lot illuminated the darkness, but it still took him a couple of seconds to spot the figure on the sidewalk, covering the ground with quick strides as he headed toward the parking garage.

Fortis hurried after him. His pulse was the highest it'd been since his piss-poor attempt at racquetball last summer with an old CPD buddy, pounding in his ears like one of those awful rap songs his son liked. Until this moment, he hadn't realized how much he'd missed the rush of tailing a suspect. Too many long nights crammed behind a computer typing up endless reports, not enough solving cases. When had he gotten so old?

Although, as he followed the man into the parking garage, Fortis didn't feel old. Not with the way the adrenaline thrummed in his veins. This was the most alive he'd felt in years.

The man glanced over his shoulder and increased his pace.

Fortis did the same, and their footsteps echoed through the deserted structure. "Hey, wait up! I want to ask you something!"

His shout bounced off the concrete walls, but the man didn't so much as hesitate before he broke into a run.

"Shit," Fortis muttered, even as his spine zinged with an electric thrill. As his shoes slapped cement, some primal instinct buried deep inside of him roared, like the cheetah in that nature program he'd watched with his daughter, right before the cat brought down an antelope.

It felt good being the cheetah again. Even if his quads burned like a sonofabitch. *Go ahead and run. That will make tackling your ass all the more satisfying.*

The man rounded a corner and disappeared behind a black SUV. Fortis pumped his legs harder. His right knee ached, reminding him that he hadn't sprinted like this in years, but he pushed through the pain.

His lungs burned as he skirted the SUV's bumper and scanned the lanes ahead. No sign of the man on the ramp leading up to the next level. Damn. Now he'd have to check behind every nearby car.

Fortis slowed his pace and reached for his gun. A flash of motion to his left, and he swung in that direction. He glimpsed a gray shirt before the stairwell door clicked shut.

Leading with his gun, Fortis sprinted for the door. He yanked it open to footsteps pounding up the stairs. "Freeze!"

He lunged for the first step, keeping his eyes trained on the suspect. In his hurry, his boot caught the lip of the second step, and he pitched forward. His left hand shot out to break the fall, and after a few wasted seconds to regain his balance, Fortis was back on his feet and bounding up the stairs.

When he reached the first landing, the man was gone.

Fortis peered up the second flight of stairs. Nothing.

He hesitated as silence stretched around him. If the suspect had fled upward, Fortis would have heard footsteps. He couldn't recall any, so he shifted away from the stairs and eased open the door that led to second-level parking. He swept his gun left to right, searching the depths of the dim garage for any signs of life. Perking his ears for the snick of a car door opening or hoping for the sudden glow of an interior light, he stood silent for several long moments.

When neither of those things happened, Fortis entered the parking area. His pulse continued to pound like his heart hadn't caught the memo that his legs had stopped running a ways back. So what if he was out of shape, though? None of that would matter if this fucker turned out to be who Fortis suspected he was. Hell, if the man was Kingsley, the entire damn department, maybe even the city, would throw him a party and call him a hero.

If that happened, he wouldn't have to trade in his badge for a fedora after all. Marie would remember why she'd married him in the first place, and the kids would look up at him with excited, proud eyes. The way they had when they were still little. Ellie would finally be safe, and so would Bethany.

Excitement urged him to hurry, but Fortis knew better. Rushing after a perp had led to more than one cop ending their career in a body bag. He had no desire to be next.

Quiet and methodical, Fortis began his hunt, stalking down the aisle, clearing one car at a time. First the red Honda Civic, then the white Ford Escape. Every few steps, he stopped. Held his breath and strained his hearing.

The only sound was the faint electric hum of one of the lights overhead.

He stalked forward, this time darting in-between a Subaru and a Prius. After another quick scan, Fortis dropped to the ground, pressing one palm to the cold cement while he peered between the tires in both directions. An empty McDonald's bag and a few oil stains but nothing else. No bodies hiding under cars or even a pair of shoes.

With a frustrated groan, Fortis shoved back to his feet, winced when his knee complained, and continued his slow search. He reached the end of the row with no luck, and his shoulders began to sag.

Where had the bastard gone? Forget being a hero. If the

guy did turn out to be Kingsley and Fortis had let him get away, he'd never hear the end of it. The other detectives would whisper behind his back that he'd lost his edge.

Shit, forget behind his back. Browning would tell him straight to his face.

Dammit to hell.

Fortis stalked back down the aisle, rechecking behind and between the cars as he passed them. He reached for his phone to call for backup, but doubts froze his hand midway to his pocket. What if he called in the troops and they caught the guy, but he turned out to be a nobody? Just some Good Samaritan who talked kinda snooty and was just tired from a long trip?

His gut squeezed, insistent that the man was a person of interest. But at the end of the day, that was all Fortis had. His gut, and a single delayed reaction. Was that really enough to put his reputation on the line?

Now that the adrenaline was wearing off, the pain in Fortis's left knee grew sharper. Still, he limped along, double checking every single car on the level before finally conceding defeat.

Fortis didn't know how, but the man was gone.

"Dammit."

He holstered his gun and headed back toward the stairwell to where his own car waited on the first level. By the time the door shut behind him, and he'd limped his way to the driver's side door, Fortis had convinced himself that he'd overreacted.

The man probably had an outstanding parking violation or owed back child support. Or maybe he'd had a bad encounter with the police in the past. Lots of explanations for fleeing that didn't involve him being a serial killer. Fortis had let visions of a heroic, movie-style takedown cloud his judgment.

He stepped a little too hard on his left foot and winced. Now the only things on his mind were a long, hot shower and a tube of topical ointment that burned his skin.

Fortis's keys jingled as he unlocked the door. When he swung it open, the side-view mirror reflected shadowy movement behind him. Adrenaline surged, and he grabbed for his gun.

His side seized up first.

You have got to be shitting me. A measly quarter-mile run, maybe less, and he had a side stitch? Pathetic. Starting tomorrow, he was hitting the gym.

Those were the thoughts circling his head as Fortis gasped through the pain to massage the area just above his waist. He froze when his fingers touched something warm and wet. Sticky.

Fortis yanked his hand away and gazed at the red substance smeared across his skin in disbelief just as the pain increased a hundred-fold. His training kicked in an instant later. He lifted the gun in his other hand. Or tried to. As though incased in iron, his arm felt like it weighed a hundred pounds all of a sudden. Too heavy to raise without help.

The overhead lights spun as Fortis staggered into the car door. He summoned every remaining bit of energy to raise his gun hand, but it was like trying to push an anvil up a mountain. His legs buckled next.

As he slid to the ground, Fortis wished that he'd called his kids when he'd had the chance. *Marie* crept to his lips, but forcing sound from his throat required too much effort.

For a few seconds, his surroundings all but disappeared as his vision turned to a sheet of bright, blinding white. As the light faded, a shadow squatted by his head.

"Poor Detective Fortis. Your instincts were spot-on. For all the good it will do you now. Don't worry, though. Ellie will be joining you in the afterlife soon enough."

Ellie. No.

Fortis gathered his remaining strength to grab for the shadow, but his hands refused to work.

The shadow's laugh filled Fortis's ears while the lights spun above him.

No.

His lips tried to form the word again, but consciousness faded first, plunging him into the silent dark.

6

When the detective's eyes closed and didn't open again, I fished the gun out from under his coat and tucked it into the interior pocket of my own jacket. Grabbing him beneath his armpits, I heaved him up and plunged him into the driver's seat. Once I'd maneuvered his limp body behind the wheel, I stepped back and allowed myself a moment to enjoy the fruits of my labor.

Only a moment to gloat, though, because despite the glee bubbling through my body like champagne, my time here was limited. It was just about the only downside of murdering an officer in the parking garage of the police department where he worked.

Using my jacket as a glove, I pushed the button to recline the seat a bit more. There was no dignity in allowing Detective Fortis's head to loll forward on his neck like a rag doll.

I snickered and wiped the knife handle clean of prints before tossing the weapon into the passenger seat. After straightening my jacket in the side-view mirror, I nudged the door shut with my hip and headed out of the parking garage, with my hands in my pockets and whistling the tune of a favorite Queen song from my younger days.

Two uniformed officers passed me in front of the precinct, but I was no one to them. Just another person reporting a crime. I smiled and kept walking until I reached the street, taking a left on the sidewalk. Once the brick building that housed the precinct disappeared from view, the jacket came off. The medical-grade putty I'd inserted into my cheeks to create jowls was dislodged with a few hard pokes of my tongue.

Two blocks away, I spied the thrift store I'd scouted the day before. The large box labeled "Donations!" sat in the same spot beside the entrance, so I tossed the jacket inside without breaking stride.

The next block up, I pretended to cough, spitting the putty and dentures I'd used to alter the shape of my jaw into my hand. Regret slowed my pace as I approached the trash can, and my hand clenched around the tools. This new disguise hadn't lasted as long as I'd hoped, but that couldn't be helped.

My mind flashed back to the shocked expression on the detective's face when he'd reached for his side, and his hand came away bloody, and my spirits soared. Short duration or not, the disguise had been worth every cent I'd paid, and then some.

Whistling once more, I tossed the putty and dentures into the bin and continued my stroll through the city, my footsteps lost in the rumble of car engines and tires that streaked up and down the streets. Exhaust mixed with Indian spices and another sweeter scent, perhaps chocolate, drifted past and I inhaled the heady ambrosia while soaking up the riot of colors that painted Charleston at night.

As I neared the next corner, a black and white patrol car cruised by, slower than the surrounding traffic. A shiver raced over my skin. Had they discovered the body so soon, and if so, were they searching for me?

Not that they'd find me. The average police officer's intelligence didn't come close to mine. A few cities even put a cap on the maximum IQ an aspiring cop was allowed to have to join the force, and the courts had upheld that decision. I supposed it made sense in an odd sort of way. Higher IQs led to independent thinking, which led to questioning authority. Like the military, the success of law enforcement relied in large part on group think.

That was one of the reasons why Ellie Kline had been such a breath of fresh air.

My hands curled into fists. Until she'd thwarted me, like all the rest.

Ahead, the patrol car stopped at the red light, so I turned down a side street and headed for the bustling open-air market one block over. Just because most officers couldn't begin to match wits with me didn't mean I should make their job easy for them. Within minutes, I'd merged with the crowd milling through the stalls, turning myself into just another shopper on a chilly winter night.

I feigned interest in a jewelry vendor's gaudy silver and turquoise wares before moving along to the next booth.

"But I don't want to shop anymore. I'm tired! I want to go home!"

A young boy, from the high-pitched voice.

Another youthful male voice piped up. "Me too! I'm bored. I wanna go home and play Minecraft!"

"Stop whining! This is the first time I've left the house at night in over a month. You two will survive if we stay another twenty minutes!"

I craned my head until I spotted the thin woman with her hands on her hips. She stood by a booth that advertised handcrafted bags and purses, glaring into the tear-streaked faces of two elementary-school-aged children. Based on their almost identical heights, the kids were no more than a year apart in age.

The temptation to scold the young mother that perhaps her children would be better behaved if she didn't take them out shopping past their bedtimes was near unbearable, but sadly, I couldn't risk the unwanted attention such a scene might generate.

Almost like she had a sixth sense, the woman glanced up and narrowed her eyes at me, as if warning me to mind my own business.

One of the boys started to cry while the other one sniffled. The whining reminded me of another boy I'd known many long years ago…

I stood with my head bowed in the headmaster's office while his wife, Letitia Wiggins, prowled around me in a tight circle. I could practically feel the anger radiating off her, even though when I chanced a quick glimpse of her face, her expression gave little away. Another student would have been too distracted by the mounds of fiery red hair and those lush lips to notice the tiny signs of her rage, but not me.

Not when I knew her better than anyone.

A sniffle drew my attention toward the two boys standing shoulder to shoulder before the headmistress. Both of them were much younger than me. Only year-six students, while I was in year ten. The snot-nosed one's shoulders trembled like he was one sniffle away from sobbing, unlike the sandy-haired boy next to him, who curled his fingers into fists and glared holes into the headmaster's wife.

"Well, Mr. Kingsley? What do you suggest we do with these rule breakers? We can't allow fighting to go unpunished, wouldn't you agree?"

I did, although they hadn't been fighting, not really. Along with most of the school, I'd witnessed the so-called battle in the cafeteria.

The tough kid had been picking on the wimpy one by grabbing the milk and apple off his tray, the same way he did every day. The wimpy one's whine had been the same as usual too. More of an annoyance than anything.

I licked my lips and searched for a clue in the beautiful face that, even after all the terrible things I'd watched her do, still made it difficult to breathe. Her green-gold eyes glowed with that unholy light that told me something exciting was in store.

"Why don't you suggest the punishment this time, Mr. Kingsley? After all, you are the one who reported the incident."

The blood soared through my veins, injecting me with a sense of power that went straight to my head. This was it, my chance to make her proud.

I threw back my shoulders and fixed the two boys with my meanest glare.

"Let's start with you." I nodded at the quivering boy who went by the name of Reggie. "Tell us what happened."

"I..." Reggie peeked at the bigger boy and hunched his shoulders like he was attempting to disappear. "He...uh...he took my milk." The last part was mumbled to the floor.

Pitiful. So pitiful that sympathy flickered to life inside me. I slid my gaze to the headmistress to gauge her reaction, flinching when I spotted the curled upper lip and narrowed eyes.

Shame spread like oil through my veins. Here she was, handing me an opportunity to prove my strength, but instead of rising to the occasion, I'd almost blown it. The headmistress loathed weakness. I'd spent enough time around her to realize that. In her eyes, if I defended a wimpy boy who allowed himself to get picked on, then I'd be guilty by association, and she'd be right.

I turned back to Reggie with a hardened heart and a sneer. "How is anyone supposed to take you seriously when you speak like that? Stand up straight!"

Reggie's pale face turned even more ashen, but he obeyed. His shoulders snapped back, and his head jerked up. Controlling him was so easy, like pressing a button on a doll to make her talk. Beside me, Headmistress Letitia purred her approval, and my chest puffed with pride.

Skin flushed with renewed confidence, I advanced a step closer. "Now, tell us again what happened without muttering like a mouse. Enunciate."

Reggie's Adam's apple bobbed as he swallowed and cleared his throat. "I said that he took my milk." His shoulders still trembled, but he spoke with more volume this time, his voice high-pitched and clear.

Her chin lifted. "Took my milk...what?"

The Adam's apple bobbed again. "He took my milk, Head-mistress."

That was what she wanted everyone to call her, even though she was really only the headmaster's wife. I didn't care.

"Much better." I shifted my attention to the bigger boy a few feet away, who was pretending to be bored. Sean. "And what do you have to say for yourself?"

Sean met my eyes with a defiant glare and shrugged. "I was thirsty for milk, and I didn't have any, so I took his, um, Head-mistress."

Pleased at how quickly I'd gotten to the bottom of the incident, I turned to Headmistress Letitia to discuss the punishment I'd decided upon. Before I could make the suggestion, though, she leaned in and murmured in my ear. "Doesn't it seem odd to you that Mr. Tanner didn't fight back?"

"Uh..."

My first instinct was to say no. Not really. Even at my age, I understood that the world was full of Reggies, and they never fought back. But I worried that the headmistress would be displeased if I disagreed with her. Plus, I was struggling to focus.

Up close, the musky-sweet perfume she wore was even more distracting, leading my thoughts down forbidden paths. For a dizzying instant, I breathed in her scent and toyed with the possi-

bility that the headmaster's wife realized the effect she had on me, or better yet, felt the same about me.

"'Uh' is not a complete sentence, Mr. Kingsley. You disappoint me. Would you care to try again?"

As she retreated and space opened up between us, I gouged my nails into my palms until the pain snapped me back to my senses. Idiot. If I wanted to impress Headmistress Letitia, I had to prove myself better than the rest of the horny teenagers who walked the academy halls. Superior. Uncommon. Strong. "Yes, Headmistress."

It was the correct answer because she edged closer again. "Don't you think we should ask a few more questions and find out what made them play out these particular roles?"

I whipped my head up and down, eager to show my agreement and climb back into her good graces. "Yes! Exactly. I'm sorry, I should have thought of that right away."

She skimmed my jaw with a fingernail and smiled with so much warmth that I desperately wished for a pause button so I could live in the moment forever. "That's why I'm here, to give you the training you need to succeed in life."

I drank in her validation the way the lacrosse team guzzled stolen beers and probably felt every bit as inebriated.

"Go on, then."

The headmistress gave me a playful little nudge. Cheeks burning from her attention, I began pacing in front of Reggie, more to snap my brain out of its Letitia-induced haze than anything else. "When Mr. Foster stole your milk, how did that make you feel?"

Reggie licked his lips, his little mouse eyes darting between the headmistress and me as if he might find the correct answer written across one of our faces. "Bad?" He offered the word in a tentative voice, but when neither of us reacted, he found the courage to elaborate. "I like milk."

A heartbeat passed. Then five. Enough time to allow Reggie's forehead to bead with sweat. I'd absorbed enough of the head-mistress's tactics to learn that playing with the mouse was half the fun. "If that's true, then why didn't you fight back when he stole it?"

The boy froze. Less a mouse and more like a deer in the headlights. "I...because fighting isn't allowed."

I double-checked Headmistress Letitia's reaction. Her lips turned down, and I agreed. Rules were for wimps. For the dimwitted boys and those without an original thought in their heads. "I understand that, but Sean took something that belonged to you. He stole from you. Don't you think that's grounds for defending yourself?"

"I..." Reggie's freckles stood out in his face like splatters of brown paint on a white page. "My dad gets really mad whenever I break a rule. I'd rather lose my milk every day for the rest of my life than make my dad angry. We're not...he's not going to hear about this, is he?"

His legs started trembling again, but I ignored him and pivoted toward the sullen boy beside him. "What about you, Mr. Foster? Is there something in particular about Mr. Tanner that makes you want to bully him?"

Sean Foster jerked his chin at Reggie's shivering body and sneered. "Yeah. Look at him. He's a wuss. My stepdad would beat me with the belt if I walked around like him all day, scared of my own shadow. You don't stand up for yourself, then you deserve to get beat down, that's what he says."

The larger boy pushed out his chest, and his chin lifted defiantly.

The headmistress made an excited noise in her throat and clasped her hands together. "Wonderful. Now we're really getting to the heart of the issue." When she addressed Sean, her voice was husky and encouraging. "Mr. Foster, why don't you show us how you stand up for yourself?"

Sean blinked up at her. "Headmistress?"

She nodded. "That's right. I'd like you to hit Mr. Tanner."

The room filled with silence. Electricity raced along my nerves as I waited for the boys to react, but neither one of them moved. Not even Sean, who'd just been granted a get-out-of-jail-free card to take a swing at Reggie.

She sighed. "Please, don't be shy. Did you know that, inside every little boy, there's a beast just waiting to be released from its cage? Even the smart boys have one. Even the sad ones. Even the scared ones."

Letitia strolled forward and began to circle the two boys. Their bodies tensed, but neither of them dared to turn to follow her path as she walked behind them, her left hand extended so that her fingers could graze their backs.

The room temperature shot up. Conscious of the sweat staining my shirt, I tugged at my collar and lifted my arms away from my sides when she wasn't looking.

"Once upon a time, all men were beasts and magnificent in their unabridged, natural beauty. Sadly, as societal structures evolved, we began imposing rules and laws on our people, forcing the beast into hiding." Her voice was like honey and warm milk, seductive in its smoothness. "They only hibernated, though, never disappeared. A good thing, if you ask me."

She prowled in front of the two boys, who both held so still, I wondered if they remembered to breathe. "We need our inner beasts, sometimes. During wars, for example. Or if we're being attacked at knifepoint. The problem is, when we keep our beasts locked up for too long, they slowly starve to death, the same way our bodies would. We need to nourish them whenever possible, lest our beasts wither away and die."

As she weaved her seductive story in that perfect voice, I stood rooted to the office floor, transfixed. I'd learned about sirens in our Greek mythology studies, and it wouldn't have surprised me one bit to learn that the headmaster's wife was a descendent of those seductive beauties.

"If the beast languishes from lack of nourishment, boys will become meek and frail, which is an abomination against God and nature. Men were crafted to be strong." The headmistress trailed her fingers along Reggie's shoulder, making my gut twist with jealousy.

"Powerful." She sidled up to Sean next, allowing her fingers to linger a bit longer.

Jealousy raised its ugly head, and my fingers twitched as I pictured grabbing a steak knife from the cafeteria during dinnertime and stabbing the boy at that same spot.

The rage eased when she drifted back to my side to finish the story. "From the dawn of mankind, women's power has resided in their ability to procreate and perpetuate the human species by bearing children, so it makes sense that they would be the gentler of the two sexes. Whereas men's power resides in their ability to serve as providers for their mate and children. Protectors too. To become a true man, you must be able to overcome the people around you and take what you desire. And to accomplish that goal, you must make sure to feed your beast."

Her words were like arrows, piercing my skin and shooting straight into my soul. The truth in them resonated on the deepest, most primal level, in a way that nothing had ever come close to resonating before. I'd experienced so much guilt and shame over the years, from giving in to my inner beast. Now this beautiful, cunning, vibrant woman was telling me that there was nothing wrong with me. That the actions others regarded with disgust were actually signs of strength.

I was tempted to kiss her feet. I might have, if we'd been alone and she hadn't raised a pale, delicate hand toward Sean.

"Do you understand now? If you don't learn to be strong, you will always suffer."

"Yes, ma'am."

Sean's hands curled into fists, and Headmistress Letitia smiled her pleasure. "That's it," she breathed. "Release your beast. You know you want to."

Sean's chest lifted and lowered, which was his sole warning

before he whirled to Reggie and struck. His fist sank into the other boy's gut, hard enough to make Reggie wheeze and wince, but not to knock him off his feet or inflict any real damage.

Headmistress Letitia's tiny frown conveyed her opinion.

Not nearly enough beast.

Skin buzzing, I raced over to the desk, pulled open the drawer, and with shaky hands, withdrew the strap stored there. After a loving stroke of the silky leather tassels, I hurried to Sean and offered him the headmistress's favorite weapon.

Sean stared at the tawse cradled in my hand but made no move to accept it.

I sidled closer, crowding the younger boy. "You can either take this and use it on Mr. Tanner, or I'll use it on you. The choice is yours."

My warning did the trick. Wide-eyed, Sean flinched but reached for the tawse.

I chanced a peek at Headmistress Letitia, who gifted me a luminous smile, her eyes gleaming their approval. Heat mixed with the buzzing sensation in my cells, turning my body into a lit firework, a match strike away from exploding.

"You don't have to use that. Please!" Reggie cowered from Sean as the larger boy approached him with purposeful steps and the tawse clenched tight in his hand.

The leather whistled and landed with a loud slap across his shoulder. Reggie squealed and jerked away.

"Again, and harder this time." Headmistress Letitia pressed her hands together, and air hissed in and out of her ripe lips. Until then, Reggie's mouse-like squeaks had disgusted me, but the headmistress's excitement triggered my own. Blood pulsed in my ears, and there was a new tightness in my groin. "Remember, if you don't show strength, you will end up broken. If you don't take power, you will end up suffering. Do you really want to suffer?"

She uttered the words with conviction, but her glittering eyes seared right into Reggie's.

The truth took another moment to sink in. Not Sean. Reggie.

Stunned, I performed a mental rewind of her speech. It checked out. Her talk of taking power and channeling inner beasts had never been meant for Sean, but Reggie.

I could have kicked myself because, of course! In retrospect, this made perfect sense. A bully like Sean already knew how to access his power. Meek, mousy little Reggie was the one who needed the wake-up call.

The strap whistled again, and the resulting slap cracked like thunder. Reggie screamed, but Sean didn't stop, not now that the seal was broken. Lips bared from his teeth like a wild animal, he lashed out again and again, striking the other boy across the back, shoulders, neck. He struck everywhere he could reach while Reggie did his best to curl his body into the smallest possible target, covering his head with his hands.

"Good." Headmistress Letitia clapped her hands. "Again. Let your beast out or suffer the consequences!"

Sweat beaded on Sean's forehead, but he kept swinging. The strap hit Reggie one, two, three times more.

Blood running hot, I curled my hands into my thighs to curb the urge to yank the tawse away from Sean's hand and take over. Beside me, the headmistress's breathing quickened too.

"Soon," she whispered. Only loud enough for my ears. "Very soon."

After the fourth strike, a scream ripped from the smaller boy's throat. It was so full of pain and explosive rage that the sound reverberated off the walls like a jungle cat's roar. Reggie whirled and launched himself at Sean, headbutting the larger boy in the chest. As Sean staggered backward, Reggie charged again, pummeling Sean's chest and gut with his fists.

I held my breath, anticipating the moment when Sean would strike back and knock Reggie to the floor with a single punch. But the bigger boy lifted his hands to protect his face and shrank away, blubbering like a two-year-old. "Stop! Make him stop!"

An object thumped my hip, returning my attention back to the market.

"Excuse me!" A gray-haired woman called the apology over one shoulder as she hurried away, the large shopping bag that had accosted me swinging from her arm.

After separating the old hag's neck from her shoulders in my mind, I located the young mother again. Looking exhausted, she was crouching and cradling both sniffling boys to her chest. "Shhh, we'll go home soon. I know you're tired. Come on, let's go get an ice cream cone."

Like magic, the tears disappeared, and the two boys skipped along, each clutching one of their mother's hands.

I tracked their progress through the crowd until they disappeared around a corner. One day in the not-too-distant future, when the brothers matured enough to comprehend their inherent power, they would cease using tears as a primary tool and switch to violence instead.

Boys were so easy in that way. Society encouraged them to tap into anger and aggressiveness to such an extent that we'd even adopted a special saying to excuse any injuries that might occur as a result of testing their inner beasts.

Boys will be boys.

Smiling to myself, I slid my hands into my pockets and searched the crowd until I spied a young woman wandering through the booths, wearing a sleeping baby on her chest in one of those special carriers. A tiny pink knit hat that covered the infant's head and ears designated her as a girl, and I clucked my tongue.

Girls posed more of a challenge, requiring more planning and skill to circumvent their natures, which were hardwired more toward nurturing and fulfilling societal expectations. Unlike boys, igniting an explosion of violence in the female of the human species necessitated a liberal application of accelerants and more than one fuse.

I eased into the meandering crowd while my mind raced ahead to the grand finale I had in store. A fireworks extravaganza that would put the Fourth of July displays to shame. Even with all of them on high alert, the three special women in my life would never see it coming.

With all the noise from the market, my murmuring as I weaved through the shoppers went unnoticed.

Never fear, Ellie, Katarina, and sweet little Bethany. Soon, very soon, I planned to strip away the rest of their armor and bare the truth of their innermost selves for everyone to see.

When the explosion came, it would detonate like a nuclear bomb.

I couldn't wait to watch the show.

7

T he painting's vivid pink and purple sky first drew Clay's attention, but the little girl running along the beach with a swath of blonde hair whipping behind her like a kite was what sucked him in.

The artist's impressionistic style made the intended age of the small figure tough to peg, but if Clay had to guess, he'd say ten or so.

Close to Bethany's age.

"Can I offer you a bottled water, Agent Lockwood?"

Clay tore his attention away from the painting and touched the tip of his cowboy hat. "Thank you, I'd appreciate it."

The fabric of Dr. Eddington's trousers swished as she crossed the office to pull two bottles of Fuji water from a small refrigerator in the corner. He thanked her again when she handed him one but didn't bother opening it. Instead, his gaze drifted back to the sunset painting.

That was where Bethany should be right now. On a beach somewhere, kicking up sand and building castles with rock walls and seaweed moats. Not in the hands of a sick man who wanted to hurt her to get even with her mother.

His hands tightened around the bottle. He should be out there, working with the Amber Alert response team to track her down, instead of sitting on his ass in offices all day, asking endless rounds of questions.

The Fuji bottle grew taut beneath his grip, so Clay set it on the floor before the top popped and sprayed poor Dr. Eddington in the face.

Check your ego, Lockwood. Plenty of good agents are out searching for Bethany. It's not like you have any special skills they lack when it comes to finding lost children.

If he did, he would have found Caraleigh years ago.

An invisible knife twisted between Clay's ribs. Bethany might have legions of LEOs out hunting her down, but his sister had no one.

No one but him.

His gaze returned to the painting. The vivid sky reminded Clay of the sunset at the fair that night. He remembered that as well as the tinny music blaring from the rides. The flashing, colorful lights, and the sugary aroma of cotton candy and churros.

He and Caraleigh had been having a great time until he bumped into his longtime crush near the Ferris wheel. After that, Clay only had eyes for Jana. Or to be more precise, he'd only had eyes for the way Jana's tight black jeans had hugged her legs and ass.

Caraleigh had tried to regain his attention, even tugged on his arm to drag him over to the games. Clay had trotted along, but only because he'd hoped to show off for Jana. His sister had squealed when he'd won the stuffed pig and thanked him profusely, and what had Clay done? He'd shoved the toy into her hands and prayed she'd shut up so that he could concentrate on getting to second base with Jana.

That was the last time he ever saw Caraleigh.

Late at night, when he tossed and turned and couldn't sleep, Clay would rewrite the scene and change the ending. His favorite version was the one where he dropped the pig into Caraleigh's hands, hugged her tight, then turned to Jana with a regretful smile and said, "I'm sorry, but this is brother and sister time. Why don't we hang out next weekend instead?"

In this fantasy, he and Caraleigh spent the next two hours together playing games and stuffing their faces with pretzels and funnel cakes before meeting up with their parents and returning home. Later, his sister fell asleep safe in her own bed with her arm curled around the stuffed pig.

"Agent Lockwood?"

Clay blinked at the woman seated behind the desk. "Sorry, I was filtering through some of the timeline."

Dr. Eddington adjusted her glasses and sighed. "I was saying that regardless of how this new information looks on the surface, I'd recommend proceeding with caution. As we discussed before, Lucas has experienced a great deal of trauma in his life, especially around the time period precipitating his escape to the cabin. His memories of living with the girl you suspect to be your missing sister might not be real."

Her gaze softened when her focus shifted to the young man hunched in the blue chair closest to the window.

"She was real. She lived with me." Lucas spoke in a flat, slightly stiff cadence that Clay attributed to his spectrum disorder.

He studied the younger man's body language. Nothing in his actions gave Clay any reason to believe Lucas was lying, but the other man didn't exactly inspire confidence, either.

He didn't bother to lift his head, just sat there, examining his own fingers as they tugged at the yellow shirt.

Clay rubbed his palms on his pants and warred with the voice in his head. Was Dr. Eddington right? Was Clay allowing hope to tarnish his judgment?

He couldn't deny that his heart had all but burst with fresh hope a week ago, when Lucas first identified a photo of Caraleigh as the girl he'd once lived with in the woods. The entire incident had been a stroke of luck. When Ellie had shown Lucas the picture, she hadn't even realized that the girl was Clay's little sister, especially since her name had been listed incorrectly. The photo had been one of many, pulled from the stack of cold case files on Ellie's desk.

Coincidence?

Fate?

Plain good luck?

Clay didn't care what the sequence of events could be attributed to, but he'd left floating on air. He hated to admit it, but every day since, a little more doubt crept into his heart.

What if the link between Caraleigh and Lucas Harrison seemed too good to be true because it was just that? A fictional story created by an autistic boy who'd needed a friend while fending for himself in the wild? "How would he identify a photo of Caraleigh if she was only a trauma-induced fantasy?"

Dr. Eddington finished sipping water and set the bottle aside. "It's possible that Lucas saw Caraleigh once. In person or perhaps on a missing child flyer or on a news alert somewhere."

"I don't watch the news." Lucas directed the statement to his hands. His leg kicked out once before he flinched and tucked both feet beneath the chair.

"Right, but maybe someone you lived with had the TV

tuned to a news station when you were younger, and you caught a glimpse of Caraleigh then." The doctor studied the top of Lucas's head with a furrowed brow. "You might not even remember, consciously, but your subconscious could have stored that visual information and used it years later to create a relationship with an imaginary friend. For all our scientific advances, the human brain persists in retaining its mystery in many ways."

Instead of replying, Lucas began bouncing his shoe on the floor.

Clay eyed the rhythmic motion for a few beats before arching a brow at Dr. Eddington. He remembered how emotional she'd gotten when Lucas had first identified the picture. He thought that the doctor's heart believed Lucas's story, while her head forced logic and reason to take its place.

"You don't know that for sure, which is why I want to take Lucas back to the cabin."

The little grooves above the doctor's nose deepened. "I don't think that's such a good idea." She reached for a manila folder to the left of her keyboard and handed the file to Clay. "Take a look."

Clay flipped the folder open to reveal a report dated back several years.

...when a second patient challenged the existence of the girl in group therapy, the patient exhibited signs of anger and aggression by throwing a chair and lunging at the patient, screaming, "she's real!" repeatedly. Symptoms are consistent with a cognitive break, likely precipitated by trauma brought on by the patient's real world and fantasy worlds colliding.

In one study of patients suffering from unspecified delusion disorders, pointing out the simultaneous existence of two opposing, mutually exclusive realities caused a similar reaction in multiple cases. The researchers concluded that the resulting mental confu-

sion manifested itself as rage, causing the test subjects to lash out at the source of his pain.

Lucas's outburst can likely be attributed to the same reasoning.

Clay frowned at the page. As much as he hated to admit it, the doctor's conclusions made sense.

50 mg of Haldol was administered IM to calm the patient following the outburst, and two orderlies returned him to his room. Patient reported no lingering side effects once the sedative wore off and appeared to return to his usual, non-aggressive demeanor by the next day.

As Clay continued to read, Dr. Eddington started speaking again. "That was one of the only times that Lucas has ever demonstrated violent behavior of any sort or attempted to physically hurt another patient."

But Clay barely registered the doctor's warning. The line stared back at him, kickstarting his hope all over again. His heart slammed against his ribs, and he squeezed his eyes shut, ordering himself to slow down and breathe.

"Agent Lockwood? Are you feeling okay?"

Clay held up a single finger, filled his lungs with air, and opened his eyes.

Please don't let me have imagined it.

The folder balanced on his lap trembled as he forced himself to read the line again. By the time he finished, his hands shook so hard that the file almost slipped to the floor. Sweat beaded on the back of his neck, and the goose bumps erupting on his skin were triggered by excitement, not chills.

Clay wanted to jump up to his feet, toss his cowboy hat into the air, and whoop for joy. Instead, he called on years of training to leash his emotions and slapped the folder onto the desk, loud enough that Lucas froze and the doctor flinched.

"Sorry." He drew in a long, ragged breath. "We can go the paperwork route if you want, but I'd really prefer you to work with me on this. Lucas is the sole witness to a crime, and at this point, he could be the only person to help me find Caraleigh."

The doctor regarded him over folded hands with an expression of concern. "I'm sorry, I'm afraid I'm not following."

Clay opened the folder to the last page. "In this report, there's a line that makes it one-hundred-percent clear to me that Lucas's girl and my sister are the same person."

A soft gasp came from Lucas's direction, but Clay's gaze never wavered from the report. He dragged a shaky finger down the page until he found the line in question and read aloud. "The patient's doubt of Lucas's account of his imaginary friend appeared to be the initial precipitating factor, but the aggressive behavior didn't begin until a toy was taken from him, a stuffed pink pig wearing a top hat."

When Clay glanced up, his vision was blurred, but he didn't care. "Dr. Eddington, my sister loved pigs. The last time I saw Caraleigh at the fair before she vanished, she was clutching the prize I'd won at the ring toss to her chest. A stuffed pink pig in a top hat."

8

B ethany's tummy ached all the time now. A hollow pain, like someone had carved her insides out and left an empty space behind.

She rolled onto her back in the hard bed with the scratchy blanket, but that didn't help, either. Nothing did.

At home, Bethany would have already jumped out of bed and skipped to the kitchen, where her mama would have breakfast waiting. On school mornings, she usually ate Frosted Flakes or Cheerios, but on the weekends Mama fixed pancakes or French toast and hot chocolate with whipped cream. The whole house would smell like yummy syrup, and they got to take their plates to the couch and eat while watching the Disney channel.

Trapped here in this dark room, there was no reason to get out of bed. Especially since she was tired all the time now.

Where are you, Mama? I'm scared and hungry. Please come find me soon.

Bethany's throat burned, but no tears came.

Another knifelike pain stabbed at her tummy. She whimpered and clutched her stomach. She was about to roll onto her other side and curl into a ball when a floorboard outside the door creaked.

Bethany froze.

Go away. Please, go away. I'll be good from now on, I promise.

But this prayer didn't work any better than the rest because the door squeaked as it swung open.

Staying still was so hard. Bethany wanted to jump up and run. Hide somewhere. But that was stupid since there was nowhere to go.

Besides, Mama had told her what to do if something like this happened.

"Sometimes, playing possum can save your life, but you have to understand a little about people's bodies and biology in order to fool them. Do you breathe quick or slow when you're asleep?"

Bethany only needed a moment to answer that question. "Slow!"

Her mama nodded. "That's right. When they're sleeping, adults breathe about once every five seconds. Children your age might breathe a little more often, but for the most part, it's slow and steady. Now, give it a try. See if you can fake me out."

Bethany giggled. Her mama was a little weird sometimes, but in the best possible way. Her friends at school had moms who taught them boring stuff, like how to play soccer, or the names of the presidents, or how to plant tomatoes, but her mom was so much cooler because she taught Bethany ways to survive a Zombie Apocalypse.

"Shhh, possums don't giggle." Mama poked her belly and made her giggle again before Bethany quieted and did her best possum imitation. She laid still on the couch, arms clamped to her sides and eyes squeezed shut so tight that her eyeballs wanted to pop out, and practiced breathing in and out on a count of five.

After two tries, her mama poked her again. "You look like you're trying to poop."

"Ew!"

When Bethany stopped shrieking with laughter, her mama

grew serious. "Remember, sleep is about giving your mind and body a chance to relax, so if you want to fool someone, you need to relax all your muscles. Your arms, your legs, your fingers, your toes. Even your eyelids. Focus. Think about that feeling you get when you lay outside on a hot, sunny day, and you're so relaxed that your body almost sinks into the ground while your mind drifts away."

Bethany repeated the exercise two more times until Mama clapped. "Better, much better." Once the lesson was done, she'd led Bethany to the kitchen and made them some microwave popcorn.

Another floorboard creaked, this one closer to the bed. Bethany's heart pounded faster, but she couldn't do anything about that, only her breathing.

Nice, deep, slow breaths.

And she tried, but this was so much harder than when she'd played the possum game with Mama. That had been pretend and fun.

This was for real, and somehow, her stupid muscles knew the difference. They kept trying to turn stiff, and her body wanted to shiver.

Her mama's voice whispered in her head, urging her to try harder.

...Focus. Think about that feeling you get when you lay outside on a hot, sunny day...

So, she did. Bethany pictured a time when the nice couple before Mama took her to the beach for a long weekend. How, after she'd played in the waves and flopped all salty-wet onto the beach towel, the sun beat down on her skin, drying her in minutes and warming her from the outside in. She remembered the heat zapping her energy and turning her so lazy that she could have stayed there for hours, floating away like one of the kites flying over the waves.

Bethany relaxed her arms and legs, fingers and toes. Even her eyelids. She sank into the bed and tried to float away.

The only part of her body that moved was her chest as she breathed.

In...out. In...out.

Something tickled her cheek, and her heart jumped, but Bethany played possum. Even when she realized the tickle was the bad man dragging his fingers across her cheek.

Even when those same fingers smoothed back her hair.

She stayed very, very still, remembering her mama's game. Remembering her classmate, who'd spent lunch telling them about her uncle the cop, who'd told her about the scary men in the world who liked to touch kids on parts of their bodies they shouldn't touch, and how that was why adults always told kids not to talk to strangers or take candy from men in vans.

Bethany's heart pounded so loud in her ears that she worried the bad man could hear it.

What if he was one of those types of scary men?

Warm sun. Relax. Float away.

The bad man stroked her cheek again, and Bethany's hands itched to grab a washcloth and soap, to scrub his touch off her skin. He was so close now that she could smell minty toothpaste. She could *feel* him hovering inches from her face. Staring.

Her breath caught, but she remembered in time, exhaled slowly, and prayed.

Don't let him be one of those kinds of bad men. I promise to be better. I'll do my homework without whining and pick up my room. I'll even eat broccoli, even though it tastes like dirty leaves.

When she prayed, Bethany dreamed of warm beaches and breathed.

In...out. In...out.

Time passed, and Bethany's fear spiked. Why was he still here? Did he know that she was awake? Maybe this was one of the bad man's tricks. He liked to play tricks on her.

She almost gave up and opened her eyes, but Mama's voice wouldn't let her.

Warm sun. Relax. Float away.

The floorboards creaked. First near Bethany's bed, then farther away.

Yes! Finally!

The door squeaked, but as much as Bethany strained her ears, she didn't hear it click shut. She wanted to peek but knew better. Her mama had taught her that too.

"Make sure you never stop playing possum too soon. Sometimes, the zombies will try to trick you and only pretend to leave, which means you need to keep pretending too. Always wait at least five minutes after you think they leave to open your eyes, and only if you don't hear any noises. When you can't use your eyes, your ears can be one of your best tools to save you."

Mama knew more about this kind of stuff than anyone, so Bethany kept her eyes shut and her breathing deep. She played possum until the front door slammed, and an engine grumbled to life outside the window. Even after the car sputtered away, she held on to her act, too terrified to open her eyes in case the man was pretending too.

In...out. In...out.

The bad man always thought he was so smart and that Bethany was just a dumb kid. She let him think that because, sometimes, adults did the dumbest stuff when they thought they were the only smart ones.

She hadn't needed Mama to tell her that. Bethany had figured it out all on her own.

Her empty tummy cramped again, as if it knew the man was gone and was ordering her to hurry up and hunt for food.

Just a little longer. Just in case.

Most of the time, the bad man was smart. That was the problem. Otherwise, she might have escaped already.

Bethany hated everything about him. Those sharp smiles that didn't reach his eyes as well as his quiet, sneaky steps. He could never be Wonder Woman, or Catwoman, even if he was sneaky enough to be a burglar. The bad man was definitely a supervillain. He needed a name, but the best she'd come up with so far was Doctor Bad.

After counting down another twenty breaths, Bethany finally opened her eyes. The sun crept between the boards over her window and painted her bed in thin stripes, enough light to show that the room was empty. She sat up and listened.

Another twenty breaths later, Bethany slid out of bed and slipped on her socks. Retracing her steps from yesterday, she took the quietest path across the room, edged open the door, and peeked out.

No bad man there, so she crept down the hall to the bathroom and frowned at the toilet. Usually, she had to pee the second she woke up, but not today. That seemed wrong somehow, but she didn't have time to waste worrying about it. Not when her body ached, and her tummy was empty, and her mouth was as dry as if she'd swallowed sand.

Her gaze fell on the faucet. After pausing to listen for the rumble of a car, Bethany hurried over to the sink. The water splashed icy-cold on her hands, and she muffled a yelp but didn't wait for the temperature to warm. She cupped her hands beneath the spray and raised them to her mouth to take big, greedy gulps.

Her empty tummy cramped even harder when the water hit, and she doubled over, gasping. When the pain subsided, she forced herself to drink again.

When she finished, Bethany shut off the faucet and used her sleeve to wipe up the counter. The bad man never kept any towels in here, and he was creepy enough to measure the toilet paper too. She left the bathroom and padded past his room and all those weird pictures on the wall until the hallway spilled into the living room.

Her legs wobbled as she rushed to the front door and yanked on the knob. No use. The bad man always kept it locked, with a key, even from the inside. Bethany remembered now, but the disappointment still made her head spin. Or maybe the spinning was because she hadn't eaten in so long. Either way, thinking too much hurt her brain.

She ran to the windows next but lifting her arms to try to pry the boards off made the dizziness worse, and the wood scraping against her torn fingers shot pain up her arms.

Bethany let go of the board and rubbed her palms on her forehead. Why was she doing this when she knew it was stupid? A total waste of time. The bad man locked the little house as tight as a jail. Without a key or a tool, she was trapped, so why even leave her room?

Her bleary gaze traveled across the living room and landed on the kitchen.

Right. She needed food.

Bethany pushed away from the window and headed in that direction, but after only two steps, the room started spinning again. She stumbled into the beat-up green couch and grabbed the back for support while she panted and waited for the dizziness to wear off.

Food. If she could just get to the food, she'd feel so much better.

Once her vision cleared, Bethany started forward again. Slower this time. If she fell, she was afraid she might be too weak to get back up.

She inched across the living room toward the kitchen. When she reached the threshold, excitement cleared her head until she peeked inside.

A thick metal chain was strapped tight across the refrigerator door. Bethany stared at the ugly black metal links and wanted to scream. Hatred curled her fists. She wished someone would wrap that chain around the bad man, as tight as one of those snakes that squeezed you to death.

Guilt followed the ugly wish. Her teacher told the class that hate was a bad word, and hurting people was wrong and mean.

Bethany didn't want to be mean, not like the bad man. If only her tummy didn't hurt so much.

She hurried to the fridge and yanked on the chain, but the thick metal refused to budge, so she gave up and stumbled to the cupboard. Climbing onto the counter was so much harder than yesterday. Her legs shook, and her arms wobbled like noodles. After three attempts, she finally stood up and reached for the cabinet doors.

She opened them, and the hope inside her died. Empty. All the cereal, bread, and yummy snacks were gone. He'd even taken the dried noodles and jars of sauce.

The bare shelves made Bethany's tummy hurt even more. She pressed a hand to her stomach and staggered back to the floor to search the rest of the cupboards, but there was nothing to eat. Not a single can of soup or a forgotten chip. No crumbs on the counter.

She even opened the trash can, hoping to find a sandwich crust or a brown piece of banana, but that was empty too.

Bethany stood by the trash can for a long time, staring at nothing. When she closed the lid and left the kitchen, her body felt funny. Kind of floaty and fuzzy, like maybe this was all just a bad dream.

With no idea where she was headed or why, Bethany drifted through the tiny living room and stopped on a worn, green rug sprinkled with flowers.

"Pretty." She squatted down to sniff the flowers, but they smelled like dust, and when she stood again, the room tilted.

She clung to the couch and waited for the furniture to

quit moving. When had Mama bought this ugly green couch? And that rocking chair?

A few seconds more, and her mind cleared. This wasn't her and her mama's cozy little home.

This was the bad man's house.

Bethany's legs wobbled, like that cute little boy in one-piece pajamas who'd been at the grocery store last time they'd gone shopping. He'd screeched at his mother to let him out of the cart, but the moment his feet touched the floor, the boy tried to run away. His wiggly-wobbly legs carried him halfway to the strawberries before he plopped onto his butt and cried.

The grocery store...

Bethany licked her cracked lips, picturing the rows and rows of food. Oreos and chocolate chip granola bars. Fresh strawberries and milk. Everything sounded so good right now—even broccoli.

I promise, I'll never complain about food again if I could just have something to eat soon.

Floating along in her happy daydream of strawberries and blueberry muffins and pineapple pizza, Bethany didn't realize that she'd wandered into the bad man's room until she stood a foot away from his bed.

You shouldn't be in here, a tiny voice in her head whispered. *This is a bad idea.* But then the ringing in her ears grew louder, and she forgot all about bad ideas.

The bed with the navy-blue comforter with thin white stripes was all made up, as neat as one in a hotel room. Bethany ran her hand over the silky material as she looked around the other furniture. No dust in here. No mess of any kind. Everything was so tidy. Not like her mama's bedroom at home, where the floor or chair was usually covered in clothes.

Bethany wrapped her arms around her waist and shivered. This room was almost too clean, like it was trying to impress someone or lure them inside. Goose bumps raced down her arms.

You should leave.

Soon. But first, she'd check for food. Or a phone, or maybe a weapon.

Bethany opened the drawers of the bedside table, but they were as empty as the kitchen cupboards.

Besides the bed, the only other piece of furniture was a large bookcase, so she drifted there next. Instead of books, the shelves held more photos, like the ones hanging in the hall. All of the poofy-haired woman and the little boy.

She squinted at the nearest one, nearly touching her nose to the glass. Could the bad man be the little boy?

No. The bad man had never been a little boy. He'd probably been sent here from outer space in an alien egg or created in an evil doctor's lab.

A giggle slipped from her lips. *Quiet*, the voice in her head whispered.

"Why?" Bethany whispered back before giggling again. Her head was really spinning now, like one of those fair rides that made you barf, so she plopped down on her butt. "Now I'm the baby in the grocery store."

As she giggled again, her gaze fell on a set of books on the bottom shelf. The books were a rainbow of soft pinks and blues and yellows, and they all had fancy gold designs decorating the spines. Moving closer, she noticed a different name on each one. She read the names, pausing at one near the end.

Ellie. That was a good name. Like a superhero or the policewoman who'd saved her once.

Bethany slid out the album and opened the cover. The first page showed two photos of the same girl with pretty red curls and pale skin. Older than Bethany, maybe high school aged. Below the photos were cut out pieces of newspaper.

The little black words crawled across the page like ants at first, so Bethany shook her head and tried again. Better.

The article talked about the redheaded girl being kidnapped one night and how worried her parents had been.

Just like me. I bet my mama's worried too.

Bethany flipped the page to find three photos of a different person. A woman. In the first picture, she scowled into the camera while holding up a sign. The other two were photos of the left and right sides of her face. The kinds of photos the police took when you were arrested. Bethany had seen it in a cartoon once.

She studied the photo. The woman didn't look like a criminal, but then again, Bethany wasn't sure what a criminal looked like. Plus, her mama was always telling her that not all crimes were the same, and sometimes, people did bad things for good reasons.

This woman had short, dark hair and wore lots of black eyeliner and purple eyeshadow, and her red lipstick was smeared half off her mouth and onto her cheek. There was an ugly black bruise on her face, and she was dressed weird, in a shiny pink top that was so tight, her boobs looked like they might pop out, and a black skirt that was way shorter than any of Bethany's.

She read the name on the sign first. Sophie "Cleo" Finn. Sophie was a pretty name, almost as pretty as Ellie.

The next part of the sign made her frown. "So-li-ci-ta-tion." Bethany sounded out each syllable but had no idea what the word meant.

She flipped through the rest of the book, stopping on the last page. Tucked inside was a shiny silver circle. Bethany stroked the DVD with a finger and wondered what was on it. Maybe there was a player hidden somewhere in the room.

Bethany lifted her head to search, and her hands went numb.

The bad man stared at her from the doorway, his face a dark cloud.

She dropped the album like a hot potato, but it was too late. His eyes narrowed on the book at her feet like he was mad, except when he glanced up, his face was blank. For some reason, that scared Bethany more. Even that creepy little smile was gone. He looked dead, or plastic, like a statue or a doll.

"Someone's been very naughty, I see. How very disappointing. I expect all of my guests to obey the rules when they're under my roof."

He spoke in a lower, softer voice than usual, which didn't seem like it should make Bethany shiver but somehow did. She scooted back, until the bookshelves trapped her. "I...I..."

"Stand up. *Now.*"

With the help of the shelf, Bethany scrambled to her feet and tried not to throw up when the room tilted.

"Come here."

He held out a hand. Bethany's skin crawled at the thought of touching him, but the emptiness in his eyes scared her too much to disobey. What else could she do, anyway? There was nowhere to run. No way out. She'd missed her chance.

His fingers curled around her wrist and tugged her into the hall. She was so tired, and her feet kept tripping like she was dressed up in her mama's shoes. He led her toward the living room, and Bethany cast a longing glance at the tiny bedroom before scurrying after him.

Where are we going?

She didn't dare ask. Wherever they were going, it was nowhere good. Not that she had a choice. The bad man was too strong, and Bethany was too weak, and anyway, if there was no food, then she didn't care much where they went, as long as she could curl up in a ball somewhere and go back to sleep.

The man pulled her into the kitchen, and for a second, hope flared in Bethany's belly. When the man unlocked the chain on the refrigerator, she licked her lips and took an eager step forward.

Finally, he was going to feed her! If she'd had the energy, Bethany would have done a little dance. Instead, she held her growling stomach and tried to boss him with her mind.

Come on, faster. Hurry up and open the door already.

The metal chain clinked. The door swung open. Bethany stared into the empty space and refused to accept it.

No. There had to be food here, somewhere. What had happened to it all?

Not only the food but the shelves were gone. Without them, the inside of the fridge looked more like a big white box.

Like a sleepwalker, she drifted closer. Maybe this was all a dream, and sometimes in dreams, Bethany discovered new things if she kept searching. Maybe she'd find food in the fridge. But no. No milk, no cheese, no fruit or pudding appeared. The only thing left were a few Tupperware containers in the door.

"Why?" Her voice cracked.

Instead of answering, the man dug his fingers into her waist and shoved her inside. Her hip smacked the back wall, and the pain sucked her breath away.

The pain also woke her up, like a pinch in a dream, and fear clawed at her skin. "No! Stop!" Bethany twisted and lunged for the opening. The man's scary smile stretched his lips before he slammed the refrigerator door on her fingers.

She screamed again, and the door snicked open, just long enough to yank her hand out. When the door slammed shut this time, the refrigerator plunged into darkness. Bethany pounded the wall with her good hand for a few sobbing breaths before giving up. Her hip ached, and her fingers throbbed, and her throat burned, but none of that mattered because she needed to get out.

Take slow, easy breaths. Especially when you're afraid.

Her mama's lesson helped. Bethany worked on breathing and reminded herself to be brave.

Once she was quiet, the man spoke through the door. "You're going to stay in there until you've learned your lesson. Did you know that people can live in refrigerators for a long time? Maybe we should see how long you last in there. And maybe I should plug it back in so that you turn into a popsicle."

Bethany's throat knotted up like it did when she was about to cry, but no tears came. She remembered how she hadn't needed to pee that morning and wondered if it was possible for bodies to be too thirsty to make any new water.

It was too dark inside to see her hand in front of her face, and the air tasted stale. Bethany was so tired, and the dizziness was back. Her legs trembled, and she was about to sit down when she remembered.

Containers. There had been containers in the door.

Panting, she groped around until her hands hit plastic. At this point, she didn't care what was inside. Anything. She'd eat anything.

It took three tries with her shaky hands, but the lid finally popped off. She lifted the container to her lips. The reek hit an instant later.

Bethany gagged, inhaling even more stink of rotting, moldy food. The sour scent filled the entire space, and Bethany imagined spoiled particles flying up her nose, in her mouth. Down her throat. The idea squished her stomach, and what little water she'd drunk from the faucet earlier burned on the way back up.

By the time she finished hurling, her legs shook too much to stand. Bethany collapsed to the floor, which was wet with puke, but what difference did it make? There was nothing to clean up with, and she'd barfed on her shirt. The smell of vomit and rotten food made her tummy flip again, so she buried her head in her knees and closed her eyes.

How long would he leave her in here? Days? Weeks? Would he let her die? What if her mama was the one who opened the door and found her dead body?

With the little energy she had left, Bethany kicked at the door and pounded the wall with her uninjured hand. "Let me out! Let me out of here! I hate this place! I hate you! You're going to be sorry!"

She raged until her head spun again, until her lungs burned, and she gasped for air. Her body shook hard enough to rattle her teeth, like she was freezing, even though the air felt stuffy inside the box. She curled into a damp ball, wondering if she was going to die now.

How long had she been trapped already? One hour? Two? Five?

The door creaked open, and daylight rushed in, bringing air along with it. Bethany swallowed down long, deep breaths. Too deep, because she started coughing, hard enough to make her ribs ache.

When she finished, the bad man was staring down at her. The scary blank mask was gone, and the tiny smile was back. "That was five minutes."

Bethany blinked at him in confusion, and the tiny smile grew.

"Five minutes. That's how long you were inside. I timed it. I carried a load of laundry to my bedroom and brushed the breakfast from my teeth, and then came back. Can you imagine what would happen if I walked away for ten minutes? Fifteen? An hour? What if I locked the door, picked up my keys, and went out for a little drive? To the grocery store, or the mall, or perhaps a hike? What if I stayed away overnight?"

Huddled in a ball, shivering, Bethany stared up at him without speaking.

"You must remember that your life is mine to give or take as I please."

She stayed very still, terrified that the wrong word or movement would lead him to shut the door again.

After a moment, he nodded, then set a bucket on the floor in front of her. "Fill it with soap and hot water and use it to clean out the fridge. It's disgusting in there."

Bethany crawled out and carried the bucket to the sink. When water from the faucet slapped the plastic bottom, she glanced down at her arms.

Chunks of the rotten food and her stomach bile splattered her bare skin and sleeves and the front of her shirt. Sour and rotten, and green with mold.

Her stomach somersaulted again, but Bethany swallowed hard and shoved her arms under the spray.

Rotten, she decided as the chunks washed away.

The bad man's supervillain name was Doctor Rotten.

9

"I don't know, Ellie. With that little girl missing now, I'm worried this case might be too much for you right this second. Are you sure you're okay?"

Helen Kline's doubt flowed from the Bluetooth speakers as Shane steered the Explorer into the precinct's parking garage. Her bodyguard lifted an eyebrow at her, silently asking what she wanted him to do.

She mimicked parking in a space before turning her attention back to her mother. "I'm fine, Mom."

"I'm sorry, but I find that hard to believe."

Ellie gritted her teeth. Why bother asking the question, then? But she held her tongue. Getting drawn into an argument with her mother was about the last thing she wanted to do.

Shane guided the SUV past the disabled spots while Ellie waited for her mom to elaborate.

A long sigh filled her ears first. "You just got back from burying someone you cared about. How can you possibly be fine?"

The reference to Val's death wrenched Ellie's heart. She

slammed her fist against the dashboard, startling Shane enough that he thrust his foot on the brake, causing the SUV's tires to squeal.

Easy. Totaling the Explorer won't bring Val back.

"What was that noise?"

"Nothing, Mom." Ellie examined her knuckles, glad the skin hadn't broken. "Thought I saw a squirrel."

Crossing her fingers over her second white lie of the day, Ellie gave Shane a *sorry* smile and relaxed her muscles as the SUV edged on. None of this was her mother's fault. Ellie had lied about being fine because her mom was an expert-level worrier, but maybe honesty was the better option.

If the chief understood her reasons for not taking a break from work, her mom could too. "And you're right. I'm not really okay. The truth is, I don't think I'll ever be okay again until we catch Kingsley and put him behind bars."

"Oh, honey." A deep sigh. "I sometimes wonder…"

Shane pulled into an empty space near Fortis's black sedan and shifted the Explorer into park. Then he pointed, silently communicating that he was going to give her some privacy. She smiled her thanks. "Come on, Mom, spill. You've never been shy about sharing your thoughts before. Why start now?"

Helen Kline holding back an opinion was such an anomaly that Ellie's curiosity was piqued.

"I suppose you have a point, Eleanor, dear. I was going to say, I sometimes wonder if jail is even the right place for a man like that. Like…*Kingsley.*" Her mom whispered the name like she was afraid that saying it out loud might summon the sociopath from thin air.

Ellie frowned. "I'm not sure I'm following. If jail isn't the right place for a man like Kingsley, then where is?"

A hesitation. "That's just it, Eleanor. I wonder if nowhere

on this earth is the right place for a vicious monster like that."

This time the message registered. "Oh."

Leave it to her mom to find a delicate way to suggest that instead of law enforcement arresting Kingsley and bringing him to stand trial, society might benefit more from an extra-judicial kill. A murder.

Not that the idea of putting a bullet in Kingsley's brain hadn't occurred to Ellie…it had. Multiple times. Especially on days when memories of her own kidnapping tormented her. Kingsley's evil game would haunt Ellie forever. The worst emotional scars came from the role she'd been forced to play.

They'd been tied up opposite each other, and the other woman's face was permanently etched into Ellie's memory, her image carved into Ellie's subconscious through fear and blood and pain.

Her battered face and the screams. The agonized noises ripped from the woman's lungs were a soundtrack of terror. So traumatizing that even the thought of them now, over ten years later, fried Ellie's nerves and made her desperate for escape.

Kingsley's mocking voice was always the encore, as he urged Ellie to make an impossible choice.

If she said nothing, the woman's torture and bloodcur-dling screams would continue as Kingsley hacked away at her body, limb by limb.

If she uttered the right words, the other victim's suffering would end for good. No more shrieks. No more pain. Just bittersweet silence.

Life or death, all on the basis of a single phrase. *Die, bitch! Die.*

A devil's bargain that no one, especially a fifteen-year-old, should ever have to make.

At first, Ellie had refused, screaming that he couldn't make her play. Kingsley had merely laughed and informed her that there was no escape because, "Not choosing is still a choice." Hours and hours of witnessing the woman's pain had worn Ellie down.

In the end, Ellie had shouted the words.

The screams stopped.

She'd had to live with that choice ever since.

For the decade following the kidnapping, Ellie had suffered from amnesia, and for once, the doctors all agreed. To protect itself from further trauma, her teenage brain had blocked those events out.

After repeated encounters with one of Kingsley's henchmen, who'd worked for a brief time as the department psychologist, the memories started flowing again.

Some, at least. A few murky spots remained. Even now, a memory niggled at her brain, but the second she tried to tease the information out? Poof! Gone.

Ellie bit back a curse. Each time she worked on detailing the hours spent in Kingsley's warehouse, she failed. Those memories were trapped somewhere deep in her subconscious.

So much time had passed now that Ellie doubted they'd ever be recovered.

"Ellie? Are you still there?"

Her mother's voice pierced the dark storm of the past. "I'm here. And I understand where you're coming from, but I'm a detective, not an executioner. My job is to gather evidence, make arrests, and trust our justice system to take care of the rest. If I kill someone just because I think they deserve it, then how am I any better than the criminals I hunt?"

That exact question had stopped Ellie from descending

too far into gruesome fantasies involving guns and scraping Kingsley's brain matter off the wall.

Helen Kline huffed into the speaker. "Don't compare yourself to them. That's absurd. Now, I'd like to see you soon and reassure myself that my only daughter isn't on the verge of collapse. Can we please arrange a day?"

Ellie stifled a groan. She loved her mother, but the last thing her frayed nerves needed was a head-to-toe, eagle-eyed inspection scrutinizing her for the tiniest hint of any cracks or fatigue.

Her neck tensed just thinking about it. She rolled her head to the side to stretch, and her gaze landed on Fortis.

She frowned. That was odd. Fortis hadn't moved the entire time she'd been yacking away with her mom.

"So, can you take a peek at your calendar and see which day—"

Ellie knew the nagging would never stop. "How about lunch on Friday?"

No sense dragging this out. Her mom would win in the end, plus Ellie wanted to check on her boss. Napping on the job wasn't like him.

Poor guy. He'd cautioned her about burning out over the Kingsley case, but maybe he needed to take his own advice.

"Friday works, but it'll have to be a late lunch. One or after? I have a meeting at eleven with a potential donor for the museum fund."

Fortis still didn't move. Had he slept at all last night? "One is good, see you then."

When the call ended, Ellie grabbed her bag, and hopped out, leaving the engine running for Shane when he went back to babysitting duties. She spotted him at the stair entrance and knew he was scouring the place for people who were stupid enough to try to take down a cop in a police precinct's parking garage.

Ellie wasn't worried.

"Hey, boss. Looks like you're the one who needs that vacation if you're falling asleep behind the wheel. Want me to send you my travel agent's number?"

Once the joke quit echoing off the concrete walls, silence stretched out. Nothing from Fortis. He was out cold.

Her frown returned. Hadn't Fortis worn that same gray sport coat yesterday? She peered into the tinted window and the hairs on her forearms lifted. Her boss's skin, usually a warm brown courtesy of his mother, appeared several shades paler today. Too pale, and his lips held a blueish tinge.

Wrong, wrong, something is very wrong.

Ellie whipped the gun from her holster and dropped into a shooter's stance. "Fortis! Wake up! Fortis!"

Barrel extended, she swept the garage and edged around the trunk, praying for a response. None came. Not even when she banged on the driver's side window.

The gun steady in her right hand, Ellie used the left to fumble with the door handle. After several attempts, her boneless fingers succeeded. She nudged the door open with her hip and tapped her boss on the shoulder.

No. No. This isn't happening. It can't be.

She jumped when Shane came around the car, gun up and ready. "What's going on?" he demanded, his eyes scanning the vicinity.

Ellie didn't take her eyes off her boss as she shook him this time. "Come on, wake up."

Fortis's head slumped forward, causing his sunglasses to slide off his face and into his lap. Up close, his skin was wrong. Waxy.

Ellie waved her hand in front of him, but she already knew. Those sightless eyes would never see again.

"No, please, no," she moaned.

Futile pleas her boss would never hear because Lead Detective Harold Fortis was dead.

Ellie shuddered and pressed her fingers to his throat, checking for a pulse just to be sure.

She waited...praying...putting all her senses into the two fingers pressed to his skin. Cold and silence was her only response.

"Shit." The curse came from Shane, who kept his gun up and ready while grasping his phone with his other hand. "I'll call it in."

She pushed a fist to her mouth and started to turn away, but her anguished gaze snagged on a strip of white.

There, in his jacket pocket. A paper of some kind.

If she'd been thinking clearly, Ellie would have stepped back without touching anything else and waited for the crime scene techs to do their jobs, but her brain refused to function. Pure instinct drove her hand to pluck the note from her dead boss's pocket.

She read the message and went numb.

Hate that I missed you,

-K

10

Beyond the yellow crime scene tape that stretched across the parking garage, forensic technicians scoured the area surrounding Fortis's car like busy little ants.

Stranded on the wrong side of the tape, Ellie clenched her teeth in helpless frustration. She should be over there, helping the department search for clues. Instead, she was a hostage to Valdez's endless interrogations. The detective asked the same six questions posed in slightly different ways.

"When did you last see the victim alive?"

Like that one. Ellie twined a loose curl tighter and tighter around her finger, tugging until her scalp stung from the pressure. "Yesterday afternoon, just before I left the precinct to go home. The same thing I told you the last three times you asked this question, and all the rest of them."

When did you become aware that something was wrong?

Did you notice anyone suspicious?

To the best of your knowledge, had the victim been acting strangely over the past few days?

What did you touch?

That one made Ellie grimace. Grabbing the note from Fortis's jacket had been a rookie mistake.

Do you know of anyone who'd want to hurt the victim?

The last question was a complete joke. Fortis was a lead detective who'd put his fair share of criminals behind bars. Like most LEOs, there were plenty of bad guys out there who'd love to take revenge, given half a chance.

But Ellie and Valdez both knew that Fortis's murder wasn't the work of some random criminal. Even before spotting the note, one killer in particular had risen to Ellie's mind.

Kingsley. This had his fingers all over it.

Valdez rocked back on his heels. "Do you want to take a break and finish later?"

Ellie released the curl and expelled a noisy breath. "No. I'm sorry. Here I am, complaining about the same questions witnesses are subjected to every day. I just hate this, all of...this."

She winced up at Valdez. The artificial lights washed some of the color from his brown skin, but the Latino man's dark eyes were calm and steady as he regarded Ellie over the top of his notebook.

"It's okay. This has been quite a shock for all of us, but especially you."

She tried and failed to force her lips into a smile. "Thanks." Until recently, Ellie and Valdez had been at each other's throats, arguing about the multitude of Kingsley cases. For months following Valdez's transfer to CPD, he'd made veiled accusations about Ellie being involved with Kingsley's criminal enterprise, leaving her so furious on certain occasions, she'd come close to trading her job for the satisfaction of landing a punch.

During a private conference, Valdez had eventually come clean, admitting he was an undercover FBI agent sent to investigate corruption within the Charleston precinct after the explosive discovery that a former detective was on the take. Ever since the truth aired, suspicions between the two of them had simmered down to a more bearable temperature.

"Let's prepare the area to move the victim."

The command drew Ellie's attention to where the medical examiner and her assistants were arranging thin plastic sheeting on the ground.

Victim.

The word pinged through her head, like an old record that always skipped at the same spot. But no amount of repetition could inject reality into the word. How could her grumpy, tough boss be a victim? The man was a force of nature. Relentless and strong. There'd been times when her boss's by-the-book methods drove Ellie bonkers, but no matter how much they'd clashed, she'd always admired him. Always.

Harold Fortis had been a damned good cop and an even better man.

Sorrow swelled in Ellie's throat. Fortis hadn't deserved to die like this. None of Kingsley's victims had.

She shied away from the scene, too heartsick to witness her boss being zipped into a body bag. "How did you get assigned this case if you're still undercover?"

Valdez shrugged while scribbling something in his notebook. "I'm done with that job, and I guess the powers-that-be figured my knowledge of the CPD made me the best choice to lead this particular murder case."

A small, injured noise escaped Ellie, and Valdez glanced up from his writing.

His brown eyes softened when he studied her face. "Like I said before, I know this is difficult, especially for you, but I liked Fortis too. I admired the hell out of him, and I trusted him. Please, let me take care of the case. I give you my word that I will devote myself to bringing the bastard who did it to justice."

She nodded. "I know you will."

"Any news yet?" Chief Johnson interrupted them, his expression as grim as Ellie had ever seen it. "Ellie, how are you holding up?"

"I don't know. I think I'm still in shock that he's gone."

Gone. What a useless euphemism.

"I can imagine. You're not alone, either. It's been a shocking morning for all of us." The chief patted her on the shoulder in an awkward attempt at comfort. "Are you sure you won't reconsider what we talked about in my office yesterday? If anything, this makes a stronger case for you to take some time off."

Ellie bit her lip as the pain spiraled into her chest like a drill. When they'd met in the chief's office yesterday, they'd formed a trio, not a duo. Fortis had faced Chief Johnson across the desk and gone to bat for Ellie by defending her choice to work through the grief of Val's murder.

Now less than twenty-four hours later, he was dead too. Wiped from the earth by pure, unadulterated evil.

"I haven't changed my mind since yesterday. When we talked about it with Detective F-Fortis." Ellie squeezed her arms as fresh sorrow washed over her. "If anything, I'm more determined than ever to keep working."

"I understand." The chief rubbed his jaw. "But maybe—"

"In fact, after this, I'd like to dedicate all of my working hours to Kingsley's cases."

Valdez cleared his throat. "I think this is my cue to leave before I offer unsolicited advice."

"Right, sorry. Ellie, walk with me back to the office." Chief Johnson gestured toward the exit, and Ellie fell into step beside him, putting his muscular frame between her and an unobstructed view of the crime scene.

When they rounded the corner, Ellie's shoulders eased a little. "So?"

The chief shook his head. "I don't think clearing your schedule to only work Kingsley cases is a very good idea. What about your cold cases? You still have crimes to solve, missing children to find."

Guilt pinged in Ellie's gut, but she lifted her chin. The missing children had disappeared over a decade ago. The world wouldn't catch fire if the files sat on her desk for another few months. "The only cold case I can focus on right now is the one involving the girl Kingsley pitted me against when he held me prisoner in that warehouse."

They continued walking and were steps away from the precinct's front door before the chief replied. "As much as I'd like to deny you that case for your own safety, I feel like it wouldn't be the right thing to do. So go ahead, work that case if you must. But Ellie?"

He paused on the sidewalk a few yards short of the door, so Ellie stopped too. "Yes?"

His forehead creased. "Please, be careful. We've lost too much to this monster already. I will not accept losing you too. Do you copy?"

Ellie managed a wobbly smile. "Yes, sir."

"Good."

The chief nodded, and they both started walking again.

"Detective Kline, hold up!"

Shoes pounded the pavement behind them, and they turned in unison as a skinny man in a white lab coat barreled down the sidewalk.

He staggered to a stop and doubled over, gasping for air. When he'd recovered enough to straighten, his forehead and neck glistened with sweat, and his entire face was red.

"Sorry...haven't been to the gym since before Thanksgiving. This...was in the car...for you. Passenger...seat."

The forensics tech extended the manila file that had been secured in a plastic evidence bag to Ellie, but Chief Johnson swooped in first, blocking her.

Ellie held out her hand. "Please, I think it's safe for me to look. I highly doubt there's an explosive masquerading as a piece of paper."

Chief Johnson arched a brow at her outstretched palm until she sighed and crossed her arms. "Fine. I'll wait until you've decided that a folder isn't a threat."

As if she had a choice.

Ellie sank back on her heels as the chief pulled a pair of latex gloves from his pocket. Once he'd slipped them on, Chief Johnson took the file from the tech and began inspecting the exterior folder.

They found her name on the side, in large, bold letters:

Kline, Ellie

Dread crawled across Ellie's neck. Both that format and font were familiar.

Chief Johnson's lips thinned into a flat line as he arrived at the same conclusion. "This looks like your cold case file from thirteen years ago."

Ellie agreed, and her stomach soured. Could that really be her cold case file, and if so, how? How had Kingsley gotten his hands on it, and why return the thing now?

Chief Johnson turned to the waiting tech. "I'll need an evidence kit. Bring one to me down in the lab."

Cheeks still flushed, the skinny tech nodded and scurried off, and the chief focused on Ellie. "I'll have the CSI team take pictures of each item and send them to you."

11

With her mind spinning at a million miles per minute, Ellie paced the lobby floor clutching the folder of photocopies to her chest, ignoring the curious glances thrown her way by the desk clerk and passing patrol officers.

The door whooshed open, and Jillian Reed, Ellie's best friend and sometimes roommate, rushed over and threw her arms around Ellie without a trace of self-consciousness. "Are you okay? I can't believe this is happening."

Ellie closed her eyes and squeezed her friend hard before pulling away. "None of this is okay."

Jillian's blue eyes were rimmed in pink, and blonde strands escaped her usual neat ponytail. "I know. Poor Detective Fortis. It's not right. How many more lives is that asshole going to destroy before the end?"

That question had been haunting Ellie for months. "None, if I can help it. I need you to let me into the file room."

Jillian nodded. "I was headed there now. Anything in particular you're looking for?"

On their way to the basement where Jillian worked as the

evidence desk clerk, Ellie explained about the file that Kingsley had left for her.

Jillian paused in the stairwell, her eyes round. "Oh my god, he left that for you? In Detective Fortis's car?"

"Apparently."

Ellie had already hit her quota for concerned looks from coworkers today, so she continued down the stairs. Outside the door, the hallway that led to the evidence room was darker than the rest of the building and held a faint musty odor, like maybe once upon a time, a leak had never been fixed properly, and the damp air allowed mold to flourish.

The touchpad beeped as Jillian typed in the code, then the lock clicked open. Ellie dumped the copies that Chief Johnson had sent to her office on Jillian's desk before bypassing the current case evidence and heading straight for the back room, where the older cold cases were stored.

Ellie shivered as they perused the white evidence boxes stacked on the shelves. The temperature down here was always chillier than everywhere else, and the frigid air bit through her blazer and thin top.

"Here it is!"

Jillian pushed onto her tiptoes to grab a box off the top shelf labeled *Kline, Ellie*. "I have no idea how Kingsley could have gotten his hands on the information in here. Unless… do you think there's another mole in our office?"

Ellie tagged behind as Jillian carried the box to her desk. "I don't know, but I promise to ask him once I drag him out of whatever hole he's hiding in."

Jillian set the box down near the folder of photocopies and pulled out a chair. "All right, here we go. You ready?"

Ellie sank into a second chair. "Let's do it." While she opened the folder to the copies of papers Kingsley had left for her, her friend removed the lid from the box and fished Ellie's original report out.

Once the first pages were arranged side by side, Ellie began scanning, starting with the legitimate report in front of Jillian. The inconsistencies between the two popped out before she reached the second half.

Ellie wrinkled her brow. "Ready for the next page?"

"Yeah." Jillian was frowning too, but they continued their inspection, waiting until they were both finished with a page before flipping to the next.

About halfway through, Jillian expelled a breath. "Well, at least we know that the file Kingsley left you wasn't copied verbatim. There are parts that sound like something out of a bad movie script."

Ellie nodded. "Right? This definitely wasn't written by anyone in law enforcement."

"I don't get it. What was the point of creating such an obviously fake file, much less risk leaving it at a crime scene for you to find?"

While she'd examined the last few pages, Ellie had racked her brain over that very same question. "I honestly have no idea on either count, and that worries me."

Surprises and Kingsley never mixed well.

Jillian shoved the file aside and shifted sideways in the chair to face Ellie. "On a scale of one to ten, with one being floating away in a state of pure bliss and ten being hurling yourself naked and screaming into the abyss, how are you doing?"

Despite the awful morning so far, Ellie's lips twitched. "Just for my own personal reference, what happens at level nine? Hurling myself screaming into the abyss, but I'm fully clothed?"

"Obviously. Now, quit stalling and answer."

"Okay. But for the record, I have more questions about this rating scale." Ellie's amusement faded. "I'd say I'm at a six. But that score will improve once we find Bethany. And improve even more when we haul Kingsley's ass in."

"But for the most part, you're okay?"

"I will be, just as soon as everyone stops asking me that question." Ellie was half-joking when she said it, but Jillian reached over and gave her another hug before burying her head back over the file.

Ellie pushed the folder away and stared up at the ceiling, wishing she understood what Kingsley was playing at this time. Because without a doubt, that was exactly why he'd left the file on Fortis's passenger seat. The doctor loved nothing better than to force unwilling participants to take part in his macabre mind games.

One thing was almost certain, though. The clues to solving this latest riddle were hidden inside the phony file.

Ellie cracked her neck before scooting forward and getting back to work, starting from page one and scrutinizing every line.

The beginning was pretty cut and dried. Names, locations, dates. Nothing much jumped out at her until she flipped to page two. "Hey, check this out."

Jillian craned her neck to inspect the line above Ellie's finger. "All I see is an address. What am I missing?"

"That's not my home address."

Jillian peered closer and frowned. "It's not an old one either?"

Ellie shook her head. "No. I've never lived there. I don't even know where that is."

The laptop squeaked when Jillian dragged it across the desk. "Let's fix that right now." Her fingers clicked on the keys as she typed the address into the search engine.

A list of entries popped up. Ellie zeroed in on the first few and discovered that the address belonged to Far Ridge Boy's Academy.

As she read, her pulse picked up.

Not just any boy's academy, but one with a sordid past.

The top hits were all articles with salacious headlines.

Three Boys Dead Under Mysterious Circumstances at Exclusive Boarding School

Headmaster Gives No Explanation for Student Deaths at Far Ridge Boy's Academy

Students Locked Out of Rich Prep School Overnight Die of Exposure

"Yikes," Jillian murmured.

"Can you open that fourth one?" Ellie pointed to the entry she wanted, and Jillian slid the mouse and clicked. The page opened to the About Me section of a blog. The author bio beneath the banner claimed the blog owner was a former student and survivor of the Far Ridge Boy's Academy.

Ellie's pulse kicked up as she read on. Beneath the bio was a section titled "Support My Work," which contained brief descriptions and links to a podcast and book. Based on the list of awards next to both the podcast and book, Nickolas "Hank" Crawford was well-regarded in the field of true crime.

"We need to talk to this guy, see what, if anything, he knows. Can you pull up the contact info?"

Jillian clicked on the heading. "You think he's linked to Kingsley somehow?"

"He has to be. Why else leave me this Easter egg hunt?"

"With Kingsley, who knows? Didn't he send you on a wild goose chase once already, when he had someone pretend to be the long-lost daughter from one of your cold cases?"

Beyond her screaming gut, Ellie couldn't explain how she knew this time was different, so she didn't waste time trying. "Yes, but that tip did lead me to solve another case."

"After sending you to a meth trailer that could have exploded if you'd sneezed wrong."

Ellie bristled at the memory. "The bomb squad went in first, so I was okay on that front. Dying from inhaling toxic fumes was the real concern."

Jillian jabbed Ellie's ribs with her elbow. "Gee, I feel so much better now that you've cleared that up."

After a brief lull, the page pulled up. Ellie frowned at the contents. "An email address, that's it?"

"Sure looks that way."

Grumbling under her breath, Ellie tugged the laptop closer, copied the address into her email account, and began typing up a message.

"Do you really think this Hank guy will be able to help? He clearly has his own trauma issues to work out."

"All I know is that Kingsley directed us this way for a reason. If this Hank Crawford knew him, or if Kingsley had something to do with that boy's academy, then questioning him can only help. Maybe they were old school buddies or something, and he's aware of one of Kingsley's hidey holes. I feel like the fastest way to find him is by talking to the people who knew him best."

Ellie finished composing the message and hit send before glancing up and catching Jillian's pointed look. "What?"

"I was just thinking…if that's the case, then shouldn't you head out to the psych hospital? Because I'm pretty sure there's a patient there who knows Kingsley better than anyone."

12

K atarina stared at the visitor who stood at the foot of her hospital bed in stony silence, amazed once more by how different she and the redheaded detective from the Charleston Police Department were. As far as Katarina could tell, the only significant trait she shared with Ellie Kline was the fact that both of them were members of the very exclusive Kingsley Survivor Club.

As for the rest, well…that was still up in the air. Until recently, Katarina had been certain she'd gotten the better end of the stick. Her upbringing, while unconventional, had granted Katarina the type of freedom that few children experienced. It lacked the stifling rules and restraints Ellie had grown up with. Rules that would have driven Katarina bananas.

Her lips curved in a humorless smile when she went to scratch her nose but was stopped short by thick straps on her wrists. Then again, who knew? Maybe she was predestined to end up in a straitjacket whether she'd been raised in a mansion or a meth house.

"Something funny you want to share?" Ellie stepped to

the side of the bed, causing the fluorescent lights overhead to reflect off the badge pinned to her hip. The metal shimmered like fourteen karat gold, an image that forced a sigh from Katarina's lungs.

Whatever she'd believed before, the truth now was clear.

The winner of their unofficial competition was the woman who could come and go from the hospital as she pleased, and who didn't have to hit a call button to use the toilet. "Not really."

Other than flaring her nostrils, Ellie ignored Katarina's rude response. She stood as stiff as a wooden doll by the foot rail, with her hands fisted by her sides.

Katarina narrowed her eyes. Thanks to her unorthodox upbringing, studying surroundings and people was second nature. Their previous encounters revealed that Detective Kline practically simmered with hyperkinetic energy. One of those loud, bubbly types who found it near impossible to sit still.

Not on this visit. The other woman's spine was rigid, and the fire in her green eyes had been replaced by ice.

Something had happened since the last time they'd met. A big enough event to take a drastic toll on the detective.

Katarina jerked her chin to gesture at the empty chair. "Quit gaping at me like an awkward carrot and sit down already. All that hovering is giving me the willies."

That prompted a snort as the detective folded her long legs and sat. "I didn't realize carrots could be awkward. Or that Katarina Volkov ever said 'willies.'"

Katarina shifted her hips in a futile attempt to get comfortable. She'd never admit the truth out loud, but now that she was in the psych ward, she kind of missed the air mattress. The thing had been noisy as hell, but at least she didn't wake up feeling like she'd slept on a sack of bricks. "Why are you here?"

"I was hoping you might have some idea of where Kingsley is hiding."

Katarina barked an irritated laugh and rattled her arms. "Do you really think I'd still be chained to this stupid bed if I had any clue at all where my daughter was?"

"Oh, I don't know. You don't really strike me as your average, run-of-the-mill mother."

The detective delivered the remark in a teasing tone, but the barb sank its hooks into Katarina's chest anyway. A sharp reminder that all her efforts to keep Bethany safe had failed. Her daughter had fallen into the hands of the one man she'd vowed to protect her from, and the knowledge all but split her chest in two.

"Yeah? Well, at least I am a mother. Speaking of, how is the lovely Mrs. Kline doing? Has she accepted the reality yet that her only daughter can't seem to hold down a boyfriend to save her life?"

That insult had been a shot in the dark, but when Ellie's jaw tightened, Katarina knew she'd hit the target. Surprising, really. From the puppy dog eyes Agent Lockwood made at the detective, Katarina had figured they'd be an item by now. The jab had been aimed at her ex-boyfriend, the fancy rich philanthropist who was often splashed across the papers.

Ellie's chest raised and lowered in five long, slow breaths. "Believe it or not, I didn't drive out here just to trade insults. I have better things to do with my day."

Katarina opened her mouth as wide as she could and yawned. When she finished, she blinked up at the detective. "Oh, I'm sorry, were you saying something? I would have covered my mouth, but you know how it is with these kinky psych doctors. They just can't stop themselves from indulging in a little patient BDSM."

Ellie ducked her head and made an odd noise in her throat. If Katarina didn't know better, she'd accuse the detective of having a sense of humor. "So, why did you really come here?" she asked. "I know! Maybe you came to spring me out."

Slowly, the detective lifted her gaze to meet Katarina's. "I don't have the authority to release you. It's up to the doctor."

Katarina rolled her eyes before closing them. "Sure. Like I don't know that if it were left up to you, I'd be locked up in a prison with no hope for parole."

"You're right. I do like to lock up bad guys whenever possible. But I also know better than to argue with the Attorney General when he grants someone a 'get out of jail free' card. Besides, the past is in the past. You haven't killed anyone lately, have you?"

Clayne's face appeared behind Katarina's eyelids, flashing that same confident grin from the afternoon they'd first met, back in the dark bar that squatted in the shadows of the Grand Tetons. His eyes had brimmed with humor and life then, even lust.

Unlike the terror in those gray depths in his last moments, when he'd begged for his life...or the dull acceptance an instant before she'd slit his throat.

Katarina flinched, but the image refused to fade. No less than she deserved.

Flawed or not, the man had stood by her side and helped her hunt down Kingsley to reclaim her daughter. Katarina had done lots of unforgivable things in her life, but this one topped the list.

She opened her eyes and glared. "Either tell me what you're doing here or get the hell out. I'm tired of this visit already."

The detective didn't respond right away, so Katarina filled the downtime by subjecting her nemesis to a thorough once-over. That crisp tailored charcoal suit she wore easily cost more than most of Katarina's closet combined, and

Ellie hadn't even earned that fancy wardrobe through hard work.

Her fair skin was smooth and perfect, no doubt thanks to a drawer full of expensive beauty products, and those baby pink nails appeared fresh from a manicure because only the best would do for the daughter of the wealthy Kline family. All due to a stroke of luck at birth. Some twist of fate that plopped her into the hands of loving, loaded parents.

Meanwhile, Katarina had been passed around from home to home like the hand-me-down clothes she had to wear. Each time, the new set of parents wanted to recreate Katarina into their image of a perfect daughter. No one ever asked Katarina what style of clothes she'd prefer to wear or which hobbies she might enjoy, but any failure to display an appropriate amount of enthusiasm for whatever they chose for her led to trouble.

Good thing she was a quick study. It only took one slap across the face and one accusation of *ungrateful brat* for Katarina to learn that her needs and wants didn't matter. Not even when foster parents claimed they did. The safe option was to slip on the new clothes and personality like a mask and play a never-ending game of pretend.

Bitterness welled like blood to a scratch as Katarina glared at the elegant, expensively dressed trespasser who'd barged into her hospital room like she owned the place. Who knew? Maybe she did. Nothing would surprise Katarina less than to discover one or more Klines owned a stake in the building that trapped her. At the very least, their twenty-four carat asses probably all sat in seats on the board.

Lucky bitch. As she eyed Ellie Kline in her beautiful suit, perched on the ugly brown chair like a princess lowering herself to visit a peasant, Katarina bet that the detective had never spent a single day of her life pretending. Must be nice growing up with doting parents who accepted you the way you were.

"Why haven't I been given any updates on Bethany? What are you guys even doing to find her, beyond annoying the hell out of patients trapped in the loony bin?"

Ellie's nose wrinkled at that last bit, which only irritated Katarina more. Screw her highness's disapproval. Katarina was the one stuck here. As far as she was concerned, that gave her the right to call this hellhole whatever she liked.

Or maybe the detective wasn't reacting to her wording at all, but the smell. Katarina couldn't remember the last time she'd showered. She lifted one arm and sniffed. Oof. Definitely ripe. But what the hell could anyone expect, tied to a bed all day and night?

Eyes narrowed, she bent her elbows and flapped her arms like a chicken, hoping to push the reek of BO in Ellie's direction. *Take that, Princess.*

The detective's nose twitched, but she was too polite to comment. "The Charleston Police Department is working in coordination with the FBI to pool resources and find your daughter as soon as possible. We have officers and agents working around the clock and chasing down every credible lead."

Katarina sneered. "Blah blah blah, give me a break. You sound like a trained seal. If I'd wanted to hear that kind of politically correct department speak, I'd flip on the ten o'clock news."

Not that she could flip on the news in this stupid place even if she wanted to, because apparently those sort of real-world events were deemed too upsetting for the patients' fragile mental states. Katarina would be lucky if they let her watch the cartoons.

Ellie's lips tightened as she tugged on a loose strand of

hair. "I'm sorry if I came across that way, but we really do have agents—"

"Cut the bullshit already. I just want the truth. Why haven't they found Bethany yet? Or are only kids from fancy families with McMansions and seven-figure stock portfolios considered worth the effort to find?"

The detective's spine stiffened, and her hands balled in her lap. "That's not true. Money doesn't matter at all in kidnapping cases."

Katarina narrowed her eyes. "Spoken like someone who comes from money because they're the only ones clueless enough to say shit like that."

Red splotched the other woman's cheeks. The gray jacket Katarina admired lifted and lowered several times before she replied. "I agree that money often makes a difference when it shouldn't, but I don't believe that kidnapping cases are one of those times. Just about every officer or agent who puts on a uniform dreams of being a hero, and nothing is more heroic than rescuing a pretty little girl from the clutches of a sick and twisted sociopath. So, to answer your question...everything. Everything is being done to find her."

Katarina grunted her disbelief, earning her a frustrated glare.

Ellie exhaled another long breath. "That's the main reason I'm here, to help chase down any possible lead. No one knows Kingsley better than you, so I'm hoping that by talking, we can shake some little detail or memory free that will help lead me to Kingsley, and Bethany by default."

The laugh that burst from Katarina's lips rang harsh in the sterile little cell of a room. "That all sounds great in theory, except for one little problem. No one truly knows Kingsley. Not even Kingsley himself. Besides, even if I did know something, telling you would be a waste of breath. We both know you wouldn't believe me anyway."

Ellie braced her palms on her thighs and leaned forward. "Try me."

After a brief internal debate, Katarina was swayed by the feverish intensity in the detective's green eyes. *What the hell?* Worst case, Ellie would shake her head at the end of the story, draw the same conclusions about Katarina's sanity as the doctors, and finally leave her in peace.

"He came to visit me. Right here in the hospital. Well, not in this room, but in my ICU room downstairs. He waltzed in like he owned the place and started asking me questions only Kingsley would know to ask, but when I screamed for the nurse, no one believed me. So, yeah, I guess I do know Kingsley. At least, enough to recognize him when he's wearing a disguise and no one else had a clue."

The story had an effect, just not in the way Katarina had anticipated. Ellie sprang to her feet, but instead of running, she surged closer to the bed. "You'd better not be messing with me right now." Those manicured hands curled around one of the side rails that formed Katarina's cage. "Are you telling me the truth? Did you really see Kingsley in your room?"

Katarina gaped at Ellie's glittering eyes and flushed cheeks. Her heart skipped a beat. Was it possible that someone in this awful place finally believed her and didn't chalk her story up to a mental breakdown?

"Oh, it was real, all right. What the hell reason would I have to lie? But if you require further convincing, go check the surveillance footage. I'm guessing a place like this has camera feeds that actually work."

Katarina held the detective's glittering stare for a good ten seconds before Ellie nodded. "Okay. I believe you. Or at least that you believe that's what happened."

"Gee, thanks. I'm ever so grateful that you believe I'm

telling the truth, even if you're half convinced I'm hallu-cinating."

Ellie tapped her foot and sighed. "Look—"

"No, you look!" Katarina broke in, urgency making her talk fast. "You were partially right when you said I know Kingsley better than anyone because I do know better than anyone what he's capable of. Even with little girls he feels affection for. He started grooming me on the first day he walked in the door of the Davidsons' house, the latest in a long line of parents. Not in a kiddy diddling way, but in a psychopath crazy as shit way."

Katarina closed her eyes, forcing her mind away from that day.

"What happened?"

Katarina forced herself to meet Ellie's green gaze again. "Those people, the Davidsons, were worse than shitty parents, but they didn't deserve to burn to death...or to have that sick bastard prey on all my loneliness and anger and press a knife in my hand and make it obvious that I either cut them or die alongside them. I was just a kid."

The words rang soft and hollow in her ears, so she repeated them. Louder, with more conviction this time.

"I was just a kid. Parentless and scared and sad and confused. That asshole got me when I was older than Bethany, and already harder, and that was just the first horror in a whole string of them."

"I'm sorry, Katarina."

Katarina cringed at the gentleness in Ellie's voice. Screw that. She didn't need anyone's pity, least of all the red-haired princess bitch. Messed up or not, she'd survived.

"Spare me your sympathy. I only told you that story to remind you of what's at stake here. My daughter is innocent and good. We can't let him ruin her like he did me. Please *find* her."

"Tell me more about her. What are some of her favorite things? What's she like?"

Through her rising panic, Katarina pictured her daughter's smiling face, and her mouth softened. "She loves pancakes and waffles, especially the kind you make yourself at those free all-you-can-eat breakfasts they have at hotels. Her favorite superhero is Wonder Woman. She's a pro at getting you to read her a second bedtime story, loves playing games of pretend and learning new facts. That kid is incredibly resilient, and at eight years old has more ingenuity in her little finger than I've had in my entire damn life."

She stopped talking to drag air down her constricted throat as waves of helpless frustration threatened to overwhelm her. Bethany had been missing for over a week now. Long enough for Kingsley to have inflicted permanent damage on her tender eight-year-old psyche.

Ellie rose from the chair. "I'm sorry, I know this must be awful, but I swear I'm not lying when I tell you we're pulling out all the stops to find her."

Katarina tugged on the wrist straps. "If that's true, then you'll help me get out of here."

The detective hesitated, studying Katarina's bound arms like she was tempted before lifting her shoulders. "Like I said before, it's not up to me. Do what you need to do, say what you need to say to get yourself out of here." Her long legs made quick work of the room, and within moments, the detective was at the door, where she paused. "I promise I'll be in touch the second I hear anything."

The door clicked shut behind her, and she was gone.

Angry tears sprang to Katarina's eyes, but she choked back the cry, fighting the emotion until she was sure Ellie was out of range. She counted ten seconds before the dam burst, and the bed shook from the force of her sobs.

Bethany was out there, trapped with one of the most

demented men on the face of the earth, and Katarina's fleeting hope that the police would find her soon had died the second Detective Kline opened her mouth.

Her daughter was in danger, and there wasn't a damn thing Katarina could do to protect her. Not while strapped to this bed.

I'm sorry, baby girl. I'm so sorry.

She sobbed and sobbed until a male voice intruded on her pain. "Hey, now. It can't be as bad as all that."

The kind voice only made her cry harder.

"Is this about your little girl? I promise the doctor will let you out as soon as you show that you're stable."

A harsh laugh scraped her raw throat. She lifted her head and blinked until Jasper's features were no longer blurry from tears. "Stable? How could anyone in my position be stable, knowing that their daughter is in the hands of a killer? Please, tell me what the acceptable behavior is for this scenario, and I'll get right to work. How about smiling, is that what the psychologists want to see right now? Here, how's this?"

Katarina grinned so wide that her cheeks ached, making Jasper flinch and glance away. "I'm sorry."

"Don't be. It's not your fault. But do you get it now? The most unstable thing I could do is spend my days smiling and giggling and looking on the bright side. That would be the real show of crazy." Katarina's fingers latched onto his forearm when he moved close enough. "Freaking out is the normal thing to do. I need to get out of here. Now. Please, help me."

As she pleaded with her eyes, Jasper's expression softened. "I'll talk to the doctor for you, okay? I promise. I'll try to help you in any way I can."

Katarina gripped his arm a few seconds longer, savoring

the prolonged contact with bare, warm skin before pulling away.

She knew better than to hope. Hell, she knew there were laws that should stop this damn hospital from keeping her tied up so long, but there was nothing she could do about that either.

No one could help her. No one had ever been able to help her.

Defeat crashed over her like a tidal wave, destroying every lingering speck of energy. Katarina closed her eyes.

"Just go away. You can't help me now. No one can."

13

T he hospital elevator eased to a stop and dinged before the doors slid open. Ellie waited on the two chatting nurses in blue scrubs to exit first before following them into the lobby, her mind reeling from the visit with Katarina. So many shocks in such a short amount of time.

The transformation of the tough-as-nails criminal into an adoring, worried mom had thrown her more than it should have. Now, she had to sit with the discomfort that the other woman might have a point about Ellie's privilege blinding her to reality sometimes.

Later, though. She needed her mind clear to deal with the other surprise...Kingsley. If Katarina was to be believed, he'd shown up at her bedside.

Ellie didn't care what the doctors said about Katarina. Apart from that weird chicken wing thing, the woman had seemed lucid. Furious, scared, and snarky, but not at all delu-sional. Sneaking into a hospital room under everyone's noses was exactly the type of maneuver Kingsley would get off on.

Her gut tightened as she hurried past the waiting area full

of soothing seafoam-green couches and abstract blue and green paintings and headed for the front desk.

A silver-haired man in wire-rimmed glasses offered a polite smile as she strode up to the window. "How may I help you today?"

Ellie showed the CPD badge tucked in her jacket pocket. "I was hoping you could help me view some hospital surveillance footage."

The employee fumbled his smile but managed a last-second save. "I'm sorry, but I'm afraid hospital policy requires a warrant be provided first, due to the private nature of the footage. Do you have a warrant?"

She'd figured as much but had to try. Hopefully, the chief was already working on that warrant request she'd sent via text message while waiting on the elevator. "Not yet, but it's being processed as we speak. If you could have your security or admin department get that footage ready by the time I get back, I'd appreciate it."

The employee's noncommittal "hmm" failed to get Ellie's hopes up, and she muttered to herself as she left through the sliding doors.

"No, really, don't put yourself out. It's only the life of an eight-year-old girl at stake, that's all. No big deal or anything."

Shane frowned from where he shadowed her a few feet away, but she ignored her bodyguard's concerned expression and continued toward the parking lot, shaken by what Katarina had shared back in the room. Kingsley's old protégé might not want her sympathy, but too bad.

I was just a kid.

Her chest hurt when she remembered how the woman had whispered the words at first, like she was trying to convince herself. How many times had Ellie tried to tell herself the very same thing? Late at night, when guilt over the woman she'd sentenced to die held sleep hostage?

That had been one surprise. The way Katarina had talked about Bethany had been another. The tightness had faded from her jaw, and her eyes had softened with a warmth that Ellie had never expected to witness on that shrewd face. And the things she'd shared about her daughter, well…

Ellie shook her head. Damned if they didn't remind her of her own mother.

Over the years, Helen Kline had uttered many of those same things about Ellie. About her inner strength and resilience. Heck, her mom probably still bragged about Ellie like that when her daughter wasn't around to groan and roll her eyes.

In the parking lot, a couple passed her, heading toward the hospital. The man's brown skin and hazel eyes made Ellie's mind flash to Fortis's sightless eyes and pale skin, and she stumbled her next step while she prayed.

She hoped, for the little girl's sake, that Katarina wasn't prone to the typical mom hyperbole, inflating their kid's strengths to make them seem more impressive than they actually were. Because Bethany would need to draw upon a deep well of inner strength if she hoped to survive Kingsley long enough for the police to find her.

With Shane at her side, she ducked her head and hurried forward, anxiety a slow, steady drip down her spine. Soon. They had to find Kingsley soon, to possess a remote chance at preventing him from breaking yet another child.

A battered face beneath a shock of short, dark hair materialized behind Ellie's eyes, and pressure lodged in her chest. The woman pitted against her all those years ago in Kingsley's Die, Bitch! Die game hadn't been so lucky.

Ellie would move heaven and earth to ensure that Bethany was.

The ringing in her pocket sliced through the memories of past traumas. Ellie stopped a few feet from the Explorer to dig her phone out and caught Jillian's number flashing on the screen. "Hello?"

"Hey, it's me. That podcaster from Far Ridge Boy's Academy emailed back. He says he's willing to meet, but he's not local. He lives in Savannah."

Ellie started to groan but stopped when an idea popped into her head. "I have a contact there. Maybe she can help."

"A friend?"

Was friend the correct word to characterize her relationship with Charli Cross, the petite Savannah detective whose prim demeanor hid a cunning, possibly devious mind? Probably not, but now wasn't the time to quibble over semantics. "Sure. Hey, don't wait on me for dinner tonight. I'll be working late."

"Let me guess, a last-minute work trip to Savannah just came up? No worries, I'll plan a dinner date with my furry friend tonight. She's been complaining about our lack of couple time lately."

Ellie smiled at Jillian's reference to her goofy Labrador. "Good luck with that."

"You're just jealous because Sam has better table manners than you."

"Whatever you do, don't tell my mom you said that. She'll start to wonder what I was doing during all those etiquette classes she forced me to take growing up."

Jillian snickered. "I'm not even going to ask." When she spoke again, her voice was soft. "But all joking aside, please, be careful."

"I will."

Ellie tapped her foot, waiting on a truck to roll by before stepping onto the crosswalk that led to the parking lot. Rows and rows of cars lined up along the asphalt, with the Explorer parked all the way in the back.

She nodded at the middle-aged couple who hurried past and avoided glancing left at the parking garage that towered five levels up. It would have been a shorter walk to park inside the looming structure, but when Shane had signaled to enter it earlier, she'd panicked and barked at him to use the lot.

The visions of Fortis's slumped, motionless body threatened to swamp her again, but she shook them off and dialed Charli Cross's number. Forward, not back. That was the only way to push through this.

The Savannah detective answered on the second ring.

"Detective Cross speaking."

"Hi, Detective Cross, it's Ellie Kline from the Charleston PD. I'm headed to your neck of the woods soon to interview a witness, and I was wondering if you might have any information on him already that you could share."

"It's Charli, and sure. Give me a name, and I'll tell you if it rings a bell."

"He's a true-crime podcaster, goes by Hank Crawford. First name Nickolas."

A long pause followed, and the hesitation caused Ellie's skin to buzz. Charli Cross was nothing if not direct, so the detective's uncertainty told Ellie that Crawford's name wasn't new.

Charli confirmed Ellie's conclusion a moment later. "Yeah, I know him. Mr. Crawford isn't especially popular around these parts. His podcast leans pretty hard into victims' rights, which means he can be a real thorn in our side when it comes to pushing for more resources and effort on cases with no leads."

Ellie frowned. "That doesn't necessarily sound like a bad

thing. Cold case victims deserve as much effort as anyone else."

"No argument from me there, but it's more the way Crawford goes about pushing for those rights that ruffles feathers. He considers himself to be an investigative journalist, and I think his past traumas and enthusiasm can sometimes get the best of him."

"So, what you're saying is, he's another crackpot turned armchair sleuth who sticks his nose where it doesn't belong and gets in the way of investigations?"

"A succinct yet accurate assessment, yes."

Laughing at Charli's droll delivery, Ellie stopped next to the Explorer. "Thanks. I think. Anyway, it's looking like Crawford might have some information on Kingsley, so annoying or not, I need to have a sit down with him."

"Mind if I join you?"

Ellie lifted her eyebrows at her bodyguard, who nodded and opened the passenger door. "Please do. When it comes to Kingsley, two heads are definitely better than one. See you there in an hour and a half or so?"

"Yup."

Charli hung up before saying goodbye, a fact that somehow didn't surprise her.

Shane walked around the SUV and settled his burly body behind the wheel. "I take it we're headed to Savannah?"

"You take it right."

14

On the street leading into the trailer park, Southern live oaks reached across the road with gnarled branches, the Spanish moss dripping down and whispering over the car like phantom fingers. Combined with the dreary gray sky overhead, the overall effect was eerie. Almost like they were driving straight onto the set of a horror movie.

Not the most auspicious start to this excursion. "Let me guess, this is the part where you tell me the trailer park was built on ancient burial grounds full of angry spirits."

Charli Cross didn't take her eyes off the road. "Believe it or not, this trailer park hasn't had much in the way of crime, apart from a few drug busts and domestics. They rank lower than average on crime statistics here, despite the fact that the median income is thirty percent below average for the area."

Ellie raised a brow. "I'm impressed. Did you know those stats off the top of your head, or did you look them up after I called?"

"We're detectives. Shouldn't we know the numbers that are relevant to our jobs?"

The matter-of-fact tone convinced Ellie that the detective

wasn't messing with her. She settled deeper into the passenger seat, considering. "I don't know. Sometimes, I think numbers can get in the way."

Charli shrugged, clearly not persuaded, and silence settled in as they crawled down the wide street, passing rows of yellow and white trailers squatting behind tidy patches of artificial turf or rock gardens. Little bits of personality were on display out front, ranging from American flags, colorful flowerpots full of green plants or blooms, birdbaths, and little concrete statues, pinwheels, and in one case, a parade of pink metal flamingos.

The car hugged the right turn, making room for a bald man pushing a walker with two tennis balls on the front and a gray-haired woman leading a small white dog on a pink leash. The man lifted a trembling hand to wave before continuing down the street.

They rolled to a stop in front of a trailer that wasn't quite as festive as its neighbors. An oversized gray satellite dish shadowed a dismal square of brown rocks in lieu of grass or a flower bed and two sun-bleached plastic chairs.

Charli shifted into park, pushed on the emergency brake even though the street was flat as a pancake, and tucked the keys into her pocket before opening the driver's side door. "This is it."

Ellie scrambled out of the passenger seat and stepped over to the narrow path that led to the tiny porch area just as Shane pulled the Explorer up behind them. As she waited for Charli's short legs to round the front of the car and join her, the trailer door swung open, and a man appeared.

Hank Crawford was skinny, dressed in a gray sweatshirt and navy sweatpants faded in the knees, with hair that thinned to a prominent bald spot on top and a scraggly, ill-kempt beard. The feature that jumped out at Ellie, though, was the man's eyes. The dark shadows beneath them dominated his entire face like round, twin bruises.

He popped a black cigarette between his teeth and waved them over. "Come on in. We'll be more comfortable inside."

Until Hank Crawford opened his mouth and that rich, melodic baritone emerged, Ellie hadn't realized she'd been expecting a raspy, defeated voice to match his worn-out appearance. Though, duh, the discrepancy made perfect sense. He was a podcaster. Of course he gave good voice.

Crawford's gaze followed Ellie as she trailed behind Charli up the walkway, and something in those dark eyes unsettled her, giving her the feeling that Crawford saw far too much.

Charli introduced herself first. When Ellie's turn came, Crawford brushed the introduction off. "I know who you are. You've been on my radar ever since your name was tied to Kingsley in the papers."

No, that wasn't creepy at all, finding out a stranger had been tracking your life via the media for years. Ellie's polite smile froze, and the moment she turned away, her mouth reshaped itself into a grimace.

Inside, the trailer held a distinct odor, like a combination of cigarette smoke and old Chinese takeout. A scan of the interior confirmed Ellie's suspicions. White cartons and pizza boxes mixed with empty plates and glasses in the compact kitchen area. An ashtray that was overdue for dumping sat on top of the tiny, four-seat dining table. More half-empty cups were scattered along the surface of an ancient coffee table, along with several books. Half the couch was covered in discarded sweatshirts and a pair of striped socks.

"This way." Crawford walked past the living area and into a narrow hallway.

Charli glanced around at the mess before following, Ellie

on her heels. They passed a small bedroom that looked like a clothes bomb had been detonated inside before ending up in a larger space at the end of the hall.

Ellie crossed the threshold and stopped short. Crawford had transformed the master bedroom into an office space, but more surprising than that was the area's tidiness. Two walls were covered from almost ceiling to floor in neatly arranged rows of photographs, newspaper and article clippings, and handwritten notes on cards or post-its. All that was lacking were red lines and scribbled arrows leading to circled photos with question marks beside them, and the wall could double as the secret lair of a conspiracy theorist searching for the Zodiac killer.

Or an obsessive detective hunting down a sadistic psychiatrist.

A large L-shaped desk took up much of the third and fourth walls. From the array of sound equipment, professional microphones, and headsets organized on top, the area served as Crawford's miniature recording studio for his podcast.

Puffing out a cloud of smoke, Crawford sank onto the rolling chair behind the desk, kicking his feet out in front of him while gesturing at two plastic chairs that matched the ones on the patio. "Go ahead and sit if you'd like. I brought those inside for you."

"Thank you." Charli brushed a speck from the chair before perching on the edge while Ellie settled into the other one without checking.

"So, what brings two detectives out to my humble studio?"

Charli shrugged. "It's Detective Kline's case. I'm just along for the ride."

Crawford huffed as if to say *yeah right* before turning his shrewd gaze on Ellie. "And how can I help you?"

Ellie frowned at the tense vibes. Maybe letting Charli tag along had been a mistake, but it was too late to worry about that now. "I'm guessing it will come as no surprise to you that I'm investigating Kingsley's crimes—"

"When you say crimes, I'm assuming you're talking about the ones involving the three boys from the Academy?"

Ellie's frown deepened. "What three boys?"

Crawford made an impatient noise. "The boys who died. Isn't that why you tracked me down?"

Confused, Ellie shook her head. "I'm sorry, I think our wires are getting crossed somehow. Which academy are you talking about? The one Kingsley attended in Europe? If so, I'm afraid I don't know anything about crimes committed against three boys there."

Crawford finished puffing on his cigarette, exhaled smoke, and laughed. "Come on, I thought you were smarter than that. One of the reasons Kingsley blends in so well no matter where he goes is because he grew up all over. He might have ended up in a fancy school in Europe, but his life started out at public school in a Podunk, middle-of-nowhere America. It wasn't until his mother married rich that he was packed off to Far Ridge, and after everything went down with those boys, Europe."

Heart racing, Ellie leaned forward. "Are you saying that Kingsley attended Far Ridge Academy and played a role in the deaths of those three boys?"

"That's exactly what I'm saying."

"Hold up." She lifted a hand as the pieces clicked together. Three mysterious student deaths at a school linked to Kingsley? She could have kicked herself for not suspecting. If Kingsley was involved, though, his family must have paid off a lot of people and pulled an entire puppet show's worth of strings to keep it under wraps. In all of Ellie's time investigating, she'd never gotten a whiff of young Kingsley being suspected of anything more than a few tardies.

This wasn't the first time boarding schools had come up as Kingsley-related cases, though. Over the past year, one of the missing children she'd investigated had ended up at a special academy away from home. Poor William.

The Warrens had wanted the best for their son, the type of care for a kid who struggled with multiple spectrum-related issues that extended beyond the local public school's capabilities. To his parents, the special boarding school had sounded like a godsend, so they'd packed William up and sent him off, praying for the best.

The hopeful couple never set eyes on their son again, because instead of a boarding school, William had been sold into one of Kingsley's child trafficking rings.

Crime seemed to always circle back to Lawrence Kingsley.

"Okay, let's back up and start from the beginning. What can you tell me about Far Ridge, particularly Letitia and Walter Wiggins?"

Crawford's expression turned broody. He sucked on the cigarette while he stared off into space, slowly rotating the chair back and forth with one foot. "The things I could tell you about the Wiggins would curl your hair."

"Her hair's already curly."

Crawford's eyes narrowed on Charli while Ellie kicked her chair and shot a warning look. The detective met both with a blank face and innocent shrug.

Torn between laughter and annoyance, Ellie tensed and prepared to jump in as referee if necessary. Luckily, Crawford chose to ignore Charli's ill-timed quip. "I can say with absolute certainty that neither Letitia nor Walter Wiggins belonged anywhere near children. I shudder to think how much cumulative damage they inflicted onto young, impressionable psyches over the years, mine included. Those three boys never should have died."

He stubbed out the cigarette in an empty ashtray, then pulled a new one from the pack in his sweatshirt pocket. The lighter sparked, and the new cigarette glowed red at the tip. "Poor Walter Wiggins ended up as the fall boy for everything."

Ellie puzzled over the phrasing. "But wasn't he responsible? I read through the case, and it seemed pretty clear that Walter Wiggins abused those three boys and left them outside in the middle of winter to die."

Crawford's laugh turned into a hacking cough that wracked his emaciated body. When he caught his breath, he waved the cigarette with a grimace. "I know, I know. One of the downsides of self-medicating with nicotine. Hang on a sec. It's getting a little stuffy in here."

He set the lit cigarette in the ashtray and tugged the sweatshirt over his head. The t-shirt beneath rode up with it, exposing such sharp, bony ribs that even Charli flinched. After folding the sweatshirt and setting it on the floor, Crawford tugged his t-shirt down and grabbed the cigarette.

"Back to Walter Wiggins's culpability in those deaths. The man was definitely no angel, but in this particular case, he got railroaded. That entire damned trial was a lesson in how privilege and wealth protects people from facing consequences for even the most heinous crimes."

It was eerie how closely Crawford's comment about privilege echoed Katarina's from earlier. Ellie shoved the distraction aside. *Later.* "What do you mean?"

This time, the hand that lifted the cigarette shook a little. "One time, I was called into Headmistress Letitia's office to be—"

Ellie held up a hand. "Headmistress? Isn't she the headmaster's wife?"

Crawford rolled his eyes. "She insisted we call her head-mistress, the bitch. But anyway, she reprimanded me for putting on too much weight."

Ellie recoiled. "What? That's terrible."

The podcaster nodded. "I know, we've hopefully left those days behind, but back in those days and at a private institution, that bitch had carte blanche to inflict her sadistic punishments."

He settled back in the chair, his gaze distant. "First, she lectured me about the dangers of sneaking candy at night, then shoved me in the Blue Room."

Ellie's eyebrows rose. "The Blue Room?"

"Yeah. A fancy name for a crappy little hellhole where the headmistress or headmaster's wife or whoever she was shoved students she felt needed to spend some time 'reflecting.'" He air quoted the last word. "After leaving me in there with no food for days, she trotted me out and forced me to stand in her office in a uniform that was several sizes too small. I remember the pants dug into my waist so much, the red marks lasted for days. And the shirt was uncomfortably tight across my chest and so short that I was afraid to lift my hands away from my sides because I knew my stomach would show. I was already self-conscious. Not a big shock, I guess, that students at private schools can be every bit as cruel to bigger kids as anywhere else."

His rich, podcast-worthy voice lost its usual inflection, turning monotone and flat. The brittle recitation made Ellie sense that while he'd likely shared this story a number of times, he'd never rid himself of the ghosts roused in the retelling.

Her cheek itched, but she was afraid to move, worried that the slightest distraction might shut him down. Charli sat in silence too, with her hands clasped in her lap.

"First, they brought in tray after tray loaded with delicious-smelling foods and feasted right in front of me. I was so hungry that it was hard not to cry, but I tried my best, because I knew they'd only use any show of weakness against me."

He trailed off, so Ellie risked a question. "They?"

Crawford's mouth tightened. "They, as in Letitia Wiggins and Kingsley. My mind was fuzzy, but I'm pretty certain that was their first official meeting. She recruited him to witness my torture and humiliation."

Beside her, Charli rustled in the chair, likely as caught off guard by the revelation as Ellie was. "He ate the food while you watched?"

"Yes, although ironically, the worst part came when they actually fed me. I'd like to claim that if I'd understood the twisted punishment they'd had in store, I would have refused the food when it was offered, but I'm not sure that's true. I was so hungry, you see."

The hairs on Ellie's neck lifted in anticipation of the story's ending. "What happened next?"

Crawford's chapped lips cracked open in a smile that had nothing to do with humor. "They made me eat so much that I threw up, and then berated me for being wasteful and made me eat my own vomit too."

Ellie's own stomach turned at the punchline, and it took all her training and self-control not to shudder. She stared into her lap to give herself time to banish any signs of disgust from her expression. That poor man. What a monstrous thing to do to a child. To anyone. "I'm sorry, that's terrible. That never should have happened to you."

"Thanks. I'd like to say I'm over it, but…" He gestured around the room and shrugged. "You've probably already reached your own conclusions about that."

That, and his unhealthy skinniness. What was that saying, something about the body keeping score?

Ellie shook her head. "But I still don't understand. Why wasn't any of this included in the reports?"

Crawford tapped ash into the ceramic circle. "That's the part where the privilege and wealth comes in. Kingsley's stepdad had both, and he paid heaps of money to keep his stepson out of the scandal. And like most abusers, Letitia Wiggins was also skilled at playing the victim card. Those deaths took place during a stretch of time when nothing at Far Ridge happened without the headmistress and her little pet being involved."

"Kingsley being the pet in question," Ellie guessed, and Crawford nodded. "And Walter Wiggins?"

"A horrible human being who inflicted more than his fair share of suffering and deserved punishment, but I'm not convinced that he took part in that particular crime. At the very least, Letitia and Kingsley shouldered most of the blame. But Kingsley got off scot-free, and Mrs. Wiggins was sentenced to four years for criminal neglect, served a little over half her sentence, and now lives out her days in a swanky retirement community."

While Ellie digested that, Charli nodded. "Statistics show that women are more likely to be child abusers than men. About fifty-three percent of the perpetrators in cases of child abuse are women. I'll never understand it."

Crawford scoffed. "Me either. Man, woman, or alien, statistics don't mean shit when you have to watch the evil bitch who forced you to eat your own vomit cruise around in a Lexus in front of her expensive house."

The anger radiating off the podcaster made Ellie cringe, but Charli's expression and posture remained unchanged. She regarded him with those piercing blue eyes. "I'm sorry you experienced all that, and I'm sorry the system failed you. I'm also sorry that Letitia Wiggins received nothing but a slap on the wrist."

Crawford's hand shook harder now as the anger faded to sadness. The glance he shot at Charli over his cigarette was enough to make even a strong person flinch.

Not Charli. The detective's forehead remained smooth, her chin lifted. The only potential sign of the detective's discomfort was the slender hands twisting together in her lap.

Had she experienced something similar? Ellie couldn't help but wonder.

Since Crawford seemed ready to cry at any moment, Ellie made the executive decision to cut the interview short. She stood. "Well, I need to get back on the road, but thank you so much for your time, Mr. Crawford. You've been incredibly helpful. Come on, Detective Cross."

Charli stood too and followed Ellie to the door. She paused on the threshold and craned her head toward Crawford, who hadn't bothered standing to escort them out.

"Please, don't hesitate to get in touch if you remember anything else."

He nodded at Charlie without sparing her another glance, his gaze trained on the photo wall. "Yeah."

Ellie and the other woman left the trailer and headed outside. Shane stood next to the Explorer, his head on a swivel as if he expected a monster to jump out at them at any time.

The thought made Ellie shiver.

As she climbed back into Charli's vehicle, she looked back at the little trailer. The man inside had also known her monster when he was just a boy.

How many lives had Kingsley destroyed over the years?

Probably more than she could ever count.

15

Ellie let out a low whistle when Charli led her through the front doors of the Savannah Police Department. "Damn, this place is huge compared to the Charleston precinct."

A good three times the size and with triple the number of police officers filling that extra space. All those additional bodies made the building much noisier than home base, but Ellie didn't mind the increased volume. She was too busy plotting as Charli led her past the clusters of desks and cubicles.

All that manpower and none of them bogged down trying to locate Bethany. If she could recruit some of them to team up with her to help solve cases, no telling how much more efficient they'd be?

The extra hands on deck weren't the only potential benefit, either. Ellie never underestimated the value of a fresh pair of eyes on a case.

Charli's posture retained its military perfection as she practically sprinted up a set of stairs to the second floor. Her office was small and contained two desks, one of which Ellie assumed was her partner's. Charli sat at the one with nary a paperclip out of place.

"Damn. Remind me to clean my desk before you ever come to visit, okay?" On any given day, Ellie's workstation back in the Charleston precinct could be counted on to showcase an array of empty takeout coffee cups, Skittles, and Milky Way wrappers from midafternoon vending machine snack runs, and endless piles of papers and files teetering in precarious stacks near the edge.

The petite detective shrugged. "I like my things tidy. I don't care if yours aren't."

Two uniformed male cops sauntered by, whispering and shooting Charli sideways glances as they passed. She ignored them, so Ellie followed her cue. Another time, she might snoop a little more and attempt to unravel one of the other detective's many layers of mystery, but not today, when she was on a mission.

Not when Bethany's life was on the line.

Ellie's chest tightened. Deep in her soul, she sensed time was running short. They had to find the little girl and fast. Before Kingsley had a chance to inflict irreparable damage.

Or worse.

Images of Kingsley's other victims flashed like phantoms behind Ellie's eyes, and for a moment, her vision blurred. Val. Gabe. The poor, nameless woman Kingsley had murdered because Ellie had told him to.

She clenched her jaw and gave herself a mental shake. The memories disappeared, but the sense of urgency lingered.

Charli stood over her laptop and tapped at the keyboard. Ellie winced. If she worked in that position, her back would rebel almost immediately, but the Savannah detective was a good eight inches shorter in height. Charli finished typing, and a nearby printer buzzed to life.

Ellie cocked her head as Charli strode over and gathered the pages the printer spat out. "Don't you have tablets here?"

"We do, but I prefer hard copies."

Report printed, Charli dragged an empty chair behind her desk for Ellie before plopping into her own. She handed Ellie a stack of pages before burying her nose into an equally thick pile.

Side by side, they thumbed through Letitia Wiggins's case file. Several other officers and a detective passed by Charli's office door while they read, but no one stopped to share details on cases or even smile or say a quick hi. The one time Ellie glanced up, two officers averted their eyes and kept walking.

Charli never gave the slightest impression that she noticed or cared one way or another, but Ellie wasn't so sure. Cops could be real assholes sometimes, and the vibe reminded Ellie a little too much of her early days in the Charleston precinct. Back when she'd first started on the job, all the other officers were convinced that her family's money had bought her that place in the department and stolen a spot from a more deserving candidate.

Despite being surrounded by a room full of coworkers, those first few months as a patrol officer were some of the loneliest in Ellie's life. The old saying about how you often felt the most alone when you were in a crowd had proven true, at least in Ellie's case. Sucked if Charli was experiencing a version of the same thing.

"Must be nice, working without many interruptions."

Ellie offered the overture up as a joke. Either Charli would accept the invitation to talk about her tense workplace, or she wouldn't.

Charli raised her head from the file, her gaze resting on the two officers who'd just walked past without an acknowledgment. "My presence makes people uncomfortable." She shrugged, like their comfort or rudeness was of no significance to her.

Sympathy stirred in Ellie's chest. "I can relate. I dealt with something similar in Charleston when I first started working there."

Charli's spine stiffened almost imperceptibly. "Actually, I doubt very much that you did."

Ellie blinked at the abrupt shutdown. Oh boy, she'd put her foot in her mouth now. Charli did a good job of hiding it, but the standoffish treatment of her peers was obviously a sore point.

She opened her mouth to apologize, but Charli cut her off. "Here, take a look at these."

Paper rustled as the detective set new pages on top of the file. Ellie leaned in to get a closer look. "Transcripts?"

"From the Letitia Wiggins trial. If you turn to page ten, you'll see testimony from a psychologist called as an expert witness for the defense."

Ellie flipped to the page in question and scanned the excerpt. Partway through, she began reading out loud. "After spending time with the defendant, my clinical observations have led me to conclude that Mrs. Wiggins exhibits symptoms consistent with battered woman syndrome."

She glanced up from the transcript. "I wonder when they changed the name to Intimate Partner Violence?"

Ellie had intended the question to be rhetorical, but she should have known better. In the very brief time Ellie had known the detective, she'd learned that Charli could pluck that information off the top of her head. "The WHO mass distributed a pamphlet in 2002 that utilized the term, and IPV became more commonplace after that. Intimate Partner Violence works better because even though men are more likely to kill their partners, women are also common perpetrators of partner abuse."

Charli's attention never wavered from the finger that moved down the page as she read, so she missed Ellie's wide-eyed appraisal. Was there anything law-related that this pixie-ish dynamo didn't have tucked away in that giant brain of hers? If so, Ellie would require proof to believe it.

The detective's finger halted partway down the page. She wrinkled her pert nose. "This next part basically claims that due to fears for her own safety, Letitia Wiggins had no choice but to take part in the abuse. Especially near the end, when she discovered she was pregnant."

Bitterness burned Ellie's gut. "That psychologist and defense attorney really pulled out all the stops to play on that jury's sympathies, didn't they? Yet another skeezy psychologist twisting everything into a sob story and helping a guilty person walk free. Yay, justice."

When she shook her head in abject disgust, she gasped as the motion sent the room spinning out of control. Mind swimming, she squeezed her eyes shut and inhaled through her nose.

"When's the last time you ate or slept?"

When the wave of dizziness passed, Ellie dared to check the clock on the far wall. Yikes. "A while."

Charli crossed her arms and lowered her eyebrows. "There's a direct correlation between hunger and focus, or lack thereof, to be more specific. You should eat something and try to get some sleep."

With the other detective's black pixie cut, bright blue eyes, and delicate features, it was a little like being scolded by a fairy.

Not that Ellie would ever dare to voice that opinion aloud. "I'd love to rest, but there's a little girl out there who's been kidnapped by a killer, and her life could come down to how much time I dedicate to sleeping instead of trying to find her."

Ellie's statement thrummed between them, striking a forgotten chord in her heart. This couldn't be...but it was...*oh, God.*

She dug her nails into her thighs and tried not to succumb to the shame that coiled inside her chest in tight, suffocating loops. She'd been so hellbent on making Kingsley pay for his crimes that this was the first time she could remember putting Bethany's safety above her quest for revenge.

Charli didn't argue or mouth some worthless platitude about how Ellie could only do so much. She simply nodded, as if she accepted Ellie's analysis of the time constraints as logical. "What's your next step?"

Ellie filled her lungs with air and came to a decision. "I want to visit Letitia Wiggins. We read what the psychologist had to say. Now, I need to speak with the accused in person and form my own opinion."

"I anticipated that you might say that." No surprise there. "The Lake Walters Retirement Community where she resides now is almost four and a half hours away. In light of this new information, I suggest that you revisit your previous conclusion and consider getting some rest first."

Ellie's body sagged. Four and a half hours? Even Shane would be exhausted by now, and that was too far to drive powered on fumes, coffee, and determination. Not if she didn't want to risk ending up as another one of Charli's statistics. *Fatal car accidents caused by overtired drivers.*

"Fine, you win. I'll book a hotel room and sleep for a few hours before heading out."

Charli responded in her even tone. "I wasn't aware we were playing a game." She paused a beat before granting Ellie a mischievous smile. "But for the record, I do enjoy winning."

16

A weird looking animal sprawled on the kitchen floor, its snakelike tail twitching every few seconds.

The bad man held the shiny silver knife out to Bethany. "All you have to do is pick up the knife and start cutting, wherever you like. Each cut will earn you a snack of your choice."

She backed away, shaking her head. "What is it?"

He laughed. "It's an opossum, my dear. One of the stupidest animals on the planet. You'll be doing it a favor and saving it from becoming roadkill."

She took another step back. "No."

"Don't be silly. I gave the marsupial medicine, so he won't feel a thing. Each cut will earn you a small snack. Aren't you hungry?"

The promise of food made Bethany's heart beat faster, and she glanced up at the bad man's face. His smile was weird tonight. Softer than normal, and his voice was nicer too. Like he wanted to be friends.

He moved, and she flinched, but he was only squatting

down over the animal. "Here, I'll show you that it won't hurt, okay?"

Before Bethany had time to protest, the knife flashed and sliced into the opossum's fur near his tail. She covered her eyes, but when it didn't make a sound, she peeked between her fingers. He laid in the same position, his eyes closed and chest gently rising and falling. The only change was the blood welling up where the knife had cut.

"See? He's perfectly fine, aren't you, boy." Doctor Rotten patted the furry head before rising. "Now, it's your turn."

When he pushed the knife toward her, a red streak glinted on the silver. The opossum's blood. "No."

"No?"

His voice changed in that one word, wrenching Bethany's gaze up to his face. She yelped at the angry line of eyebrows and tried to jump away, but she was too late. His free hand snaked out and grabbed her wrist, dragging her closer to the sleeping animal.

"How about this? I'll give you an entire meal in exchange for three cuts deep enough to draw blood. Deal? Your mother would tell you to accept, you know. She wouldn't want you to starve over some dumpster diving pest."

Bethany licked her lips. The idea of an entire meal sounded too good to be true. She glanced at the animal's face, and her heart sank at the pink tongue sticking out of its mouth. Its long hairless tail twitched again in his sleep.

The meal sounded too good to be true because it was.

"Here, take the knife. See how it feels in your hands. How powerful and strong."

Doctor Rotten shoved the knife into Bethany's hand and pressed her fingers around the handle as anger filled her so full she forgot to be scared.

No matter what he said, she knew this was wrong. He was wrong.

Strong was doing the right thing, and the right thing to do was to leave the poor thing alone. She didn't care if he couldn't feel any pain for now, because what happened when he woke up? He'd be hurt and crying, and it would be Bethany's fault, and no amount of food in the world was worth that. No matter how scared or hungry or tired she was.

Her mama had told her to always be brave, and that was exactly what she was going to do. Brave people didn't hurt sleeping animals, or any animals.

The bad man sucked in an excited breath. "Yes, that's right. Go on, do it."

Bethany realized he was staring at the knife in her hand and believed she would cut the poor thing. For some reason, that made her so mad she tightened her fist around the handle harder. She wound up her arm and threw the knife at the bad man, but he moved too quickly and sidestepped out of the way.

"I won't! I won't hurt anything. Not animals, and not even snails, and you can't make me, so leave me alone! I'm going to be like Wonder Woman and wait for my mama to come!"

The bad man only stood there, waiting for her to finish. When she did, he pulled her by the hand across the floor, over to the ugly green couch.

"I'm afraid that this is an area in which you require further education regarding the true nature of superheroes. Of course, all children want to be heroes. They have a deep, innate desire to be special. The problem stems from the belief that all they have to do is throw on a cape or drive a fast car with lots of cool features, or gain a secret power, and, presto! They can save the world. But they always forget about the price of tapping into those superpowers. *Pain*."

The bad man's eyes gleamed when he breathed the last word, and Bethany shivered. She could tell he liked the idea of pain, instead of thinking it was awful, like a normal person. She wanted to cover her ears and block out every horrible thing he said, but he'd only rip her hands away or shove her back into the refrigerator.

She refused to agree, though. Wonder Woman didn't need pain to save people. "I don't believe you."

Doctor Rotten smiled the tiny smile. "Don't you? Tell me then, what happened to Batman before he decided to fight evil?"

Bethany shrugged. How would she know? The *Batman* movies were too old for her. Besides, she liked Wonder Woman better.

"His parents were murdered right on the street in front of him when he was a little boy, so he internalized all that pain and channeled it into helping other citizens of Gotham. Without that tragic backstory, Bruce Wayne would be just another billionaire, exploiting workers for his own gain. Now, what about Spiderman? Do you know if he had a happy life growing up with his parents?"

Bethany bit her lip. She'd watched that movie and was pretty sure the answer was no. Peter Parker grew up with his Aunt May, so that probably meant his parents were dead...or bad. Plus, he'd been picked on a lot in school.

Even though she didn't say anything, Doctor Rotten nodded like he'd read her mind.

"There, you see? Poor Peter." He clicked his tongue like he was sad, but Bethany knew he wasn't sad at all. "What about those dismal X-Men? If you've read the comics or watched any of those movies, you'll know that none of them led very happy lives to start. Persecuted and locked in cages, experimented on by their own government! All for powers outside of their control. Then there's the one you mentioned before, the marvelous Wonder Woman."

Bethany had been staring at the floor, but her head jerked up at that. *Shut up. Shut up, shut up, shut up.*

But Doctor Rotten wouldn't shut up. He never did. "Tell me, did your caped superhero live out her days on her beautiful, hidden home island, all safe and cozy with her Amazonian family and friends?"

Bethany's heart raced, and her fingers curled at her sides. She wouldn't answer. She *wouldn't*. The bad man must think she was really stupid to fall for his trick. She wished he'd just hurry up and finish already.

"Cat got your tongue? That's okay, I'll answer for you. Wonder Woman was forced to leave her homeland and never return. Never see her family again. And do you know why? Because the only way for a superhero to reach their true potential is by experiencing a traumatic trigger. Without pain and suffering, they'd simply go about their everyday lives and not spend a single minute worrying about ways to help others or save the world."

Doctor Rotten moved closer and held out a hand. "Do you see now? If you let me, I'll help bring out the superhero in you. Think of how much good you can do once you have rage and anger and pain to draw your powers from."

Bethany stared at the hand like it was a snake, except even snakes were nicer than him. "I'm not a baby. I know superheroes aren't real. Someone wrote them, like books. They're make-believe." She shoved out her chin. "My mama is going to come and save me, though. Just wait."

The bad man clucked his tongue again. "I wish you were right, but the truth is, Katarina is no hero, super or otherwise. If anything, I'm afraid your dear mama is a villain. Would you like me to share some of the horrible crimes she's committed over the years?"

This time, Bethany did cover her ears. "Stop! I won't listen."

But Doctor Rotten grabbed her wrists and wrenched her hands away. "Oh, but you will. Starting with when I first met your mother as a little girl. She was only two years older than you but already so incredibly bloodthirsty. Did she ever tell you how she cut up her poor adoptive parents, the Davidsons, and once she'd tired of her fun, lit them on fire?"

Bethany's hair whipped in the air as she shook her head. "I don't believe you. I don't." But her voice came out squeaky and small when she remembered all the Zombie Apocalypse stuff Mama had taught, and his smile widened.

"Oh, but I think you do. And if she killed someone at such a tender, young age, can you imagine how many people she's killed since? Why, only last week, she slit her boyfriend's throat and watched him bleed out on the floor. I believe you met him once or twice. Clayne."

Her stomach clenched tight. Clayne? Why would Mama hurt Clayne?

He hadn't been her favorite person in the world, and she'd hated the yucky old bed in his guestroom, but her mama had liked him, so she'd tried her best to be polite. "You're lying. That doesn't make any sense."

But the triumph in his dark eyes made her think that maybe the bad man was telling the truth. "Bad people don't always make sense when they do terrible things. But one truth you can count on, my dear, sweet girl, is this…Katarina is one of the villains."

Bethany wanted to punch him right in the nose but settled for balling her fists. All those stories he'd told about her mama made her chest hurt, and her throat felt funny. She wasn't sure whether or not to believe him. Whether her mama had done all those awful things or if he was trying to trick her again.

One thing Bethany was sure of, though. Her mama would

never hurt her. She loved Bethany, and Bethany loved her mama right back.

"So, what if she is?" Bethany looked Dr. Rotten square in the eye. "Even bad guys can be good guys when they need to be."

17

B ranches from an overgrown section of trail clawed at Clay's shirt as he trekked back down the mountain. He moved to the side and held them out of the way for Lucas to pass through before rejoining the descent.

They'd spent hours traipsing along the trails already, starting close to the river where the ranger found Lucas all those years ago. The drawings Lucas had created from his time in the cabin were tucked away in Clay's backpack. At several points along their hike, Lucas had stopped in his tracks to scrutinize certain sections of the mountain, asking Clay to hand him the drawings to compare.

His gaze would travel back and forth from the sketch to the landscape, sometimes for up to a minute before he'd finally nod and hand Clay the paper while pointing out the landmarks. "See...there and there." He'd indicate the land-marks on the mountain, then show Clay where to find them on the drawing.

Sometimes, the landmarks were so overgrown that Clay needed additional help to spot them, and Lucas would guide him closer, or to a different angle, until he could finally make the connection too.

The kid had endless stores of patience, and a damned good eye.

Man, Clay corrected, not kid. Not anymore. Lucas's youth had been stolen long ago by the people who'd snatched him. He was a young man now.

Clay had worried the hike would be too rigorous for Lucas, both physically and emotionally, but out on the mountain, the other man was in his element. What could have been a grim day turned out surprisingly enjoyable, with Lucas halting on the trail every so often to point out a squirrel, or a fox, or a hawk spiraling up in the sky, along with the best items to use to start a fire, and how to build a shelter from branches, plants, and moss.

Only once had the other man needed assistance, and that was when they'd meandered along the river and come to a bend where boulders protruded from the flowing water like stepping-stones.

Lucas's eyes stuck on one stone in particular, and he'd begun rocking back and forth on his heels. "I'm sorry, I'm sorry, I'm sorry."

Clay had finally calmed him down by asking for his help to identify a nearby bird perched on a tree limb. His sister had sometimes gotten stuck in a mind rut like that, and the thing that had worked the best for her was distraction.

No luck so far in terms of finding any sign of Caraleigh, but Clay had managed to accrue an impressive number of mosquito bites. There was always tomorrow. And the day after that. Clay would spend as many days as necessary to track his sister down.

The sun was only an orange smudge on the horizon by the time they finished hiking back down and reached Clay's truck. He was dusty, sweaty, but most of all, starving. The power bars they'd devoured on the trail weren't cutting it, so once they'd snapped on their seat belts, Clay turned to Lucas. "You hungry? Why don't we find somewhere to eat? We can start searching again in the morning."

"Okay."

"Anything sound good to you? I'm sure there are plenty of places around."

The other man stared straight out the windshield, rubbing his palms up and down his jeans. "It's Tuesday. They serve burgers on Tuesdays at the center."

He stated that bit of information in a stiff, solemn voice, like burgers on Tuesdays was an unbreakable vow.

Clay smiled. "Burgers sound good to me. Let's see what Yelp has to say." He consulted his phone to search for a local spot with high ratings. "How about Billy's Burger Barn? It's only a mile away and has rave reviews. Here, listen to this one: 'A real hole-in-the-wall gem of a place. If you care more about taste than fancy tablecloths and snooty waiters, then this is the spot for you.'"

Lucas frowned. "Is hole-in-the-wall good?"

"Depends, but some of my favorite diners and bars are tiny little spots that you'd miss driving along the street if you blinked."

"Okay. But that doesn't seem like very effective advertising if you could miss seeing them by blinking."

Clay laughed at Lucas's logic. "That's very true. Also, I can see why you and Caraleigh got along so well. She used to say stuff like that all the time."

Of course, as a teen, Clay had often found some of his little sister's quirks annoying. He only hoped he'd get the chance to appreciate them now that they were both adults.

When they pulled into the crowded parking lot five minutes later, Clay whooped at the miniature barn-shaped building. The red paint peeled all over, and the last two letters were out on the neon sign. *Billy's Burger Ba.* "Now that's what I'm talking about! They weren't joking when they said hole-in-the-wall."

"And that makes you happy?"

"Yup. In my experience, they cook up the best burgers in places that look like they've been around for the past eighty years."

Lucas tilted his head as he gave the shack-like building a dubious once-over. "Do they cook up the best burgers in places that look like they're about to fall apart too?"

"That just adds to the ambiance."

The other man shook his head. "That doesn't even make sense." He smiled when he said it, though, transforming his face into something that could grace a magazine cover or TV screen.

Clay's return grin faded when he remembered that Lucas's pretty face was likely part of the reason he'd been trafficked as an older kid. That, along with the spectrum traits that could sometimes make him seem younger than his actual age.

Fear tugged at him as his mind veered down dark paths, calculating odds that his sister had suffered a similar fate, but for once, Clay refused to speculate. Spending the day with Lucas on the trails had gone a long way toward restoring his optimism, and for that, Clay owed the other man a debt of gratitude. Caraleigh had gotten lucky once, when she'd ended up with Lucas on that mountain.

Maybe her luck had held.

Like Lucas, his little sister had been whip-smart. Stubborn as hell, even difficult at times, but smart. Great with numbers and memorizing facts. She'd loved to learn, and he could picture her hanging on Lucas's every word and acting like a little sponge while she soaked up his knowledge of survival skills.

Who knew? Maybe the survival training she'd learned while living with Lucas had saved her life. And maybe, just maybe, Caraleigh was still putting those skills to use, somewhere out there in the mountains. One way or another, Clay would find out. Even if that meant he'd spend the next two years hiking every square mile of those woods.

Lucas entered the restaurant first through the ancient, scratched-up red door but stopped only a few steps across the threshold.

At first, Clay guessed the country music twanging in the background was too loud, or the number of people packed inside, but then he followed Lucas's pointing finger to the wall behind the register. A cartoon illustration of a massive burger with eyes was next to a sign that declared *Biggest Burger in the State!* The print below read, *If you finish the burger in 30 minutes, it's free!*

Lucas's eyes were round as he stared at the ad. "I don't think I could finish a burger that size in thirty minutes."

Clay laughed. "Me either. Not in thirty minutes or even thirty hours."

"Probably in thirty days, though. Unless they left it sitting out the entire time. Then I wouldn't because of all the bacteria. Did you know that the amount of bacteria on food doubles every twenty minutes when the temperature is between forty and one hundred and forty degrees Fahrenheit?"

"I did not. That fast, really?"

Lucas nodded, his eyes wide and serious. "Really. That's why so many people get sick at buffets or barbecues, because the food is left out so long or not warmed at the proper temperatures."

"Good to know."

"Hello, welcome. This your first visit to Billy's Burger Barn?" The pretty blonde hostess beside the podium was young, probably mid-twenties, and wearing a red-and-white checkered shirt paired with denim shorts, suspenders, and cowboy boots. Her polite smile skimmed Clay before widening to an appreciative grin on Lucas.

Clay tipped his hat. "Yes, ma'am, it is. We were in the area and in the mood for a good burger, so figured we'd give it a shot."

"Well, you'll be happy you did. Follow me. I'll get you gentlemen seated in two shakes of a lamb's tail, so you can get on to the important stuff…eatin'!"

Lucas's brow wrinkled as they trailed her toward the rear of the packed, ramshackle space, but Clay was too busy biting back a laugh at the extra bounce the waitress added to her step to ask. When they reached the empty booth, Lucas scooted into the closest seat, so Clay maneuvered around the waitress and slid into the opposite side.

The waitress fluttered her false lashes as she handed Lucas a menu, her mouth drooping when he grabbed the laminated page without ever glancing up from the table. Once again, Clay was reminded of his sister. On report cards, Caraleigh's teachers often commented on how bright she was but that she could stand a little extra work on eye contact and social skills.

"I'll be back in a few to take your order."

Once the waitress strutted away, Lucas lifted his gaze. "Does 'two shakes of a lamb's tail' mean fast?"

"It does." Clay was puzzled by the random question until he remembered the waitress had used the phrase.

Lucas's brow remained creased. "Why?"

"Why does two shakes of a lamb's tail mean quick? Well, let's see…" Clay racked his brain and came up short. "You know what, I have absolutely no clue. We can google it later, but first, let's figure out what we want to eat."

Luckily, the menu was pretty limited. Burgers, chicken

strips, a couple of different sandwiches, and chili plus sides. That was it.

Once Clay made a decision—classic cheeseburger with bacon and a side of onion rings—he set down the menu and studied Lucas. The other man was chewing his lower lip and frowning down at the page. "Everything okay?"

"Yes." Still biting his lip, Lucas glanced around the restaurant as if searching for someone, then hunched his shoulders. "No. Can...would you mind ordering for me?"

Caraleigh hadn't liked ordering at restaurants, either. "Sure, no problem. What would you like?"

"A burger that's cooked until it doesn't bleed at all. With cheese but nothing else. And French fries. And maybe..." Lucas fidgeted with the menu. "A soda?"

"A soda, huh? Just a regular, plain old soda, with no flavor in it? Or were you wanting a flavored one?" He snapped his fingers. "I've got it! How about...pickle flavor."

Lucas made a gagging noise. "Gross. Why would anyone want pickle soda?"

"Hey now, have you ever tried pickle soda?"

"No."

"Then how do you know it's gross? Don't knock it 'til you try it."

Lucas pulled another face. "I don't want to knock it *or* try it." The indignant way he repeated the phrase provoked a surprised laugh from Clay, causing Lucas's eyes to narrow as he studied him from across the table. "There's no such thing as pickle soda, is there?"

Clay lifted his hand and grinned. "There really is. I've just never tried it before. Apparently, there's also a dirt soda, and eel."

"Eel soda?" When Clay nodded, Lucas's mouth gaped in horror. "But...why?"

"Dunno and can't say I ever plan to find out. Well, maybe the pickle juice soda. Definitely not eel."

"Yeah, me either. Not even pickle. I hate pickles." Lucas shuddered before scanning the other tables. "You don't think any of them are drinking eel soda, do you?"

The suspicion-laced question made Clay laugh. "No. Pretty sure Bob's Burger Barn sticks to boring old flavors. Orange, cola, lemon-lime, those types."

"Good." After another shudder, Lucas picked up the menu and scrutinized the options. Probably to double-check that Clay was telling the truth. "I'll take a regular brown soda."

"Sounds like a wise choice."

A couple of seconds passed. "Are you sure you didn't make those sodas up?"

"I swear. Here, I'll prove it to you." Clay typed "pickle soda" into his phone and showed Lucas the results.

The other man leaned on the table, peering at the screen. "Wow."

Clay repeated the process with eel and dirt soda. "Trust me now?"

Clay meant the question as a joke, but when Lucas didn't answer right away, he kicked himself for the teasing.

Before he could apologize, Lucas grinned. "I don't know if I can trust anyone who thinks pickle soda sounds like a good idea."

The force of the relief that swept through Clay surprised him. Until a second ago, he hadn't realized how invested he was in gaining the other man's confidence. "Fair enough."

The waitress came, and as promised, Clay ordered for both of them. Once she left, their conversation switched to favorite beverages, but part of Clay's mind dwelled on that unexpected surge of relief. He'd put the same friendly, joking technique to use countless times in the past in order to place both suspects and witnesses at ease.

This was different, though. Winning Lucas's trust and high regard mattered, and he wasn't sure why. No doubt part of the urgency was because of the man's connection to Caraleigh, but there was more to it than that.

It was the way Lucas talked, his little mannerisms and interactions. They reminded Clay of his sister.

During a lull in the conversation, Clay risked bringing her up again. "Can you tell me anything else about Caraleigh when you two were together? Anything at all. It's been so long since I've seen her that I'm scared I won't even recognize her now that she's all grown up."

He grimaced when he voiced the fear out loud. He hadn't meant to put a damper on their meal like that, but Lucas's eyes lit up. "I read that babies are challenging for people to recognize later because their facial structures grow and change so much. Prepubescent faces lose fat but change at a much slower rate. Caraleigh wasn't a baby."

Clay knew all that already. As an FBI agent, he'd worked with facial progressions more than once. But somehow, Lucas's steady, matter-of-fact recital drove the truth home. "Thank you, that makes me feel better."

Lucas beamed, but by the time Clay finished sipping his water, the happiness dimmed. His shoulders rounded while he drew circles on his glass. "Sometimes, I believed the doctors when they said she was too good to be true. That she wasn't real. They kept asking me how it was possible that, out in the mountains with barely any other people around, how I'd found a girl my own age who didn't make the world noisier or more stressful? They didn't believe the girl existed, and I started to think that maybe I did make the whole thing up." His hand stilled. "But I didn't, did I? Make her up?"

Lucas's soft plea was full of hope. The same hope that had been fueling Clay. "No, you didn't. Good luck, karma, guardian angel, whatever you want to call it. I think some unexplained force helped the two of you find each other. And let's hope that didn't use up our quota of luck because we're gonna need a helluva lot more of it."

The waitress waltzed up with a tray and placed their plates on the table. "You need anything else, just holler."

Clay thanked her and turned back in time to catch Lucas lifting up the top bun and peeking underneath. "They got it right. No ketchup…or pickles."

That made Clay laugh again while Lucas picked up his burger and nibbled off the tiniest of bites.

"What, you afraid it might be poisoned or something?"

Lucas swallowed before shaking his head. "Not poisoned, but why take a big bite if I'm not sure I'll like it yet?"

Hard as Clay tried, he couldn't come up with a good answer for that. "Valid point. So, how is it?"

Lucas had already bitten off a much larger chunk and mumbled around a mouthful. "Delicious."

Even so, damned if Clay didn't try a smaller bite to start with than usual, just in case, but the instant the burger hit his taste buds, he had to concede. He waited until he swallowed to gloat. "What did I tell you? Hole-in-the-wall joints make the best burgers."

Lucas was too busy gobbling down another bite to speak, so he nodded. He polished off the burger in half the time Clay took with his and started in on the fries. They talked for the remainder of the meal, with Clay sharing a funny story about how Caraleigh had refused to leave the petting zoo when she was six or seven unless their parents agreed to let her bring a baby pig home.

The pig chased her around the enclosure, which was full of mud from a recent storm. His mom had ended up slipping right on her butt in the dirtiest part, and their dad had started laughing, and then Clay. Caraleigh had finally stopped throwing a giant hissy fit and laughed too.

They'd bought a stuffed animal pig on the way out, which Caraleigh had aptly named Baby.

Lucas smiled. "She always loved all the animals. Sometimes, she'd climb the big tree near the cabin or go to the sunning rock and sit there for hours, just watching the animals go by. There weren't any pigs, though, but I told her that some places do have wild pigs, called javelinas. She said she wanted to go there one day and see them."

Clay could almost picture her begging Lucas to take her to see the wild pigs. "That sounds like Caraleigh."

Lucas pushed a French fry around on his plate. "When we find her, can we take her there sometime? To see the javelinas?"

When...not if.

A lump formed in Clay's throat. "Yeah. I'd like that a lot." And it was true.

Lucas visibly brightened at the reassurance, and the lump in Clay's throat grew. After spending the day with the other man, it was impossible not to like him. He hoped, for both of their sakes, that Lucas's optimism wasn't misplaced and that they'd find Caraleigh alive and well.

Or they'd find her body and find closure in knowing her fate.

Somehow.

"Thanks for coming with me today, Lucas. I really appreciate your help."

Lucas shrugged. "I wanted to come." He pushed the last fry around his plate once more before peeking up at Clay. "And you can call me Luke."

After they both finished eating, Clay grabbed the check and followed Lucas...*Luke*...past the other diners to the cash register. The waitress was gone, replaced behind the counter by a young man in a plaid shirt and overalls with a gray bandana wrapped around his neck.

"How was everything this evening?"

Clay passed him the bill and a credit card. "Delicious, thanks. Could you recommend any local places to stay the night? We were thinking of doing a little more hiking in the morning."

"Sure, no problem. There are a couple of decent hotels less than a mile—"

"Gah!"

The high-pitched exclamation cut the cashier off. Clay whirled to check on Luke, who'd gone stiff as a pole. His mouth moved like he was trying to speak, but no sounds came out, and his gaze was fixed to a spot to the right of the cashier's head.

"Is he okay?"

Clay wished he knew. "Not sure. Luke, what's wrong?" He traced the trajectory of Luke's stare to the corkboard. The picture of the cartoon hamburger was still front and center, but how did that make sense? They'd laughed about the stupid thing earlier. Nothing else was there but a bunch of customer and employee photos. "What is it?"

In response, Luke darted forward, straight for the cartoon burger. He curled his hand and clawed at the pictures, as if trying to rake them off the board.

"Uh, he can't do that. Should I call 911 or something?"

"No! Don't call, and for god sakes, don't touch him. He'll be fine. It's probably just sensory overload." Clay rushed forward, kicking himself the entire time. He should have known better when they'd walked in. This place was too crowded and too damned noisy by far.

When he reached Luke, the man was smacking his palm against one specific picture, making deep, guttural noises in his throat. Clay lifted a hand to touch him before dropping it again, remembering how physical contact would sometimes make Caraleigh's meltdowns worse.

Think, dammit! What used to help Caraleigh?

Clay relaxed on an exhale and allowed his body and voice to fill with calm. Before he could help, he first needed to identify the problem.

"Hey, Luke. Everything's going to be okay. Can you help me understand what's going on? Is it too noisy in here? Because it's nice and quiet outside. We can get some fresh air or hop in the car and turn the radio on to any channel you like."

Luke cried out and gave his head a violent shake.

"No, you don't want to go outside? What is it, then? The photo? Is there something in that photo that's upsetting you?"

That question prompted Luke to reach for the photo with both hands like he might tear it off the wall.

"Hang on, we need to leave that up there for now. Here, let me take a look too. You can show me what's so exciting." Clay leaned forward and peered at the photo, wondering what in the hell had upset Luke so much. The big man with the trucker hat, who was smiling into the camera over an empty plate? Or the pretty blonde waitress who stood behind him with her hand on his shoulder, wearing a check-ered shirt and a phony why-do-I-have-to-be-in-this-picture smile?

Frustrated, Clay scanned the rest of the frame, seeking a clue as to what set Luke off. He reached the far left corner, and his heart stuttered to a stop before starting again at triple speed. He rubbed his eyes and leaned in closer to ensure the dim lighting wasn't playing tricks on him.

The checkered shirt and denim overalls marked the woman in the frame as a waitress, but it was the face that rendered Clay unable to move.

Half a face. That was all that showed, like she'd turned

away from the camera a fraction too late to avoid being in the shot entirely.

Still, half a face was enough for Clay to recognize his sister.

Caraleigh.

Pressing a hand to his trembling lips, Clay read the hand-written numbers at the bottom.

The photo had been snapped an entire year after Luke was fished out of the river.

18

That morning when I opened my eyes, my mind was already abuzz with the coming day's festivities. The soft, green glow of the digital clock confirmed that I'd woken up one minute early, per usual.

Good. Punctuality was a must when planning.

I tapped off the alarm on my way out of bed and headed straight for the shower. The warm spray soothed me a little too much, so I turned the lever down until the water turned icy cold. The shock on my bare skin reinvigorated me enough to dry off and go in search of clothes. After sparing a few moments to peruse the closet's offerings, I selected a pair of gray slacks and a gray, blue, and white pinstriped shirt. Even with no public appearance on the agenda for this morning, there was no excuse for a shabby appearance.

Headmistress Letitia had taught me that.

The walk down the hall and through the living room was silent and shrouded in shadows, with only a few stripes of weak early morning sunlight creeping in through gaps in the boards. Instead of heading to the kitchen for breakfast as my usual routine dictated, I went to the door and used the key in my pocket to turn the lock. A click later, and I was outside, rubbing my arms against the frigid morning air as I strolled past the winter-brown grass, intent on the tiny structure squatting on the far side of the yard.

The lawn triggered a rush of memories. Once upon a time, I'd been a little boy, content to dig in the dirt for worms and roll my thrift-store trucks around the postage-stamp yard of the house my mother and I had shared. In those early days, I'd still had a mother who'd loved me. We'd struggled to make ends meet and been poor in possessions, but we'd had each other, and I'd believed that was enough.

And love very well may have carried us through life, if not for the foolish man who'd swooped in and bedazzled my mother with wealth and material objects. She'd transformed before my eyes. Her love for me hollowed out and rotted, a casualty of her new husband's disapproval.

Another cold gust cut through my shirt, rousing me from my sordid past and planting me firmly in the present. That was all ancient history and of no consequence now. I'd procured a suitable replacement for my distant mother, at least for a while.

I stomped a dried leaf on the pathway and savored the satisfying crunch beneath my shoe, delighting in the reminder of how a finger felt when snapped beneath my hands, or a wrist. I continued on to the wooden shed, humming as I unlocked the door and ducked inside to reach the refrigerator. Two eggs, a slice of ham, and a piece of bread went onto one of the clean plates stacked on the collapsible metal table. Mission complete, I locked the door behind me and carried the plate back to the house to cook.

The eggs sizzled as I added them to the hot pan, but it was the sweet-savory aroma of ham that brought me back to that morning at the academy...

My eyes drank her in from across the crowded cafeteria.

Her hair gleamed like a freshly polished shoe when those burnished copper waves caught the light, all sleek and tidy, without a single strand out of place. As always, her outfit was immaculate too. Crisp, with no wrinkles or creases, like she'd come straight from the dry cleaners, with the overall effect somehow both reserved from the buttoned-up collar and yet also enticing with the way the fabric skimmed her curves.

I pressed the lever to fill the cup with orange juice while my stomach did that funny flip it liked to perform whenever she was around. Not that I blamed my body for the reaction. She was the perfect representation of femininity, her appearance a how-to guide for the way women should look.

She played the little game we'd been forced to adopt in public. Ignoring me completely or letting her gaze skim over me as though I wasn't there. But as I carried my tray into the dining area, her blue eyes connected with mine. Once, and excruciatingly brief. Just long enough to send the message, loud and clear.

I kept walking, my heart swelling to twice its normal size.

Tonight. Our training would continue tonight.

On my way to the usual spot at a table near the back wall, I approached three boys from my year. They elbowed each other as I drew closer, and the two seated closest to me sneered.

I ignored them. Impudent idiots. They were so far beneath me that they weren't worth the bother.

That thought vanished when one of them muttered something under his breath as I passed, his eyes narrowed with malice.

I stopped and slowly turned in their direction. "Excuse me, I didn't quite catch that. Can you say it again?"

Two of the boys exchanged uneasy glances, but the loud-mouth only sat up taller. "You heard me. *Freak. Perv.* Everyone knows you've got a boner for the headmaster's wife." He practically spit the word out this time, his mouth twisted into a cruel smile.

Heat blazed through me, and my hands gripped the tray so hard, the plastic rattled with my anger. A hand curled around my shoulder before I could react. "Whatever is going on here, gentlemen?"

All three of the other boys' gazes flew to Headmistress Letitia, who'd managed to creep up behind me without my knowledge. Fear widened their eyes before two of them stared at the floor. Only the one who'd insulted me was brazen enough to maintain eye contact. "Uh, nothing, Headmistress."

"Mr. Kingsley, is that true?"

Her perfume reached my nose, musky and sweet, and the hand still resting on my shoulder infused my entire body with warmth. I wanted to tremble, but years of practice and control held me steady. "No, Headmistress Letitia. I'm afraid they weren't behaving in accordance to academy rules."

"That...that's not true!" the boy sitting in the middle yelped before turning to glare at his loudmouthed companion. "Tell her, Freddy!"

Freddy's skin paled beneath its usual tan, the latter a result of his frequent trips to Key West and the Bahamas, thanks to his parents' vacation homes there. "He's right. Nothing happened. Kingsley here is lying, to get us in tr—"

"Enough." Headmistress Letitia silenced him with a single word. Seconds ticked by while she played on their growing fear, enjoying their squirming and twisting their dread into yet another weapon in her arsenal.

My pulse thundered. Genius. Our headmistress was a genius.

When the tension drew out enough to meet her satisfaction, the headmistress tapped a glossy, manicured nail to her chin. "I know, why don't you three come meditate on this situation in my office once the school day is complete?"

Another display of brilliance, the way she pretended the punishment was spontaneous and posed the command as a request. Even though by now, every student within these stately halls understood that even when uttered by such perfect lips, the phrase *meditate in my office* never, ever amounted to anything good. A truth reinforced by the collective silence that descended over the entire cafeteria, like all the students were holding their breath at once.

And there I was, standing at Headmistress Letitia's side, in the thick of it all. Commanding attention and fear while basking in her approval.

The power inherent in that moment vibrated along my skin, filling my head with an amphetamine-like high. These were the thrills that fed my soul. That injected my life with meaning and had, from a young age on.

Rules were so important. Out in the real world and here in the academy. These students needed to learn that not following the rules meant consequences. That acting out against academy policies led to repercussions, doled out by those of us who were willing to do whatever it took to ensure order prevailed.

Under Headmistress Letitia's careful guidance, I'd learned that not everyone was well suited to become enforcers, because that particular role required a strength of will and an ability to inflict pain when necessary.

No, not everyone was well suited to inflicting pain, but Letitia had recognized a kindred spirit in me.

I scooped the eggs, ham, and toast onto a clean plate, carried them to the tiny table just outside the kitchen, and began eating, allowing my mind to drift to later on that day.

We'd wasted hours in the headmistress's office that afternoon, giving the three rule-breakers a chance to carry out their punishment. So simple. All they'd been required to do was designate one among their group to receive the punishment while the other two carried it out. Wield the tawse, and they'd be free to go. Nothing too gruesome or horrifying.

And yet, they'd stood stiff-backed and stubborn in that office and refused every opportunity given to cooperate.

Headmistress Letitia had finally lost patience and sent them out into the frigid dark, telling them that spending a night outside in the elements would likely clear their heads.

For the first time to my knowledge, Headmistress Letitia was wrong. When she let them back into the building the next morning, the threesome were shivering and pale, but after spending all day locked inside the Blue Room, their stubborn pride had reared up again.

Apparently, even the Academy's notorious punishment room was no match for Mother Nature in the dead of winter.

"Which one of you will be disciplined today?"

The question garnered the same response as the day before. "None of us, Headmistress."

I recalled my stunned fascination as the same scene played out over the next three days and nights. The question asked and refused. Over the passing time, my fascination turned to anger, and possibly even a flicker of jealousy, because the only reason those three fools had to cling to their ridiculous moral code was some sort of misplaced devotion to each other.

After the second night, I was so sure they'd crack. But they didn't, despite not being fed during the entire period when the battle of wills raged on and despite the lack of sleep that showed on their shadow-lined faces. Certainly, they'd been exhausted and bleary headed with hunger, but they were also teen boys and able to rebound from those minor hardships without fear of permanent damage.

Or at least, they would have ended up perfectly fine, were it not for the cold front that descended upon the mountain late that fourth night, so sudden that even the weathermen had failed to predict it.

That night, they went out into the cold as usual. When they didn't return the next morning, the headmistress sent me out to fetch them. I'd hurried out to scour the area, grumbling at the icy wind that cut through my layers and the frost crunching under my boots. I hadn't ventured far when I discovered all three of them. Dead.

The first two were huddled together for warmth like sleeping puppies beneath the sculpted hedges lining the building in back.

Freddy, I located about twenty feet away. Lying on his back, stripped down to nothing but his boxers, his tan flesh pale with frost. I'd later learned that hypothermia played tricks on people, often convincing them they were burning up when, in reality, their bodies slowly froze to death. Nature's little prank, and a rather poetic one at that.

They died due to nature and their own disobedience, but of course, the local police had disagreed.

I left the last bite of toast and pushed the plate away. The resulting chaos their deaths brought down upon the academy was in large part my responsibility. My failure.

Had I been more skilled in breaking people back then, the boys would have fallen into line and carried out their punishment without a peep. That could have been my gift to Letitia, for all the lessons she'd taught me.

Instead, she'd turned her fury on me in a brutal attack that made me shudder, even after all the suffering I'd inflicted on others since. The scar on my back tingled, a reminder of the agony that blistered my flesh when she'd pressed the hot knife to my skin as punishment for my failings.

With a heavy sigh, I rose, rubbing the scar as I walked over to the refrigerator. The chain clinked to the floor when I released the lock, and I swung the door open to reveal Bethany.

She was huddled so close to the front, knees drawn to her chest and shivering, that she tumbled onto the kitchen floor, reeking of vomit.

Over the course of the night, I'd opened the door for brief periods on a schedule to ensure she didn't perish from lack of oxygen, sacrificing my own sleep for the sake of her safety. The ungrateful brat had greeted my kindness with kicks and tears and pleas.

This time was different. While she hacked and filled her lungs with noisy slurps of air as usual, she didn't bother to cry or fight.

Satisfaction warmed my bones. Progress. Good. Katarina's offspring needed to learn that her sweet, fragile life was nestled like an eggshell in my hands, every bit as easy to crush as it was to nurture.

"Good girl, you're learning. Now, if you can promise to stay calm and quiet and get yourself over to the table, I'll reward you by letting you finish the leftovers on my plate."

Her dazed, hungry eyes drifted a little before focusing on the food. A third of a fried egg, a few bites of ham, and half a crust of toast. That was all I'd left her, but she licked her chapped lips like the crumbs were an elaborate buffet.

On quivering legs, she stumbled for the table. When she got close enough to reach, she hooked her hands over the back of the chair for extra support. Painfully slow, she eased her weak body onto the chair, almost slipping off the side but righting herself at the last second.

Before I'd even finished setting the plate in front of her, those black and purple swollen fingers reached for the food.

My slap rang out, sharp against those bruised knuckles in

the quiet room. "Eat like a human, not an animal. Use the fork."

Pride stirred when she swallowed her cry because the blow on that damaged skin had to hurt. The fork shook in her hand, but that sweet forehead wrinkled with concentration, and she managed to spear a bit of egg and lift the bite to her mouth.

I allowed myself another moment to relish the picture she made before heading to the freezer and withdrawing a Hot Pocket. The microwave hummed as the frozen meal heated and infused the area with a delicious cheesy aroma.

Behind me, Bethany released a small, animal-like whimper, and I smiled.

When the timer dinged, I transferred the Hot Pocket to a fresh plate and carried it to the table. Round with longing, Bethany's eyes followed my every move, not realizing that her swollen hand gripped the fork like a weapon.

I slid the plate before her, and she went still, her gaze glued to the crispy sandwich. She looked like a fox too terrified of a trap to lunge for the piece of meat poking out from shiny steel, but too hungry to flee, either.

"Good girl for waiting for permission, but go ahead now. Eat. I need you strong for what's coming next."

19

The digital clock on the Explorer's dashboard read 11:03 when Ellie's bodyguard pulled up to the entrance of the Lake Walters Retirement Community.

From the passenger seat, Ellie arched her back and stretched. Finally. Their four-hour drive had turned into six. Half an hour into the trip, they'd hit road construction that funneled the highway down to a one-lane crawl, followed by stop-and-go traffic around the four-hour mark, thanks to an RV engine fire.

Shane rolled the SUV to a stop beside the guard kiosk. Giant palm trees flanked the street on both sides, rising beyond the wrought iron gates at regular intervals like green-haired giants. Interspersed between them were terra-cotta roofs that gleamed orange-red in the Florida sun while the lush, manicured grounds and large homes beyond the gate oozed with wealth.

Ellie powered off the stereo, cutting off Hank Crawford mid-word. Her expectations for the true-crime podcast hadn't been very high, so she'd been pleasantly surprised when the episodes turned out to be both in-depth and insightful. Impressive, especially for a guy whose psychology background consisted of his own past traumatic experiences and a few books.

Crawford had sketched a clear, fact-based portrait of Letitia Wiggins, along with his conclusions as to what made her tick, and Ellie recognized many of the former headmaster's wife's traits in some of the women she'd grown up around. The attributes he described were common in the elite and privileged, especially women who derived a sense of power by focusing outward to control others rather than working on their own self-control.

Shane rolled the window down as the security guard stepped out of the kiosk, approaching their vehicle with a polite smile and a tablet in one hand. He was much fitter than the daytime security detail Ellie was accustomed to staffing residential communities in Charleston, with broad shoulders, muscled arms, and a military bearing to match his buzz cut. A 9mm hung in plain view from his right hip.

"Morning, folks. Can I get the name of the guest you're visiting today?"

Ellie leaned across the center console and smiled. "Good morning. We're visiting Letitia Wiggins."

The guard nodded as he finger-scrolled along the tablet's screen. "And your name is?"

Ellie flipped the sun visor down to grab her badge. "Detective Kline."

The guard stopped scrolling and lifted his gaze from the tablet. "Detective Kline. Can you move that badge a little closer for me, please?"

She passed the shield to Shane, who held it outside the window. The guard leaned over, using a hand on his forehead to shield the sun, squinting at the badge before straightening back up. "I see you're from Charleston, Detective

Kline. What business brings you out so far this way to visit our resident?"

As soon as he asked, Ellie bit back a sigh. Her chances of getting in without a warrant weren't looking good. "I work cold cases for CPD, and Letitia Wiggins is a potential witness to a crime that occurred several years ago."

"I see. Well, I'm sorry you drove all this way for nothing, but I'm afraid I can't let you in, not without a warrant or a guest pass."

There it was.

"Are you sure? I'd think Ms. Wiggins would want to do her civic duty and help out with our investigation."

The guard was unflappable. "She may very well want to, but without her buzzing you in or adding you to the guest list, I'm afraid we won't be able to find out."

Ellie ground her molars together. "If it's just the car that's an issue, we could park outside, and I could walk in?"

In her experience, gated communities often cared more about preventing unauthorized vehicles than foot traffic, because burglars tended to think twice about robbing a house without getaway wheels.

Not this guy. Before she even finished, the guard was shaking his head. "I really do apologize for the inconvenience, but I risk my job if I don't follow community policies. The residents here pay for gated access for a reason, I'm sure you understand. Now, you two both have a nice day, and feel free to come back when you have that warrant or a guest pass."

The security guard dismissed them by turning his back and returning to the kiosk, leaving Ellie to seethe and mutter under her breath.

"He seems nice."

Shane's dry comment shook a surprised laugh from Ellie. Her bodyguard didn't speak up without prompting much, but when he did, he often voiced snide little gems like that. "He definitely takes his job seriously."

She glared at the security guard one last time before slumping. He was only doing his job. Unfortunately for her, his job and hers were at odds at the moment.

Shane shot her an inquisitive glance. "Where to?"

"Go ahead and make a U-turn and drive us back to that little downtown area we passed on the way. I'll just have to think of something else."

She stared out the passenger window as the Explorer cruised along the sun-washed roads that led to a cute little area full of cobblestoned streets, palm trees mixed with live oaks, and a mixture of boutiques and cafes that boasted patios with outdoor seating, all under an array of colorful awnings.

The sidewalks teamed with midday shoppers and diners, and the SUV crawled along the busy road, passing a long streak of full parking spaces before Shane zipped into an empty spot a block away.

"Hungry?" Ellie asked Shane, but he only gave her the *I'm on the clock* look he normally did. If the man ever ate, she didn't know.

Ellie climbed out and headed into the bustling shopping area, irritated by the long, unproductive drive and hoping that lunch might refuel her lagging spirits and prompt a new plan. A quick glance back reassured her that her shadow was doing his job just a couple steps from her heels.

She passed three boutiques, a nail salon, an ice cream shop, and a Cuban café before popping into a pub with an open table tucked away in the corner of the brick-lined patio. After ordering a blackened shrimp salad, Ellie sipped sweet tea from an oversized glass and people-watched while reevaluating her plan.

Had her spur-of-the-moment decision to jump in the car

and head down to Florida been an error in judgment? Because it was really starting to appear that way.

Ellie flopped her chin into her palm and sighed. Instead of lowering her head like a stubborn ox and bulldozing forward, maybe the smart action right now was to accept this one failure, take the loss, and head home. If they hopped back on the road as soon as she finished eating, they'd arrive in Charleston in time for dinner, and she could figure out where to take the case from there.

Except, she was a stubborn ox. They were here now, after a six-hour drive, and the idea of turning around and leaving without taking another stab at questioning the woman rankled. Ellie frowned at her tea. If only she had the vaguest notion of how to speak to Letitia without that bulldog at the gate chasing her off. Without Letitia Wiggins, she wasn't sure how to go about finding information on Kingsley, either.

Ellie chewed the end of her straw while countless pedestrians strolled by before pulling out her phone and dialing.

"Miss me already?"

Despite her sour mood, Ellie smiled at Jillian's greeting. "Believe it or not, I'm calling to see if there've been any updates yet."

"Nothing on Bethany as far as I know, but I think Valdez is making some headway with Fortis's case."

The waitress set Ellie's salad in front of her. "Let me know if you need anything else," the young brunette whispered.

Ellie smiled. "Thanks, I will."

The waitress left.

"Who you talking to?" Jillian asked.

"The waitress, my order just came. I'm drowning my sorrows with shrimp salad."

"Yum, sounds like a sound judgment call to me. I'll let you

go so you can hop right to that sorrow drowning, unless you needed something else?"

Ellie was about to say no but hesitated. "Actually, would you mind pulling up and printing me a copy of everything we have on Letitia Wiggins and the Far Ridge Boy's Academy? I'm especially interested in any records we might have on Kingsley while he attended."

"Nope, no problem, I can do that."

"Thanks. You know, while you're at it, could you cancel my lunch with my mom tomorrow?"

"Hell no. Sorry, not sorry. I consider myself a decently brave person, but I'm definitely not brave enough to risk the wrath of Helen Kline."

Ellie laughed. "Rats. I figured maybe I could sneak that one in there, and you might agree before you noticed. Oh well, worth a try."

"You keep right on dreaming. See ya!"

After they hung up, Ellie rummaged through her purse until she located her earbuds. Once she adjusted them in her ears, she started playing the podcast again, soaking up more of Crawford's description of Letitia Wiggins while she forked a few bites of shrimp and romaine into her mouth.

The first impression the Far Ridge Boy's Academy headmistress gave to prospective students and their parents upon meeting with her was one of impeccable grooming and exquisite manners. That was my second impression too. Along with my third.

Letitia Wiggins was the type of woman who took great pains with her appearance, like she was compelled to reach some sky-high internal measurement of perfection. Not necessarily a problematic trait to possess, unless you're the type of person who demands that same perfection from others, which she did. Namely, her students.

Ellie made a scoffing sound. So far, Letitia Wiggins would fit in really well with half the upper-class women in Charleston.

But I'm getting a little ahead of myself. Back to Headmistress Wiggins. Her shoes always gleamed from a fresh polish, and her suits and tops were crisp from the iron. She sashayed around the halls with the air of a woman who realized she was attractive. On its own, that isn't an issue. Wiggins capitalized on her beauty, though, brandishing her looks as a weapon.

I've surveyed a number of former Far Ridge students over the years, and they've all agreed: Letitia Wiggins's pride and joy was her red-gold hair. While I attended the Academy, I once overheard another teacher joke that she wouldn't be surprised if Ms. Wiggins stashed a personal hairdresser at the academy to pop out and perform touch-ups throughout the day. Looking just right was clearly an item of crucial importance for the headmistress, and I believe a source of great pride and dysfunction too...

Ellie hit stop on the podcast and pushed the lettuce around on her plate, once again reminded of a few of her mom's wealthy friends. They were the kind of women who wouldn't be caught dead leaving the house in saggy sweatpants or without a full face of makeup. Heaven forbid they venture out into polite society without styling their hair first or be caught dead with split ends or unsightly roots. The joke about Letitia Wiggins sneaking a private hairdresser into her room wasn't all that far-fetched.

In the social circles her family ran in, the women who fixated on their appearances to a pathological degree rarely lowered their harsh, exacting standards as they aged.

Chewing a bite of salad, Ellie typed "hair salons" into her phone's search window. Results popped up in seconds. She dismissed a chain and a barbershop before landing on a local salon with a fancy name.

Chez La La.

The salon was located in the same little shopping village, a couple blocks up the road and less than a mile away from Letitia Wiggins's retirement community. Ellie scrolled through the reviews. When customer after customer raved about how the results were well worth the expense, she figured she might as well pay them a visit.

She shoveled down the rest of the salad, threw enough bills on the table to cover lunch plus a large tip, and headed down the sidewalk. Shane fell in step behind her.

The winter sun warmed the air and was accompanied by a mild breeze that carried the lush, sweet scent of jasmine. Walkers, tourists, and shoppers sprinkled the sidewalks, taking advantage of the good weather. Ellie passed two middle-aged women in loungewear and diamonds who'd paused to peer at brightly dressed mannequins inside a boutique and a tanned, elderly man wearing Bermuda shorts with a Hawaiian shirt and yakking into a cell phone.

If Bethany's disappearance wasn't pressing down on her, Ellie could have spent hours meandering along too, soaking up the sun and poking through any boutiques that caught her eye. Instead, she hurried around the slow-moving shoppers with quick strides that marked her as an outsider.

Three blocks later, the GPS informed her that the black-and-white striped awning embellished with gold accents located a few storefronts ahead likely belonged to her destination. She drew closer and peeked at the window to confirm it. The same gilt accent color from the awning was scrawled in elaborate, cursive letters on the glass to form the salon's name.

On the opposite side of the glass, a handful of stylists zipped around elderly women draped in black gowns, while wielding scissors and brushes and aluminum foil squares.

Ellie brushed a speck of lint off her black blazer, drew in a deep breath, and channeled Helen Kline at her most regal and imperious. Chin lifted and shoulders back, she sauntered into the salon with what she hoped was a passable imitation of her mother's reserved confidence.

The well-groomed receptionist behind the computer podium glanced up with a smile when the bell over the door tinkled a snooty warning. "Welcome to Chez La La. Do you have an appointment?"

The woman's face was expertly made-up, with thick, sculpted brows, cherry-red lips, and a soft glow in all the right places. A chunky gold necklace flashed beneath the collar of her white silk blouse, and large diamond studs sparkled in her ears, all of which screamed money. Ever since she'd joined the police force, Ellie had stopped paying much attention to her own clothes, but she was happy that she'd dressed with care that morning. Especially when the receptionist's gaze itemized her outfit.

Ellie smoothed a hand down the tailored black jacket she wore, drawing the receptionist's sharp gaze to both the expensive cut and the gold Rolex peeking out from her sleeve. The suit had been a gift from her mom. Helen had attended Fashion Week in New York and decided her daughter simply must have something from a particular up-and-coming designer. Which probably meant the outfit cost more than most people spent on rent.

Along with some tasteful gold jewelry, Ellie was glad she'd thought to pack the suit, especially since she ended up trying to convince Letitia Wiggins's gatekeepers that she was worthy of an audience. That plan had tanked but dressing up might pay off yet.

Ellie tossed her head before leaning on the marble counter, ensuring her jacket sleeve hitched up enough to showcase the Rolex again. "Actually, I'm hoping that someone is available for a last-minute job. I'm new to the area and on the hunt for a good salon. I'm sure you know how stressful that can be." Ellie fanned herself with one hand, and after a lingering glance at the Rolex, the receptionist's expression turned sympathetic.

"Oh, I do. Isn't that the worst, trying to figure out who you can trust with something as important as your hair?"

"Right? Hair is so important. I thought I'd have more time to search, only someone sprang a surprise engagement on me tonight, and I need to look my best."

The receptionist nodded. "Trust me, I completely understand. Hang on, let me check and see what I can do." She tapped at a few keys and beamed. "It looks like you're in luck. We're usually booked weeks, sometimes months out, but we happen to have a brand-new stylist with an opening. Would that work for you?"

"Oh, that's fantabulous, thank you." Ellie cringed inside. Fantabulous? She didn't think she'd ever said that word in her entire life. Even Helen Kline wouldn't be caught dead forming the word. "I only need a wash and a trim, so that should work out fine."

"Perfect. Go ahead and take a seat, and I'll let her know you're here."

Ellie settled on one of the two fancy loveseats crafted from red cushions and gold metalwork and inspected the salon during the wait. Glossy black workstations stretched toward the back wall, each dominated by a massive gilt mirror. A stylist swept hair clippings from a cream-and-black floor that appeared to be genuine marble, or at the very least, a damned good imitation.

If Letitia Wiggins didn't frequent this salon, Ellie bet she was a client at one every bit as lavish. This place even smelled good thanks to the lit candles scattered all around. Like peaches and cream instead of the typical color solution and hairspray.

"Ellie? Hi, I'm Holly, and I'll be your stylist today. I can take you back now."

The woman who bounded up to Ellie appeared younger than the rest of the hairdressers, somewhere closer to Ellie's own age. Her short hair was dyed black and razored into multiple layers around a heart-shaped face. Holly led her to an empty chair closest to the back wall, chatting the entire time as she draped Ellie in a black gown.

Ellie laughed and replied and nudged her to keep talking. The more loose-lipped her stylist, the better.

Once they both faced the mirror, Holly fingered one of Ellie's waves. "So, what are we doing today? Your hair is so pretty."

"Just a wash and a trim."

The stylist pressed a hand to her chest. "Oh, thank goodness. I was half-afraid you wanted me to cut it all off."

Ellie reached for her hair, flinching. "No, no, just a trim. An inch at most." Not that she believed hair was as life-and-death as the receptionist seemed to, but still. Ponytails and braids were simple and quick and suited her busy lifestyle. Short hair required too much work. Plus, okay, she admitted that maybe she was just the tiniest bit vain about her long curls.

The stylist washed Ellie's hair with a delicious mint-scented shampoo and chattered away about her boyfriend and his new job and the weather. Ellie coaxed her along every once in a while, peppering in questions about how Holly enjoyed working at Chez La La so far and if the clients were nice.

After that last question, Holly paused her snipping. "A lot of them are really great. I love my little old ladies who come in and tell me all about their grandbabies and dogs. Of course, there are always a few who can be a little...demanding."

She brushed out a new section of Ellie's hair and clipped off the ends while little red pieces fell to the floor. "I understand completely. Actually," Ellie lowered her voice, like she was sharing a secret, "my aunt can be a little like that sometimes. She sprang a last-minute dinner party on me for tonight, and I didn't dare show up with split ends, or I would have never heard the end of it. She's the one who told me about this place."

Holly made a sympathetic hum. "Oh boy, do I know the type. Who's your aunt?"

Ellie waited until the stylist met her gaze in the mirror. "Letitia Wiggins."

Holly winced, and her mouth formed a circle. "Oh." She ducked her head and busied herself lining up a new section of Ellie's hair.

"I'm guessing from that reaction that you know her. Come on, you can tell me. She's my aunt, remember? I know she's a pill, so it's not like you'd be sharing something new."

The stylist bit her lip and checked the workstation closest to them, but her coworker was busy chatting away with a white-haired elderly woman. Still, Holly scooted closer and lowered her voice. "Everyone knows Letitia. She comes in every four weeks to get a root touchup and make sure her style stays perfect."

Ellie rolled her eyes in the mirror. "Yup, that sounds like Aunt Letitia. She can be a lot. So demanding. Don't tell her I said this, but I feel sorry for her poor stylist."

Holly snipped away. "Me too. I guess she always stares at her hair in the mirror for like five minutes after Bev finishes. She twists every which way and frowns, like she's never quite satisfied with how it turned out. She even points out spots that Bev needs to touch up."

"Oof. Though, I'm not surprised. I remember when I was younger, she used to make her housekeeper cry. She can be pretty terrifying." Ellie clapped a hand over her mouth. "Please tell me she's not due in today. I'd die if she marched over and started bossing us around. She always has very particular ideas about what I should do with my hair."

Holly's eyes rounded. "Oh, Lordy, I hope not. What day of the week is it again?"

"Wednesday."

The stylist heaved out a breath. "You're so lucky. You missed her by one day. She always comes the third Thursday of the month. Ten thirty, like clockwork."

"Whew! I definitely dodged a bullet there."

While Holly finished touching up her hair, Ellie thanked providence for smiling down on her. And when she walked out of the salon ten minutes later, she smiled while patting her curls.

Sixty-seven dollars for a wash and a trim plus information on how to bump into Letitia Wiggins despite an overzealous security guard? That was money well spent.

20

K atarina spent a good chunk of the night and all the next morning creating and rejecting escape plans.

Her first idea centered on waiting for a busy period like lunch to provoke a fight between two of the more volatile patients, one or both of whom could be counted on to freak out. When the staff rushed in to neutralize the situation, she'd use the resulting chaos to sneak away.

The bed whirred when Katarina hit the control panel. She scowled through the open doorway as her top half lifted into an upright position. Great idea, except for one tiny detail. This stupid place hadn't seen fit to put her into any group therapy sessions yet, or a communal lunch.

No, Katarina was sentenced to this miserable room, chained to the bed like a naughty puppy. The nurses barely even visited, popping in only a few times a day to check her wound dressings and change them if necessary unless she hit the call button.

When she was released, she was going to call whatever healthcare regulatory agency oversaw conditions like these.

Right after she found her daughter, which took her right back to forming escape plans.

Jasper was her second idea. Given a few weeks, she was confident of her ability to charm the cute CNA under her spell. Except, she didn't have a few weeks. Even a few days seemed too long to remain trapped in this bed while Kingsley had Bethany. Way too long.

Besides, she'd taken a few shots at sinking her hooks into Jasper, and each time, she'd quit too soon to stand a chance of reeling him in. All because of a dead man. Her heart and mind were too painfully full of Clayne.

Katarina shifted her shoulders back and forth on the bed, attempting to scratch an itch on her back that her bound hands made impossible to reach before slumping. Great. Maybe she could stand some mental health care, after all. That first session with a new therapist would be a real gem. Katarina could picture it now.

So, the thing is, I kinda offed my boyfriend on purpose in order to save my daughter from this psychopath who was basically a father figure to me. He's the one who taught me how to slit someone's throat in just the right place to kill them...the very technique I used on my boyfriend. Got any exercises or meditations to help me fix that? Don't get me wrong, I've killed other people before him and even enjoyed it sometimes. For some reason, though, this particular murder keeps bothering me.

Yeah, right. They'd report her ass to the police before the session even ended, and Katarina would wind up in prison. She seriously doubted that the AG was waiting in the wings again with another get-out-of-jail-free card, so she'd do hard time.

Not an option when Bethany needed a mother.

"Jesse? Where are you? Jesse!" A wail drifted into her room from the patient next door, an elderly woman who called out day and night for some phantom person named Jesse.

Katarina whacked her head against the pillow. Escape was the only option, and soon. The longer Bethany spent under that monster's control, the more time he had to inflict permanent damage.

"Jesse? Jesse!"

Plus, the longer Katarina was subjected to that screeching, the more likely she was to actually lose her damn mind. She slammed her head into the pillow again. But how? How the hell did she get out of this shithole? Not like she could climb out the window, since this pit of a room didn't have one. And no chance of getting out of the locked psych ward without an employee to open the doors.

She wiggled her toes in the neon yellow socks. Plus, on the off chance she managed to overcome the wrist restraint and door problems, these stupid Day-Glo socks marked her as a runaway mental patient.

Katarina groaned and dug her heels into the bed. There had to be a way out. There had to be, and if there was, she would find it. No excuses. The man who'd raised her might be twisted as hell, but he was smart too. Genius-level. That was how he'd evaded capture for so many years.

If Kingsley were in her position, he'd have ditched this dumpy room and freed himself days ago. All she needed to do was think like him, and she could ditch this place too.

When you decide upon a goal, my sweet Katarina, the most crucial element to reach that goal is your plan. If your goal is large, you'll likely need to break it down into a series of smaller goals. Start at the beginning and map them out in order, step by step. Once you have your plan, take time to memorize each component, then once you're certain of your success, execute.

Right. Start at the beginning. In this case, the restraints. Her gaze landed on the material binding her to the bed frame. Overpowering them with brute strength was out. She either needed a knife or sharp object of some sort—a joke in this place, where they didn't even allow drawstring pants or freaking plastic forks—or to grab her opportunity during a time when the restraints were removed.

So far, that only happened when she ate the slop they called food, or on toilet trips, or when they paraded her like a pony through the halls every afternoon for daily exercise.

Bathroom trip it was. If she got lucky, they'd send a small female nurse. Someone easy to overpower, who was wearing any color sock besides yellow.

She puffed her cheeks with air before blowing it out. Okay, supposing she managed to steal socks and overpower the nurse...what would prevent the staff from issuing a lock-down before she ever reached the door?

Step two: distraction. This escape plan required a distraction, one that happened while she was restraint-free in the bathroom.

"Jesse? Are you there? Jesse!"

Oh my god, not this again. Katarina had no clue who Jesse was or why the woman wanted him or her so bad, but she wished someone would find the asshole already. "Would you please shut up? I can't think straight!"

She banged her fist twice on the bedrail for good measure, but stopped before the third strike when an idea materialized.

Oh, this could work. This could definitely work.

Without pausing to assess her idea further, Katarina slapped the nurse call button. So what if she'd skipped Kingsley's memorizing-all-the-pieces-of-the-plan step? The asshole wasn't here to lecture, and patience had never been her strong suit.

The nurse took seven minutes to respond, and Katarina

used every last one to plan. By the time Jasper hurried in, her body buzzed with anticipation.

"You rang?" He smiled down at her, and her excitement grew. Forget a small female nurse. The flirty, young CNA could definitely work in her favor.

"Yeah. Sorry to bother you, but I need to use the bathroom."

He gasped and slapped a hand on his chest. "How dare you interrupt my busy schedule with such a frivolous request." Jasper grinned as he began loosening the restraints. "Trust me, there's no need to apologize. You should hear some of the reasons patients give for calling us into their rooms."

The left strap fell free. Katarina shook out her wrist as he moved around the bed to the right. "Like what?"

His fingers worked at the material. "Like, 'oh, can you help me find my glasses? I've looked all over, and they aren't anywhere!' Narrator's voice: 'The patient did not look all over.'" Jasper laughed. "Half the time, they're sitting on top of the patient's head."

The right restraint loosened enough for Katarina to slip her hand free. She caught a hint of body odor when she lifted her arm and slammed that sucker back down. Her goal was to attract this man, not run him off from her foul smell. "Oh wow, bet that's frustrating as hell, especially when you're so busy."

Metal creaked as he pulled the bedrail down so she could stand. She was glad that she'd been working her muscles as much as she could from her prone position, or she might not have had the strength to get onto her feet.

"Nah, it's honestly okay. Part of my job. Just don't feel bad about calling for anything, especially when the restraints make it impossible for you to do stuff on your own."

"Thank you, you're so sweet."

As he escorted Katarina to the tiny bathroom opposite the bed, the pink tinge to his cheeks told her the flattery was disarming him. Good. She flashed him a bright smile before shuffling inside the cramped space. The second the door shut, she jumped to work. No locks, but that shouldn't be a problem as long as she was quiet.

Katarina slipped off her underwear and shoved them in the toilet first. An army of paper towels from the metal holder followed. Once a small mountain formed inside the bowl, she crossed her fingers and flushed.

The contents swirled, and her heart picked up tempo. *Come on, come on. Show me the water.*

The water level surged and overflowed an instant later, spilling down the white porcelain into puddles on the linoleum floor. Katarina purposely soaked her socks before opening the door. "Help! The toilet is backed up!"

The toilet kept gurgling and running as Jasper hurried over to investigate. His shoes splashed in the growing stream that spilled over into the main room. "Dammit!"

He raked his hands through his hair before turning back to her. "Come with me. Let's get you somewhere dry until we can fix this." He led her out to the hall and pointed to the room next door. "You okay to wait here with Mrs. Thomas? She likes to chat when she's not looking for her son. Hang on a sec."

Jasper grabbed a passing nurse. "Hey, can someone get a janitor on the line? We've got a busted toilet next door that's leaking all over."

The woman, who looked to be nearly a hundred years old, nodded. "I'm headed back to the nurses' station now. I'll call."

"Thanks, I'll be there in a minute."

He ushered Katarina into the room. "Good morning, Mrs. Thomas. I brought you some company."

A frail, birdlike old woman with a thin neck and sagging skin speckled with age spots peered at Katarina with round eyes. "Well, hello, dearie. Goodness, are you here for a luncheon? We're not set up for that quite yet, and I still need my hat. Where is my hat, anyway?"

She patted her straggly gray hair with a frown while glancing around the room.

Jasper cast an anxious glance at the bed. "Sorry, she gets a little confused sometimes."

Katarina shrugged. "Don't we all? Hey, do you think I could get some new socks? Mine are soaking wet." She bent down and stripped off the squishy socks, tossing them into the laundry bin before leaning closer to Jasper and lowering her voice. "As long as you think it's safe in here. You never know, maybe she only pretends to be a confused old woman to lure in unsuspecting patients."

"Well, it's either her or the guy who has a fondness for stabbing people with pens. Don't ask me where he keeps finding them."

"In that case, sounds like I'm chilling with Jesse's mom." Her gut cramped as she forced a smile. *Hurry up. Leave.*

Jasper's shoulders relaxed. "Wise choice. I need to pop out for a few minutes. Hang tight and hit her call light if you need anything."

"Will do."

As soon as he disappeared out the door, Katarina scooted closer to the bed. Usually, she'd take her time with this part, finesse the old woman a little, but that wasn't an option today. She had minutes before the janitor arrived and Jasper reappeared with a fresh pair of fugly yellow socks in tow.

This had to work.

She inhaled and slipped into the old Katarina persona with ease. The same way she'd molded herself into the type of daughter each new set of parents wanted back before Kingsley swooped in and carted her away.

With her heart fluttering like a hummingbird's, Katarina reached out and grabbed the old woman's chin, wrenching the wrinkled face around until she stared into those dazed blue eyes. Her other hand dug into the woman's shoulder and gave her a brisk shake. "Jesse is dead. Do you hear me? Dead. I killed him. I slit his throat with my knife and watched him bleed all over the floor."

Confusion clouded the woman's eyes at first...then her gummy lips opened wide, and she started to scream. Shrill, nerve-shredding shrieks burst into the room from that frail body, surprising Katarina with their force as she darted behind the door and waited.

The old lady continued screaming until footsteps pounded down the hall.

"Mrs. Thomas, what's wrong?" The nurse ran straight to Mrs. Thomas's bed, allowing Katarina to slip out of the room unnoticed as the old woman yelled and thrashed.

"Code yellow, we have a code yellow in room six twenty!"

The call spilled from the intercom, filling Katarina with an odd pang of regret as she speed-walked to the nurses' station. A middle-aged, dark-haired nurse muttered under her breath before pushing the chair back. She made a shooing motion at Katarina with her hands. "Go back to your room. I can't help you right now."

"My room's the one with the overflowing toilet. I'll just stand right here until you get back."

Muttering under her breath again, the nurse scurried down the hall. Katarina leaned against the wall and pretended to be bored while she tracked the nurse's progress into Mrs. Thomas's room. The back of her head was still visible in the doorway when Katarina raced into the nurses' station and slapped the button that opened the locked double doors.

She whirled as they swung open and raced for the opening. If anyone spotted her now, she was screwed.

Three steps. Five steps. Seven. On the eighth step, she burst through the open doors and into the outer hallway. Out of the psych ward, but not yet free. She fled for the stairs, taking two at a time, circling down to the third-floor door before shoving the metal bar and popping out near a waiting area. Her pulse thundered like she'd been climbing for days as she checked for threats.

A forty-something man sat on one of several couches, talking on a cell phone while staring at a TV. "Yeah, I'm just waiting on them to discharge her. No, they said her hip should be fine to go home now. She's been using a walker to get around and has decent range of motion. We just need to make sure she keeps up her exercises once she's back home..."

Rehab floor. Perfect. No locked doors.

Katarina veered left at the nurses' station, heading straight toward the open door that led to the patient rooms. Unlike the psych floor, neither nurse here spared more than a passing glance as she hurried by, allowing Katarina's breathing to return to a regular rhythm. She peeked into the first open doorway but kept walking when she spotted the patient sitting upright and flipping through channels on the TV. The second room had visitors clustered around the bed.

She paused in the third doorway. Soft snores emitted from the elderly man who sprawled in bed with his eyes closed, but what really caught Katarina's eyes were the blue hospital socks on the empty chair.

Slipping inside, she tiptoed to the chair and slid the socks on her feet. After glancing at the bed to make sure the patient was still asleep, she rummaged around in the tiny closet and drawer.

Clothes, two books, a family photo. No wallet or money.

She went back to the clothes. No pants that worked, but the gray Berkeley sweatshirt would do. After turning the sweatshirt inside out to hide the logo and pulling it over her head, Katarina scurried from the room.

Socks and shirt, check. Now she needed something to cover her bare legs.

In the hallway, another elderly man in a hospital gown was pushing a walker past while a white-haired woman kept pace and chattered in his ear. "Coco is doing fine, but I can tell she misses you and wants you to come home. She's been crying at night and peeing on the floor."

Katarina adopted a stiff-legged, clumsy walk as she headed toward them, hoping that Coco was a dog. At just the right moment, she let her right leg buckle and stumbled into the woman's oversized purse. "Oh no, I'm so sorry about that. Still getting the hang of this new knee."

The woman smiled. "That's like my John here, except he's getting used to his new hip. See, John? Getting a joint replacement doesn't make you old." John mumbled and continued pushing the walker. "Oh, don't be such an old grumpy pants. Coco will be mad at you if you come home with that attitude."

Katarina retraced her steps down the hallway with the woman's wallet tucked beneath her sweatshirt. Thank god the woman hadn't paid enough attention to notice Katarina's lack of a bandage or surgical scar.

Sweat dampened her armpits as she hurried back past the nurses' station. Any minute now, Jasper would notice she was gone. If Katarina was still inside the hospital when that moment arrived, she was toast.

She raced down the last three flights of stairs, slowing her pace to a quick walk when she hit the lobby. Arrows pointed the path to the gift shop. Resisting the urge to peer over her shoulder, she rounded a corner and burst into the sweet-smelling space.

Almost there.

The clothing was near the front. She grabbed the first pair of sweatpants she found and moved on to slippers next. At the register, she grabbed a cheap pair of mirrored aviator-style glasses and a pink knit beanie. She paid for the purchases with a one-hundred-dollar bill she found tucked into the wallet.

Less than five minutes later, Katarina hustled out the sliding glass doors, confident she was unrecognizable to the casual eye as the psych patient from the sixth floor. Especially not when she was wearing a pair of pink "New Mommy" sweatpants.

The winter sun warmed her skin, and she paused for a moment to tilt her head back and drink in the natural light and fresh air.

Freedom at last.

Seconds later, she was moving again, losing herself among the other pedestrians and putting distance between her and the hospital.

Now it was time to rescue her daughter.

21

The older woman headed down the sidewalk toward Chez La La's black and white awning with the high chin and confident strides of someone accustomed to commanding attention. The rose-pink shade of her elegant pantsuit accentuated both a slender waist and taut, unlined skin that Ellie would bet money was thanks to regular Botox injections.

She checked her watch. 10:26. Letitia Wiggins had arrived right on time for her hair appointment.

No surprise there. Hank Crawford's podcasts and articles, which Ellie had spent all last night poring over in her hotel room, had suggested as much. According to Hank, Letitia cared about appearances—physical and reputational—more than anything else. Ellie had been expecting an immaculately groomed and dressed woman, and so far, the former head-master's wife didn't disappoint.

The morning sun glinted off Letitia's hair, turning the platinum strands a brilliant shade of white gold. In older photos, her hair had been coppery, more like Ellie's own, but blonde was much better at hiding gray. If Ellie didn't know better, she'd guess the woman's age a decade or two younger than her sixty-some-odd years.

A façade that Letitia obviously invested impressive amounts of money into maintaining.

From the passenger side of the SUV, Ellie tracked the woman's progress down the sidewalk a little longer, hopping out when Letitia was still about ten feet short of reaching the salon. She'd already argued with Shane about her safety, which was why he was standing over by the salon, pretending to play with his phone.

She took two steps and cupped her hands to her mouth. "Aunt Letitia!"

The woman's shoulders stiffened. She turned, and Ellie waved and flashed her badge.

"I'm Detective Kline, and I need a few minutes of your time."

Letitia Wiggins's forehead remained smooth and unflustered at the announcement. Ellie couldn't tell if that was because she had ice water in her veins or her aesthetician had gone a little overboard with the anti-wrinkle treatments.

The tap of the woman's silver kitten-heeled shoe against the pavement displayed her impatience, though. "I'm afraid that won't be possible. I have an appointment, and besides, unless I'm under arrest, I have no legal obligation to speak to you."

Ellie strolled forward with an easy shrug. "You're right. Go ahead inside. I can't stop you. I was trying to spare you the embarrassment of asking questions about the Far Ridge Boy's Academy as well as your husband Walter and Lawrence Kingsley in front of all the stylists, but you do you."

When Ellie first started speaking, Letitia was reaching for the door, but that last name made her hand fall to her side. She sighed before pivoting to face Ellie with her arms crossed over her chest.

Those icy blue eyes traveled over Ellie's outfit, hair, face, inspecting and dismissing her as unworthy in less than five seconds. Her toe resumed its rhythmic tap.

None of her antics fazed Ellie in the least. She'd attended hundreds of dinner parties with women far more imperious than Letitia Wiggins and had always managed to stand her ground during interactions ranging from disinterested to snobby to downright rude. Without fail, all those individuals suffered from the same mistaken belief that their lives were oh-so-important compared to others' and loathed having anyone waste their valuable time.

When Letitia cast a pointed glare at the diamond-encrusted watch on her wrist, Ellie lifted the white takeout cup to her lips and pretended to savor a sip of old coffee. She made Letitia wait through two more sips, the other woman's seething annoyance over her unhurried pace worth every cold, bitter drop. "I'm looking for information that might help lead us to Kingsley's whereabouts."

No change in Letitia's expression, but the silver shoe stopped moving. The woman cast a furtive glance at the sidewalk, as if worried someone might overhear. "My boarding school days ended long ago, Detective. I haven't been in contact with Mr. Kingsley for many years now."

"I find that surprising, Ms. Wiggins. I was under the impression that the two of you were...very close once."

Her lips flattened, and her green-gold eyes turned glacial. "I take it you've been listening to that boy."

Ellie leaned her shoulders against the decorative street-lamp and crossed her ankles. "I'm sorry, I'm not allowed to discuss my sources outside of the department. I'd be curious to know which boy you're referring to, though." Setting her cup down on a nearby bench, she fished a small, unused notebook and pen from her blazer pocket and flipped open to the first page.

Letitia's uneasy gaze remained on the notebook a beat too long. "You coming here and harassing me like this is a form of abuse. I was a victim of my husband's horrifying behavior. Scared half to death. Did you know I was pregnant at the time all that nonsense happened?"

The quivering lower lip was a nice touch. Ellie pretended to buy the story, projecting sympathy into her voice. "I imagine that was a very difficult situation for you."

Letitia nodded, blinking in rapid succession. "It was."

"So, how is your child doing these days? Well, I hope."

The woman hitched her shoulders up and looked down her nose. "I'm afraid I wouldn't know because I gave her up for adoption. After that ordeal, I could hardly be expected to keep the child now, could I?"

Her arrogant bearing and calculated delivery tugged at Ellie's memory.

Kingsley. This woman held herself and spoke almost exactly like Kingsley.

The realization triggered a memory, and Ellie was transported back to the cold, damp warehouse where the battered woman with the short, dark hair was tied to the chair opposite her. The other prisoner's face was clearer this time, allowing Ellie to glimpse the Cupid's bow mouth and wary, wide-set eyes. Strip off the thick layers of makeup, and the woman became a girl. Three, maybe only four years older than Ellie had been.

Combined with the skimpy clothes and caked-on eyeshadow, her jutting collarbones and skinny arms and legs pegged the girl as living on the streets.

Ellie recalled one particular moment when Kingsley had sneered down his nose at the woman after she'd called him a sick fuck who probably got off on torturing women. Kingsley had looked at her in almost the exact same manner as Letitia and said, "You can't expect me to give credence to the opinions of a slut like you."

Spoken in the exact same derisive tone that Letitia Wiggins had used to describe her own child.

Not an endearing quality in someone whose past job was tending to other people's children.

By the time Ellie cleared her head, Letitia Wiggins was turning away. "If you have anything else to ask, you'll have to speak with my lawyer." The bell jingled as she swept into the salon.

Ellie stood her ground outside the door long enough to wiggle her fingers at the aggravating woman through the glass wall when she peered out. Once Letitia whirled away, Ellie dumped the nasty coffee into a trash can and returned to the waiting SUV.

The usually taciturn Shane caught up with her and spared her a glance as she climbed into the passenger seat, his eyes hidden behind a pair of aviator-style sunglasses. "She's not your favorite person."

"Whatever gave you that impression?" At his grunt, Ellie shook her head and strapped the seat belt across her chest. "You're right. She's not. She reminds me too much of a monster."

Shane knew better than to pry. "Where to now?"

Ellie scrolled through her phone until she located the necessary information. "Next, we're going to pay Dorothy Hindman a visit."

She rattled off the address, staring out the windshield while her bodyguard programmed the details into the GPS. Minutes later, the Explorer was cruising down the interstate toward the residence of the former Far Ridge Academy's secretary.

Ellie used the forty-minute trip north to rehearse questions. They arrived before noon, with Shane pulling the SUV up to the curb in front of a simple, one-story home in an attractive but ungated retirement community. A little duck pond was located across the street, where two senior citizens lounged in camping chairs and cast fishing lines into one end.

A welcome mat decorated with daisies sat beneath a cheery red door, but the woman in the baby blue track suit who opened the door was anything but. Her mouth was turned down into a permanent frown, and she glowered when Ellie introduced herself.

"I don't give a single hoot if you're the president of the United States let alone some lady detective. I don't have anything to say about Far Ridge or anyone who worked there."

Dorothy Hindman planted her sturdy legs wide and glared through maroon-rimmed bifocals. The top of her pink-tinted white head didn't even reach Ellie's shoulder, but what she lacked in inches, she more than made up for in attitude.

"What about Lawrence Kingsley, then? Can you tell me about him or where I might be able to find him?"

If Dorothy's mouth turned down before, now it positively drooped. She threw her hands up in the air. "And now you're asking about that poor boy? What is this?"

"I'm sorry...poor boy? Why poor boy?" To the best of Ellie's recollection, no one had ever referred to Kingsley like that before.

The former secretary smacked her forehead and made a frustrated noise. "Why do you think? Because of the way Letitia abused him, of course. Isn't that why you're here?"

"Letitia abused Kingsley? As in physically?"

While Ellie tried to wrap her head around that revelation, the secretary scoffed. "I don't know, you tell me. Is that what they're calling child molestation these days?"

The accusation dealt Ellie a stunning blow, leeching the oxygen from her lungs. Letitia had molested Kingsley? Was that possible? Hank Crawford hadn't so much as eluded to that in his podcasts or during their in-person meeting.

"Let me make sure I have this straight. You believe that Letitia Wiggins, the former headmaster's wife of Far Ridge Boy's Academy, had sexual relations with Lawrence Kingsley while he was a student there?"

Dorothy harrumphed. "That's right. I believe it, and so does just about everyone else who was at the academy at the time. It was the talk of the school."

"And Walter Wiggins? Did he know?"

The older woman threw her hands up in the air. "Well, who can rightly say? But he sure didn't let her keep that baby she whelped later on that year, did he?"

Baby? A terrible suspicion poked at Ellie. *No...surely not...*

"The baby was given up for adoption, right? Can you tell me more about that?"

"No, I cannot, because, unlike some people," the woman scowled at Ellie, "I know how to mind my own business."

"I understand. Can you—" Ringing from her jacket pocket interrupted her. Ellie waited until the noise stopped to finish the question, but a chirp followed the call. "Excuse me."

She pulled her phone out to read the text from Clay.

Call me back ASAP. Important.

Her gut clenched. "I'm so sorry, but I need to return this call quickly."

Leaving Dorothy to harrumph and glower from the doorway, Ellie turned and retreated a few steps back toward the curb while the line rang.

"Clay? What is it?"

"Katarina." He sounded like he was running. "She's escaped from the hospital."

22

E llie unlocked her apartment door to seventy pounds of exuberant, slobbering dog. Sam wiggled from head to toe with her tongue dangling out, threading between Ellie's legs and whining until she stopped and patted her black, furry head. "What, did Jillian make you eat Kibbles 'n Bits while she feasted on lobster and steak on your date night?"

"Please! That dog probably ate more of my dinner than I did. We saved the Kibble 'n Bits for you." Jillian popped around the corner, already dressed for bed in a pair of pajamas covered in grinning sushi rolls. "Also, hi, honey. How was your trip?"

Ellie dropped the laptop bag to the floor and arched her tight back, letting the warmth of the familiar surroundings and her best friend's smile wash over her and ease some of the day's tension away. "Longer than expected. I think I spent more time in the car than I did anywhere else."

Jillian pulled a sympathetic face and tucked a loose blonde strand behind her ear. "Sorry, those are the worst kind of road trips. Want something to drink? I've got a kettle on."

"Herbal tea sounds great, please." Ellie trailed Jillian into the kitchen, ignoring the stools to lean against the granite countertop. She'd had more than enough sitting over the past twenty-four hours. "Any updates yet?"

Jillian shook her head as she grabbed the kettle off the stove and poured water into a Sherlock Holmes mug. "Not really. Everyone's still out searching high and low for Bethany, but there hasn't been any sign of her yet."

Not good, in terms of Bethany's chances. Every passing hour in a kidnapping case reduced the probability that a child would be recovered alive. If she gave Charli Cross a call, the Savannah detective could undoubtedly rattle off the likelihood of finding Bethany in time within two seconds flat. Tempting, if Ellie wanted to sink into a pit of despair.

So maybe not.

Jillian set the mug on the counter. Ellie warmed her hands around the porcelain and blew on the fragrant, citrusy steam while Jillian returned to the sink.

She turned on the faucet, splashing water over the plates. "I'm just washing up from dinner. Did you eat yet? I made a pasta salad. Leftovers are in the fridge."

Despite the worry squeezing her temples, Ellie's gaze softened on her roommate's back. Jillian was always fussing over Ellie and feeding her. "Thanks, I had a burrito." No sense kicking those mother hen instincts into overdrive by telling her it was a breakfast burrito purchased from a drive-through over twelve hours ago.

Once Jillian loaded the dishwasher, she dried her hands on a sunny yellow towel and joined Ellie at the counter, stifling a yawn. "I printed all that stuff out that you asked for about Kingsley and the Far Ridge Boy's Academy, and whatever I could find on those student deaths. Oh, and I went ahead and reprinted your case file, on the chance it might come in handy."

Ellie finished a sip of tea and pushed the mug aside, overwhelmed by a cascade of emotion. "What would I do without you?"

"Oh, I don't know. Spend less time lint-rolling black hairs off your ass, for one."

At Jillian's snicker, Ellie shook her head. "No, I mean it."

Unlike most people, Ellie didn't have many friends. Not growing up, and not as an adult. That was okay, though, because Jillian was one of the best friends anyone could ever ask for. "One of the luckiest days of my life was the day I met you."

Her friend pretended to frown, leaning across the counter to press the back of her hand to Ellie's forehead. "You sure you're feeling okay? Oh god, please tell me this isn't leading to a big reveal of a cancer diagnosis or something?"

Ellie batted Jillian away. "Stop! I promise I'm not about to spring a Nicholas Sparks twist on you, okay?" She rubbed her eyes with her fists. "The long drive and stress from the case must be making me sentimental, that's all. Now, thanks for waiting up, but shoo! Go to bed and take that hairy beast with you."

"I already have one hairy beast in my bed."

Ellie smiled. "Are you talking about Jacob or Duke?"

That earned her a laugh. "Correction. I already have *two* hairy beasts in my bed, so this one will make three."

Ellie wished that Jacob was awake because she barely got to see him anymore since they worked opposite shifts. "Tell both Jacob and Duke that they aren't supposed to be sleeping on the job."

Jillian rolled her eyes. "I don't need a bodyguard, man or canine, thank you very much."

Ellie wished that was true. "Sleep well."

Jillian yawned. "You too." She snapped her fingers. "Come along, hairy beast."

Sam trotted at Jillian's heels as her roommate wandered toward her bedroom. Right before she rounded the corner, she paused and grinned over her shoulder. "I think I'm pretty lucky too. Night."

"Night."

Once the door clicked shut, Ellie stretched again and headed for the fridge. After staring at the contents for over a minute without a single item tempting her, she shut the door again. Selection wasn't the problem. Jillian's pasta salad was to die for, and the fridge was packed with an assortment of easy-prep meals and snacks. Ellie just wasn't hungry.

The shock of Dorothy Hindman's gruesome accusation concerning Letitia Wiggins and Kingsley when he'd been a student had stolen her appetite.

With Jillian's printouts in hand, Ellie headed for her own bedroom, frustrated when that little niggle in the back of her head returned, telling her she was missing something. But what?

She flipped on her light and went straight for the bed, kicking off her shoes before flopping onto the thick, squishy comforter. Names and faces circled through her brain, round and round without stopping.

Letitia. Kingsley. The three dead boys. Bethany.

Why did she sense a connection there? How did that even make sense? She concentrated, searching for common threads, but each time she came close to grasping one, the thought slipped away like a shadow in the night.

"Ugh." Ellie flung an arm over her eyes, but sleep was a joke when her mind buzzed like this. After lying there a few minutes, she sat up, grabbed her case file, and flipped to the first page.

Maybe sheer boredom would help lull her to sleep. She'd

gone over all the information before, on multiple occasions. The time and date of her kidnapping, her confused mental state when she was found, the victim statement the officer had taken at the hospital. Nothing new there.

As Ellie scanned through the file, her mind wandered to the psychiatrist who was once employed by the department. Dr. Ernest Powell. During mandated sessions, Dr. Powell had worked with Ellie on recovering lost memories around her kidnapping, and though the visits were tough and often painful, she'd been grateful at the time.

Right up until she discovered Dr. Powell was one of Kingsley's lackeys, planted in the department to keep tabs on her.

She rubbed her neck, frowning at the pages without really seeing them. Why was she so stuck on this? As awful and invasive as the revelation about Dr. Powell had been, she'd processed that trauma already. But her brain refused to drop it. Psychiatrist. Her psychiatrist had been crooked. Why was that ringing a bell?

Ellie stiffened. Another psychiatrist had come up in the past couple of days. Back in the Savannah PD, Charli had pointed out a section of Letitia Wiggins's trial transcript, where an eloquent psychiatrist spoke on her behalf. His conclusion that Wiggins suffered from Battered Women's Syndrome had likely gone a long way toward procuring her the light sentence.

She dialed Charli's number.

"Did you arrive home safely?"

Ellie blinked. No hello, just straight to the point. No one could accuse Charli Cross of beating around the bush. "I did, thanks. I was wondering if you could send me copies of those transcripts we went over? Pictures are fine. You can text them if that's easiest."

"Yes. I'm in the middle of something, but I should be able

to get those to you first thing in the morning."

"Thank you, that's perfect."

"Good."

Once again, the line clicked without Charli saying good-bye. Ellie shrugged, already growing accustomed to the Savannah detective's abrupt send-off. She gathered the papers into a pile and set them on the bedside table, then went to her dresser and pulled a t-shirt and a pair of soft-knit pajama pants from the drawer and carried both into the bathroom.

She was about to twist on the faucet to wash her face when the doorbell rang. Who the hell?

When the bell rang again and again, she hurried to the front entrance, a *hold your horses* on the tip of her tongue.

Ellie peered through the peephole and gasped. Fumbling for the lock, she twisted the knob and swung open the door.

Katarina stood in the hall, illuminated by the soft glow of an overhead light. The woman's hair was mussed and a little oily, like it was in need of a good wash, but her ridiculous, very un-Katarina outfit of pink beanie and matching sweat-pants paired with slippers stood out more.

As silly as she looked, nothing was more prominent than the navy-blue baby carrier strapped to her chest.

Ellie gaped at the woman, wishing she'd thought to grab her gun. "For the love of god, please tell me there's not an actual baby in there."

Katarina removed the thin pink blanket draped across the top of the carrier. Nestled inside was a plastic doll. "But shh, don't tell little Suzy. She thinks she's real. All the better to go with my sweatpants."

She stuck out a leg so Ellie could read the white letters running up the side. *New Mommy.* "Why are you wearing...*that?*" Ellie waved her hand to encompass the entire ensemble. "Better yet, what the hell are you doing here?"

Katarina nudged her shoulder with her chin, drawing Ellie's attention to where the gray sweatshirt was stained red with blood.

"I was hoping you had some clothes I could borrow."

23

K atarina sat behind the table in the fancy dining room, keeping her hands in plain sight and doing her best to seem as nonthreatening as possible. Not the easiest job when Ellie's roommate scrutinized every move she made with the gun in her right hand held at the ready. That'd be rich, if, after her wild and crazy life, Katarina ended up getting taken out by a tiny blonde in cartoon sushi pajamas.

She surveyed the room, pausing on the wide-legged stance of Ellie's bodyguard. Definitely not her biggest fan. The death stare he drilled into Katarina from across the room was unnerving, and in her opinion, a little misplaced. She'd stooped to begging and pleading to prevent Ellie from calling the cops, not a loaded gun.

The rest of the apartment was roomy and elegant, decorated in that tasteful sort of way that rich people used to mask the fact that they were rolling in dough. Please. Katarina bet the carpet was some top-of-the-line, premium crap, created in limited supplies and handcrafted from the wool of prize-winning sheep that were only fed organic wheat, or whatever the hell sheep ate.

"Here."

Ellie tossed a pizza box onto the table near Katarina, next to a massive bowl of pasta salad. When she opened the cardboard lid, Katarina almost moaned out loud at the heavenly scent that wafted free.

Cheese. Pepperoni. Sausage. So much deliciousness in one package. After the cardboard flavor of the hospital food and endless containers of Jell-O, fresh pizza was a miracle.

She lurched for the box but drew up short when movement caught her eye. The roommate's gun arm had twitched. That woman was too jumpy by half.

Meanwhile, the red-haired detective was also keeping close tabs on her from across the table, even though she acted more nonchalant. No obvious gun, but Katarina had zero doubts she was armed too. Goody. Stuck between a trigger-happy runt in kid's jammies and a stuck-up detective with an ax to grind. She could sense the indigestion setting in already.

Her mouth watering, Katarina made a big show of inching her hand toward the box. Torture, when all she wanted to do was cram a slice into her mouth, but no pizza was worth a bullet in the skull. No matter how delicious it smelled.

She retrieved a piece with equal care, and finally, sank her teeth in. Tomatoes and cheese and spicy meat swarmed her taste buds, and her eyes fluttered shut as she savored the experience. So, so damn good.

Katarina polished off half the slice before opening her eyes to find the two other occupants both sitting at the table now, acting a little more relaxed, like her obvious hunger had eased their overactive nerves. Good. She had too much to do to afford getting tackled by Carrot Top and Sushi Girl.

Bodyguard man, though, looked like he would spring at her at any second.

After plopping another piece on her plate, Katarina zeroed in on Ellie. "Where's my daughter?"

"That's what I'd like to know too."

"You're telling me you've got nothing yet?" Katarina scoffed. "So much for Charleston PD going all out when needed or appointing the best and brightest."

Ellie stopped sipping her water and smacked the bottom of the glass on the table. "I'm about two seconds away from putting that criticism to test by calling your presence in. Which is exactly what I should have done the moment I saw you outside my front door."

Uh oh, she'd hit a nerve with that one. Usually, nothing would give Katarina more delight than ruffling the redhead's feathers, but for now, she needed the detective's aid. She lifted both hands as a peace offering. "Hey, it's not like I'm doing anything illegal by being here. Sure, I left AMA, but I wasn't under arrest."

Ellie's eyes narrowed. "Leaving a hospital against medical advice isn't a crime, but the last time I checked, breaking and entering a locked building was absolutely illegal. How'd you get in? Wait, never mind. I can guess. The same way you got past Shane over there," she gestured toward the grumpy bodyguard, "with your mom disguise."

Katarina only shrugged. Turned out, a new mommy outfit was almost as good as having a key to the door. Katarina had remained hidden from view until one of Ellie's female neighbors approached the building. She'd fallen in beside her long before the bodyguard ever glanced in their direction.

With the baby carrier, outfit, and blanket conveniently covering her bloody shoulder, no one had come close to second-guessing her ruse. By the time they'd reached the locked door, Katarina had sold the woman on her frazzled new mom act. The middle-aged brunette had expressed nothing but sympathy when Katarina shared that she was visiting her cousin Ellie's apartment, but silly, sleep-deprived her had locked her keys inside.

If Ellie were a friend, Katarina would recommend that she hire less gullible bodyguards, but since the detective was more of a necessary evil, Little Miss Perfect could figure that out on her own. "Look, once we find Bethany, I promise I'll be a good little patient and let you trot me straight back to the psych ward on a leash if that floats your boat."

The blonde roommate muttered something along the lines of, "I'd like to float your boat right out to sea," but Katarina kept her eyes locked on Ellie.

"I'm the best chance we have of finding Bethany, and you know it." Katarina swallowed, working her jaw to force the next part out. "Our chances are even better if we work together."

Asking for help made her insides squirm. She'd learned as a kid that the only person you could rely on was yourself. In her world, team players were the losers who couldn't cut it on their own.

The idea of working with anyone, and especially Ellie, clashed with Katarina's every last instinct, but if there was another avenue that led to saving Bethany in time, Katarina couldn't find it. She was a psych hospital fugitive. Low on resources. Ellie didn't face either of those stumbling blocks. So, she'd grit her teeth and put up with these two for as long as was necessary to rescue her baby girl.

Ellie sighed but didn't argue with Katarina's logic. Katarina took that as a win. As the detective scooped a pizza slice onto her plate, something nudged Katarina's thigh.

"Well, hello there."

The black dog whined before plopping its head into Katarina's lap. She stroked the velvety ears before raising her eyebrows at the other two women. "I hate to be the bearer of bad news, but this dog is a terrible judge of character."

The blonde roommate snickered. "You're not wrong."

Ellie kept chewing a bite, but a faint smile eased the tension from her face. Her roommate finally relaxed her death grip on the gun long enough to grab her own slice of pizza.

Saved by a mutt. Katarina gave the dog an extra head scratch. *If this all works out, buddy, I promise to send you a giant bone.*

As if the canine understood her silent promise, the dog thumped its tail twice on the floor.

Emboldened by the doggy's support, Katarina sucked in a breath and got the discussion rolling. "So, any speculation at all on where Kingsley is right now?"

Jillian jumped in first. "My guess is that he grabbed Bethany and took off somewhere to lay low. Someplace too far away for people to hunt or even guess, like the Bahamas or Barbados."

Katarina was about to shoot that idea down when Ellie beat her to the punch.

"I don't think so. Kingsley is arrogant as hell and has a superiority complex a mile long. He'd chafe at the notion of running away." She drummed her fingers on the table. "I think that's why he always comes back. If he'd planned on running away, why risk coming to the police department? He thinks he's too smart to get caught, and he delights in rubbing that in our faces, far too much to leave. Do you agree?"

The detective directed the question at Katarina, and she nodded. "I do. The only time I can remember him ever being out of the country for an extended period of time was when he needed plastic surgery. His roots are here. He used to talk about living in this area specifically when he was a kid."

"I remember. We were just at that fancy house he grew up in a little over a week ago." Ellie sighed. "We've had undercover agents stationed outside, just in case, but he hasn't been back since."

Katarina gave an impatient jerk of her head. "No, not there. I'm talking before that. He told me about some piss poor place he and his mom lived in before the rich stepdad came along."

Ellie sat up straight. "Do you know where?"

"No, don't you?" When the detective shook her head, Katarina had to bite back a snarled *why the hell not* and replace it with a less combative, "Well, I'm sure you'll figure it out."

She grabbed her napkin to give her itchy fingers something to do. It was better than lunging across the table and denting the expensive wood with the detective's pretty red head.

This teamwork shit sucked.

Katarina was thankful when Jillian distracted her from shredding the napkin into tiny white fragments. "Maybe we should discuss what else we know about Kingsley. Like, is it safe to say that he has a preference for choosing female victims?"

Jillian glanced at Katarina for confirmation. She nodded. "Definitely. He liked really pretty men, and he doesn't have any problems hurting men if they get in the way, but I think his real satisfaction comes from torturing and killing women."

"I'd agree with that." Ellie toyed with her glass. "After reading transcripts from his Letitia Wiggins's trial and talking to some former employees, I think it's a safe guess that he might have been a victim of abuse at one point, at a female's hands. Wiggins allegedly molested him while he was a student at the Far Ridge Boy's Academy. According to the witness I interviewed, pretty much everyone on campus at the time knew about it."

Both Ellie and Jillian turned to Katarina, as if the psychotic asshole who'd raised her had opened up about the experience over ice cream one night. "If she did, he never told me, but that doesn't mean anything. We didn't exactly have one of those TV relationships where the people are always sharing their innermost secrets and sobbing on each other's shoulders. He raised me to be just like him, strong and deadly. He would have seen all of that touchy-feely shit as counterproductive, a weakness."

Katarina broke off when she caught Jillian's softening expression. Great, now the roommate looked about two seconds away from asking if Katarina needed a hug. She curled her lip. "I don't need your pity. What I need is someone to find my daughter."

An awkward silence descended while Katarina sank into her chair with hot cheeks, frustrated over her loss of control. Why was she acting like she gave a single damn what these women thought when she didn't? She wasn't here to impress them or join a knitting group. So what if they pitied her? Instead of letting that get to her, she should figure out how to twist that sympathy to her advantage.

"Sorry," she mumbled, trying not to choke on the word.

"That's okay," Jillian's reply was stiff.

Good. Better that than the sad puppy eyes from before.

Ellie cleared her throat. "Did he mention Letitia at all to you?"

"Yeah. Not so much by name, more about how he'd had this great mentor at the academy who helped him reach his potential, and that's the role he planned to fill for me, and so on. God, he really did like to hear himself talk sometimes."

"He never got married, right?"

Katarina snorted at Jillian's question. "Him? No. As far as

I know, he never came close. Never even dated women. I figured he either hated them too much to try, or he'd had his heart broken so badly once, he never recovered." She picked her thumbnail and shrugged. "Probably for the best. Good chance he'd have whacked anyone he dated once he got tired of them."

Jillian flinched. "I wonder if this Letitia woman is the reason why."

"I was wondering the same thing. A spouse would have been useful as a cover, but he never bothered." Ellie twisted her hair and gazed at Katarina like she expected her to pull the information out of some long buried place.

"Like I said before, dunno. Could be, though. Fits with my theory, that's for sure."

Ellie nodded. "Okay, let's go with that theory for now. Anything else we know about him?"

Lots of shit. None of it good, and most irrelevant. Little she was willing to share. Katarina suppressed a shudder by taking a sip of water.

"You mean, apart from the fact that he's evil?"

Jillian's smart-ass reply almost made the water shoot back out Katarina's nose. She choked and smacked her chest. Once she stopped gasping for air, she glared at the blonde. "First, you're Attila the Hun, then the sad mom from some shitty cable movie, and now you're a comedian. Give me a warning next time before you switch personalities. I'd like to skip another stint in the hospital over aspirating my drink."

She coughed once more while Jillian shot Ellie a puzzled look. "Sad mom from a shitty cable movie? What's that supposed to mean?"

Katarina rolled her eyes. Jillian whispered louder than a two-year-old in a movie theater.

"I wouldn't sweat it. Katarina's not known for her sunny disposition, even at the best of times. Besides, it's late, and we're all probably feeling a little punchy by now." Despite the reassurance, Ellie's lips were twitching, and the roommate scowled before throwing her hands in the air.

"Okay, fine, I admit it. I'm a mother hen sometimes. So, sue me already." Jillian folded her arms and stuck her lower lip out, but a second later, both she and Ellie were snickering.

"And yet I'm the one they locked up in the psych hospital."

That only made them snicker harder. Their antics made Katarina want to chuck her plate at their heads. Had they forgotten so soon? This wasn't playtime. Bethany's life depended on them. If this was how the investigation was run, no wonder the police hadn't found her daughter yet.

Beneath the impatience, envy swelled, and Katarina gripped the chair to keep her nails from biting into her flesh. Must be nice to have someone so in sync with you. She'd never had a close friend, male or female. Growing up with a sociopath didn't lend itself to opportunities for relationships that weren't transactional. "If you two can tear yourselves away from the little BFF moment, I did have something to add."

Ellie's smile evaporated. "Go ahead."

"Kingsley also has a tendency to fixate on young girls. Around ten, eleven, or even younger. Not in a sexual way, more like a dad." Katarina grimaced as old memories of Kingsley's version of paternal affection wormed into her consciousness. "A super shitty, messed up dad, but whatever."

Ellie's brow furrowed. "Why do you say that? The dad part, I mean?"

"Why the hell do you think? Because of how he talked to me after I went to live with him. He treated me like a parent, like I was his kid. Like we were actually related or something. Besides, in the whole time I lived with him, I never noticed him ever so much as think about sex, let alone seek it out, and he's had plenty of opportunities with women over the years. He doesn't seem to care about physical connection, only pain. Pretty much any kind but the sexual variety."

Ellie rubbed her neck, her forehead lines deepening as she frowned down at the pizza box.

Seconds ticked by while Katarina waited for the detective to share what was on her mind. When she couldn't stand the tension any longer, she pounded the table with her fist. "What is it?"

Ellie lifted her eyes to meet Katarina's. "I was just wondering about your mother."

Her eyebrows shot up. This? This was the question plaguing the detective? "Which one are we talking about? I had lots of mothers when I was little."

The detective exchanged a glance with her roommate before placing her palms on the table and leaning forward, almost vibrating with intensity. "But are we one-hundred-percent sure who your birth mom was?"

What was Ellie trying to get at? Katarina narrowed her eyes, answering slowly as she attempted to unravel the detective's sudden fixation on her genealogy. "Yeah. My biological mom was Alice Becker, and my dad was John Becker. But you know all that already, so why the...oh, hell no!" Shock rippled through her body like an afterquake, rendering her incapable of speech. When she overcame her frozen vocal cords, her skin was flaming with anger. "Are you kidding me right now? I see where you're headed with this, and just stop already. It's complete and utter bullshit."

Even voicing the speculation that she and Kingsley might be related by blood seared her stomach with acid and sent nausea barreling up her throat. She pressed a hand to her belly and fought back a heave. Absolutely not. She refused to entertain such a disgusting idea.

Her parents were Alice and John Becker, who'd died when she was two, at which point she'd ended up with her great aunt, Euphemia. Anyone suggesting otherwise deserved a swift kick to the head.

As if sensing how close Katarina was to losing her shit, Ellie lifted her hands in surrender. "Okay, sorry. It was just a thought that popped into my head."

Katarina dug her fingers into her stomach and glared. "Well, un-pop it, and let's get back on track to Bethany. I think he's using her as the bait." Enough with the batshit conjectures. They needed to focus on the real task.

"Using her as bait for what?" Jillian asked.

"Any of us, all of us. The fuck should I know? I just know that it makes sense. He has a track record of using little girls as decoys or lures for his dirty work." Her lips twisted. "I should know. When I was still a kid, he used me too many times to count as a way of getting people to drop their guards and venture close enough to trip into his web. Think about it. Bethany is the best bait he could possibly use to draw any or all of us to him, wherever he wants us to go."

Wait. If in some horrible twist of fate Katarina truly was his daughter, then that made Bethany his...

"Motherfucker!" Horror, rage, and fear erupted, and Katarina banged her fist on the table until her hand throbbed. When that didn't serve as an adequate release, she grabbed handfuls of her hair and pulled until her scalp burned and tears stung her eyes. How could this be happening, after she'd spent so much time and effort to free herself from him?

She sensed the other two women's startled looks but didn't care, and the bodyguard had taken a step closer. Let them believe she'd lost her marbles, or shoot her, even. Physical pain would be a relief, compared to this onslaught of bitter, soul-crushing futility.

They were still murmuring to each other when she began speaking, her voice low and hoarse. "Do you have any idea how hard it was for me to break free of him? Almost impossible after growing up with him manipulating me, brainwashing me, telling me how much I meant to him and that a good, grateful 'daughter' would never leave her 'papa.'" She used air quotes around the words to make sure they understood she was talking figuratively. "Of course, that was when sweet-talking suited his mood. He used threats just as much. Told me how if I ever tried to leave him, he'd hunt me down like a rabid animal and put me out of my misery. But I finally did it. I dug deep and found the willpower after I found out that Bethany wasn't really dead."

An acrid laugh scraped up Katarina's throat as she lifted her gaze from the table to meet Ellie's eyes.

"How stupid could I have been? I knew what he was, knew the horrible things he did to people, yet I somehow went so many years, never guessing that he could be cruel enough to steal my newborn daughter from me."

Ellie shook her head. "Hey, it's okay, you don't have to—"

"I know what you all think of me, that I'm a cold, vicious bitch, and you're not wrong. But I can't tell you how much I hate," Katarina choked out the words, "*hate* being linked to him, how much I despise this connection we have. And I hate myself for wanting to run to him for protection, even when he was the one shooting at me. Isn't that the most pathetic thing you've ever heard? That even after every awful thing he's done, that I still somehow look to him for comfort and help? Shit, maybe I am crazy after all."

She stuffed her fist into her mouth to choke back a sob.

"That's not pathetic." Jillian's hand curled around her forearm. The contact made Katarina flinch, but she didn't move away. "It's a normal response to trauma in kidnapping victims, a form of Stockholm syndrome."

"Jillian's right. There are studies of former kidnapping victims who described those exact same behaviors and feelings. And that was in cases where the victims were adults, and the kidnapper didn't also act as a parent substitute."

Katarina used her shirt to dry her eyes. What a pathetic idiot. She hated that she'd melted down, especially in front of these two. Kingsley would have punished her for weeks over such a huge lapse of self-control. "God, I'm never like this. I'm just worried about Bethany." She glared up at Jillian, who still hovered near her shoulder. "I swear, if you try to hug me, I'll headbutt you in the nose."

The blonde backed away with her hands up. "No hugging, I promise. You don't smell all that great anyway."

Relieved by the shift to a lighter topic, Katarina sniffed her armpit and winced. "Yeah, didn't get around to showering much in the hospital. Deal with it."

"You can use mine once we're finished talking about Kingsley. What do we think his endgame is? To get us all together in the same spot and pick us off, one by one?"

Katarina scoffed at Ellie's suggestion. "Please. He's not some freak strung out on bath salts who runs around eating random people's faces for shits and giggles. He wants to feel powerful, which he achieves by outsmarting everyone around him. He gets off by taking people and molding them into the exact person he wants, into someone who will perform in a big way for him, at his bidding." She sneered to shove back a fresh burst of pain. "Nothing gives a man a greater sense of power than bending a strong woman to his will."

"And did he? Bend you to his will?"

The quiet question came from Ellie. Katarina debated answering, then shrugged. Why not? What did she care if they rehashed or judged her old traumas? Maybe one of the stories would further their investigation, and she'd flay the skin off her own back if that could help rescue Bethany.

Staring at her hands, she opened her mouth and let the

stories spill out. Starting with the first one, when Kingsley stole her from the Davidsons and manipulated her to wield a knife on them before she started the fire that burned their mangled bodies and continuing on through all of the crimes that followed.

The endless hours of training and preparation he'd subjected her to first to make sure she was ready, like martial arts, knife work, and breaking and entering. She shared how he'd taught her to scam people and steal and ended their lessons with real-life training. When she was still green, he tested her out on easy marks like half-deaf little old ladies with canes and graduated her to tougher scores by the time she hit thirteen.

As she recounted the early crimes he'd put her up to, her throat clogged. She'd never even had a chance.

Another hand curled around Katarina's shoulder, but this time when she glanced up, it was Ellie's face that hovered over her. Their eyes connected and understanding flashed between them. For the first time, Katarina wished things could have been different between them and wondered if, in another life, with different pasts, the two of them could have become friends rather than enemies.

The sensation was fleeting, slipping away in the blink of an eye as Ellie stepped back.

"There was this one kidnapping victim I handled, back when I was just starting out as a beat cop. She was a little girl not much older than Bethany, who'd been snatched by a friend of the family. A mother whose own child had just died." Ellie gripped the back of an empty chair, her voice soft as she told the story. "The little girl felt scared and sad about being taken away from her family and angry at the family friend for stealing her, and also guilty. There was even a part of her that felt bad for the woman who snatched her because of the daughter who'd died."

Against her will, Katarina was pulled into the story. "What happened to her?"

"Eventually, all those emotions proved too much for the little girl to take, made her feel so helpless that she ended up shutting down and going completely numb. As a survival mechanism, she went on autopilot and started to obey her kidnapper and do whatever she was told. Sometimes, that's what you're forced to do to stay alive, especially when you're young. You place your survival in the hands of the exact person who terrifies you."

Katarina struggled to connect with the detective's message but ended up sinking into the chair in frustration. Her body was spent, more wrung out than a wet towel, and her skull throbbed all over. "Is that supposed to make me feel better about what happened to me?"

Ellie gave a single shake of her head. "No. I told you that story to help you feel better about what's happening with Bethany."

24

The waitress's white sneakers squelched on the sticky concrete floor as she sauntered toward two burly men sporting ZZ Top beards and leather biker jackets. Like most dive bars, The Shanty was dark and reeked of stale beer, but the thick roll of cash poking out of the waitress's black cutoffs suggested the grimy interior didn't stop the patrons from leaving generous tips.

She leaned lower than necessary to set pints on the table between the bikers, a move Clay suspected she'd perfected to ensure an impressive amount of cleavage spilled from her skintight tank top. He passed the next few minutes fighting for patience while she tossed her blonde hair and chatted. Finally, after laughing at something the larger of the two bikers said, she patted his shoulder, winked, and strutted up to the small table where Clay and Luke were seated.

"Well, hello there. Don't think I've seen either of you at The Shanty before. Pretty sure I'd remember a couple of handsome mugs like that. You boys new in town?" She cocked one hip and flashed a dazzling grin.

Clay returned her smile. "Just visiting. How about you? Are you from around here?"

"You know it. Spent my whole life within thirty miles of this area, give or take a few. What about you? Where you from?"

Close up, the waitress appeared older than Clay had originally guessed. Lines bracketed her mouth and fanned out around her eyes, and her thin, painted-on eyebrows were sharply arched, giving her face a perpetually surprised expression. Her skin was that cigar-shade of tan common in aging sun worshippers. "Here and there. Lived in Texas for a stint before moving to Charleston."

Luke added nothing to the exchange but absorbed everything with alert ears even though his eyes were firmly on the table.

"Texas, the state where bigger is better." In case her verbal flirting wasn't blatant enough, she winked at Clay. He widened his smile. Best to lower her defenses, let her think she was reeling him in.

At least now he understood the massive wad of tip money.

He slid the sketch artist's portrait of Caraleigh across the table. "I'm hoping you can help us out. Have you seen this girl before?"

When the waitress dropped her gaze to the sketch, her eyebrows lifted. For a couple of heartbeats, she went still. By the time she handed the picture back to Clay, her expression was wiped clean. "Sorry, never seen her before."

Clay worked to keep the skepticism off his face. One of the earliest lessons he'd learned at the FBI Academy was... forget the words, read the body language. And the waitress's body language said she was lying.

Luke must have sensed it too, because he bristled and balled his fists.

"You know, it's not nice to fib to a federal agent." Clay pushed the Polaroid of Caraleigh from Bob's Burger Barn in front of her.

The waitress huffed at the photo and stuck her jaw out. Her lips thinned, but she didn't reply.

That was okay. Clay was happy to do the talking for now. He draped his arm across the back of the chair to show just how little her antics fazed him. "The great thing about local business owners in these small towns is how they run the same places for decades. Like Frank. Funny, I figured his name would be Bob, given it's Bob's Burger Barn, but apparently Bob was his great-grandfather."

She started when Clay dropped the name. *Good. Progress.*

"That's right, Frank Slater, your old boss at the hamburger joint. Turns out he's a real talkative fellow. In fact, Frank was more than happy to tell us all about Cara. Why, he even mentioned that he didn't mind overlooking her lack of government-issued ID because she was such a good kid, if a little on the odd side. Said she was a real hard worker too, but the most interesting part was when he told us that she roomed with another waitress named Lori while the two of them worked together."

Clay reclined in his chair with a friendly hat tip and waited. Frank hadn't been quite as forthcoming from the get-go as Clay had portrayed, but the waitress didn't need to know that. The older man's initial reluctance to share that he'd paid Cara under the table made sense since tax avoidance was a federal offense. Once Clay reassured Frank that his inquiry was a labor of love on behalf of family versus a criminal investigation, the man had opened up. Claimed he was a family man himself and wanted to help.

The waitress stared at the sketch for a long time before her shoulders drooped. "I didn't do anything wrong. Frank was the one who hired her. All I did was let her crash on my couch. Not like she could get an apartment anywhere without ID."

Even though Frank had told them as much, Clay's heart still leapt when the waitress confirmed the story. That made two people now who'd interacted with Cara after Luke was picked up by the rangers. His worst fear—that she hadn't survived in the wilderness on her own—was put to rest.

His sister had found her way down the mountain and back to civilization. Alive and safe. At least for a spell.

"So, she couch surfed at your place while she waitressed at Bob's Burger Barn. How long did that arrangement last?"

Lori pulled a surly face. "Not very long. She was weird, so she never settled in with the rest of us all that well."

Out of the corner of his eye, Clay caught Luke's glare. He squeezed the other man's shoulder again. A reminder to keep his cool.

Now, to take his own advice. The waitress's callous, offhand remark about Caraleigh was ruffling his feathers too. "When you say weird, what do you mean by that?"

The waitress sighed and cast a glance over her shoulder, like she hoped someone behind the bar might rescue her. "Just, she got upset over stupid stuff. Like when the music got too loud, or if guys tried to hit on her." She rolled her eyes. "What kind of nineteen-year-old girl doesn't like music and men? I mean, unless she was into chicks or something, but she never gave me that vibe."

Clay bit back a sharp reply and gave the waitress a chance to elaborate. *Easy, you need her to open up, and jumping in to defend Caraleigh will do the opposite. Pretend this is like any other investigation, and you're asking about a stranger.*

The problem was, his heart knew better.

When the waitress didn't offer any additional explanation, he prodded. "Let me make sure I've got this right. The only reason Caraleigh moved out is because you didn't see eye to eye on musical tastes and flirting?"

The waitress hooked her thumbs into her pockets and adopted a belligerent pose. "That, and a bunch of other little things. It all just added up until we had a big blowout. I just couldn't deal with all of her nitpicky bullshit demands anymore, so I told her she needed to find a new place to crash." She shrugged. "After that night, she never showed up at work again."

Clay's temper flared. Training took over, and he turned his focus inward and worked on controlling his breathing. *Act professionally. Professionals don't take asshole witnesses personally.*

His inhalation rasped in his ears while his heart disagreed.

Screw professional. This jerk kicked Caraleigh to the streets.

With his own inner debate raging, Clay forgot all about Luke until his chair screeched back. Cheeks flushed, Luke sprang to his feet and planted them wide, his entire stance combative. "It's okay not to like the same things as other people! Everyone is different! Why did you have to kick her out? Why?"

Oh boy.

Clay winced at Luke's volume. Heads turned, both drinkers and staff alike. Clay jumped up and clapped a soothing hand on Luke's shoulder. Luke jerked away like the touch burned. His hands balled into fists, and his entire face was now a mottled, angry red.

The waitress sidled back a step.

Clay scooted between Luke and the woman. Wouldn't be the first time he'd used his body as a buffer. "Easy, buddy. I know this is upsetting but yelling at the waitress won't bring Caraleigh back."

His attempt at damage control came too late. A square-shouldered bartender with close-cropped hair and a goatee was already striding up. He folded his arms, causing a pair of brawny, tattooed biceps to bulge from beneath the sleeves of a black t-shirt. "Everything okay over here?"

He directed the question at the waitress.

She flashed him a grateful smile. "Thanks, Jack, I'm good. I think they were just leaving."

Jack grunted before studying Clay and Luke through narrowed eyes. "You heard her. It's time for you two to head toward that door."

Clay lifted his hands, palms out. "Don't worry, we're leaving now."

For a tense moment, Luke planted his feet and acted like he'd refuse to budge.

"Come on, Luke. If we want to find Caraleigh, we need to leave."

The other man flinched when Clay grabbed his forearm but didn't resist being led across the sticky floor. More heads turned, briefly tracking their progress toward the exit before returning to their booze. This likely wasn't the first time they'd watched patrons get ejected from this particular dive, and he doubted it would be the last.

"You know, it's not my fault Cara was a weirdo!"

The waitress's parting shot caught them right at the door. Clay stiffened but didn't deviate from the goal. His main concern was getting Luke outside before he melted down or the bartender called the cops.

He ushered Luke through the exit, welcoming the relief that flooded his body when the door clicked shut behind them. The fresh, chilled air was soothing after the fermented stench of the bar. He stayed close to Luke, who was stomping on the asphalt and flapping his hands.

"It's not okay! It's not okay!" The other man repeated the

same accusation as he stormed around in tight circles, his face scrunched up like he was close to tears.

Watching him vent his frustration in the parking lot set off that familiar ping in Clay's gut again. He'd witnessed Caraleigh go through similar meltdowns when she was younger. Just like with Luke, the trigger was usually sensory overload or when her feelings grew too big to handle.

"I can see that you're upset, Luke, and I understand. What the waitress told us was really upsetting, wasn't it?" Clay vocalized the question in a calm, soothing voice.

When Luke didn't respond the first time, he repeated himself. He remembered times with Caraleigh when he'd needed to repeat himself five or even six times before she was calm enough to focus. No guarantees that he'd be able to get through to Luke at all, but he figured a little validation and empathy couldn't hurt.

"Yes! It wasn't okay."

Progress. Luke was still stomping and flapping, but at least he'd responded.

A man exited his car and cut across the parking lot, giving them a wide berth. Clay met his wide-eyed gaze without a hint of embarrassment. The stranger shook his head in disgust before disappearing inside.

Clay flipped him the bird before turning back to Luke. Same shit used to happen with his sister all the time. Let them judge. The only thing he cared about was making sure Luke was okay. "Trust me, I get it. I was hoping the waitress would have more information, so I'm really disappointed too, and sad for Caraleigh. I keep thinking of how lonely she must have felt, being all on her own and then getting kicked out of the apartment like that."

After a few seconds, the stomping slowed. "Really lonely and scared. I'm scared." Luke shivered and flapped his hands harder.

"Scared for Caraleigh?"

Luke stood still long enough to nod, his expression solemn. "Yes. I've heard that bad things can happen to people who live outside because they don't have anywhere indoors to stay. Especially young people. I don't want bad things to have happened to Caraleigh."

"I hear you. I don't want bad things to have happened to Caraleigh, either. But as of now, we have no reason to believe that they did, okay?"

Luke's chin quivered. "But if bad things happened to her, it's my fault. I shouldn't have let the rangers take me away. I left her all alone."

Clay's heart broke at the anguish reflected in Luke's face. He could relate.

He'd tortured himself with those same guilty lies too many times to count.

"You were just a kid, Luke. You didn't fall and break your arm on purpose, and you didn't have a choice when the rangers took you away. Please believe me when I say it's not your fault."

Now, if only Clay would take his own advice to heart.

Luke's throat bobbed as he swallowed hard. "Do...do you think we're going to find her?"

The younger man trembled under the night sky, scared and hopeful and looking to Clay for reassurance. More than anything, Clay wanted to wrap his arms around Luke and hold him close. The exact way he'd hugged Caraleigh when she was on the verge of tears.

His experience with his sister also taught him that unsolicited touch could make things worse, though, so Clay opened his arms and let Luke decide.

Luke's face crumpled as he surged forward, slamming into Clay's chest with enough force to rock him back on his heels. Unashamed, his throat thickened as he stood in the parking lot, embracing the other man while gazing at the dim outline of the mountains in the distance.

Hope stirred in his chest. If Caraleigh had survived those mountains, she could survive anything.

"Yes, I think we can find her. One thing is sure, I know we're damned well going to try."

25

"Now, go ahead. Hop into bed."

Bethany followed my instructions without complaint, climbing into bed with the listless energy of a worn-out, one-hundred-year-old woman. Along with the wan complexion, the purple half-moons beneath her eyes, sharp cheekbones, and waiflike frame reminded me of one of those pictures of starving children that good Samaritans used to guilt people into monthly donations.

The only thing she lacked to pose as a poster child for one of those campaigns was the hollow-eyed, beaten stare. Even now, Katarina's daughter overcame her weakened, calorie-deficient state long enough to glare defiance at me from the pillow.

Pride curved my lips as I gazed into that tenacious little face. Over the course of my life so far, I'd experienced the pleasure of knowing several strong-willed women. Bethany topped that impressive list. The eight-year-old was demonstrating herself to be more stubborn than Letitia, Morrigan, or her disappointment of a mother. Pure, brazen fire crackled within the depths of that young body and mind.

The flames shined bright in her eyes. Dimming such a bright flame as I wore her down into submission would prove exquisitely rewarding.

Delicious warmth coiled in my gut at the prospect of her inevitable defeat. Easy victories were hollow and unworthy of my efforts, but I did so enjoy a good challenge.

The mattress sank when I perched on the edge. Bethany scrabbled to the far side of the bed. "You did quite well with your training today. I'm very proud of you. I appreciate that all of this must be very confusing. I merely want the best for you, my sweet girl. The reason I push so hard is because I can sense how very special you are. There's so much potential in you, even more than I saw in your mother when she was around your age."

That remark grabbed her attention. She peered at me from beneath her lashes, chewing on her inner cheek as if debating whether or not to engage. Curiosity won out. "You knew my mama back then?"

"I did indeed. She looked a lot like you." I allowed a benevolent smile to soften my face.

A brief hesitation. "Was she…was Mama brave when she was a little girl?"

Aha. As I watched her bony fingers pluck at the blanket, satisfaction unfurled inside me like a cat sunning itself on a warm deck. To her daughter's naive young mind, Katarina's brash courage was aspirational. Precisely the tool I needed to facilitate winning her trust. "Your mama was quite brave, yes. But here's a little secret between you and me." I lowered my voice and leaned in, delighted when she didn't shrink away. "I think if we work together, you'll turn out to be so much braver and stronger than even your mama was. But we must never tell her that. Katarina was always very competitive and has a tendency to get upset if she believes someone is outdoing her."

Bethany drank all of that in, her eyes wide and owllike in her gaunt face.

"Now, would you like me to tell you a story?"

No response. Better than the screams I'd received earlier in the week, but still not as gratifying as a yes.

My gaze wandered over her pajama top, to the mangled collar full of gouges. Teeth marks, from where she'd gnawed on the material in a losing battle to hold hunger at bay. Every day she grew a little weaker, and in turn, closer to complete capitulation. Fighter or not, Katarina's brat would eventually accept the difficult lesson that all the other stubborn women in my life had learned, some more painfully than others. Attempts to thwart me were futile.

No, I possessed nary a doubt that in the end, Bethany would yield to me as the master of her destiny.

For now, I would savor the process.

"Good girls who listen to stories get a snack."

Bethany's breathing hitched on a tiny, hopeful intake of air, and she licked her lips. Likely fearing another trick, she hid any other signs of excitement well. That little demonstration of self-control was better than women double, even triple her age, a reality that tickled my pride once again.

While weakness bored me, I did so appreciate a quick learner.

I reached into my pocket and extracted a plastic-wrapped granola bar. As I dangled the prize in the air, her features sharpened with hunger and turned her appearance almost feral. An atavistic gleam entered her eyes, like the promise of food had summoned some long dormant beast from hibernation.

Gaze glued to the bar, her breathing rate quickened. She offered me a single nod, and being the magnanimous sort I was, I chose to accept her gesture in lieu of a verbal agreement.

"Excellent choice. So, I suppose we'll start this tale in a similar fashion to all great stories. Once upon a time, there was a little boy who lived alone with his mother in a tiny house. Though the boy never quite fit in with the other children, and he and his mother couldn't afford much in the way of creature comforts or possessions, it was okay because the boy knew his mother loved him very much, and that was what mattered the most. Sadly, that all changed when a filthy rich man with more money than character crashed into their lives. Like many rich men, this intruder was greedy and had never learned how to share. He wanted the little boy's mother all to himself, so once he and the mother married, he sent the boy off to a school far, far away."

Lured into the story in spite of herself, Bethany's gaze crept from the granola bar in my hand to my face. "Did the little boy not want to go away to school?"

I shook my head. "Not at first, no. Remember, the little boy loved his mother. He wanted to stay home with her and was scared of living without her in some strange new place. But gradually, the boy became accustomed to his new home at the school and grew to enjoy certain aspects of his life there. You see, the boy had always enjoyed learning, and this particular school had exciting new lessons to teach. The sort of lessons that went far beyond what he could have learned under his parents' roof while attending the public school back at home. Over time, he even fell in love with a brilliant woman, who taught him more of the true nature of people and life than he'd ever dreamed possible. The important lessons that most students were never lucky enough to learn."

Katarina's whelp's eyes were wide and trained on mine as she soaked up every word. As a reward for her interest, I extended the granola bar toward her, holding tight when her greedy hands shot out to grab the other end. "Now, what do you suppose happens next in the story?"

She tugged at the bar, but I held firm. Catching on to my game, she relaxed her grip. Her smooth brow furrowed as she considered my question. "Did the little boy and the woman get married?"

I released the snack. "Well done. That is an excellent guess."

The wrapper crinkled as she tore at the plastic with trembling hands and teeth, like a raccoon raiding a campsite picnic. She ripped off a hunk and swallowed the bite after two chomps.

So perfect, how she was falling into my trap without the slightest inkling. Though dated now, Skinner and Watson's operant conditioning theories had yet to fail me. Shaping behavior with both punishment and rewards was a technique still implemented by animal trainers for one simple reason... it worked.

So cute, the way humans believed they were elevated beyond monkeys or Golden Retrievers when, in actuality, they reacted the same as baser mammals when stripped down to survival mode. I'd accepted the truth long ago. The members of our supposedly superior species were nothing more than animals awaiting the right trainer.

The quicker little Bethany understood that her most basic, essential survival needs relied upon exhibiting the behaviors I desired, the quicker she'd acquiesce to my reins.

Lulled into a good mood by this recent success, I allowed Bethany to scarf down the granola bar without interruption and lapsed back into storytelling mode. "No, I'm afraid the boy and the woman never did get married, although there was a time when he would have liked nothing better. Alas, the woman already had a husband, even though she loved the little boy more. The pair of them were so in love that they created a baby together, but the woman lied to the boy when he asked and pretended like the child belonged to another man. Wasn't that horribly, terribly wrong of her?"

I broke off when my own voice penetrated my ears, taut and sharp as a guitar string wrapped around a gasping throat. A glance at Bethany revealed no observable symptoms of fear at all. Rather, the child agreed with my summation of Letitia's vile act with a bob of her head.

My fingers dug into the blanket like claws.

See, Letitia? Even an eight-year-old agrees that you behaved in a despicable manner.

"She tried to hide the child from the boy, but he was too smart for her tricks. Far smarter than she gave him credit for. You see, she'd forgotten that she'd already taught the boy most of her tricks, so he was hard to fool. And, as often happens, the student had surpassed the teacher. Knowing that she lied, the boy hunted high and low for his child. Along the way, he stole a few other children he stumbled across too, snatching kids from undeserving parents who didn't appreciate them and selling them to parents who did."

The story tumbled out faster now like an outside force was pressing on me, insisting that I hurry to the conclusion. Bethany polished off the food in silence and hunted for crumbs in the sheets. When she finished, she pulled the blanket up higher, as if protecting herself from my growing unhappiness with the direction the story was taking.

Her reaction was inconsequential. All that mattered was that I spew the remainder of this sordid tale into the world before I burst.

"Of course, the boy did end up finding the child, but not until he was a grown man, and his daughter was almost a full-grown woman herself. The reunion went nothing like he'd hoped. His daughter had no idea she'd been given up for adoption as a baby and didn't believe the boy. When he tried to tell her the truth, she called him a dirty liar, crazy, all sorts of repugnant names. The boy bore her ignorance without faltering, though. The moment he laid eyes on the girl, he knew, and none of her denials could change his conviction. She was the spitting image of some photos he'd seen in albums of his mother at that same age."

With my mind lost in the past, I was barely aware when I rose from the bed and paced across the hardwood floor.

"But no matter how many times the boy tried to reveal the truth, the daughter denied him, just like her birth mother had done years before. The boy lost his temper then, and who could blame him? Morrigan was a foolish little whelp who ran wild and ended up getting herself pregnant, just like her mother. The boy never meant to hurt her. Of course he didn't, because attacking a pregnant woman is a cowardly act, and the boy was a man by then, and the farthest thing from a coward."

My spine stiffened at the mere suggestion. Me, a coward? Ludicrous. The unfortunate turn had been Morrigan's fault. The haughty, arrogant bitch took after her mother a little too much.

"She hit the boy first, you see. Called him all sorts of vile names. His reaction was instinctual, his lashing out reflexive. One little push, that was all. How was the boy to know that pregnancy had caused her center of gravity to change and impact her balance? He couldn't possibly have guessed that his tiny shove would make her stumble and strike her head on the flagstones. If he'd injured her on purpose, would he have rushed her to the hospital, visited her every day in a disguise, to ensure that the innocent baby survived? The answer is no. Of course not."

Old frustration cascaded through me as I recalled the unfortunate chain of events.

"Everything would have worked out fine if the boy hadn't

suspected that Morrigan recognized him during a visit and forced his hand. She was spiteful enough to ruin his life by crying assault, and then what would the boy do? In the end, she left him no choice. The boy couldn't stomach a future in a prison cell, so once she returned home, he waited outside her house, hidden away in the bushes. One night when she ventured outside to grab her mail, he struck. He stifled her cries with a hand over her mouth and slit her throat. He remembers how warm her blood was when it gushed over his fingers. He laid her limp body on the walkway when she stopped struggling and slipped away."

"What…what happened to the baby?"

The small, high voice made me whirl in my tracks. The shape of the lump beneath the covers suggested that Bethany was curled into the fetal position, and the eyes that peeked over the top of the blanket were wide with fear.

I'd been so swept up in the past that I'd failed to notice I'd shared the entire story out loud. I strolled back to the bed and smiled down into her pinched face. "Of all the babies the boy ever stole, Morrigan's child was the one he took care of the most."

Bethany's eyelids drooped as fatigue settled in, but she jerked them open again, too wary to succumb to sleep when I was still so close.

"Clever girl." A strange tenderness surged into the hardened space beneath my ribs. Keeping my touch gentle, I swept the hair off her forehead before grazing my knuckles along her sweet, soft cheek, whispering as her eyelids drifted shut again.

"*Ma petite fille.*"

26

Blue, purple, and red paint slashed across the white canvas in a riotous, violent outburst, dominating an entire wall in the gallery of the Gibbes Museum of Art. Helen Kline tilted her head to the left, then right. She tapped a French manicured nail to her chin as she attempted to puzzle out the meaning behind the nebulous shapes. The painting's vivid colors had captured her attention from the moment she'd entered the special modern art exhibit in the third-floor gallery, but she had yet to make up her mind as to what she thought of the piece.

Hands on her hips, she stepped closer to the painting. When that didn't do the trick, she sighed. This was why she preferred classical or more realistic art over most contemporary pieces. How was one to form an educated opinion over a painting's merits when you weren't even sure what you were viewing?

The beginning notes of a Bach concerto intruded on her ruminations. Helen plucked the phone from the zippered pocket of her Italian leather handbag and ended the alarm. Ten minutes until her appointment time with the new donor.

She'd best start for their designated meeting spot in the second-floor atrium.

After one last glimpse of the confounding painting, she headed for the elevator, her low heels clicking across the blond hardwood floors. When the doors opened, a young mother pushing a towheaded toddler in a stroller exited, smelling of baby powder and spit-up.

Helen's gaze tracked the woman and child until the doors slid shut and blocked them from view. She guessed the mother's age at twenty-five, perhaps thirty. Around the same age as Eleanor.

She exhaled a long breath as the elevator squeaked its descent to the second floor. Why couldn't that be her daughter pushing a stroller and enjoying a leisurely day at the museum? Helen sniffed, longing for one of those sweet beings to be on the agenda in the foreseeable future for Ellie.

Baby or not, why couldn't Eleanor consider working in a nice, safe, culturally rich environment like the Gibbes Museum? Although Helen supposed any job would suffice, as long as the duties didn't include Eleanor thrusting herself into harm's way every five minutes.

Her daughter was so beautiful and intelligent. Helen entertained no doubts that she could succeed at whichever endeavor she chose.

Why, then, did her only girl insist on tormenting her mother by picking one of the most dangerous careers possible?

Helen smoothed the peach collar of her designer blazer in the mirrored wall and patted her carefully styled blonde hair before clicking out of the elevator in the direction of the Patrick Dougherty installation. As a member of the museum's charity foundation, she'd wandered these airy, clean halls enough to turn left through the Twentieth Century Charleston exhibit without consulting a map.

She arrived at the atrium with five minutes to spare. The treelike sculpture inside was another example of contemporary art, but one that appealed to Helen's sensibilities. With this piece, the artist had managed to strike that delicate balance between the whimsical and the absurd. The sculpture was a crowd-pleaser, which was why Helen had selected the atrium as the perfect meeting spot.

Donors tended to loosen their purse strings more when they got a taste of the art their contributions funded.

The sculpture's woven twigs and branches often served to soothe Helen, but they had little effect today as she meandered through the exhibit. Her head was far too full of those awful news reports about Eleanor's boss to relax. She fiddled with her sleeve, fretting. Such a gruesome murder, and in the police department's own parking garage, no less. What kind of criminal risked that type of exposure?

Only the most brazen. The kind who would let nothing stop him from attacking again, Helen suspected. And who was to say that her Eleanor wouldn't be the next target? She wrung her hands together and shuddered. No wonder she'd found more gray hairs this morning. This whole situation was simply too dreadful to consider.

Helen returned to the front of the atrium to wait, fighting the uneasiness in her stomach. She'd tried so hard to accept Eleanor's career choice, to set aside her qualms and be supportive, but how could anyone expect a mother to endorse a job that seemed dead set on killing her child?

She fiddled with the tasteful tennis bracelet on her wrist and smoothed the frown from her features. At her age, too much frowning would deepen the wrinkles by the hour. Along with the gray hairs, her wrinkles had grown by leaps and bounds since the day Eleanor signed up for the ridiculous detective job.

Her heel tapped an anxious beat on the floor before she

steeled her spine and adjusted her blazer's hem. This absurdity had carried on quite long enough. It was past time for her to schedule a chat with Eleanor about her future. Of course, the conversation would require a delicate touch. Even as a toddler, Eleanor had dedicated herself to proving the old redheaded stereotype about stubbornness true.

A rueful smile curved Helen's coral lips. Good thing for her that the apple didn't fall far from the tree. She might not be as obviously muleheaded as her feisty offspring, but she was plenty strong-willed in her right, if more polite with how she voiced her positions.

They didn't call Southern ladies steel magnolias for nothing.

She toyed with the links on the tennis bracelet and plotted. Her husband had been pestering her for the past two months to start planning a family vacation in celebration of their upcoming anniversary. Helen liked to pride herself on rarely resorting to manipulation to get her own way. In this instance, however, a little guilt wouldn't hurt anyone. Not when Eleanor taking a break from that ghastly job could very well be a matter of life and death.

Besides, the stress of fretting over her daughter's safety was taking a toll on Helen's health, and Eleanor was long overdue for vacation from work.

And if Helen could convince her daughter to change careers during the trip? All the better.

Who knew? Perhaps she could persuade Eleanor to assist her here at the museum. When it came to fundraising, extra hands on deck were always beneficial. Helen enjoyed the planning, organizing, and community outreach that accompanied her position as head of the charitable foundation. Maybe Eleanor would learn to appreciate working in the nonprofit sector too.

The satisfaction of achieving goals and seeing her visions

become reality filled Helen with satisfaction. Once they met their next fundraising goal, the museum could hire contractors to fix the out-of-date electrical wiring that hindered parts of the western wing. Without the much-needed repairs, the risk of accidental fire loomed over the museum like a hovering funnel cloud.

Two hundred thousand dollars. That was the amount that Mr. Ray needed to sign on his check today in order for the museum to reach its goal. She smoothed her palms along the jacket's lapels and fixed her mouth into an encouraging smile.

Helen Kline imagined that soliciting donations was similar to heading into battle. Outfits and attitude were crucial. The main difference was that the bloodshed in the business world was financial instead of physical. Here, a nice suit or a Louis Vuitton purse took the place of armor, while compliments and quick wits were the weapons of choice.

High-pitched stage whispers snagged her attention, and her smile widened as a frazzled teacher wearing glasses and a ponytail herded a horde of elementary-aged students in matching orange t-shirts down the hallway. So young now, but they grew so quickly. Some days, she could scarcely believe her own children were fully grown. All three of the boys were men now and had entered into safe, respectable professions with nary a fight.

It was only her headstrong daughter who'd rebelled against the more gentile life she'd envisioned for her offspring and insisted on courting danger at every turn.

A baby's wail pulled Helen from her musings. She glanced at the antique, white-gold watch circling her wrist and frowned. Twenty minutes past the hour. Where on earth was Mr. Ray?

She scoured the faces of nearby patrons, but none matched the photograph Mr. Ray sent in his email. A brief trip through the closest gallery didn't turn him up, either. With an impatient harrumph over his rather rude behavior, Helen dialed his number on her phone. The call went straight to an automated voice service.

Her mouth tightened before she remembered to relax her muscles. Frowning would only hurt her, not the donor who hadn't bothered to show up to their meeting on time. After a round through the entire second floor without a sign of him, Helen decided enough was enough.

Her nails drummed an annoyed beat on her forearm as the elevator descended to the first floor. Chin high, she marched past the museum store and stopped at the Visitor's Service desk.

The pretty young clerk smiled a greeting. "Hi, Mrs. Kline. Is there something I can help you with?"

Helen returned the smile despite her irritation. When she was a little girl, her mother had taught her that there was no excuse for bad manners. "Greta, would you be so kind as to contact me immediately if a Mr. Ray comes looking for me?"

"Of course, Mrs. Kline."

"Thank you, I appreciate it."

When she exited the museum into the dreary day and descended the first three steps, her mind had already moved past the missed meeting and onto planning out the remainder of the afternoon's activities. No sense dwelling on events over which she had no control. Like her grandpappy always said, that was a recipe for unhappiness and a broken ticker.

There was always a positive to every negative if one searched hard enough. Like now, for example. Suddenly, she had ample time to fit in some shopping before the one o'clock lunch date with Eleanor. And if her daughter canceled at the last possible minute, as she was wont to do?

Helen shrugged her slim shoulders. Well, more shopping time for her.

She descended the last two steps and headed for the parking lot at a brisk pace. This afternoon, she had phone calls to make about two fundraisers scheduled for later in the month to ensure the events were proceeding without a hitch. Early evening was dedicated to dinner with her husband, of course, followed by a warm bath and a few chapters of the current romance novel she was reading.

The sun peeped out from behind the cloud cover, warming her cheeks as her heels clicked across the pavement to the parking area. All in all, a good day beckoned. With or without Mr. Ray's donation.

Her Mercedes was in sight when the child's cry reached her ears. Helen ignored the caterwauling at first. Museums weren't most children's first choice of entertainment options, and Helen could scarcely recall a visit that hadn't included one sobbing preschooler or another.

When the volume climbed higher, though, Helen's confident stride faltered. With four children under her belt, she prided herself in being rather adept at distinguishing phony, attention seeking cries from sobs of genuine distress.

The child cried out again, and the shrill wail sent a chill feathering down Helen's spine. She paused, scanning the grounds for the source. No small, shivering bodies jumped out at her until her gaze swept along the deserted alley that led to a catering entrance on the side of the building. There, huddling in the building's shadow, was a petite figure. Almost certainly a child based on the height and slim build.

After a quick glance of the surrounding area didn't produce any other adults, Helen took a hesitant step toward the alley. "Hello? Do you need some help?"

As Helen's voice echoed off the concrete, the girl's head whipped in her direction before she went rabbit-still. She whimpered and scrambled two steps back, as if even more terrified now.

Good going, Helen. You all but frightened the poor dear away.

Helen sighed and continued down the alley in the girl's direction. The waif held her ground this time as Helen approached the deserted area near the wall. As she drew closer, she clucked her tongue in growing concern.

The girl's pasty skin stretched taut over spiny cheekbones, like she hadn't eaten a good meal in weeks, and her eyes were so shadowed that they almost appeared bruised. Helen's maternal instincts clicked into overdrive. She knelt on the pavement to make herself less intimidating.

"You poor, poor thing. Are you okay? Are you lost?" No response, so she tried again. "Where's your mommy or daddy?"

Helen extended her hand to the urchin, who hesitated, staring at her with wide, cautious eyes before placing her small hand in Helen's palm. Something about the elfin face framed by lank blonde hair tugged at her memory. Where had she seen those delicate features before?

"Are you here with your class from school?" Helen recalled the frazzled teacher leading the small army of kids. If this girl was part of that group, Helen wanted to have a word with the principal to see how to go about donating food and supplies to needy students. This child appeared so frail that a light breeze might pick her up and blow her away.

Helen frowned when she recalled the students in that group wearing matching orange shirts. Not part of the school trip, then.

The girl tugged at Helen's hand. "My papa fell and needs assistance, please."

Alarm bells surfaced in Helen's head. The girl's intonation was stilted, almost robotic, as if the line had been fed to her and rehearsed. And she voiced the request without urgency.

More like she was being forced to carry out an unpleasant chore than seeking emergency aid for her injured father.

The clouds blotted out the sun, and another chill swept across her skin. Something was very, very wrong.

Helen checked her surroundings again but didn't notice anything odd. Still, the little voice in her head kept insisting that she hurry back to the car. "Sweetie, what's going on here? Don't be afraid. I won't hurt you."

The girl stroked her left arm, inadvertently drawing Helen's eyes to the dark bruises marring the fair skin. A quick scan revealed similar marks on the opposite side.

Helen's eyes narrowed as her worry gave way to anger. Hurting a child was despicable behavior. Whoever did this had better believe she'd unleash some choice words on them if they dared to show their cowardly face. "Poor baby, who did this to you?"

Helen lifted her gaze back to the gamine face, and this time, recognition hit. She inhaled a sharp gasp. "Sweetie, what's your name?"

The little girl returned Helen's stare with the sunken, empty gaze of a drug addict or abuse victim triple her age, causing goose bumps to skitter across Helen's chest.

She needed to get this child out of the alley. Escort her to the safety of Helen's car or back inside the museum.

A breeze kicked up, whisking a dead leaf down the alley. The girl jumped and tugged at Helen's hand.

"It's okay, baby, I'm here now. I'll take you somewhere safe and get you something good to eat. How does that sound? A nice big meal, and maybe a cup of hot chocolate or a shake. What do you like? Spaghetti? Pizza? We can have anything at all, my treat."

At the mention of food, hope lit up the girl's eyes for one heart-stopping instant, and Helen sucked in a breath. The transformation was unbelievable. Just as quickly, the expression vanished, and the dead-eyed wariness returned. Had someone lied to the girl about food before?

Helen was this close to spitting nails. What kind of monster would tease a precious little angel like that? Starve her half to death? "I promise, I'm not playing a trick. I'll buy you whatever you want."

The girl began to quiver all over. Her throat moved several times, and her lips parted, and the expression on her little face when she glanced over her shoulder could only be described as pure terror.

Her fear made Helen's urgency return. "Come on, sweetie, let's get out of here. You'll feel so much better once you eat."

And Helen would feel better once they were out of this creepy alley and back in the open. Hopefully, once Helen removed the girl from this grim spot and tucked her into a booth in her favorite diner, the child would relax a little. There wasn't much a little good, Southern cooking and a big bowl of peach cobbler couldn't fix. Once her belly was full again, Helen was sure to coax the story out of her.

As soon as they were locked inside the car, Helen would call Eleanor and let her know who she'd stumbled upon.

But first, she needed to get the girl to move.

Helen tugged on the girl's hand and tried to pull her into a run, but the girl's legs wobbled and stumbled after only two steps. Too weak. Probably from hunger.

That left only one option. Helen bent down and scooped the girl up, the same way she'd done years ago with her own children. Her knees creaked and her spine complained, but the girl was light. Too light. Helen clutched the frail body close to her heaving chest and staggered toward the parking lot.

She'd been so wrapped up in the girl that she hadn't

noticed the silver car come to a stop at the exit of the alley until the motor sounded over the beating of her heart.

She was trapped.

Fear clawed at her breast, but Helen Kline did what she did best...pressed forward. There was a foot or so of space between the wall and car. If she hurried, she could slip past and rush to her own vehicle.

She only made it a few steps before a man leapt out, and Helen gasped. She recognized the face from the photo attachment he'd emailed her.

Mr. Ray.

There was no smile on his face now. No apologies for arriving so late for their scheduled appointment, or explanation for how he'd located Helen here, out of sight from the museum foot traffic.

Helen Kline prided herself on being the type of person who wasn't given to flights of fancy or allowed her imagination to run wild, but the victorious expression on the man's tanned face was truly the most frightening thing she'd ever seen.

Hurry. Hurry.

Holding the child tight, she rushed to get past him. Three steps, and then her ankle wobbled, twisted. Cursed heels! She'd chosen her fancy, impress-the-wealthy-donor footwear today, not her Cole Haan sneakers.

Frantic, she kicked off the first shoe, then the second, before hugging the girl and gathering her legs to launch into a run.

They only had to get to her car. They could make it. She might need an oxygen tank afterward, but she would get them there.

She lunged forward, but a strong hand grabbed her arm from behind. Terror clawed up her throat. She sucked air into her lungs and opened her mouth to scream, but another hand clamped across it, muffling the sound to a squeak.

No.

Helen Kline twisted, lurched, fought with all her might. As she struggled, she felt a pinch in her upper arm.

No.

She staggered. Craned her head in time to witness the hypodermic needle extruding from her favorite peach blazer.

The man withdrew the needle, and she stumbled away.

Hurry. This was her last chance to get them to safety.

She managed one more step before her knees buckled, and the blue sky ahead tilted in a sickening way.

As her vision blurred, the man she knew as Mr. Ray finally spoke.

"Hello, Mrs. Kline. I am so very pleased to see you."

27

An undercurrent of urgency electrified the silence in Ellie's living room, which was broken only by an occasional cough or paper rustling when someone flipped a page. Katarina's surprise arrival on her doorstep had led to both Ellie and Jillian letting work know they'd be staying home for the day. Neither of them trusted leaving Katarina to her own devices, so instead, they were sprawled out across the apartment, each of them claiming a different area to serve as a temporary workstation.

Thanks to her work on the Burton case, Ellie had access to a treasure trove of adoption documents that would have proven difficult to acquire otherwise. The dining room table doubled as her desk, with all the files on Burton's illegal adoption victims stretched out before her like an assembly line.

Ellie tugged at the elastic holding back her ponytail to tighten it while frowning at the quick and dirty timeline she'd attempted to form. Her idea was that by arranging the illegal adoptions in chronological order and cross-referencing that with the geographic location of where the child was reported missing, she might get lucky and determine Kingsley's comfort zone.

If she found a comfort zone, then they might be able to triangulate and ascertain a probable location of Kingsley's safe house, give or take a dozen square miles or so.

Ellie bit her cheek until she tasted blood. Might. Probable. Dozen square miles. Not very reassuring, but what else could they do?

She traced her finger over a line of text that she'd read too many times already and exhaled through her nostrils. Staring at these documents all morning and afternoon was making her eyes start to cross. So much of this felt like a wild goose chase. Hopefully, her accomplices were having better luck.

Stretching her arms overhead, she glanced up from the sea of papers to check in with the others. Jillian's blonde head was bent over the laptop, and adoption records were strewn across the kitchen island as she searched for a legitimate adoption by Letitia Wiggins. Ellie didn't envy her that job.

Adoption records were usually sealed, so uncovering the one that was linked to a specific person would be a hell of a feat. Sam laid at her feet with her head slumped on her paws, heaving deep doggy sighs every once in a while, her expressive eyebrows twitching.

Ellie's gaze traveled across the room to one of her overstuffed living room chairs, where Katarina sprawled with a yellow legal pad in her lap and her bare feet stretched onto Ellie's coffee table. She'd spent half an hour in the shower and had discarded the atrocious "New Mommy" sweatpants ensemble in favor of a pair of Ellie's old baggy jeans and a long-sleeved t-shirt. Her brown hair hung loose, obscuring part of her face as she scribbled notes with a pencil.

Katarina had shot down the suggestion that there was a

blood link between her and Kingsley, refusing to even entertain the idea to the point that she scoffed at Ellie and Jillian's
focus on the adoption records as a waste of time. Instead,
she'd told them she'd rack her brain for anything and everything Kingsley had ever shared or revealed about his history
during her time with him and jot the details down, no matter
how irrelevant, vague, or inconsequential they might seem.

Ellie studied the other woman's profile, frowning. Was
there really no deeper connection between Katarina and
Kingsley? Because Ellie wasn't convinced.

Truth be told, she was pretty sure Katarina wasn't
convinced, either. Why else had she breathed fire and all but
charred their heads to ashes when presented with the
possibility?

Ellie understood why Katarina reacted that way, though.
Turned out, not even Kingsley's protégé wanted to entertain
the idea of additional bonds to the man who'd raised her.
She'd had years to accept the nurture part of their relationship. Expecting her to immediately jump on board to tacking
on a genetic, nature link to the sociopath was a lot to ask.

The more Ellie toyed with the idea, though, the more she
wondered. Kingsley had a proven track record of fixating on
father-daughter relationships, of obsessing over the unrav-
eling and corruption of interpersonal connections. All of
which fit perfectly with a man whose lover lied about a pregnancy and gave up a child for adoption without his knowledge. Plus, there was his dysfunctional focus on the
bifurcation of women into two groups...good girl or slut.

Slut. She shuddered at the word. At the horrible, horrible
memories it conjured up. Memories she still couldn't fully
access, thanks to her brain's protective mode repressing
them. The game, though. She'd never forget that. Even the
horrible name—*Die, Bitch! Die*—testified to Kingsley's misog-
ynistic, twisted ideas about women.

His sinister voice stuck in her mind. Sometimes disappearing for a while, but always coming back, like an evil boomerang. One day Ellie hoped to eliminate every trace of him from her brain entirely, but that would never happen unless he was locked up or dead and no longer a threat to her family or anyone else.

Like Bethany.

Her teeth tugged at her bottom lip while she straightened the closest papers. Time to focus. Hopefully, they'd get lucky and find the clue leading to Kingsley's whereabouts. It wouldn't help Ellie manage her memories, but at least they could prevent him from featuring in any new ones.

A wet nose nudged her elbow, and she absently stroked the dog's soft head with one hand while she marked a location on the map with her other. After a few minutes, Sam abandoned her in search of a more attentive ear scratcher, but Ellie barely noticed as she hunched over the table and tapped the pen on the wood. Hours had passed, yet no leads. No nothing.

Maybe Katarina was right, and this adoption angle was them sprinting down a dead end.

A gasp from the kitchen made Ellie's head whip up. "Did you find something?"

When Jillian lifted her gaze from whatever paper had elicited her reaction, her mouth hung open, and her blue eyes held an expression that sent tingles racing across Ellie's neck.

Katarina sat up slowly in the chair. Her lips were pinched, but she was quiet as she waited for Jillian to share.

"So, Letitia Wiggins did give birth to a baby. A little girl, no record of a name. Two days later, the Rhett family from Charleston announced the birth of their own daughter, Morrigan Rhett."

Wrinkling her brow, Ellie turned the name over in her

mind. *Morrigan Rhett. Why did that sound so familiar?* "How have I heard of that name before?"

"Morrigan Rhett was featured in the society pages for a long time, as one of those feel-good stories that everyone could get behind. You know, poor unwanted baby gets adopted by a rich family and turns into a beautiful debutante. It's one of those rags-to-riches fairy tales that most people love, like *Little Orphan Annie* meets *The Princess Diaries*."

"Most people are idiots."

Jillian ignored Katarina's less-than-helpful contribution. "After her society debut, Morrigan started to gradually disappear from the public eye. Rumors were everywhere, speculating that a problem had come up with the adoption or that she'd been sent to a residential program for eating disorders, or drug addiction, or any number of mental illnesses. But locals whispered that her disappearance at fifteen was related to something else altogether."

Ellie's pulse kicked up. "They think she was pregnant?"

She hazarded a glance at Katarina to gauge her reaction, but the other woman's expression was inscrutable.

Jillian nodded. "Yup. When fifteen-year-olds from wealthy families disappear for nine months, it tends to set tongues wagging." Her smile faded. "Except, she wasn't pregnant anymore when the newspaper delivery boy stumbled upon her body. She was dead, though. Stabbed so many times that whoever documented the crime scene used the word 'overkill' to describe what they found."

The gears in Ellie's head started spinning faster. "They never found who did it?"

"Nope. No one was ever even arrested, much less convicted. The police were stumped for suspects."

Ellie chewed on her cheek. A brutal crime scene. Stumped for suspects. Potential ties to Kingsley. This was all adding up in a horrible way. "So, Morrigan Rhett could have been Letitia and Kingsley's daughter."

Katarina smacked the arm of the chair. "Or she could have been the daughter of about five million other people. This is so stupid. How is speculating on them helping to find my daughter? I doubt this Morrigan person was related to Kingsley, anyway."

Jillian studied a paper and shook her head. "I don't know. I think it's a real possibility. The timing of the adoption is perfect, plus, the nature of the murder later?"

"I'm with Jillian. This feels right."

Katarina scowled at Ellie. "Is that what the Charleston PD is teaching their officers these days?"

Ellie rubbed her temples. "Look, I know this probably sucks for you, but try to remember that we're not doing this for funsies, and we're not doing this to try to upset you more than you already are. We're discussing theories that might be useful in finding your daughter."

Katarina's eyes flashed, but she snapped her mouth shut.

Good. Ellie turned back to Jillian. "So, if Morrigan was pregnant and then murdered, what happened to her baby?"

In unison, Ellie and Jillian's heads swiveled to Katarina. Her nostrils flared, and angry red splotches climbed up her neck. She sprang up from the chair, shaking her head. "No. No way. I told you before, this is all bullshit. *Christ.*"

She turned her back and began pacing up and down the length of Ellie's living room, hugging her arms around her waist and muttering under her breath.

Ellie locked eyes with Jillian again, the two of them coming to a nonverbal agreement. They'd give Katarina a little time to come to terms with the notion that the reason Kingsley had kidnapped Bethany wasn't simply to seek revenge on Katarina but because he was Bethany's flesh and blood.

Bethany's great-grandfather.

Which made Katarina his granddaughter.

Ellie's phone rang while Katarina was still wearing a path in her carpet. When she glanced at the screen and saw her dad's number, her gaze flew to the clock. It was after four. Crap, crap, crap, she'd completely spaced on that one o'clock lunch with her mom earlier. Her dad was probably calling to tell her to quit acting like such a terrible daughter and ditching her mom all the time, only in much nicer words.

"Hi, Dad, I already know what you're going to say, and I'm so sor—"

"Is your mother there with you?" Her dad's voice was clipped and anxious.

Ellie sat up straight, her nerves firing off in rapid succession. "No, I haven't seen her all day."

A strangled noise reached her ear, and Ellie's hands turned to ice. Her dad was a rock, so if he was acting scared, something was really wrong. "What is it? What's happened?"

"Your mother went out for a meeting this morning, and I haven't seen or heard from her since."

28

The security command center housed inside a small room at the Gibbes Museum was as streamlined and clean as the rest of the building, but the lack of colorful art gave the room a sterile vibe. That was fine with Ellie because sterile meant fewer distractions. Katarina tagging along with her was almost more distraction than she could handle already. Especially considering the fried state of Ellie's nerves.

Ellie had already called the restaurant where she was supposed to have met her mother, but she hadn't arrived for the reservation, either. Helen's car was still parked in the museum's lot and her phone had been powered off. With little else to go on, reviewing video might give her their only clue.

A long desk held three monitors, arranged in a slight curve. Behind the desk was a wall of even more monitors, all displaying video feeds from various sections of the museum.

A soft-spoken security guard with a thin white scar that slashed through his left eyebrow and a timid smile hovered near the desk as he explained the setup. "We upgraded our security around three years ago by implementing a custom integration to work with the existing Bosch system. We're digital and wireless now and have multiple cameras in every gallery, plus additional cameras near admissions, the gift shop, and along the building outside."

Ellie held up a hand. She didn't care about the history of the museum's security systems, only the information relevant to her search. She motioned to the video files on the closest monitor. "So, I just click on the correct date and search through the files until I find something?"

"Pretty much. The files are arranged by date and individual camera. I pulled up this morning's footage for you already, so you should be good to go. You can scroll through and double check every bit of footage we recorded."

"Great, thanks." Ellie dropped into the open chair behind the monitor, clicked on the first file, and began scrolling through the feed, searching for a glimpse of peach. Bless her dad's heart for paying attention to what her mother wore. Not all men would have noticed, and that small detail made the difference between Ellie having to slo-mo her way through every second of the feed until she recognized Helen Kline or being able to search at a quicker speed.

Even with that advantage, the process was painfully slow. Every minute that passed ratcheted up Ellie's anxiety to the next level, because every minute she wasted here was another minute her mom was missing.

Countless people streamed across the monitor. Men, women, an entire class of elementary-aged children in bright orange shirts. She hit stop when peach caught her eye and slowed the speed, but it was only an elderly woman in a peach sweater.

Another few minutes elapsed before she paused the

recording again. Her heart lurched. There she was, near the visitor's desk. Looking chic and elegant in her favorite peach blazer and a pair of slim gray slacks. "Got her entering the museum."

In the chair next to her, Katarina grunted a nonverbal reply.

Ellie's nostrils flared, but she channeled her annoyance into the search. The next glimpse of Helen Kline came ten minutes later when she approached a modern painting comprised of bold slashes of color in one of the third-floor galleries. So brief that Ellie could have blinked and missed her entirely.

She dug her fingers into the wooden desk to help temper her rising frustration. "Most of these cameras are pointed at the cashiers or the art pieces on display instead of the patrons."

The guard slanted a glance at her monitor before clearing his throat. "Right, um…well, the security is here to protect the museum's assets, not really the patrons. I'm sorry about that."

Ellie's blood heated. "Are you saying that my mother's countless contributions to this place are irrelevant? That all of the time and effort she's donated to fundraising don't qualify her in your eyes as an asset?"

The security guard cast a bewildered glance at Katarina, who ignored him and picked at her thumbnail. Her apathy toward this entire endeavor wasn't doing much to improve Ellie's mood, either.

The man tugged at the collar of his starched uniform. "I, uh, that's not what I meant. I'm sure the museum values the work your mother does for them." He checked over his shoulder, but there was no one else in the room to run interference for him.

Logically, Ellie realized that none of this situation was his fault and that she should let him off the hook. But at this precise moment, logic was taking a back seat to stress. Fine, so maybe she wasn't handling this well, but who could blame her? Her mother was missing, and she didn't have the time or inclination to mince words.

She settled back to work, checking the time stamp she'd jotted down from the first clip of her mom by the entrance and rewinding the parking lot footage to ten minutes before that. Two minutes in, she spotted Helen Kline's Mercedes pulling into a parking space.

After watching her elegant mother exit the lot and finding nothing amiss, Ellie switched to the footage from the front entrance. Her mom climbed the museum's steps one minute and forty-three seconds after the parking lot footage ended. Nothing unusual jumped out at Ellie. No strange men lurking around, and definitely no Kingsley.

From there, she skipped ahead again, to the time when her mom first appeared in the upstairs gallery. Combing through the images was tedious work and strained Ellie's eyes. Forty-five minutes in, her temples started to ache. She rubbed the spot with her hands and continued to watch.

So far, she'd caught glimpses of Helen Kline in both third-floor galleries and again on the second floor, peering at a nineteenth-century portrait. After that, she'd shown up multiple times on the camera situated near the atrium. Three times in twenty minutes, which led Ellie to conclude that she was waiting for someone to meet her there.

As she continued hunting through the feed, Ellie's hurried conversation with her mom that day in the parking garage before she'd found Fortis sifted through her mind. There'd been a lunch date that she'd agreed to and missed. Apart from jokingly asking Jillian to cancel for her, Ellie had been so wrapped up in the investigation that the meet-up had completely escaped her mind. Until now.

Her stomach knotted. If only she'd remembered that stupid lunch earlier, they'd have noticed her mom's disappearance much sooner. Possibly even recovered her by now because Helen Kline's perfect Southern manners meant never no-showing for a meeting or engagement. Ellie racked her brain, trying to recall what her mom had said about why she'd needed to schedule for a late lunch. Had she mentioned the museum or a meeting? Ellie hadn't paid enough attention to remember, a fact that she could smack herself for now.

She never gave her mom enough credit for all her accomplishments. Not that a mom should need to achieve a bunch of stuff in order to gain her daughter's attention. The truth was, though, that Helen Kline gave endlessly to both their family and community. Only Ellie had been such a crappy daughter lately that her mom's achievements barely registered.

Not until after she disappeared.

Ellie's heart was a giant boulder in her chest, crushing her ribs with the expanding weight. What if she'd squandered her chance to tell her mom how proud she was of her? Helen Kline was a force of nature. Ellie bet there were queens who hadn't ruled their kingdoms nearly as well. Her mom had always run the family like a well-oiled machine, somehow managing to keep track of the house, appointments, school, family obligations, and charity work without ever appearing flustered or breaking into a sweat.

Ellie pressed her fingers to her throbbing temples in hopes the pressure would stop the tornado from tearing through her head.

Now her mom was missing, along with Bethany. Almost certainly snatched by Kingsley, yet they were no closer to sniffing out his hidey-hole than before.

Ellie dropped her hands and glared at Katarina, who idly swiveled back and forth with her eyes closed. As if the situation weren't bad enough, she had a known criminal tagging along on the job. Who knew what the other woman was planning? Ellie certainly had no clue.

Katarina was as slippery as a wet seal, and Ellie trusted her about as much as she would one of the animals with a net full of fresh fish. "You said you wanted to help, but every time I look at you, you're not even pretending to check the video feed. I realize you probably don't give a damn about my mom, but I at least expected you to try, for Bethany's sake."

The chair abruptly stopped spinning when the soles of Katarina's combat boots smacked the floor. "First, fuck off. Second, fuck off again. Third, Kingsley is too smart to be caught on camera, and on the minuscule chance he was, no one would recognize him. Fourth…"

She arched her brows at Ellie, who rolled her eyes. "Let me guess…fuck off?"

The corner of Katarina's lips nearly reached her ears. "There, see? You really are smarter than you look."

Ellie stifled an irritated sigh and snuck a peek at the security guard to gauge his reaction to their extremely unprofessional exchange. His eyes were trained on the monitors like his life depended on it, though his body language spoke wonders. Poor guy had scrunched himself into the half of the chair farthest away from them as if trying to avoid their negative vibes.

She pressed her palms to her eyes and released a soft moan. She couldn't blame him. Even she didn't want to be here. The worst part was that the sick knife twist in her gut told her that Katarina was probably right about Kingsley being too smart to show up in the footage.

"Tell me about your mother. Is she strong?"

Katarina's quiet command triggered another low protest to slip from between Ellie's lips. Ugh, what fresh hell was this? Was the other woman so bored that she'd decided tormenting Ellie with stupid questions was preferable to scouring the recordings? "Why?"

"Because with Kingsley, strong women last longer."

Shock zinged down Ellie's spine. Was this some kind of sick game, or was Katarina actually attempting to reassure her? She regarded the woman's profile with suspicion. "How so?"

Katarina's jaw tightened. "Weak women don't hold his interest for long. He bores easily, and once he's bored, they're of no more use to him. It's different with strong women, though. He appreciates the challenge. Enjoys breaking them first, so they last longer." She swiveled her head to stare at Ellie, the hard glint in her eyes proving that this was no game. "So, I ask again, is Helen Kline strong?"

A lump lodged in Ellie's throat as her mind flashed to the hundreds, maybe thousands of times over the years when she and her mom had butted heads. Nothing made Helen Kline back down from a challenge other than personal choice.

Was Helen Kline strong? That was like asking if the Charleston summers were hot.

With difficulty, Ellie swallowed around the lump. "Yeah. She's one of the strongest women I know."

Katarina nodded. "Then focus on that. More than anything else, it will buy us time."

Some of the pain behind Ellie's eyes eased. "Thank you."

An unreadable expression flashed across the other woman's face and vanished again when she smirked. "Don't bother making me a BFF bracelet yet."

"Wasn't planning on it."

"Good." A brief silence yawned between them. "Do you and your mom get along?"

The surprise question prompted Ellie to laugh. "Uh, define 'get along.'"

"That good, huh?"

"Pretty much. Don't get me wrong, my mom is a great person and is a great mom. We've just never really agreed on...well, much of anything. Even as a kid, I was different. A tomboy, always dirty and bringing home bugs or frogs. My mom already had two boys and was so excited for a girl. Except I turned out to be wilder and more rebellious than any of the boys in our family, and my very socially correct mother wasn't quite sure what to do with me."

Half of Katarina's mouth tipped up. "Well, as someone who's still figuring all this motherhood shit out, I can say with certainty that being a mom isn't as easy as it looks on TV. And I've only been with Bethany for a few months and missed all the difficult baby and toddler stages."

The other woman acted like missing those stages was no big deal, but the hands twisting together on the desk told a different story. Ellie studied her former nemesis. "That has to be hard on you, missing all those milestones."

Katarina stared at her hands. "Yeah. There's not a day that goes by that I don't wonder about that, about how things might have been different. But I try not to get too caught up in that line of thinking. Sometimes I even wonder...if maybe it was for the best."

Ellie's heart went out to the woman. "How so?"

Katarina lifted a shoulder. "I was sixteen when I had her and completely unprepared for all the responsibilities that go along with caring for a kid. From the first day they're in your care, you are one-hundred-percent responsible for keeping them alive. For meeting their needs, not hurting them, helping them grow into decent humans who have a real shot at a happy, semi-normal life. Don't get me wrong, I'll never stop hating him for taking my daughter from me and lying about her being...gone. But at least Bethany ended up in decent homes and wasn't damaged."

To give her privacy, Ellie focused on the monitors while Katarina swiped at her eyes. "I think that's a pretty impressive realization to have."

Katarina waved a hand. "Nah. You know what's impressive? That your mom managed to raise four kids. Sure, the money helps, but it sounds like all your siblings turned out to be reasonably well-adjusted human beings. Not quite sure what happened to you, but hey, at least you're not in jail. Yet."

Ellie's laugh was genuine. "Gee, thanks for the vote of confidence."

"Anytime." Katarina smiled before shooting Ellie a sideways glance. "Seriously, though, you should cut your mom some slack. Having a small human completely dependent on you for every single need is an enormous pressure. You two might clash, but it also sounds like you respect the hell out of her. Yeah, I'm new at this gig and have a shit ton left to learn, but I can tell you this for sure. Nothing is more satisfying than having your kid give you a heartfelt compliment or a simple I love you. When Bethany says that, my heart melts, and I don't even have a damn heart."

Ellie studied Katarina for a long time. "Funny. Once upon a time, I would have agreed with you, but I don't know, Volkov. I think the motherhood gig is softening you up like a campfire marshmallow."

Katarina screwed up her face. "Whatever. Let's throw down sometime soon, and we'll see who's soft."

Despite the challenge, Ellie sensed an undercurrent of relief in the woman's voice. "Oh, and if you ever need to learn mom tips, I'm sure mine would be more than happy to share. Once we find her."

"And Bethany."

Both of them sobered over the reminder of what was at stake. Katarina scooted closer to the desk and focused on her monitor.

Another ten minutes passed before Ellie located her mom heading for the museum's exit. "She's leaving. Let's check the footage from just outside the front entrance and the parking lot. You take the parking lot. I'll do the entrance." Pulling up one feed on each monitor saved time.

After a minute of silence, Ellie surged forward. "There. I've got her walking down the front steps."

"Anything look weird?"

"No. Nothing at all. She doesn't talk to anyone, doesn't stop to check her phone. What the hell?"

Tension hitched Ellie's shoulders toward her ears as she tracked her mom's progress as far as that camera allowed. What if this entire endeavor turned out to be a huge waste of time? For all they knew, her mom could have been abducted after leaving the museum.

Katarina pointed. "Here she is, close to the parking lot."

Ellie crowded closer to Katarina and leaned forward to get a better view of the monitor. "Okay, she's walking, walking, walk…wait, why's she stopping?" She'd been the source of Helen Kline's impatient head tilt enough to identify the gesture, but the annoyed gesture was quickly displaced by a far more troubling expression. "Freeze it. There, does she seem worried to you?"

Katarina frowned. "I don't…yeah, maybe. Or confused? By whatever caught her attention off screen. What's she looking at? Can we find out?"

"I think so. Let's finish this feed out first, though. Use slo-mo."

About ten seconds in, Helen Kline turned away from her car and headed toward an alley that lined the far side of the museum.

What the hell are you doing, Mom?

"Is your mom usually impulsive like that?" Katarina asked as Helen's image disappeared from the camera's view.

"No. I'm not even sure impulsive is in Helen Kline's vocabulary." Ellie's stomach filled with lead as she turned to the security guard. "Hey, can you tell me what's over here?"

He scooted his chair across the floor to peer at the screen. "That's the delivery bay, where the vans come to bring the food."

"Then there should be a camera feed there, right? Since it's an entrance into the museum?"

"Yeah. Check number eight, I think?"

"Thanks."

Ellie clicked on the file for the number eight camera and fast-forwarded to the correct spot. Her mom appeared in the frame, striding past the kitchen entrance and disappearing from view again. Ellie smacked the desk. "Dammit."

She went to rewind the footage, but Katarina's hand stilled hers. "Look." Katarina pointed to the edge of the screen.

A car cruised into the frame, following the same path Ellie's mom had walked only moments before. Something about the silver vehicle's deliberately slow pace made Ellie think of a predator. Like a hungry shark approaching a swimmer.

She shivered as the images continued to stream. The car rolled to a stop, blocking the only exit. A door opened, but the parking job had been well planned, far enough from the camera that only the intruder's legs showed.

She let the video play through. Sixty seconds passed. Two minutes. Nothing happened, but then—

Ellie hit stop and rewound. "Watch closely. Tell me what you see."

Katarina nodded, and Ellie hit play, unsure whether or not her imagination was running haywire. She'd half convinced herself of that when Katarina pointed at the rear tire. "You mean, that bounce there? Like something heavy just got dumped in the trunk?"

"Yeah." Neither of them needed to voice their fears out loud to understand what the other one was thinking.

The heavy item deposited in the trunk was very likely an adult body.

Ellie's mouth went dry. If that was true, then Kingsley had abducted her mom at eleven-thirty-seven that morning. And because of the stupid camera angle, they had no way of knowing if she was injured or even breathing when he shoved her in the trunk.

A tiny hiccup of distress escaped from between her clenched teeth. Katarina slanted her an alarmed look.

"Shoving the victims he abducts in the trunk is one of Kingsley's go-to maneuvers, and they're almost always healthy and alive. Remember, it's all about the game for him, and dead people make for shitty players."

"Thanks." Ellie was glad there were no mirrors around. She figured she must be giving off serious breakdown vibes for Katarina to bother with reassuring her. She gazed helplessly at the screen. "I just wish we could see something useful. All we have now is a silver car, and knowing him, he ditched it already."

As she was speaking, another figure appeared in the frame. Much skinnier, and short enough that the camera caught the better part of her head.

The girl's face was only in profile a brief moment before she turned her back to the camera, but that second was enough.

Just to be sure, Ellie rewound, hit play, and froze the feed when the girl's face came into view.

"Bethany?" Katarina whimpered the name, the sound so unlike her usual smug tone that Ellie's heart twisted. The other woman reached for the screen as if to stroke the pale cheek, but she jerked her hand back before making contact.

"Hey, are you o—"

Quick as Dr. Jekyll, Katarina whirled on Ellie, her amber eyes blazing. "Don't you dare ask me if I'm okay because I'm not! Nowhere close! What good is all this?" She flung her hand in the direction of the screen. "So now we know for sure he has my daughter, so what? We're nowhere closer to finding her than we were before we sat on our asses watching TV like a couple of stoned teenagers."

Breath quickening at the surprise attack, Ellie reminded herself that not even an hour ago, she'd worried that they'd been wasting time too. Kingsley had Katarina's daughter. The woman had every right to be upset. "This is all just part of the process of how we hunt people down. Sometimes it takes time, but we'll get there."

"Time? We don't have any time!" Katarina jumped to her feet, her teeth bared beneath her snarling upper lip.

Ellie stood too, jamming her fists on her hips. She understood all too well that time was a luxury they didn't have, but she was tracking the leads the best she could. "Do you have a better idea? If so, let's hear it. Either put up or shut up."

Katarina's face contorted, and her right hand balled into a fist. Ellie braced for impact, but the other woman pivoted first and clenched her fingers around the chair instead. "Enough with this two steps behind bullshit and letting him call all the shots. The only way we're going to catch Kingsley is if we quit giving chase and figure out how to get ahead of him. We need to dig into his bag of tricks and draw him out."

"Good in theory, but how do we do it?"

Katarina stared at the image of Bethany's profile a long moment before turning to Ellie. "Do you still have that cell phone Kingsley sent?"

A pit opened up in Ellie's gut. "I'm not sure I like where this is going."

"Tough shit. Do you want to find your mother or not?" Ellie gave a reluctant nod, and Katarina's eyes hardened. "That's what I thought. Get me the phone, and I'll find Kingsley."

29

The two female guests tucked into the chairs behind the cheap, scarred dining table were like night and day in both mannerisms and attitude. The duality pleased me so much that when I reemerged from the kitchen with a plate, I paused to appreciate the intriguing picture they made.

Emaciated and wan in the chair closest to me was Bethany. Her hypervigilant twitches reminded me of a frightened mouse. All she needed was a set of whiskers and a long, skinny tail, and she'd make the perfect pet. Her wary eyes tracked me from beneath the curtain of blonde hair that obscured her face, the strands lank and stringy from lack of a recent shampooing.

After those initial few snafus when she'd been determined to fight me, her training was progressing nicely. Those refrigerator sessions had proven invaluable in my quest to bend her to my will. Not too much longer before her weaker, childish will snapped like a dry twig beneath my foot, leaving her poised to do my bidding.

My gaze shifted to the dining room's other occupant. I couldn't quite repress a sneer. Ellie's mother sat upright in the chair, her posture more suited to tea with the royal family than the predicament she was in. Still so high and mighty, staring chilly disdain down her nose at me at every opportunity, as if her hands and feet weren't tied to the chair, and that wasn't a gag preventing her from speaking. Her haughty attitude couldn't conceal the fresh grease streaks that marred the once elegant peach blazer or the coral lipstick smeared across her left cheek.

The regal tilt of her chin, the patronizing stare, the exquisite posture, all traits that reminded me of Letitia. Except Helen Kline couldn't hold a candle to Letitia Wiggins because the woman seated at my table achieved power through no actions of her own but as a byproduct of her husband's and family's wealth. The far bigger sin, though, was in how she'd squandered her advantages.

No wielding, no manipulating, no bending others to her will. No, Ellie's mother flitted from charity to charity, wrapped up in the erroneous belief that such fundraising efforts for the downtrodden would fill her vapid life with meaning.

Letitia never made such repugnant, wasteful choices or took her power for granted. No, my cunning headmistress wielded hers like a weapon. Had devoted herself to teaching the lessons of power and control to the soft, spoiled adolescents at Far Ridge.

I was proof of that, and due to my former headmistress's meticulous training, Helen Kline would soon learn her money was useless here.

The image of that proud woman bound in such a similar fashion to Ellie when she'd graced my warehouse all those years ago sent delight feathering across my skin.

Like mother, like daughter.

I stepped between my two reluctant guests and set the plate down in front of Bethany. When she spotted the thin sandwich cut into identical halves, her chalky tongue poked out and dabbed at cracked lips. Her body quivered, but in testimony to the progress I'd already made, she didn't fall on the offering like a rabid beast.

"Good girl. You've learned how much Papa dislikes it when you eat before asking. Kids these days can be so entitled, wouldn't you agree, Mrs. Kline?"

The snobby old hag refused to even acknowledge that she'd heard me. I was tempted to grab my pliers and teach her that such insolence wouldn't be tolerated, but no, too soon. The stronger they were, the more I enjoyed stripping their illusion of strength from them, bit by delectable bit.

Today we'd start with a less physical lesson.

"My dearest Bethany, there are far too many people out there who believe that taking care of one another is the key to making the world a better place. Sweet, I suppose, but egregiously misguided because, in fact, the exact opposite is true. The more we give people things for free without forcing them to earn them, the worse the world is for all of us."

I nudged the plate toward Bethany and smiled benevolently at her dirty blonde head.

Her nostrils twitched, but she didn't move a muscle.

"You see, in the end, strength is what matters most. Strength and power. If we provide for the weaklings among us, how will they ever learn to grow stronger? There's a reason that the saying 'survival of the fittest' has persisted over the centuries."

After allowing her a moment to digest that kernel of wisdom, I launched into the current lesson. "As I'm sure you've noticed, there are three people at the table this lovely afternoon, but alas, only two halves of a sandwich. Your task is to select who will dine on peanut butter and jelly and who will go to bed with an empty belly."

Bethany released a tiny, excited squeal. "Really?"

I lifted a finger to caution her. "Now, before you choose, it's my duty as your teacher to point out that your actions will have consequences. First, I understand how tempting it will be to eat the entire sandwich yourself. I also suspect that, having a sweet heart, you will be tempted to split the sandwich with the pretty woman who tried to come to your rescue at the museum. Before you go with either of those options, though, I urge you to consider the potential repercussions very carefully. I beg you to double and triple check that you aren't making poor decisions based on hunger, which can lead even the smartest person to act irrationally. One crucial point to keep in mind at all times is…" I lifted a single finger. "Who wields the most power and," I lifted a second one, "will my choice put me on their good side or bad side?"

Bethany's hollow eyes skittered from the sandwich to my face and back again. Her teeth ripped at her lower lip until the chapped skin bled as she battled out the options in her head.

She had yet to choose when the doorbell rang. The shrillness whipped my head in that direction, my spine rigid with a combination of annoyance and misgiving. I wasn't expecting any callers.

"Stay put. I'll be back in a flash."

As I passed Ellie's mother, I patted her head like I would a stray dog and savored the instant mood boost when she tried to jerk away.

Oh, I'll bring you to heel yet, bitch. Just wait and see.

Apprehension took over as I bent down to peer through the peephole. Once I comprehended the perfectly groomed woman who graced my porch, the only sensation my frozen body experienced was complete and utter shock.

Three sharp, perfect raps on the wood followed, and the

racket knocked me from my stupor. Digging the key from my pocket, I unlocked the bolt and pulled the door open. My heart hammered in my chest, though I managed to keep my reaction from my voice. "Well, well, well. I see we're as demanding as ever, aren't we, Letitia?"

The icy intensity of Letitia Wiggins's eyes as they raked over me from head to toe hadn't thawed a bit in the two-plus decades of our separation, nor had her immaculate appearance. Age had yet to claim her regal bearing or delicate beauty, though her fiery red mane had been swapped for platinum blonde.

Even after so much time had passed, her presence struck a hammer blow to my lungs. I gaped, dizzy as the oxygen rushed free in a startled gasp.

"So, it is you," she murmured. "When you first opened the door, I wondered." She nodded to herself, then switched to a snappier tone. "Now, don't just stand there gawking at me, Mr. Kingsley, invite me in."

Without giving me a chance to do exactly that, she swept inside, pivoted, and pushed the door shut.

Rattled, it took me three attempts to fit the key into the lock. When I faced her again, her elegant hands were balanced on her still slim hips. One dainty shoe tapped a staccato rhythm on the floor. "I cannot tell you how dreadfully disappointed I am that the first occasion we've had to meet since our academy years occurred because I felt compelled to scold you for acting like an absolute fool. Because of whatever antics you've gotten up to, a ridiculous policewoman with even more absurd hair showed up and ruined my salon day."

As surprised as I was, I managed a clever retort. "Not your spa day, how very taxing."

With a huff, her frosty gaze traveled across the house, scrutinizing the contents of the living room with that critical air that dredged up long dormant memories. When she finished, she granted me an approving nod. "I'm pleased that you haven't forgotten my lessons about organization and tidiness."

"I wouldn't dream of it."

"Good. You know, I was quite surprised when I received your invitation to visit you in the mail, though it has been such a very long time. But, silly me, now is hardly the right moment to dwell on such things, is it?"

That same siren's smile I'd spent countless nights dreaming of lit up her face. When her warm palm cupped my cheek, that ancient thrill sizzled beneath my skin.

"My darling boy, have you missed me over the years, the way I've missed you?"

I disliked the sudden difficulty I experienced when I swallowed or the clamminess that broke out beneath my shirt. "You know I have. I never wanted us to be separated the way we were."

"Of course not, although I'm sure you've managed perfectly fine without me. I do hope you think back on our time together with fondness every once in a while. All of those afternoons we spent in my office as I helped transform you from a weak, needy boy who lacked self-control into a strong, disciplined young man." She pressed a palm to her impressive bosom and heaved a theatrical sigh.

"I do remember those days fondly. I credit you, in large part, for the man I am today, and my accomplishments over the years."

At my compliment, she arched her back and all but purred. "Let me have a better look at you." The slow circle she prowled around me was so reminiscent of one of our secret academy sessions that nostalgia filled my mouth like warm honey. "My my, did you make a deal with the devil?

Because time has been ever so gracious to you. Quite a trans-formation, bravo."

Her fingernails grazed my neck as she circled. The touch roused unwanted feelings that forced me to call on my hard-earned reserves of self-control. "And you look almost exactly the same."

"What a lovely falsehood." Her coquettish smile hinted otherwise.

I went utterly still. "I neglected to ask, how were you so sure it was me when I answered the door? Since, as you mentioned, I did undergo a rather extreme transformation."

"Love, I'd recognize you no matter how much you altered your appearance. Did you forget what I always used to say? Like calls to like."

Perhaps the realization that Letitia was the only person who'd recognized me despite my extensive plastic surgery should have come as no surprise, but it did. In all my moments of reminiscing, I'd never once bothered to specu-late over whether or not the eerie power this woman wielded over me would remain intact decades later. Like a dormant volcano poised to erupt.

This wouldn't do.

I stepped away and faced her squarely. "Why are you really here?"

She pouted, and when that didn't yield the desired effect, sighed. "I came to tell you that you should turn your-self in."

After the initial shock of recognizing her on my porch, I'd predicted she wouldn't catch me by surprise again. I'd predicted wrong. "Is this your idea of a joke? If so, might I suggest you search for new material? Because the punchline on this one didn't quite hit."

Her eyes turned glacial. "Don't get smart with me. You're the one who's acted like an utter dolt. Really, how could you be so stupid? Leading an officer to me like that? After everything I've done for you?"

My vision narrowed on her face. "I see. So, this visit is merely because I'm inconveniencing you?"

"Of course not! I already told you that I missed you so very much. More than you could possibly know." She peered at me from beneath her lashes, but I wasn't a green adolescent anymore. I saw right through her tricks.

She kept at them, though. Like I was the same little boy from the academy. A lump of clay ready for her to mold.

"My darling boy, I just want you to be safe. If you turn yourself in, at least I'll know the police won't show up on your porch one day, firing guns into your windows."

The rage built in my veins and acted like antivenom, flushing her poison from my blood. "And then poor, mistreated Letitia could go back to getting her hair done without fear of the big, bad cop ruining her relaxing outing, is that it?" A muscle throbbed in my jaw, but years of practicing self-control rendered my voice calm. Pleasant. "And why would the cops show up on my porch? Not because you'd tell them where I lived, I hope?"

Perhaps like truly did call to like, though, because Letitia seemed to sense my fury. Alarm flickered across her beautiful face before she launched herself into my arms.

I stood like a statue, not moving as her hands roved over my shoulders, my back, my sides, and those sweet, lying lips blew warm air in my ear and whispered seductively. "You know I only ever want the best for you. Let me help you again, the way I did so many times in the past. Without me, you'd still be a shadow of a man, but look at you now. So strong and powerful. I promise not to steer you wrong."

She plastered her bosom to my chest as she blabbered on while I came to a painful realization. In her eyes, nothing had changed. This was no different than that night all those years ago when the boys were locked out in the cold. When we'd woken to the news that our punishment had misfired, gone so much further than we'd intended.

"I still need you." Her hand moved down my chest. "We need each other, now more than ever. We'll keep each other safe, just like we always have."

The words she whispered echoed the ones she'd said that morning.

With a pang of sorrow, I understood now what I'd been too immature, too naïve to comprehend back then.

Letitia wasn't the woman I'd believed her to be. She never had been.

As a lonely, weak boy, I'd bestowed upon her attributes that simply didn't exist, turning an ordinary woman into a figment of my imagination. A superhero, so to speak.

Gazing upon her with a man's eyes, all those fictitious embellishments fell away. She was a beautiful woman, but nothing special. No better, in fact, than Helen Kline.

My hands were gentle as I pushed her away so I could gaze into her eyes. I swept a loose strand of platinum hair behind her ear. "Sweet Letitia, thank you for being there when I needed you."

I basked in the light of her radiant smile for several heartbeats before I snapped her neck.

She collapsed to the floor, and without another glance, I stepped over her dead body and returned to the dining table.

Such a nice surprise I found there.

The plate that waited in front of my empty chair contained the entire sandwich.

30

This late in the day, even the lilting strains of the Mozart symphony spilling through the SUV's speakers made Clay's skull pound, especially when combined with the *tick-tick* of the turn signal as he waited for the stoplight to change.

With an irritated jab of his finger, he shut off the stereo and reveled in the silence that followed. Music was usually a constant companion in his SUV, but Clay couldn't remember the last time he'd been so exhausted. Physically? Sure, but not emotionally. If someone informed him that he and Luke had covered half the state visiting soup kitchens over the past couple of days, he'd believe them. But the driving was only a tiny part of the fatigue.

Failure was by far the larger component weighing him down. Each time he and Luke showed up and checked a soup kitchen off their list without coming closer to finding Caraleigh, a little more hope died.

What happened when they reached the end of the list with no sign of his sister?

The light changed, and Clay swung the SUV into the left turn. The buildings that lined the streets here had gradually turned seedier, with weed patches growing through cracks in the sidewalk and trash collecting in the gutters. Near the end of the block, he pulled into an empty spot by the curb and switched off the engine.

"Here we are." The soup kitchen was located in a warehouse just ahead. Luke gazed out the passenger window without speaking, and Clay turned to the man, concerned. "How are you holding up?"

He didn't expect an answer, and he didn't get one. Luke hadn't uttered a single word since noon that day, right after another unsuccessful visit. Clay wasn't too concerned. Thinking back, Caraleigh used to go nonverbal every once in a blue moon too, especially when she was overstimulated and overtired. It was almost like her operating system was powering into recovery mode.

Clay resisted the urge to reach over and pat Luke's arm or offer any other physical comfort. "I hear you loud and clear. Truth be told, I'm hanging by a thread myself." He heaved a sigh and studied the building through the bug-splattered windshield. "I've spent too many hours to count imagining the moment when I'd find Caraleigh again, in hundreds of different ways. In lots of those fantasies, I fill the hero role and rescue her. In others, she just shows up on my porch out of the blue, or I'm walking down the damn street, and there she is."

Luke still didn't say a word, but Clay noticed that his face had relaxed a bit. Taking that as a good sign, he continued to talk, hoping to soothe him even further.

"Half the time, she's still the same little girl who was at the fair that day she disappeared. The other half of the time, she's a grown woman who's the spitting image of those age-progression sketches. The only thing that stays the same in all of my fantasies is that, the second I realize it's her, I wrap my arms around her, lift her feet off the ground, and swing her in a circle while she squeals with joy."

He shook his head with a rueful smile and let himself fall deeper into the daydream, talking about how they would spend their reunion and all the places they would go when they were back together.

"Too many movies, probably. I've never told anyone that, but I figure you understand better than anyone."

Clay glanced over to check Luke's expression and found half his forehead plastered to the passenger window and his lashes fanning his pale cheek. His t-shirt rose and fell in a slow, steady rhythm.

The tight knot in Clay's chest loosened. "Good for you, buddy. You need sleep even more than I do."

Writing a quick *I'll be right back* note and placing it in Luke's lap, Clay eased open the door and slipped outside. He hit a button on the remote. The click of the doors locking rang loud in his ears, but Luke didn't stir.

He pocketed the keys and headed down the weedy sidewalk toward the white building that housed the soup kitchen. When he opened the door, the scent of warm tomatoes hit him first, masking the ripe odors associated with bodies that lacked regular access to showers.

A line snaked out from a series of tables arranged in a row, with big bowls and plates of steaming food heaped atop them buffet style. Servers, young and old, doled out helpings with smiles as the patrons shuffled by, some quiet and hunched while others stood tall as they laughed and chattered with each other and the volunteers.

After performing a quick survey of the faces in line and the ones already seated at the plastic camping tables and coming up short, Clay swayed on his feet as the tiny flame of hope extinguished. He'd been through this same ritual so many times now that he was starting to feel like Don Quixote. Except, unlike the hero in Cervantes's classic novel, Clay's folly involved running down soup kitchens rather than windmills.

Buckle up, Lockwood. You know how this works. All it takes is talking to one person, the right person, and this case turns on a dime.

That was the same optimistic line he'd shared with any number of colleagues and families over the years. A truth he still believed. But being so emotionally invested in this case made each aspect about a thousand times more intense and each stumbling block that much more painful.

He wasn't sure how much more of this he could take.

After two deep breaths to clear his head, Clay shook off his fatalism and was ready to go again. He meandered among the crowd with the sketch of Caraleigh in hand, asking if anyone recognized her.

As usual, a few of the diners refused to interact with Clay or glance at the picture at all, but most were accommodating. The first three who answered studied the image before shaking their heads, so Clay moved on to a gray-haired man wearing a ratty raincoat over a tie-dyed sweatshirt.

The man scratched his scruffy chin. "Yeah, I reckon I've seen her around."

The first time Clay heard that reply, his heart had leapt in his chest. Twenty similar replies later, he knew to hold his excitement in check. "Any idea when that was?"

A slow shake of his head. "No, afraid not. A couple months ago? Maybe longer?"

Clay thanked the man with a smile and moved on. Every soup kitchen so far had resulted in similar stories. At each location, a handful of people recognized Caraleigh, or at least claimed to, but none of them could recall when.

As upsetting as the response was, Clay tamped down his frustration. Being houseless led to a transient lifestyle, where people were forced to move around a lot based on external factors beyond their control, including weather, food access, police activity, changing safety, and so on. Clay could hardly blame them.

Once he finished with the people in line, he meandered through the tables. A couple of people agreed that she looked familiar, but nobody remembered when they'd spotted her.

His feet were dragging by the time he reached the wizened old lady with hair so thin her scalp showed through. A dowager's hump rose between her frail shoulders. She pursed her lips as she studied the sketch. "Why, yes, I do recall seeing her. Hard to forget a face as pretty as that."

Clay refused to let himself get excited. "Do you remember when you last saw her?"

The woman lifted a bony shoulder, and the sad smile on her face answered first. "I'm sorry, dearie, I can't say that I do. Pretty girl like that, I imagine she moves around more than the rest of us to keep safe. It's hard to be a single woman alone, you know."

"Thank you for your help."

Clay clutched the sketch to his chest as he turned away, hopelessness weighing down every step. Pretty soon, they'd have hit all the soup kitchens, and then what? Would he be forced to throw in the towel and admit defeat?

He fumbled in his pocket for his phone and keyed in Ellie's number. She picked up on the first ring.

"Clay?"

The plaintive hitch at the end of his name was enough for Clay to shove his own worries aside. "What's wrong?"

"It's my mom. Kingsley took her. She's been missing since this morning."

Before she could finish, Clay was striding out the entrance, dipping his shoulders against a gust of chilly wind as he hurried back to the SUV. "Tell me what you need me to do."

31

More moonlight than usual trickled between the cracks in the boarded window, enough that Bethany could make out the nice lady who sat beside her on the bed. Bethany missed the moon, and the stars, and the sun. It felt like she hadn't played outside forever or breathed in fresh air.

But at least she wasn't alone anymore in this tiny, sad room. She was glad for the company. Especially tonight. The woman helped keep her mind from wandering off.

Crack. Thump.

Like that. Bethany whimpered and hugged her knees tight to her chest, shivering.

"Shh, it's okay. We're okay for now, sweetheart. Here, let's cover you up."

Bethany let the woman pull the blanket over her legs and tuck the scratchy material around her waist. "Thank you." She couldn't seem to stop shivering, though. Or reliving those awful moments.

The sharp crack when the bad man twisted the fancy blonde lady's head and the ugly thump when she hit the floor. How after that, the lady's neck was funny and bent too far to the side, and she stared at everything and nothing at all. They were dead and glassy, like one of Bethany's old baby dolls.

Crack. Thump. Those awful, empty eyes.

The woman patted the covers until she found Bethany's hand and squeezed. "What's your name, sweetheart?"

Bethany clung to the woman's hand. *Don't think about that other lady. Talk to this one. She's nice.* "Bethany."

"Bethany? That's such a beautiful name. And how old are you, Ms. Bethany?"

A small, surprised giggle flew from her mouth. "Not Mizz Bethany, silly. Just Bethany. And I'm eight."

"Eight years old? Why, you could have fooled me. You act so grown up, I thought you were at least twelve, maybe thirteen."

Bethany puffed up. Her mama would like that, she bet. "Mama says that sometimes I'm eight going on eighteen, and other times, I'm as silly as a goose."

"That sounds just about right to me. When my daughter was your age, she was exactly like that. Mature as could be one second, and the next, running through the house with dirty feet and shrieking like a girl half her age. Kept me on my toes, that's for sure."

As the woman talked, Bethany relaxed a little. She liked the sound of the woman's voice. So warm and normal. Nothing like creepy Doctor Rotten. "Is being on your toes a good thing?"

The woman made a humming noise in her throat, like she thought Bethany was funny. "You know, that is a very smart question. I suppose it all depends on whether or not a person enjoys a good challenge."

She continued to talk, but the words began running together, like the buzz of those giant bumblebees that used to fly from flower to flower outside Bethany's old school. Lately, Bethany had a hard time concentrating for very long. Her head spun in circles even when she was sitting still, and her stomach ached all the time, like someone had drilled a hole inside.

Still, the woman's voice was so soothing. So much better than being trapped in the bad man's scary dark bedroom by herself. Bethany let the woman's chatter wash over her like a warm breeze as she lifted her fingers to her nose and breathed in.

There. She could still smell the nutty sweetness of the peanut butter sandwich she'd come so close to eating. Bethany inhaled again and imagined the two perfect rectangles on that plate. She could almost feel the bread under her fingers when she picked one half up just before sinking her teeth into the soft, squishy bread and chewing.

She sniffed a third time while pretending to chew. If she tried hard enough, she could almost convince herself that she'd taken a bite.

Crack. Thump.

Bethany dropped her hand and scooted closer to the talking woman, moving across the bed until their shoulders touched.

"Everything okay?"

No. Nothing is okay. I want to go home and see my mama. But Bethany didn't want to sound like a baby. "What's your name?"

"Helen. Helen Kline."

"That's a nice name. I don't have any friends named Helen."

"Then I am very honored to be your first. What do you like to do for fun, Just Bethany?"

Bethany giggled again. "No, not Just Bethany. My name is Bethany. No Mizz, and no Just."

"Oh dear, my mistake." The woman...Helen...had such a nice laugh. "I guess I'm the silly goose now, aren't I? We can be silly geese together."

Bethany could hear the smile in the woman's—*Helen's*—voice and knew she was teasing. "Did you know that boy gooses are called ganders?"

"As a matter of fact, I did know that, but I'm very impressed that you know it too. Is learning about animals what you like to do for fun?"

"No, this kid in my class named Justin did a report on geese, though, and he told us that. His family lives on a farm. They have pigs, goats, geese, chickens, and a horse. Isn't that neat?"

Another of those nice laughs. "Very, although I suspect they spend a lot of time cleaning up animal poop."

Bethany scrunched up her nose. Ew. She'd never considered that. Maybe she didn't want to live on a farm, after all. "I think maybe I just want a dog."

"Dogs sound like a much more manageable pet. Did you know there are some breeds that don't shed very much? That's less time you'd have to spend picking hairs off your clothes."

Interesting. "But they still poop."

The woman's soft laugh filled the room. "Yes, I'm afraid they do. What does your mother say about having a pet?"

Good question. Bethany nibbled her lip as she tried to predict her mama's reaction. "I don't know. I haven't asked her yet." But surely Mama wouldn't say no to one little dog?

"I see. Well, good luck with that. What's your mother like?"

"You mean, the one I have now?"

There was a very long pause before Helen spoke again. "Did you have other mothers before this one?"

"Yeah. Lots more than the other kids at my school. First, I

lived with the Jacksons, and then with Mrs. Spellman, but she was old and grumpy and always yelled that I was too loud and underfoot, so she gave me to her nephew's family."

Bethany never remembered what a nephew was, exactly. Just that it was some kind of relative.

The nice lady rubbed Bethany's hair. "I see."

"They were really nice and bought me lots of stuff, but my favorite mom is the one I have now. She's my real mama, and she searched all over the country until she found me. A bad person stole me when I was a little baby. That's why I had all those other mommies. But my real mama promised that she'd never let anyone take me away from her again."

Bethany's lip started to tremble. She didn't believe her mama had meant to lie, no matter what Doctor Rotten told her. But the truth was, someone had taken Bethany away because...look where she was now. Away from her mama and their cozy little house near the mountains, and trapped in this smelly old house with a scary man who hurt people.

This Helen woman was nice, but she was still a stranger. Bethany wanted her own mama, her own bed, the food in her own kitchen that she could eat whenever she was hungry. She wanted to run from this place, as far away as possible, and never ever have to think about the bad man ever again.

Bethany sniffed once, and again. After that, it was like she'd turned on a faucet. Her nose turned all snotty, and tears streamed down her face, no matter how hard she tried to hold them back. The sobs came next, wrenching out of her chest so hard that her ribs hurt.

"Oh honey, I'm sorry. I know you must miss your mother so much right now."

Bethany didn't resist when the woman's gentle hands gathered Bethany tight to her chest. Hugging another person felt so good, even while she was crying. Made Bethany feel safe for the first time since the bad man stole her.

Her sobs grew quieter, but Bethany wasn't ready for the woman to let her go. She snaked her arms around the woman's neck and clung with all her might, pressing her damp nose to the woman's soft skin. Not her mama, but at least Helen smelled good, like flowers and vanilla. Her hands were soft and gentle as they rubbed Bethany's back and head.

The lumpy old mattress creaked when the woman began rocking Bethany, back and forth, back and forth. She hummed as she moved, stroking Bethany's hair until her quiet sobs softened to quieter ones, and then those turned into hiccups.

The woman stopped rocking but kept Bethany safe in her arms like a caterpillar in a cocoon and continued to smooth her hand down Bethany's head.

"I remember doing this with my daughter when she was a little girl sometimes, but now she's a big girl, all grown up. I'm so proud of her. She's fierce and brave and stronger than most people can dream of. She could have had an easy life, but instead, she chose to put herself in dangerous situations to help people. And she does help a lot of people, all the time. She's beautiful, inside and out. Kind of like you."

Bethany hiccupped once more before leaning back. "She kinda sounds like Wonder Woman."

"Does she? What's Wonder Woman like?"

"Brave, and strong, and beautiful. She was born on a secret, magic island but left so she could fight bad guys and for truth and justice. Her family was upset with her, and she was very sad, but she left anyway because she knew that helping people was her destiny."

The hand on Bethany's hair stilled, and when the woman spoke, her voice sounded thick at first, like she'd swallowed a bunch of marbles. "That does sound a lot like my daughter. She's a police officer, so she fights bad guys too, and her family wasn't thrilled with her job when she first told them about her plans, either. I hope she knows how proud we are, though."

"What about the magic island?"

Helen's hand began stroking again. "No magic island, although she did grow up in Charleston, which is almost the same thing."

The woman's voice was clear again now as she continued to tell Bethany about her brave daughter. Bethany relaxed into her arms and let her mind float, trying to picture the superhero policewoman.

As she drifted off, lulled by her new friend's soft, calming stories, Bethany dreamed that Helen's daughter showed up to rescue them, riding a giant goose and circling her golden lasso in the air.

32

K atarina stopped pacing when the front door to the Charleston Police Department opened but resumed again when an unfamiliar balding man in a blue beat cop uniform strode out.

She huffed the brisk evening air and stomped her boots a little harder. What the hell was taking Officer Carrot Top so long to cut through that bureaucratic red tape? Had she gotten distracted by a rogue box of donuts?

"I'm sure it won't be too long now."

Katarina growled low in her throat and speared the roommate with a murderous glare. Not too long? Please. This trip had already taken too long, with Ellie still nowhere in sight. If Jillian and her big, slobbery mutt weren't here babysitting, Katarina would have snuck into the precinct by now. Once she'd stolen the phone, she would have slipped back out, with no one the wiser.

"But no, we had to do it the 'right' way." Katarina curled her fingers to form air quotes as she muttered to herself and stomped.

"What was that?"

"Nothing." Great, now she'd really snagged the tiny blonde's attention. Katarina hunched her shoulders and presented the woman with her back. Although she doubted the technique would help. In the short time she'd spent in Jillian's presence, Katarina had learned that the cop's energetic roommate rarely took a hint. Subtle or otherwise.

"It's going to be okay. I promise Ellie knows what's she's doing."

See? The woman was like a walking, talking positivity meme.

Not only that, but in this case, Jillian was wrong. Katarina doubted very much that Ellie had the slightest inkling what she was doing. Not in this particular situation. The redhead clung to the romanticized versions of the justice system. Fairy tales about how following legal procedures and cooperating with law enforcement would result in a happily ever after, with the bad guys vanquished and behind bars and the good guys riding off into the sunset.

Bullshit.

Katarina's boot crunched a dead twig on the pavement. She slammed her foot down, again and again, not stopping until the wood turned to splinters. Maybe that Pollyanna fantasy played out when dealing with small-time lawbreakers or minor felons, but not with criminals like Kingsley. The monster who'd raised and trained her would never be held by the law.

Her muscles twitched with the need to do something, anything, to help save her daughter, so she started pacing again. The police...Ellie...the FBI. They all suffered from the same delusion, that they could just arrest Kingsley like anyone else and lock him up for life.

She hugged her arms across her chest, digging her fingers into her triceps. They didn't understand him like Katarina did. Didn't realize that if they locked him up, he'd only find a way out. Either by impersonating a guard, or starting a prisoner riot, or injuring himself, or hell, even pretending to be dead. The how didn't matter. The point was, no prison would hold Lawrence Kingsley for long.

He'd call on other criminals who benefitted from his tangled web of shady enterprises to help him break free and end up back on the streets, playing God with people's lives in no time.

Katarina let loose an enraged snarl and kicked the pavement. The mutt barked and bounded over, lunging at her toe with her butt in the air.

"I'm not playing with you, stop!" She bared her teeth at the dog, who barked again and wagged her tail faster.

"Sam, get back here!"

Jillian yanked on the dog's lead, and with a whine, she slunk back to her side. "Sorry about that. Sam gets a little silly sometimes." She cleared her throat. "So, what's one of your favorite memories with Bethany, or the best day you spent together? Sometimes focusing on happy times can help with the stress."

Katarina stopped pacing long enough to fix the blonde with a death stare. Stress? Did this annoying little cheerleader really think she could teach Katarina about stress? She'd experienced more stress in a few months of her childhood than Jillian probably had in her entire perky-ass life.

Stress and bloodshed.

Off the top of her head, Katarina could conjure up at least seven ways to snuff the light from those blue eyes before Ellie even stuck her little toe out the door. If Jillian kept up with the intrusive questions, she might let her itchy fingers demonstrate one of them.

Play nice. You still need their help. "My memories are private."

"Got it, sorry. I was just trying to help give your mind a break from worrying."

"Maybe I want to worry."

Jillian grunted but wisely kept her mouth shut and stooped down to pet her mutt. Too anxious to sit still, Katarina returned to marching up and down the pavement. Instead of fretting over the delay, though, her mind drifted to that night back in the government office when she'd fidgeted and paced and ripped off her cuticles while waiting to be reunited with her daughter.

Her stress levels had skyrocketed that evening too, but for entirely different reasons.

In the months leading up to that night, Katarina had devoted all her time and energy to reclaiming Bethany. Joy like no other had filled her soul when the little girl appeared across the room, then had taken a tentative step toward her. What Katarina hadn't been prepared for were the fear and doubts that dive-bombed her, like a pelican swooping after a tasty fish.

Standing there, in that stuffy office, Katarina had forgotten how to breathe. What did she know about being a mother? About keeping an entire other person alive, and not even a full-grown one at that?

A sudden urge to flee had seized her legs. No. She'd screwed up. She needed to tell them all that she'd made a huge mistake. Bethany would be better off adopted by a loving family. Anyone. Just not Katarina.

She'd shaken off the panic paralyzing her vocal cords and prepared to tell them as much.

Until the little girl appeared with the tall FBI agent in the cowboy hat and piped up in her sweet, high voice. "Who are you?"

Katarina's hardened, jaded heart had melted on the spot. She was this beautiful little creature's mama.

Her legs had buckled, and she'd dropped to her knees. "I'm your real mother. Your first mother. Your last mother. Your forever mother." Eyes wet with tears, she'd opened her arms wide and waited.

Across the room, Bethany had sucked on her lower lip and hesitated.

The disappointment had hit hard, but Katarina hid the emotion. She understood better than most the confusion and chaos that kids internalized when they were constantly shuffled from home to home.

The next instant, Bethany had taken one halting step, her little face solemn. That step turned into another, and another, until her shoes pounded the floor, and she'd launched herself in Katarina's arms.

When that warm little body pressed itself to hers in the awkward hug, Katarina's heart squeezed, pumping love and protectiveness through her vessels like oxygen. She'd made a silent vow right then and there over that sweet-smelling blonde head that they'd never be separated again. That she'd go to whatever lengths necessary to keep her daughter safe.

And she had. Right up until Kingsley swept them all up into another one of his demented games.

Despair crashed over her. That psychopathic asshole who'd raised her had shattered Katarina's vow into oblivion. Stolen her daughter for the second time, and why? As punishment for her sins? Because he couldn't bear for one of his little chickens to fly the coop?

"Argh!" Katarina whirled and lashed out. Again and again, while her blood boiled with helpless rage.

"Uh, I don't think that cement block is going to care much about your rude treatment, but your toes might."

Jillian's wry comment prompted Katarina to pause and glance down. She'd been so pissed that she hadn't even realized she was kicking cement. And, dammit, now that she mentioned it, Katarina's big toe *was* throbbing.

She shook out her foot, glaring at the wall. "You're lucky I don't have a sledgehammer."

"Okay, that does it. Let's walk across the street and grab a coffee before you go all *Fixer Upper* on government property and land both of our asses in trouble."

Katarina's knee-jerk reaction was to snarl and tell the little busybody to mind her own damn business. But her toe hurt, and she was going nuts marching around out here in the cold while Ellie took her sweet ass time.

Once the phone was safe in Katarina's hands, she could give a shit if the entire building and surrounding area— including the stupid, incredibly hard wall—imploded and disappeared into a giant sinkhole right then and there. Until that time, she could use a distraction.

Preferably before she lost her shit, charged inside the precinct, and landed her butt in a holding cell. "Fine. Coffee shop. But you're paying."

A few minutes later, she straddled a chair at a small outdoor table, plucking at the cardboard sleeve on her cup in-between sips of black coffee. She'd chosen a spot with a clear view of the police station's front doors. The next time they swung open, two people emerged into the halo of illumination cast by the exterior light fixtures. Even from across the street, Ellie's red hair glowed like a beacon, and her appearance eased the chokehold on Katarina's stomach.

Finally.

A tall, muscular man in a cowboy hat exited with her. It was the FBI agent who'd helped arrange her WITSEC deal.

Katarina's eyes narrowed as she blew on the fragrant steam. Agent Studly was walking awfully close to Ellie, much closer than she'd expect two regular old law enforcement partners would. Did that mean the hot agent and Detective Carrot Top were an item now? Interesting.

"Over here!" Jillian waved at Ellie, who scoured the patio until she spotted them and waved back. The FBI agent pulled a phone from his pocket and pressed it to his ear, motioning her to go ahead.

The detective nodded and jogged across the street while Katarina sipped the bitter brew with a scowl. Great, *now* Detective Carrot Top showed a little hustle. Where the hell was that speed inside the precinct when Katarina had stood around with her thumb up her ass?

After all this time, Ellie had better not be joining them empty-handed, either. It would be such a shame if Katarina's coffee just so happened to end up all over that shiny red hair.

Katarina's fingers flexed around the cup, relaxing again when Ellie plopped into a chair and slid the confiscated phone onto the table.

"Got it."

"Good job!" Jillian beamed at her roommate like she'd performed some sort of miracle.

Katarina gritted her teeth. "If you're all done with the cheerleading, could we, I don't know, actually look at the freaking phone now?"

Instead of the irritated response Katarina expected, Ellie lifted her eyebrows at her friend. "Has she been this delightful the entire time I was inside?"

"Why do you think we're at the coffee shop? I was afraid if we stood outside the precinct door for much longer, she was going to charge inside and start tearing the place up until she found the phone herself."

In unison, their heads swiveled toward Katarina, who slouched lower in the uncomfortable plastic chair. Huh. Maybe the tiny blonde elf-girl was more observant than she'd given her credit. "What? It was taking forever! And I would have snuck in, not torn the place up. I'm not a complete idiot," she mumbled at the table.

Someone snorted, but when Katarina's head whipped up, both of them wore bland expressions. The phone chimed as Ellie thumbed the power button. "Either way, I'm here now, so let's get to work."

They poked around a bit before opening the messages between Katarina and Kingsley.

As she read, a pit opened up in the bottom of her stomach. Each message forced her to relive the emotional avalanche that pummeled her when she'd realized Bethany was gone. First shock, then denial. The worst, though, was the icy terror. A wave so intense, she'd felt like she was drowning in fear.

That same terror lapped at her now and threatened to freeze her to the chair. She slammed her injured toe into the ground, gasping at the pain. Embracing it.

Good. At least pain motivates you to move. Fear is worthless, so quit cowering behind the table with your thumb up your ass and do something.

Katarina's nostrils flared. Why the hell *was* she sitting here, sipping coffee and checking messages like she didn't have a care in the world? She needed to act. Do something. Anything.

Her muscles coiled in anticipation. She was about to spring to her feet when the last text message caught her eye. Katarina eased back into her chair, frowning at the date. "This one was sent yesterday."

Ellie leaned closer. "What the hell?"

All three of them peered at the text bubble.

18414072112258017182123110611421158222318170

"I'm guessing it's some kind of code?" Jillian squinted at the string of numbers. "I just have no idea what."

Jillian pulled three pens out of her oversized purse and

tossed them on the table. While Ellie and Jillian transferred the numbers onto their napkins and brainstormed over what the text could mean, Katarina drew swirls on hers as her mind flashed to a memory. The first day when Kingsley sat her down at the dining room table and lectured about codes.

"Codes are often the perfect tool for foiling and befuddling even those people who claim to be of superior intelligence, which is why it's important that we learn about them. The code I'm teaching you tonight is called the Caesar Cipher."

Calm washed over her as she stared at the numbers.

18414072112258017182123110611421158222318170

After transcribing the numbers into letters, she ended up with *Rdn Gulyh Qruwk Fkduohvwrq.*

Her lips parted, and her pulse drummed a furious tempo in her ears. Katarina didn't need to brainstorm and scribble countless letter-number combinations on the damp, wadded-up napkin.

She'd already deciphered the code. She knew exactly where that monster was.

Now, she just needed to hide that newfound knowledge from Jillian and Ellie.

Katarina rose and began circling the table, shaking out her arms and hands like anxiety was back for another round.

Ellie glanced up from her napkin. "Everything okay?"

"I'm fine. I was feeling stressed sitting still, so I'm walking." She stomped a few more paces for good measure. "And I don't need you checking in on me every few seconds like I'm a baby."

Ellie sighed. "Great, then maybe you could help us out with the code? This was your idea, after all."

Katarina stopped and bent over the table, making a big show of inspecting the detective's chicken scratches. Nonsense, all of them. "Maybe we should try grouping blocks of numbers together and searching for patterns that way." Of course, the Caesar Cipher didn't work like that, but it should keep them busy for a while.

Jillian rubbed her eyebrow and squinted. "Okay, but how many numbers do we think form a block?"

"I don't know, let me see." Katarina leaned over the table and pretended to grab for Jillian's notes, making sure to strike the coffee cup with her elbow. The cup toppled over, and the lid flew off, spilling hot brown liquid everywhere.

Jillian and Ellie both jumped out of their seats like scalded cats.

"Shit, sorry! Here, let me wipe it up." Plucking a handful of napkins from the metal dispenser, Katarina mopped the spill off the table. On her third pass, she swept the cell phone toward the edge and into her other hand before shoving the device into her pocket. "Ugh, now I've got more coffee on me than on the table. Be right back. I'm going to try to wash some of this off in the bathroom."

"Yeah, okay," Ellie muttered.

Both the detective and her roommate were too engrossed in reorganizing the notes that had fluttered to the ground to pay her much attention. She swept the streets and spotted the bodyguard several yards away, his back to them all. Good. Hopefully, the task would distract the two little code-breakers for long enough to give Katarina time to make her escape.

While they smoothed the napkins into neat rows on the freshly mopped table, Katarina slipped into the coffee shop through the patio entrance. She beelined for the bathroom tucked into the back corner but swerved right at the last possible second, shoving out the rear exit without breaking stride.

Turned out, teamwork wasn't for her. No surprises there. Too slow, too many rules, and too damned annoying by far.

Ellie and Jillian had served their purpose, but now it was time for Katarina to face Kingsley alone.

Hunching her shoulders against the brisk night breeze, Katarina scurried down the sidewalk, turned into the alley, and put as much distance as possible between her and the coffee shop.

In the end, this was between her and Kingsley. One sociopath to another.

For a brief period in that house in Wyoming, Katarina had imagined a new life for her and Bethany, one where Kingsley still existed, just not in her orbit. The moment he'd kidnapped Bethany, though, she'd accepted the truth.

This would never end. Not until one of them was dead.

I'm coming for you, Papa.

33

Crumpled napkins piled up in front of Ellie like discarded tissues in a melodramatic movie scene after the heroine suffered a heartbreak. The numbers on her latest attempt at deciphering the code swam before her eyes, and a knifelike pain stabbed her skull. She was a detective, not a codebreaker. She didn't even like those stupid Sudoku puzzles her dad had encouraged her to try when she was younger. Who knew how long it would take them to crack the code? Thirty more minutes? An hour? A day?

Never?

Ellie groaned and dropped her face into her hands. They didn't have time for this. Not her mother, and not Bethany, either. But of course, here they sat. Dancing once again to Kingsley's tune. Was that his plan? To force them to waste time trying to solve this ridiculous puzzle? Did he even have a plan beyond his enjoyment of serving as puppet master and pulling on their collective strings?

"Wow, you two are really focused on whatever you're doing there. In the thirty seconds I've been standing here, neither of you looked up once."

Ellie lifted her head. "Sorry. This code is a killer."

Jillian blew air from her cheeks. "Yeah, I'm glad you're here because we could definitely use the help."

Clay feigned rolling up his sleeves. "All right, let's see what we've got here." He scanned the patio. "Where's Katarina?"

The question hit Ellie like an electric shock. She bolted upright and traded an alarmed glance with Jillian before searching the patio herself. No Katarina.

Jillian sprang to her feet with so much force, the plastic chair tipped and clattered to the pavement, startling Sam, who yelped and darted under the table. "You big wimp, you're not in trouble. But you can help me look for Katarina." She tugged the lead, and the dog trotted back out, following Jillian as she hurried around the corner.

"Shit." Ellie watched her roommate and dog disappear while digging into her pocket for her cell phone. The line rang once. Twice. Three times.

Come on, come on, pick up, Ellie urged, her knuckles white on the case.

The phone rang two more times before an automated voice mail service picked up.

Ellie squeezed the phone while waiting for the beep.

"Dammit, Katarina, what the hell are you doing? Call me before you screw this all to hell." Ellie rattled off her cell number before ending the call with a stab of her finger. She laid her head on the table, silently cursing both Katarina and herself with every breath, but mostly herself. So stupid. She'd known that Katarina would jump at any chance to find her daughter, but she'd still gone and let her guard down.

After counting to ten, she straightened and pulled up a contact. The lab tech answered on the first ring.

"This is Carl."

Ellie mouthed a silent prayer. "Carl, it's Ellie. Remember

the phone I had you LoJack, oh," she checked the time, "around thirty minutes or so ago?"

The tech whistled. "Don't tell me you need me to track it down already."

"Yup, that's exactly what I'm telling you."

He whistled. "Wow, good thing you stopped by and had me take care of that before you left the station. This might be the fastest service request ever. Never fear, I'll get you that info quicker than Thor can reach for his hammer. Except, yeah, no good, I forgot about *Avengers: Endgame*."

Ellie drummed her fingers on the table and held her impatience in check. Barely. "I don't have time for pop culture references, Carl."

"Right, right, sorry! I just meant, yeah, I'll get that info to you ASAP."

"Fantastic. Oh, and once you report back with the info, can you fill Chief Johnson in on what's happening?" Hopefully, by the time the chief got around to checking in, Ellie would be close to catching up with Katarina. This definitely qualified as one of those "it's better to ask forgiveness than permission" scenarios.

"Sure thing."

"Thanks, you're the best."

"You know it."

Clay was ready as soon as Ellie disconnected the call. "What's the play? We going after her?"

Beneath her rib cage, something softened at Clay's simple assumption. *We.* How good that one little word sounded.

On the outside, though, she worked to project steely resolve. "The play is, I'm going after her. Solo."

Ellie braced herself for the eruption that was guaranteed to follow. It didn't take long. After two seconds of gazing slack-jawed at her like she'd grown a third eye in the middle of her forehead, Clay smacked his palm to the table.

"The hell you are!"

Shane appeared at their side. "What's going on?"

Jillian had just rejoined them, but after a quick glance at their faces, began to slowly back away. "Right. So, Sam and I are heading over to help Carl out. Text me when you figure everything out, bye." Dog by her side, she scampered off toward the street.

Clay ignored Jillian's retreat. His mutinous gaze never left Ellie's. She held her ground, thrusting out her chin while meeting his stare. Seconds slipped by, with neither of them backing down.

When the tension stretched Ellie's nerves so taut she feared they might snap, she broke the silence. "I don't want to put you in danger." She looked over at Shane. "You either, so…you're fired."

Neither man moved.

Clay looked like he was chewing on nails. "I understand, and that's very noble of you. But what you need to understand is that we make a good team. And we're far better together than we ever could be apart." He leaned forward and placed his hand near hers on the table, palm up. "Plus, it's kind of my job, putting myself in danger to catch bad guys."

Hesitating, she bit her lip. One glance into his gleaming brown eyes and her stubborn determination to track Kingsley alone flew right out the door.

Clay was right. They were more effective together.

Ellie pressed her palm to his. "Okay. Just promise not to die on me, okay? Because if you do, I'm going to be pissed."

Clay laced their fingers together and squeezed. "Then I'll do my damnedest to comply. I've seen you pissed before. It's not pretty."

Despite the tension clamping down on her shoulders with a vice grip, Ellie snickered. "Good." She turned to her bodyguard, who looked like he was ready to thrash her. "This could be dangerous."

Shane simply lifted an eyebrow.

Ellie sighed. "Okay...let's go."

After dumping the useless napkins into the trash, they hurried back across the street to the precinct parking lot. Shane jumped into Ellie's Explorer while they climbed into Clay's SUV. A minute later, they headed out.

From the passenger seat, Ellie connected her phone to Bluetooth and dialed Carl. "Ellie again, you ready for me?"

"Yup. The phone's up in North Charleston, just off Oak Drive."

The farther north they traveled, the smaller and less expensive the neighborhoods. As they closed in on Oak Drive, the houses turned older and more modest, showing signs of aging in the old shingle roofs and overdue paint jobs, without falling into slums.

Depending on the particular house, the front yards were either tidy and neatly mown or full of dying grass mixed with dirt. Chain-link fences were more common than white pickets, and the cars and trucks that lined cracked driveways and curbs were late models, many featuring prominent dents or missing hubcaps. An ancient pop-up camper took up space along the left side of the road. A few houses down on the right, the SUV's headlights revealed colorful chalk drawings stretching along the asphalt.

Clay turned down another residential street, craning his neck to scan the houses on either side. "Why here?"

Ellie bounced her leg on the seat, her skin tingling. "I think Kingsley may have grown up here."

Clay tapped the brakes in the middle of the road, lurching Ellie toward the windshield. She grabbed the ceiling handle and turned toward him. "What?"

"I don't like this. It feels like we're heading straight into a trap."

Arms crossed, a man in a dark t-shirt and a pair of stained jeans emerged from his garage and stood in the driveway, fixing Clay with a suspicious stare. Clay eased his foot off the brake, and the SUV rolled forward at a snail's pace.

Ellie rubbed her arms and suppressed a shiver. "I don't like it either, but we don't have much choice. Unless you have a better idea?"

Clay's knuckles blanched as he squeezed the steering wheel. With a muffled curse, he pushed harder on the gas, and the SUV gained speed.

"The final address appears to be 1303 Oak Drive," Carl said. "The phone went inside and hasn't come out."

With the next turn, they left the residential area and found themselves on a road leading back into a wooded area. Clay stopped and pointed at something glimmering ahead. The sticker on a mailbox reflecting the light.

"Twenty bucks says that's 1303."

Ellie squinted but couldn't quite see the number. "The road circles around, so keep going and don't stop."

CLAY AND ELLIE inspected what they could see of the house as they cruised past, Shane a few hundred yards behind them. Clay continued driving until he reached the end of the street, made a U-turn, and then headed back. A quarter of a mile away, he pulled the SUV off the road around a curve.

"What now?"

They both stared at the house. 1303 Oak Drive was an unassuming single-story dwelling. Like the neighboring residences, the home emitting the LoJack signal was small and modest, with blue paint faded to almost white and a little patch of grass out front shadowed by a giant tree. A few shingles were missing from the roof, and the front window appeared boarded up, but other than that, there was nothing special about the house one way or another. Nothing to suggest a serial killer had spent his boyhood years behind those walls.

"Let's get closer."

With few functioning streetlamps, the area relied on the moon to ease the darkness. The overall effect was dim and eerie, like the calm before the storm. Down the block, a dog barked before abruptly silencing.

The hairs along the nape of Ellie's neck bristled. She stroked the gun in her holster for reassurance before lunging for the door handle. She stopped short of opening it, though, pressing her forehead to the cool glass and inhaling through her nose.

Don't just act. Think.

Her impulses screamed to leap from the vehicle and charge inside. Logic dictated restraint. They were flying blind. No blueprints, no intel of any kind, no idea at all of what awaited them on the other side of that door.

But what if Kingsley was in the middle of a new round of Die, Bitch! Die? Except instead of Ellie and the short, dark-haired woman, the current contestants were Bethany and her mom?

The memory of Ellie's own scream ricocheted through her head. *Die, Bitch! Die!*

What if he'd already played his game and vanished, leaving her mom's bloody, tortured body strewn across the floor for Ellie to discover? Hacked up like the dark-haired woman, her arms bloody stumps where her hands used to be.

The terrible image seared her lungs shut, and she gasped, squeezing the door handle. She had to stop him. For good.

The leather seat creaked. "Are you okay?"

Clay's steady calm acted like a bucket of ice water, shocking Ellie free of terror's grip.

Stop. You're not a vulnerable, foolish teenager anymore. You're a grown woman. A trained detective with the Charleston PD. Start acting like one.

Ellie straightened from the window. Calmed her breathing. She could do this. She *had* to do this.

"Ellie? What do you want to do?"

She held up a hand while she considered the options. There weren't many.

Option one: she, Clay, and Shane charged inside, guns blazing, and hoped like hell they didn't walk into a trap or turn a bad situation worse.

Option two: call in and wait for backup.

Neither option was ideal, but only one was motivated by deep-seated fury and a desire to punish.

Ellie rubbed her hands up and down her pants, concentrating on the sensation of the fabric against her palms to center herself. "If we go in now, I'm scared of how I'll react if he's hurt either of them." Ellie met Clay's eyes. "I don't want to give him the chance to play me like that, to make me forget who I am, what I stand for. I don't want one of his games to trigger me to do something I'll spend the rest of my life regretting."

Throughout her hesitant confession, Clay's expression never once changed. "I hear you. Just know that no matter what happens in there, I'll be right here with you."

His unwavering support humbled Ellie, cutting through the last of the indecision trapping her in limbo. Clay was good for his word. He'd stand by her side however this played out.

The burden was now on Ellie to prove herself worthy of such unreserved confidence. "Thank you." Her voice trembled with emotion, but her hands were steady as she pulled out her phone to dial Chief Browning.

Before she could, it started ringing. *Speak of the devil.* "Chief?"

"Detective Kline. Carl alerted me to the situation. What's your current location?"

"We followed Kingsley's phone to a house on Oak Drive." She rattled off the street number.

"Is he inside?"

"No confirmation one way or another, but I suspect so, yes. Want us to do recon?"

"No, sit tight. We're only twenty minutes out."

Relief warred with impatience. Ellie was tempted to protest, but caution won. The chief was right. Waiting for backup was the smart play. "All right, I'll—"

A gunshot boomed, piercing the quiet neighborhood. Ellie froze as her imagination conjured a new vision of her mom…falling, arms outstretched with a perfect round hole in the middle of her forehead. Gasping for breath and bleeding out while Kingsley threw back his head and laughed.

No.

The thought of losing her mother to Kingsley was worse than imagining her own cold death.

Adrenaline surging, Ellie dropped the phone and unholstered her gun, almost tumbling out of the SUV in her frantic state. Clay leapt out from the driver's side while the chief's tinny voice yelled from the floorboard.

"Kline, was that gunfire? Kline!"

No one answered. There wasn't time. Ellie's shoes hit the pavement, and she was racing toward the house.

34

C reak.

      The noise penetrated Bethany's sleep from a distance, like a scream traveling underwater. Drowsy, she ignored the disturbance and cuddled up to the long, warm shape beside her.

Don't wanna wake up yet. Go away.

Refusing to be put off, the siren in her head grew more insistent.

Wake up.

Wake! Up!

With a small cry, Bethany's eyes burst open. *What was that noise?*

Her heart pounded as she laid there still and quiet, waiting for her eyes to grow accustomed to the dark. With no clock or phone to check the time, she couldn't be sure of how long she'd been asleep. If she had to guess, she'd say an hour? Maybe two? Not much more than that, based on how her body felt all heavy, like she was stuck in quicksand, and how it hurt to think.

As her vision adjusted, the pitch-black faded to gray,

allowing Bethany to scour the contents of the room. No one was creeping across the floor or crouching beneath the window. Once she'd cleared all four corners with no sign of an intruder, Bethany's fear began to ease.

See? No more creaking. Probably just a bad dream or the poky old mattress, groaning when she'd rolled over.

Soft snores coming from the lump beneath the covers calmed her worries even more. Along with the arm draped across her chest, the little snort-gasps reminded Bethany that she wasn't alone in the tiny bedroom any longer. The nice lady was here to keep her company.

After yawning so wide that her jaw cracked, Bethany wiggled closer to Helen's warm body. Time to go back to sleep. With a happy sigh, she allowed her eyelids to drift shut.

Creak.

Her eyes shot open again, heart galloping while the rest of her body was paralyzed by fear. She definitely hadn't imagined *that*. Not a dream. Someone really was sneaking down the hallway to their room.

Part of her was too scared to move. Maybe this was one of those times her mama had warned her about, when Bethany should play possum for real. If she stayed very, very still, whatever bad thing was out there might think she was dead and go away.

Except Bethany knew, deep in her bones, that Doctor Rotten was too smart to fall for that trick. Which meant she needed help. Fast.

Bethany shook Helen's shoulder and pressed her mouth to the woman's ear. "Wake up." She kept her other hand close to Helen's face, ready to cover her new friend's mouth in case she woke up noisy.

They couldn't be noisy now.

The woman stirred, and her eyelids fluttered open. "What

is it?" The question came in the faintest of whispers, which was a tremendous relief.

"Listen."

They strained their ears. Nothing. The silence stretched long enough that Bethany started to doubt herself. Maybe it had been a dream, after all. Sometimes that happened when—

Creak!

Helen's fingers tightened on Bethany's arm. She'd heard the noise too.

The quiet resumed while Bethany's heart pounded in her legs, her arms, even her toes. She counted out fifteen beats before the next creak, which sounded closer this time.

Helen shifted their positions so that Bethany was farther from the door, and Helen's body formed a barrier between the two. The footsteps continued at that same slow pace, like the intruder was either in no hurry or trying extra hard to be sneaky.

Bethany could picture both of those being true of Doctor Rotten.

Every creak of the floorboard sent Bethany's heart hammering a little faster and made her head go all dizzy and weird. Cold sweat broke out all over her skin. Her brain kept yelling at her to hide, but where? How? The room was too tiny. Besides, Doctor Rotten knew she was here. If she crawled under the covers, he'd just throw them off and drag her out by the hair. Maybe even lock her back up in the refrigerator.

Or worse.

A truly terrible idea occurred to her next. What if Bethany had been so bad at dinner that he'd decided to kill them? Like that blonde woman who'd knocked on the front door? Her teeth started chattering when she remembered the crack of the poor lady's neck. The thump when she'd dropped to the floor and never moved again.

Bethany never should have looked at the lady after that. If she hadn't, she'd never have seen the way her neck was bent all funny. As soon as she'd understood the lady was dead, Bethany had turned away. Not quick enough, though, because she'd already noticed the lady's eyes.

They were wrong, all wrong. Empty, like her soul had left her body and flown away to heaven.

Until that moment, Bethany hadn't realized people could die with their eyes open. But she knew that now because the blonde lady was definitely dead.

Bethany whimpered. She didn't want to go to heaven. Not yet. Not without spending more time with her mama first and the two of them visiting that beautiful island with the clear blue water and white sand she'd told her about.

The doorknob squeaked. Bethany cowered into a ball. *Someone was opening the door.*

Helen tilted her head close to Bethany's ear and whispered so softly that Bethany almost didn't catch the words. "Be very still and calm, no matter what. I'll get us out of here."

Bethany nodded, but it was so hard to stay calm, especially when her breaths kept coming harder and faster. She was so scared. For herself and her new friend. Helen was only trying to help, but Bethany knew Doctor Rotten by now. He'd punish the nice woman for fighting him. Afterward, he'd punish Bethany too. Just like he had the blonde lady.

Crack. Thump.

What if he killed Helen too? Bethany's gut clenched so tight she was afraid she might puke. No. Not Helen. She didn't want the cop's mama to fall to the floor and have her eyes turn all blank and glassy too.

The door creaked again. A dark shape flitted into the open space. Helen sprang to the floor and stood tall, putting her body between Bethany and the shadow figure.

Bethany wanted to crawl under the covers and hide. To cover her ears and pretend like everything was fine. That the shadow would go away.

Except, she understood by now that none of those things worked, so instead, she shook off the fear's icy grip and peeked. Her breath caught in her chest.

She squeezed her eyes shut, opened them again. No. She wasn't imagining things.

The shape was too short and too curvy to be the bad man.

Her traumatized heart skipped a beat before pounding double time as Bethany's deepest hope broke free from its cage. *Oh, please. Please.*

The intruder moved forward and whispered, so soft that the word floated like a sigh. "Bethany?"

A sigh, or a dream. Just to make extra sure, Bethany pinched her arm, hard enough that the pain made her gasp.

The gasp turned to glee as pure happiness bubbled up her throat and spilled out, echoing as loud as a door slam in the quiet night air. Bethany clapped her hands over her mouth, while both Helen and the shadow woman froze.

They looked so silly, like they were in the middle of a game of freeze tag, that another giggle tried to break free. Bethany trapped the hot breath in her palm as joy threatened to spill over.

Helen repositioned herself in front of Bethany, spreading her arms wide. "Who are you?" The whisper sounded like a snake.

Silly Helen. She didn't need to protect Bethany now.

Too excited to stay still any longer, Bethany scrambled around Helen's side, pride lifting her chin. Even so, she used her best whisper voice. "That's my mama."

"Your...mother?"

"Let's worry about introductions later." Mama peered over her shoulder before edging closer. "Right now, we need to get the hell out of here."

Helen didn't budge. "And just how do you plan on doing that?"

"Easy." She put her finger to her lips. "Through the front door."

Mama took another step forward, and the strip of light from the window washed over her, giving her whole body a soft glow, like an angel or an actual superhero.

Her mama was here. She'd kept her promise, just like Bethany had known she would.

Safe. She was finally safe again.

"Baby." Her mother held out a hand, and with a tiny sob, Bethany raced forward.

"Mama!"

She reached for that hand, shuddering with relief when their fingertips grazed. Bethany gathered strength in her weak legs, but before she could launch herself at her mama's chest, a crash shattered the night. Quick as a cat, Mama whirled, and the only thing Bethany's hand touched was air.

Helen screamed. "Get down!"

Bethany tried to move, but her legs were too stiff, her feet stuck to the floor. Mama grabbed her around the waist, and they flew across the room, twisting in the air as a bang rattled the walls.

The air rushed out of her lungs when she landed on her mother's chest. She was still gasping as another explosion rocked the room. The doorframe shattered.

Bethany ducked her head to keep splinters from stabbing her face. Too late, because something warm and wet splattered on her cheeks and into her open mouth. The taste reminded Bethany of sucking on a penny or when a tooth fell out, and she stuck her tongue in the empty socket.

Oh no.

Hand shaking, she scrubbed at the liquid and opened her eyes.

She couldn't see it well, but she knew she'd just swallowed someone's blood.

Don't let it be Mama's.

Bethany pushed up onto her hands and knees and dry-heaved as someone turned the light on in the room. Still gagging and blinking against the sudden glare, she lifted her head in time to catch Helen launch herself, her hands curled into claws, at the person in the doorway.

"You bastard, how dare you hurt my daughter! You deserve to rot in hell for eternity!"

As Helen scratched at Doctor Rotten's face and neck, Bethany's mama sprang to her feet and lunged forward, but pulled up short two steps in.

Why? Why is Mama stopping?

Bethany scrambled to her knees, to cheer Mama on, but a flash of metal froze her tongue to her teeth. Her gaze locked on the gun as Doctor Rotten swung his hand wide.

Bethany tried to scream as the gun shimmered in the moonlight before slamming into Helen's skull with a sickening thud. She flew sideways and hit the floor headfirst.

Crack. Thump.

Bethany couldn't move. Couldn't breathe. Could only stare at her new friend's limp body in disbelief.

No. This isn't happening. I'm dreaming, please, let me be dreaming.

Except, this was happening. The same way it happened to the blonde lady. Once they hit the floor, they never got up again.

The bad man had killed Helen.

Bethany's hair whipped her cheeks as she shook her head, faster and faster. "No! No, no, no!"

She thrashed like a wild creature when rough hands grabbed her, not even stopping once her mama hissed, "Stop!" Then Bethany was sliding across the floor, her pajama top riding up as Mama shoved her under the bed.

"Stay put!"

Without waiting for Bethany to agree, Mama rolled to her feet. As she did, she saw a dark stain spread across Mama's shirt like a ketchup spill. Right above Mama's elbow.

Her knees quivered. "Mama?"

But Mama was too busy facing off with Doctor Rotten to answer.

With tears streaming down her cheeks, Bethany pressed her palms to the floor and fought with herself over what to do.

If she were brave, she'd crawl out and help her mama fight the bad man.

But Mama told her to stay put, and she was smarter than Bethany.

As she struggled to decide, her heart beating too loud and fast, no one in the room moved. From beneath the bed, Bethany had a hard time seeing her mama's face, but she had a clear view of Doctor Rotten, and he was just standing there, staring and acting strange.

Her stomach lurched when he moved, but no, he was only tilting his head and ever so slowly reaching out his hand. The same exact way mama had reached for Bethany only a few minutes ago.

A chill crept down Bethany's back. Whatever new game the bad man was playing, she didn't like it, not one bit.

Quiet as possible, Bethany shimmied forward beneath the bed. She'd be ready in case Mama needed help. The overhead light spilled on Mama, and Bethany went still. She was staring at the bad man's fingers with a weird look on her face. Almost like she *wanted* to hold his hand.

Bethany rejected that idea immediately, mad at herself for even thinking such a dumb thing. *Mama would never want to hold the bad man's hand. She was probably just trying to trick him.*

The tightness across her chest eased. Yes, that had to be it. Her mama was playing the pretend game.

"Is it true?"

Bethany frowned. Was what true? And why had Mama's voice turned all soft and wobbly? The bad man deserved mean, loud words.

Doctor Rotten dipped his head. "It is."

Bethany struggled to understand. It…what? And why was the bad man speaking so nice all of a sudden?

Bethany's fists balled up tight. Mama had to realize the bad man was faking. He wasn't nice at all. He was awful and scary and liked to hurt people.

Mama's gaze dropped to Doctor Rotten's hand again. Her fingers twitched.

No! Don't do it, Mama!

If this was a new game, Bethany hated it. Maybe even more than the refrigerator game because, deep inside, a voice whispered that once her mama accepted Doctor Rotten's hand, there was no turning back.

Please, Mama. No.

Just when Bethany was sure Mama was going to make a terrible choice, she wrenched her gaze up to the bad man's face, and her hand fell to her side. Relief swooshed through Bethany like a river.

Thank you, thank you, thank—

A crash from another part of the house cut off Bethany's thoughts. She jumped, cracking her head on the metal bed frame. Pain exploded in her skull. As she yelped and grabbed at the tender spot, footsteps echoed down the hallway.

Through the pain, hope blossomed. The front door. Someone had broken down the front door and was coming to rescue them. They were going to be okay.

As she started to crawl out from under the bed, the bad man whirled and pointed his gun out the open door. When he did, Mama attacked. One second she stood close to Bethany. The next, she soared through the air like her favorite superhero. She struck the man's chest with her head, and they both went down, crashing to the floor in a tangle of arms and legs. The gun flashed, disappeared, and flashed again.

Come on, Mama, you can do it!

While they grunted and wrestled for the weapon, Bethany darted out to help but retreated again when a man and a woman burst through the doorway.

"Police, drop your weapons and freeze!"

Bethany's eyes widened when the redhead stepped forward with a gun in her hand. Wait, she recognized that lady! Helen's daughter must be the same nice cop who'd saved her before.

Right as she figured that out, motion flashed near the floor.

Bethany tensed, relaxing again as her mama climbed to her feet. She raised the gun shoulder-high and pointed it at Doctor Rotten, who knelt on the floor with his hands raised overhead.

"Don't shoot. I'm unarmed." When Mama didn't lower her hand, he tried again. "Remember who rescued you from those terrible people you were living with and helped you become something more? Something better? If I'd left you with them, you would have shriveled up and died, like a rose bush without water. Instead, you blossomed into a shrewd, capable woman. Don't I deserve some credit for that?"

Mama's arm shook before steadying again. "The only thing you deserve is to die."

The pretty red-haired cop stepped forward. "Katarina, please put the gun down. Let us do our job and arrest him, take him back to the station. Then this whole nightmare will finally be over."

Mama shook her head. "You of all people should know better by now. As long as he's drawing oxygen into his miserable lungs, the nightmare will never be over. He'll always find a new way to torment us, but he can't do that from six feet under."

"Kat—"

Her mama squeezed the trigger before the policewoman finished.

Bethany clapped her hands over her ears, but there was no loud bang. Just a clicking noise as Mama pulled the trigger, again and again.

"Tell me you loaded this thing with more than one bullet!" Mama screamed at the gun like she thought it might answer.

Like she was living in a nightmare, Bethany's arms and legs refused to move. She was trapped. Weightless. A stranger to her own body, floating outside herself. Helpless to do anything but watch as everything happened in the space of a few heartbeats.

Thump thump.

The red-haired cop yelled, "Show me your hands!" Instead of doing what he was told, the bad man lurched upright.

Thump thump.

A silver knife whizzed through the air. Mama's body jerked, and her hands flew up to clutch her throat.

Thump thump.

Gunshots erupted, and the bad man stumbled back and spun, like he was doing a dance.

Thump thump.

He grabbed for Mama, but another loud bang rang out, and Doctor Rotten fell to the floor while blood sprayed the air.

Thump thump.

Mama's knees slammed the floor near Bethany's head before she tumbled sideways, striking the wood with a thump.

Thump thump.

The pretty cop yelled for someone to call an ambulance.

"Mama?"

Inch by inch, Katarina's head rolled to face Bethany, and her lips trembled into the tiniest smile. Spell broken, tears streaked down Bethany's cheeks, and she sobbed in relief.

Mama's alive. She's going to be okay.

But when Bethany scooted closer, her body went cold, so cold, and the world came crashing down all around her.

Blood. Blood gushed from her mama's neck, spilling onto the floor and trickling along the wood like a tiny red stream.

"B-aby."

Hoarse, more of a rasp than a word. Not like her mama at all. Tears burned Bethany's eyes, but she blinked them away. She wouldn't cry, not now.

Not when Mama needed her to be strong.

"Yes, Mama?"

Mama's lips moved, but only a wet gurgle came out. The noise was wrong, all wrong. Once again, Bethany wished she were still a baby so she could close her eyes and pretend herself back into the little house by the mountains, with her mama teaching her how to survive the zombies and heating up hot chocolate.

But she wasn't a baby. Not anymore.

Bethany slipped her hand into Mama's waiting one. The skin was cool to the touch, but she pretended not to notice, smiling instead of crying even though her throat hurt and her eyes burned.

A hole opened up in her heart, like someone had taken a shovel and dug part of it out, but she let Mama guide her hand to the pretty policewoman's, who knelt on the other side.

All three of their hands were joined together, resting on Mama's belly.

The policewoman's eyes were sad when they met Bethany's over her mama's body. Bethany hated that look. Sorrow. Pity. Anger flashed, and she wanted to scream.

Don't you know anything? She's not like those other ladies. She's a superhero! Superheroes are always okay in the end.

Her throat was too clogged for the words to come out, though. To escape the policewoman's sadness, she looked down at their hands. Smeared across all three of them was her mother's blood.

Bethany stared at the red stain while the hole in her heart grew bigger. A choking pain spread through her chest.

"Mama," the words almost couldn't come out, "please don't die."

Over her bent head, the policewoman murmured two words very softly, "I promise."

Mama's fingers gave Bethany one final ghostlike squeeze before her hand went limp.

"No! Mama, *please.*"

Bethany jerked her head up in time to watch Mama release a soft sigh. Her chest rose and fell once more, but it didn't rise again.

The hole in Bethany's heart crumbled into a crater, then the rest of Bethany's body crumbled too. She flung herself onto the woman who'd given her life, giant sobs shaking her body like earthquakes.

"Mama...I...I love you, Mama. You'll...always be my... my...superhero."

She sobbed until her head started to spin, and her vision turned fuzzy. Gentle hands stroked her back, but she barely noticed them as she clung to her mama, and the room gradually faded away.

35

The forensic team crinkled through the rooms of Kingsley's childhood home on paper-booty wrapped feet, sifting through every last hair, fiber, and trace evidence with their usual brand of meticulous, by-the-book precision. Unlike Ellie, they seemed tireless in their smooth efficiency.

Cataloging the pictures on the wall. Brushing for prints to be entered into the database. Collecting blood samples and trailing string across the back bedroom and hall as they used the blood splatters and evidence to recreate the positioning of the attackers and the wounded.

They'd already taken Ellie and Clay's guns like procedure dictated in officer involved shootings, and Ellie didn't care if they never gave it back.

Ellie's bones ached from an exhaustion so deep, she worried that no amount of sleep would ever banish the fatigue completely. This night was endless. Her watch claimed it was just after three o'clock in the morning, but she wouldn't be surprised to discover this was Groundhog Day, and she'd been stuck in this same hellish night loop without sleep for three months straight.

She wanted nothing more than to go home, pop a Benadryl, and slip into a deep sleep. Forget the past twelve hours. Hell, forget the past week, month, maybe even year.

But that wasn't an option. Kingsley might be dead, but Ellie's job was to make sure that his legacy of horror and crime stopped too. The only way to do that was to collect all the evidence into custody and tie up every single loose knot, once and for all.

Besides, if she finished up here, guilt would dictate that she head straight for the hospital, to check in on her mom and keep her dad from driving the nursing staff bonkers. In typical Helen Kline style, Ellie's mom was chafing at the overnight stay, if the flurry of texts Ellie had already received were anything to go by.

The texts alternated between insisting that she was fine and no one should be stuck in the hospital over a silly bump on the head, no matter how ugly, to when was Ellie coming to visit, to claiming that Ellie couldn't dare refuse her poor, injured mother a lunch date now.

Clearly, her mother was far stronger than Ellie had ever given her credit for.

That, and Helen Kline really was as hardheaded as Ellie suspected, a fact for which she'd never been more thankful.

Making sure to stay out of the path of the criminologists, Ellie ventured farther into the living room. In order to expedite evidence retrieval, Chief Johnson had assigned a pair of crime techs to each room, plus an additional two were assigned to the car and one more pair to the shed in the backyard. That poor team had already experienced quite a shock when they'd opened the door and discovered a dead body.

They were still waiting on next of kin to officially confirm the ID, but Ellie was already certain who the woman with the platinum blonde hair and broken neck was. She should be. She'd only just met with Letitia Wiggins a couple of days ago.

With her gloved hand, Ellie picked up a photo of Kingsley as a boy. He was no more than seven in the picture, with a gap-toothed smile, close-cropped brown hair with uneven bangs, tucked under the arm of a pretty woman. His nose was bright blue from a splotch of sunscreen, and sand coated a stomach still soft with baby fat that poked above a pair of green and yellow striped swim trunks.

They looked so normal, standing in the sand and squinting into the sun with water in the background. Just your typical mom and kid spending the day at the beach.

The idea that maybe they were even at Folly Beach wrenched Ellie's heart. How did this little boy, with his happy smile, cheap haircut, and pretty mom, go from weekends playing at the beach like every other kid to notorious serial killer? What psychic injury tipped him over the edge?

A strange mix of relief and sorrow gripped Ellie as she set the photo down. Now they'd never know because the man was dead. The little boy had died long ago. Likely back within the historic, privileged brick walls of Far Ridge Boy's Academy.

Clay entered the bedroom and placed his hand on her shoulder. His wordless way of asking if she was okay.

Habit had Ellie start to slip away, but she caught herself in time and hesitated. Ever since they'd first met, there'd been something special between them. Ellie had continually shrugged Clay's interest in a relationship off, though, because of Kingsley. The monster who'd kidnapped her had consumed too much of her energy, her life, for Ellie to even consider dating again after Nick. Instead, she'd thrown up an impenetrable wall to protect herself and anyone else from being hurt.

But now Kingsley was gone. No longer a threat, to anyone. If there was ever a time for a fresh start, this was it.

Finally, time to stop looking over her shoulder and move forward with her life.

Ellie drew in a deep breath, covered his hand with hers, and squeezed. She didn't run. Didn't clear her throat or make a joke. Such a tiny gesture and yet one that conveyed a world of meaning.

No, more than that. A gesture that contained a promise for a fresh new future.

A future where a real relationship might finally stand a chance to flourish and thrive.

The best part? Clay understood all of this. The deliberate brush of his thumb on her shoulder told her as much. No verbal explanation necessary.

Ellie savored the warm pressure of his hand until it dropped away.

"The living room is finished. Kitchen too." Clay's gaze roamed over the techs as they itemized the photos hanging from the wall. "The bedrooms are going to take a while still, a few more hours at least. I'm good supervising if you need to leave and get some rest."

Rest. That concept had never sounded so good.

Ellie sighed and massaged her neck. "Tempting, but I think I've got another few hours left in me. Appreciate the offer, though."

He studied her in that quiet, steady way of his, the one that made Ellie wonder if he was peering through her eyes and straight into her soul. "Any word on Bethany?"

Her stomach twisted again. Sharper this time. Kidnapped and held hostage by an evil man who'd turned out to be her great-grandfather. Starved. Witnessing multiple murders, including her own mother's.

As long as she lived, Ellie would never forget the image of

the little girl clinging to Katarina's dead body as she sobbed, or her brave, wobbly little voice when she whispered that her mama was her superhero. Her heart ached for the poor baby, who would require a lifetime of therapy to address the trauma.

"She's asleep in the back of my Explorer. We're waiting on the social worker to show up."

Clay shook his head. "Poor kid. She's experienced more pain and horror in a week than most people do in their entire lives."

Ellie's mind flashed to those final, terrible moments in the back bedroom. With her life draining from her carotid artery and her fingers smeared with the blood, Katarina had used her final breaths to connect Bethany's hand to Ellie's. Like a blood promise.

Maybe Ellie's imagination had conjured up details, but she was sure that Katarina's last tiny sigh had been one of relief before her chest stopped rising.

"I'm going to do my best to make sure that Bethany doesn't experience any more upheaval or turmoil while she's still a kid."

"You know that won't be easy."

Ellie squared her weary shoulders. "Not for most people, but money opens a lot of doors. I've spent most of my life refusing offers of family connections or sway to help me out because I wanted to achieve my goals based on my own merits. Not those of my wealthy ancestors. But for Bethany, I'll call in every offer and favor available. Giving her a chance at a stable life with a loving family from here on out is a million times more important than my pride."

"No one who knows you would ever believe otherwise." Clay's expression was soft as he motioned to the hallway. "Check on their progress?"

Ellie fell in beside him as they wandered down the

narrow corridor. Hard to believe that only hours ago, she and Clay and Shane had sprinted down this very same hall, frantic to reach Bethany and her mother. Kingsley had died in the cramped bedroom he'd likely grown up in.

Ellie pictured that gap-toothed little boy's face. Had he rolled toy trucks in the spot on the floor where he'd bled out? Built pillow forts or played with Legos? Had the pretty woman in the photo knelt beside that bed each night when he was younger before kissing his forehead and tucking him in?

Ellie stumbled, and Clay's hand shot out to steady her. "You okay?"

"Yeah. Just tired."

Clay's expression remained concerned, but he didn't press her.

Quit torturing yourself. You don't know what Kingsley was like as a kid, and it's irrelevant now anyway. No matter how cute his baby pictures, he grew up to be a sadistic murderer. His death will save countless lives and wondering about what could have been is an exercise in futility.

They turned into the master bedroom. The adult Kingsley's domain. One forensic tech dusted for prints on the far side of the room, while the other one snapped photos.

Ellie spun in a tight circle before taking a slow lap of the room, mentally itemizing and assessing each object in turn. First stop was the closet, full of expensive suits, crisp button-downs, and pressed slacks. All neatly hung and arranged by category and color. A testament to Kingsley's need for order, or perhaps the result of Far Ridge Boy's Academy's abusive training methods.

With her gloved hand, Ellie fingered a navy sport coat. Each item was tailored, elegant, and age appropriate. Just the sort of attire that would earn the approval of a haughty perfectionist like Letitia Wiggins.

She moved on to the bed. Immaculate, like something from a model home. Not a crinkle or crease to be found, yet another remnant from his boarding school days, with their strict adherence to tidiness as a moral attribute.

If Ellie had ever needed a reason not to feel guilty when her apartment fell into disarray, this was it. The orderly, tidy nature of Kingsley's room was a front, a tool in which to hide his inner turmoil and pain from the world, and even himself.

The bookshelf was next. Ellie paused to study a series of photos before her gaze fell on a collection of pastel books with gold trim arranged in a neat line along the bottom shelf.

Photo albums or scrapbooks. Each one bearing a name across the spine.

Ellie picked up the first one and flipped through the pages. When she comprehended what she was looking at, acid scalded her gut like liquid fire. Scrapbooks had been correct, but the contents didn't contain ticket stubs or report cards from Kingsley's childhood days.

No, these were books dedicated to his victims. As she scanned the pages, the bile spread, burning up her esophagus. Newspaper clippings and pictures blurred before her eyes, outlining how Kingsley started with the stalking phase, progressed to kidnapping, and culminated in torture and murder.

Typed notes next to some of the photos illuminated Kingsley's suggestions to himself on how to prevent a victim from dying too quickly or ways to draw out a particular torture method. Comments about the psychological traits of the women he found the most satisfying and how to forge stronger specimens.

On the last page of every book, he'd rendered a judgment in bold letters.

Success.

Failure.

The successes were few...only Ellie.

The failures were the women he'd tortured to death, which he blamed on them. For not possessing the strength of will to stay alive.

Her hands quivered, and she swallowed the bile that raced toward her mouth. Forget the little boy. Right now, Ellie wished she could shoot the man all over again. There weren't enough bullets in the world to have made him suffer the way he deserved.

Enough of this. The vile torture catalogs could wait.

She was about to snap the book shut and slide it back onto the shelf when the back of her neck started tingling. Had Kingsley kept a record of every single kidnapping victim or murder? Given his pathological need to organize and catalog his exploits, the answer was almost certainly yes.

Head spinning, Ellie sifted through the albums, flipping past images of unfamiliar women before she opened to a picture of herself.

Another shiver went through her as she stared into the face of her fifteen-year-old self. To the side of the image was a note.

Freed this one because I was longing for a chase, but she dared to get away from me. I will bide my time and make her pay.

And just like that, Ellie's mind opened up, and the last moments of her captivity clicked into her mind like she'd pushed the button of a remote.

She yelled the vile words...

The screaming had ended...

Kingsley just smiled, congratulating her on discovering the beast inside her own heart.

He approached her, knife in his hand. The other woman's blood dripped from the tip like a faucet.

Pain, but not from the knife. A punch to the face.

Then...she was running, running, running.

A man chasing her. Laughing.

The bright lights of a car.

More pain.

"He freed me on purpose."

Not out of compassion or any act of humanity. To chase her. Toy with her.

"Sucks for you," Ellie muttered. "Who has the last laugh now?"

It wasn't funny, though.

Exhausted to her core, Ellie started to put the book away, then stopped, considering.

Could she finally find her answer?

Heart heavy with a mixture of hope and dread, Ellie turned the pages until a high-school-aged girl holding a flute appeared. At first glance, the photo appeared normal. Just another high schooler posing with her instrument before band practice. Except the girl's eyes told a different story than the forced, sharp smile.

Another shiver crawled down Ellie's spine. Something in those dark eyes tugged at her memory. Not so much the color, but the haunted, hopeless expression that was so at odds with the smile.

A black-and-white printout of a police report was stuck to the opposite page, detailing the dropped charges against Kent Finn, who'd been accused of assaulting a minor.

The minor's name was redacted, hidden by a black rectangle due to her age. Even so, Ellie knew without a doubt that the girl with the flute and haunted eyes was the victim.

Sophie.

A flood of emotion hit Ellie all at once as she returned her blurry gaze to the photo. The lines of the girl's face, her chin, the shape of her nose. Once again, they plucked at a blank spot in the back of her mind.

"I'm so sorry."

Her breathing hitched with the words, and she allowed herself a few minutes to simply gaze at the face that had haunted her for so long.

Ellie tugged at her collar to cool the sweat beading on her neck. Beneath the latex gloves, her palms grew moist. All of a sudden, the room turned unbearably hot, making her desperate to escape outside to the cool night air.

Instead, she forced herself to keep flipping the pages. To read the missing child report for a fourteen-year-old Sophie, less than four months after the assault charges were dropped. To study the solicitation report that followed a few years later, for a woman who went by the name Sofie and claimed to be eighteen.

Ellie finished the arrest report before moving on to Sofie's accompanying mug shot. The image hit her like a booted foot stomping on her chest. That face. She knew that scowling face.

Ellie closed her eyes and swayed as a dam burst in her head and the memories from that night came flooding back yet again.

Kingsley had tied them both up and left them facing each other. At fifteen, Ellie had been terrified and unsure, but growing up in a loving family meant she'd entered the warehouse with emotional reserves. She'd trusted that someone would come and save her. That she'd escape and survive.

Sophie, with her abusive, desperate background, had none of those positive experiences to draw upon. The second Kingsley had explained the rules of his terrible *Die, Bitch! Die* game, her thin body had sagged, and the light in her eyes flickered out. Now that Ellie could finally access the memory in full, she could see the defeat in the other girl's expression. Resignation to her fate.

Before the game had even started, Sophie had been convinced that she would die.

The photo album slipped from Ellie's numb fingers. Her knees buckled. Clay swooped in before she fell, scooping her up in his strong arms and pressing her tight to his chest, holding her upright as she choked and gasped for air.

"Breathe, Ellie. Remember to breathe."

Clay's urgent command in her ear was what snapped her out of the daze. What alerted her to the violent spasms that gripped her chest and throat.

No wonder she'd grown lightheaded. She was sobbing so hard, she'd been unable to suck enough oxygen into her lungs.

He cradled her head to his chest. Beneath her ear, his heart beat a strong, soothing rhythm. She clutched his shirt, inhaling his clean, familiar fragrance and rode out the last of her tears.

When the worst was over, she hiccupped twice and shuddered. "It's her," she whispered, without lifting her head from his flannel shirt. "The girl in the warehouse, back when he kidnapped me as a teen. I finally know her name. Sophie."

36

"I hate to burst your bubble, but Superman is most definitely the strongest superhero of the entire bunch. Prove me wrong."

Clay offered up the challenge from the back seat, and as anticipated, Bethany rose to the occasion. She squealed and turned around in the front passenger seat so she could fix Clay with the full force of her righteous eight-year-old indignation. "Easy! All you need to beat Superman is a stupid chunk of space rock. Does that sound strong to you?"

"I think she's got you there." Ellie tossed an amused glance over her shoulder before returning her attention to the road.

"Okay, so clearly, Superman was a bad choice. Batman, on the other hand, now he's one tough fellow, and space rocks don't bother him a bit."

Far from annoying Ellie, their banter pleased her immensely. Clay had elicited multiple giggles from Bethany on this road trip already, probably more during this single outing than she'd laughed in the entire three-some-odd weeks following Katarina's death combined. Ellie would have tap-danced up and down the sidewalks of downtown Charleston dressed like any of the caped crusaders in order to get the girl to smile more.

Lucky for her and the local residents, Clay and his superhero debate skills had rendered that option unnecessary.

While Bethany was distracted by the debate, Ellie shook out her right hand before placing it on the steering wheel. This was also the first stretch where Bethany had allowed Ellie free use of her arm. Ever since that awful night, the little girl insisted on clinging to Ellie's hand everywhere she went. Except for in the bathroom. Ellie had those moments to herself. But cooking, cleaning, even driving, forget it. She'd had to learn to do everything one-handed.

The good news was, if Ellie ever injured her arm in a freak accident, she was good to go. Not that she was complaining.

Ellie tapped the brakes when the Taurus in front of them slowed, before checking the rear mirror and changing lanes. Katarina's daughter was a tough little cookie, but trauma needed to be processed. The more weeks that passed, the safer Ellie hoped Bethany would feel. But Ellie didn't kid herself. She remembered her own mood swings and sky-high need for reassurance after her Kingsley trauma, and she'd been fifteen.

Ellie glanced over at the girl, who was pointing at Clay and giggling.

Katarina, you were right. She truly is one of the most resilient people I've ever met.

As she returned her eyes to the road, her heart twinged with a bittersweet pang. Somewhere out there, she hoped Katarina was watching the daughter she'd sacrificed her life to protect. She hoped she was finally at peace, knowing that Bethany was truly safe at last.

Kingsley's legacy of cruelty and horror had died with

him. Ellie would never mourn his death. She only wished that they'd stopped the monster before his final, murderous act and prevented him from killing his own granddaughter.

Her knuckles tightened on the steering wheel before she flicked the signal on and turned left at a green light. Ellie navigated the Explorer half a block and then pulled into a drive that led to a brick building and parked in an empty spot out front.

When Ellie shut the engine off, Clay draped his arm over her seat back and peered out the windshield. "What's here?"

Ellie met Clay's gaze in the rearview mirror. "You know how for the last month, I've been meeting my mom for lunch at least once a week?"

Her odd subject change sent the FBI agent's eyebrows disappearing into his cowboy hat, but in true Clay fashion, he didn't question it. "Right, I remember you saying as much. I reckon family feels pretty important, given," he slanted a quick glance at Bethany, "how things played out."

"It does. I realized I was taking mine for granted, and decided to fix that, stat." Ellie toyed with a loose curl. "I also decided that having a family with money comes in handy sometimes…like when you need it to hire three private investigators to track down a single woman."

From his bemused smile, Clay hadn't deciphered where this was leading yet. He would, though. Soon enough.

Ellie cleared her throat and leaned across Bethany to unlock the glove box. "For me, one of the toughest parts of being a law enforcement officer is how thin we spread ourselves when we work multiple cases. Lucky for all of us, Helen Kline is a damn smart lady. She insisted on paying for the investigators, believing that more eyes solely dedicated to this one missing person would help. Turns out, she was right. No surprise there, although, if you ever tell her I said that, I'll deny every word."

No laugh for her little joke. "What are you saying?" Clay breathed the sentence like a prayer, with hope and doubt underlying every word.

Ellie pulled the thick envelope and stuffed animal from the glove box. She didn't have to check the mirror to confirm that Clay's eyes were glued to both. "Last year, a homeless young woman was taken to the hospital with pneumonia. Thanks to the help from a couple of dedicated social workers, she was placed in an adult group home once she recovered, where she'll spend the next few months healing from long-term trauma before hopefully being released to live independently."

His throat bobbed. "Is that...are you saying...?"

Clay faltered, his brown eyes glimmering with unshed tears as he reached out with a tentative hand to accept the stuffed animal she offered.

A pink pig.

His mouth gaped, and he blinked rapidly, lifting his head to meet her eyes. "Ellie, I..." Something past her caught his eye and he just stared, "*Oh my god.*"

Ellie spun in the seat to see what had turned his cheeks ashen beneath his tan. The front door of the brick building was open, and two women stood on the porch. One wore baby blue nurse's scrubs and had brown hair pulled back into a tight ponytail. The other one was blonde, dressed in gray sweatpants and a pale pink t-shirt.

It was the second of the two women who Ellie knew Clay stared at like he'd seen a ghost. "Caraleigh."

The reverence with which he whispered his sister's name tightened Ellie's throat. He repeated it a second time. Louder. "Caraleigh!"

When he wrenched his gaze to Ellie, the tears spilled from his eyes unabashedly, even as pure joy radiated from his smile. "Thank you."

Too choked up to speak, Ellie nodded, then jerked her head at the door while urging him on with a silent command. *Go on, doofus, get out and see her already.*

Clay's smile widened, and he bounded out of the SUV. His long legs ate up the sidewalk as he crossed the short distance to where his sister waited.

Ellie held her breath when Clay stopped a couple feet short, and after the smallest of hesitations, opened his arms wide. *Please don't reject him.*

She needn't have worried. After a tiny hesitation, Caraleigh launched herself at her brother, laughing and crying all at once. Clay wrapped his arms around his sister, picked her up off her feet, and swung her in a wide circle.

"Who is that lady with Mr. Clay?"

Bethany had been so quiet up until now that Ellie had all but forgotten she was sitting there, taking the reunion in with cautious eyes.

"That's Clay's little sister. She's been missing for a very long time, but he's finally found her again."

Bethany studied Clay and Caraleigh as they hugged and cried. Her smaller hand snaked into Ellie's.

Guilt stabbed Ellie as she tore her attention from the emotional pair on the porch. Idiot. This was clearly too much, too soon for Bethany, after losing her own family. Ellie should have worried less about surprising Clay and more about Bethany's fragile mental health. "I'm so sorry, honey, is this upsetting you?"

After what felt like minutes, Bethany slowly shook her head. "No. I was just wondering...do you think Clay's sister likes Wonder Woman better than Batman?"

The hard, aching knot in Ellie's chest loosened, and she huffed a teary laugh. "I don't know, but I bet we can ask her one day soon."

She squeezed Bethany's fingers before turning back

toward the group home. Together, they watched as Clay handed the stuffed pig over to his sister. The delight that lit up her pale face caused the knot beneath Ellie's ribs to loosen even more before disintegrating into dust like it had never even existed.

For the first time since that fateful day at age fifteen when a single teenage rebellion had landed her in a killer's sights, Ellie could breathe one-hundred-percent freely again. She reached across the center console and pulled Bethany close, while twenty feet away, Clay mirrored the action with his sister.

Maybe not today, or tomorrow, or even the week after that, but one day in the not too distant future, Ellie knew they were all going to be okay.

37

With a gasp, Ellie's eyes flew open. Her heart hammered against her ribs while she peered into the darkness and gulped mouthfuls of air. Sweat plastered her t-shirt to her back, and her boxers clung to her thighs, so she kicked off the comforter, bunching the sheet in her hands as she waited for the panic to subside.

The specifics of the nightmare evaded her. She only remembered a flash of Kingsley's leering face, and Sophie, begging for Ellie to end the game. The dread lingered, though, like a deep, internal chill that not even the warmest blanket could banish.

He's dead. He can't hurt anyone, not anymore.

She repeated the silent mantra until her pulse stopped whooshing in her ears and her body quit shaking. The alarm clock on the bedside table glowed with soft light. Almost six a.m.

Over a month now since she'd shot Kingsley dead. A month full of nights still frequented by nightmares. Would they ever end? Ellie was starting to wonder. Terrible as the dreams were, though, she'd take bad dreams any day of the week over the old memory gaps.

Online research suggested that the nightmares were her brain's method of processing the restored memories, predicting that they'd fade in time.

Ellie hoped so, but if not? She'd survive.

Especially if the demons stayed securely trapped in her subconscious, where the only harm they could do was cost her a few hours of sleep here and there.

The mattress creaked, and an arm snaked around her waist, tugging until her back nestled up against a firm, masculine chest. Warmth and a familiar musky-clean scent enveloped her, chasing off the last remnants of the dream.

He pressed a soft kiss to her nape. "What was this one about?" The question rumbled against her skin, tickling.

"I don't remember." True enough. Besides, the specifics of the dream didn't matter. It wasn't real.

What was real was Clay's solid warmth in her bed. The drawer in her dresser, where he stashed his spare clothes, and the green toothbrush that cohabitated in the silver holder next to hers.

What was real was the patience Clay had shown when he'd waited all those long, lonely months for her to be ready for a relationship.

What mattered was how the rugged lines of his face and his brown eyes softened whenever he looked at her and how he'd never given up on them. Not once.

Ellie trailed her fingers across his forearm, reveling in the light dusting of hair and the corded muscle, now relaxed beneath warm skin. His presence didn't keep the nightmares at bay, but she recovered more quickly when she woke to his warm body nestled beside her.

Turned out, subconscious demons held less power over

her when Clay was by her side. All she had to do was reach over and touch him, and the ghosts of her past began to dissipate like dandelion seeds in the wind.

She rolled over until she faced him and pressed her lips to his. Morning light was just beginning to chase off the dusky gray when their bodies joined in a familiar, pleasure-filled rhythm. By the time he cried out and collapsed on top of her, the nightmare was forgotten. Banished into the dark fringes of her subconscious, to reemerge again another day.

Minutes later, Ellie slipped from the bed, pulled on her discarded t-shirt and a pair of knit lounge pants, and padded barefoot toward the kitchen. On her way out, the pipes squealed as Clay prepared to jump in the shower. Into *her* shower.

Maybe she should feel weird, going from zero to sixty like this. In the space of a few days, she'd essentially gone from sprinting away at the slightest whiff of commitment, to most mornings, having a man lathering up with the French-milled soap her mom had gifted her under her oversized rain showerhead, drying off with her favorite soft green towels, and shaving his stubble in her bathroom sink.

If so, too bad, because she didn't feel weird about Clay's increased significance and presence in her life at all.

Ellie headed straight for the coffee maker. Within minutes, the delicious aroma teased her nose. Once she'd poured the steaming liquid ambrosia into a punny *I Like Big Busts and I Cannot Lie* mug decorated with a cartoon police car—a gift from Jillian, of course—she carried the cup to the dining room table and flopped into a chair.

All right. Now for the challenging part of the morning.

After swallowing a few sips of the hot brew for courage, Ellie steeled her shoulders and pulled up the video website. "You can do this."

A deep breath later, she was typing "how to make perfect scrambled eggs" into the search bar.

Ah, the glamorous life.

Ellie snickered as a much too perky blonde woman prattled on about types of skillets and how to tell if an egg was fresh or not by dropping it into a bowl of water. According to Suzy Sunshine here, floaters were bad, sinkers good.

So basically, the chicken equivalent of the Salem witch trials. Strange, but whatever. Ellie shrugged as she skipped ahead to get to the actual egg-scrambling part, pausing when soft footsteps padded down the hall.

Ellie glanced up with a smile at the little girl. "Morning, sunshine."

"Morning." Bethany slid into the empty chair next to Ellie's that she'd claimed as her own.

"Sleep okay?"

"Yeah."

To double check, Ellie appraised the dark circles under the little girl's eyes. Still there, but shrinking daily now that Bethany was sleeping through the night. The first two weeks in Ellie's apartment, she'd woken up every hour screaming, but the nightmares had gradually diminished. Their family therapy appointment loomed ahead on Thursday, a necessary evil that Ellie only agreed to because the social worker insisted the sessions were mandatory.

Left to her own devices, Ellie could have happily lived out the remainder of her life without ever seeing another therapist or shrink. She'd gone the therapy route once before, and...surprise! He'd turned out to be a murderous sociopath's sidekick. Her residual trust issues hadn't just gone poof and disappeared once the sociopath died.

For Bethany, though, she'd grit her teeth and talk to a thousand shrinks if that would make the difference between the court okaying the adoption or not.

The little girl picked at the cuticle on her thumb, her eyes downcast. Sensing there was more to the story, Ellie shoved the phone aside and scooted her chair closer, until their knees touched. "Okay, now tell me the truth. How did you sleep, really?"

Bethany hunched her shoulders. "I had a nightmare."

Her posture was so dejected that Ellie's heart melted. Using her knee, she nudged the girl's leg until she raised her head. "Guess what? I had a nightmare too. Maybe we can start a club or something."

"Really, you had one too?"

"Really. Can you tell me about yours? Sometimes, they're less scary after you talk about them."

Bethany watched her index finger trace circles on the table. "I...he locked me in the fridge again. I crawled around trying to find my way out, and there was a...a dead o-o-possum. I screamed and screamed, but no one came to rescue me."

"Oh, sweetie."

Ellie opened her arms in invitation, and Bethany crawled out of her chair and into Ellie's lap like she was half monkey, her skinny body somehow generating enough heat to make an electric blanket jealous. She clung to Ellie's neck as Ellie stroked her back, whispering soothing noises while a tidal wave of emotion surged in her breast.

In the space of a month, Katarina's daughter had managed to worm her way into Ellie's heart and instill in her a mama bear's fierce protectiveness. She inhaled the strawberry-scented hair that tickled her nose before tilting her face up toward the ceiling.

I get it now, Katarina, and I'll keep my promise. Your baby will always have a home with me.

"Bad dreams can be scary, but they're just dreams, and they'll eventually start to fade away, I promise. One day, your dreams will be full of good things, like superheroes and puppies."

Beneath Ellie's hand, Bethany's bony shoulders changed from pliant to rigid. Ellie frowned down at the blonde head as she rewound her statement, searching the words for what might have upset her. "What's wrong?"

When Bethany peeked into Ellie's face, her expression was stricken. "Nothing, really. It's just…I don't want memories of my mama to fade away."

Ellie put two and two together and wanted to smack herself. *Nice one, Kline. You just made this poor baby worry that she was going to forget her dead mother.*

Maybe Ellie should call the social worker back and suggest that the family therapy session come with a lifetime of parenting classes.

She cupped Bethany's cheeks just as the little girl's face started to crumple. "What if I promise to help you remember your mama? We can put together a photo album for you to go through whenever you want, and I'll tell you stories about her whenever you ask. How does that sound?"

The girl gave a loud sniff and wiped her nose on the back of her hand, her blue eyes wide and hopeful. "Stories about how she was like a superhero and came to rescue me?"

Ellie's own eyes started to burn, and she cleared her throat. "Yes, those stories, and any others I can think of."

"'Kay." Bethany sniffed again, gazing up at Ellie with luminous eyes. "Also…do you think I could change my name one more time?"

Ellie's eyebrows rose at the out-of-the-blue request. "I think it's something we could certainly talk about." She chose her phrasing carefully, unsure where this conversation might lead. Was Bethany considering switching to a simple name, like Sarah or Willow? Or was she enamored with some wild, new-age name, like Huckleberry Sage or Antarctica?

She might be new to this parenting gig, but her cop instincts warned of the inherent dangers in agreeing to a request without first sniffing out all the loopholes. Even when the requester was elementary-school-aged, or hell, maybe especially in those cases.

"Why, did you have a new name in mind?"

Bethany gave a shy nod before fixing Ellie with an expression far too solemn for her eight years. "I want to go by Bethany Katrina. Those were me and Mama's names before the bad people took us away from each other. That way I'll be sure not to forget her, right?"

Ellie's throat swelled so much, all she could do at first was nod and take a mental note.

Next trip to the store, buy tissues. Lots and lots of tissues. Because clearly, this parenting gig is guaranteed to turn you into a big pile of snot.

Once she'd blinked back the tears and her heart stopped shredding into itsy bitsy confetti-sized pieces, Ellie agreed. "Right. I think that's a wonderful way to honor your mama's memory."

"Yay!" A smile brighter than a rainbow bursting from the clouds after a stormy day lit up Bethany's face, and like the resilient little chameleon she was, the girl scrambled off Ellie's lap and bounced up and down. "When's breakfast gonna be ready? I'm hungry."

Laughing at the sudden one-eighty, Ellie poked the girl in the belly, eliciting a high-pitched giggle.

"What's this I hear about breakfast?" Clay swooped in from behind them and leaned over Bethany, shaking his damp hair near her face and making her giggle even harder. He scooped her up and twirled around, showing off the flattering fit of his jeans while Ellie sipped her coffee and admired the view.

"Bethany was just saying she was hungry."

Clay and Ellie exchanged a glance. As they'd discovered the first day they'd brought her home, Bethany was always hungry. The doctor had reassured them not to worry. Kids who'd suffered from starvation for any length of time were often ravenous until their bodies and minds readjusted to the idea of regular meals, and that because of her trauma, it might take a while for Bethany to put on weight.

"Is that so? Are you a hungry hungry hippo?"

Bethany snickered. "No, silly. I'm a hungry hungry Bethany!"

Clay slapped a palm to his forehead. "That's right, how could I forget? Well, hungry hungry Bethany, what sounds good to you this morning?" He winked at Ellie over his shoulder, and she gave a rueful shake of her head.

Damn, he was good. The doctor had also told them that an important part of the rehabilitation process was making food fun again rather than a serious affair.

Bethany gnawed her lip before tugging on Clay's neck and whispering in his ear.

When she finished, he rubbed his chin and nodded. "Waffles, huh? What do you think, Ellie? Waffles sound good?"

Ellie's eyes wanted to pop out of her head. Waffles? She didn't even know how to scramble a perfect egg...how the heck was she supposed to master waffles, of all things? Unless they were talking about the frozen kind that you popped in the toaster. She bet she could cook the shit out of those. "I...um..."

Clay took one look at her face and started cracking up. "New plan. Miss Hungry Hungry Bethany, if you can get dressed in less than fifteen minutes, I'll take us all out to the best waffle restaurant in the world."

Bethany squealed and clapped her hands. "Yes!" She whirled in a circle. "Can Aunt Jillian and Uncle Jacob come too?"

Ellie laughed. "Don't you mean...can Sam and Duke come too?" The girl was still desperate for a dog, and little did she know that she'd be getting a chocolate lab for her ninth birthday, which was only a couple weeks away.

Bethany laughed. "Well, can they all come?"

Ellie tapped her on the nose. "Why don't you go get ready and I'll call them and ask."

"Yay!" After twirling once more, the girl sprinted toward her room.

Clay cupped his hands to his mouth and hollered after her. "And if you're ready in ten minutes, we'll swing by and visit Aunt Caraleigh and Uncle Luke."

Another squeal reached their ears before she vanished around the corner. Bethany loved visiting Clay's sister and Luke and asked them every week when the two of them were going to move out into their own house.

Ellie had been truthful with Bethany, telling her that Caraleigh and Luke could leave the group home just as soon as they were ready, but first, they needed to make sure that after all the difficulties and traumas they'd experienced growing up, the two adults felt comfortable with the idea of living on their own. Happily, according to their last family conference, that date was coming up soon.

The way Clay's eyes shined when he talked about his sister moving nearby was something that Ellie wished she could bottle.

Ellie crossed the dining room and leaned her head on Clay's shoulder. "You know, I could never have done this without you. You're so good with Bethany. She loves you already."

"Oh, I don't know, you seemed to be doing just fine on your own there before I crashed your girl party." His hands slid around her waist, tugging her closer.

She pushed up on her toes to give him a kiss, smiling

against his lips. "Does that mean you're buying me waffles too, Mr. Best Waffle Restaurant in the World?"

Clay cradled her cheeks in his big, solid hands, leaning back just far enough so he could stare into her eyes, and only the tips of their noses touched. "Absolutely. All superheroes deserve waffles."

Winding her arms around his neck, Ellie closed her eyes, allowing herself to bask in the moment. With Clay, she'd finally found her equal. A partner who understood how seriously she took her responsibilities and not only appreciated her for those choices but stood by her side no matter how bumpy the road.

She grazed her mouth across his before reluctantly stepping back. "I'm not sure I'm quite up to superhero caliber yet, but I'm glad the credits rolled on at least one villain. You know, maybe if I had one of those cute little capes, though…"

Ellie was still smiling when she and Clay left the apartment with Bethany between them. The little girl clung to each of their hands as they walked through the building and emerged into a beautiful, cloudless day, jabbering on the entire time about waffles and syrup and whipped cream.

Anyone passing by would mistake them for just another happy family, heading out for a Saturday morning breakfast.

The thought dissolved a tight ball in Ellie's chest that she hadn't even realized was still there. Slowing to a stop, she tipped her head back to let the winter sun warm her cheeks.

"Everything okay?"

Her smile smoothed the crease from Clay's brow. She squeezed Bethany's hand and allowed the impatient eight-year-old to tug her into a quicker pace.

"It's going to be."

The End
To be Continued...

Thank you for reading.
All of the Ellie Kline Series books can be found on Amazon.

ACKNOWLEDGMENTS

How does one properly thank everyone involved in taking a dream and making it a reality? Here goes.

In addition to our families, whose unending support provided the foundation for us to find the time and energy to put these thoughts on paper, we want to thank the editors who polished our words and made them shine.

Many thanks to our publisher for risking taking on two newbies and giving us the confidence to become bona fide authors.

More than anyone, we want to thank you, our readers, for clicking on a couple of nobodies and sharing your most important asset, your time, with this book. We hope with all our hearts we made it worthwhile.

Much love,
Mary & Donna

ABOUT THE AUTHOR

Mary Stone lives among the majestic Blue Ridge Mountains of East Tennessee with her two dogs, four cats, a couple of energetic boys, and a very patient husband.

As a young girl, she would go to bed every night, wondering what type of creature might be lurking underneath. It wasn't until she was older that she learned that the creatures she needed to most fear were human.

Today, she creates vivid stories with courageous, strong heroines and dastardly villains. She invites you to enter her world of serial killers, FBI agents but never damsels in distress. Her female characters can handle themselves, going toe-to-toe with any male character, protagonist or antagonist.

Discover more about Mary Stone on her website.
www.authormarystone.com

Donna Berdel

Raised as an Army brat, Donna has lived all over the world, but no place has given her as much peace as the home she lives in with her husband near Myrtle Beach. But while she now keeps her feet planted firmly in the sand, her mind goes back to those cities and the people she met and said goodbye to so many times.

With her two adopted cats fighting for lap space, she brings those she loved (and those she didn't) back as characters in her books. And yes, it's kind of fun to kill off anyone who was mean to her in the past. Mean clerk at the grocery store...beware!

Connect with Mary Online

facebook.com/authormarystone
goodreads.com/AuthorMaryStone
bookbub.com/profile/3378576590
pinterest.com/MaryStoneAuthor

Made in United States
North Haven, CT
28 February 2022

16616100R00205